Also by Suzanne Lazear

Innocent Darkness

(Book 1 of the Aether Chronicles)

CHARMED VENGEANCE

CHARMED VENGEANCE

The Aether Chronicles • Book 2

SUZANNE LAZEAR

Woodbury, Minnesota

First Edition
First Printing, 2013

Book design by Bob Gaul
Cover design by Kevin R. Brown
Cover art © iStockphoto.com:
1051777/Matthew Scherf, 10051011/Alexey Ivanov, 12128638/gaspr13, 18839996/Renee Keith, 15919556/Bruno Buongiorno Nardelli
Cover illustration © John Kicksee/The July Group

Flux, an imprint of Llewellyn Worldwide Ltd.

Library of Congress Cataloging-in-Publication Data
Lazear, Suzanne.
Charmed vengeance/Suzanne Lazear.—First edition.
pages cm—(The aether chronicles; book 2)
Summary: When sixteen-year-old Noli joins the crew of her brother's air-pirate ship, she learns that the ship has been hired by power-hungry forces from the Realm of Faerie.
ISBN 978-0-7387-3302-9
[1. Fantasy. 2. Fairies—Fiction. 3. Magic—Fiction.] I. Title.
PZ7.L4494Ch 2013
[Fic]—dc23

2013009222

Flux
Llewellyn Worldwide Ltd.
2143 Wooddale Drive
Woodbury, MN 55125-2989
www.fluxnow.com

Printed in the United States of America

For Reina and Rachel.
Thank you for never giving up on me,
even when I gave up on myself.

Dim vales—and shadowy floods—
And cloudy-looking woods,
Whose forms we can't discover
For the tears that drip all over!
Huge moons there wax and wane—
Again—again—again—
Every moment of the night—
Forever changing places—
And they put out the star-light
With the breath from their pale faces.
About twelve by the moon-dial,
One more filmy than the rest
(A kind which, upon trial,
They have found to be the best)
Comes down–still down–and down,
With its centre on the crown
Of a mountain's eminence,
While its wide circumference
In easy drapery falls
Over hamlets, over halls,
Wherever they may be—
O'er the strange woods—o'er the sea—
Over spirits on the wing—
Over every drowsy thing—

And buries them up quite
In a labyrinth of light—
And then, how deep!—O, deep!
Is the passion of their sleep.
In the morning they arise,
And their moony covering
Is soaring in the skies,
With the tempests as they toss,
Like—almost anything—
Or a yellow Albatross.
They use that moon no more
For the same end as before—
Videlicet, a tent—
Which I think extravagant:
Its atomies, however,
Into a shower dissever,
Of which those butterflies
Of Earth, who seek the skies,
And so come down again,
(Never-contented things!)
Have brought a specimen
Upon their quivering wings.

—Edgar Allan Poe, "Fairy-Land" 1829

PROLOGUE

The Sacrifice

"Welcome everyone to this special day." High Queen Tiana's voice carried over the crowd. "We gather here, as we always do, to honor the magic. Without it we wouldn't exist, and neither would the Otherworld." She paused and looked at the people assembled in front of the Lake of Sorrows, basking in the attention. "Like everything else, the magic must be nourished or it grows weak and fades away. We bring nourishment to her as thanks for all she does for us."

In her chair, Charlotte shivered in spite of herself. James stood beside her, squeezing her hand. She gave him a reassuring smile in return. She was ready to go, but the love of her life wasn't as at peace with her decision. At least they'd had this much time together. For that she was grateful. She looked at James, and at her friends Noli and V. Soon it would be time.

Today was certainly a festive occasion, and she took comfort that the end of her life was celebratory, not somber. A big arch made of greenery, purple and gold flowers, and ribbons had been constructed in front of the Lake of Sorrows, at the edge of the wildwood.

"This has been a trying cycle, as it grows harder and harder to find the right mortal girl," the queen continued. "But a girl with the Spark has been found. This mortal girl *volunteered* to be the sacrifice, offering up her life to preserve all of ours. It gives me hope that there are still young mortals willing to make such a choice."

Queen Tiana looked at Charlotte and smiled. It wasn't comforting, but triumphant.

Everyone seemed to think so much of the fact she'd volunteered. But she was already dying. And since she had the Spark—that extra bit of something, which some mortals had—why shouldn't her death at least mean something? She'd rather feed the land, sentient magic that composed the Otherworld and kept all its citizens alive, than die unwanted and forgotten.

Charlotte looked at Noli, who'd turned away, her face contorting in pain. No matter how hard Charlotte had tried, she just couldn't get her friend to understand. She watched as V pulled Noli to him, and Noli leaned her head against his chest.

"Noli, I choose this," Charlotte whispered. "This way it means something. Remember that, all of you." She glanced at James. "Take care of him, please?" she whispered to Noli and V. She prayed James didn't mourn her too long.

"Of course we will." V clapped his hand onto her shoulder.

Charlotte squeezed Noli's hand. "Live your life. Be with V, go to the university, invent wondrous things, and be a great botanist."

All Noli's dear and secret dreams. She had so much to live for.

"I'll try. I'll try so hard, Lottie." Tears pricked Noli's eyes, and she bent down and to give Charlotte a kiss on the cheek. "It's been a long time since I've had a friend like you."

Her friends. Her dear and wondrous friends.

Out of the corner of her eye, Charlotte saw the queen nod to James. Even though her belly should dip, even though she should feel fear at the idea of dying, she didn't. Between the injuries from her uncle and the brain tumor, not only had she been in more pain than she'd let her friends know, but she'd made her peace. She was ready to go.

James gulped—and *that* wrenched her heart. He bent down and his lips brushed over hers, lingering, his hand cradling the back of her neck.

When he broke his kiss off, he gazed into her eyes. "I love you, Charlotte Wilson."

"I love you too, James Darrow." She lost herself in his green eyes. Reaching up, her fingers traced a line up his jaw as she memorized his face. Her love, her savior. If not for him she would have died in an alley in Georgia instead of spending her final days loved, cherished, and the center of attention here in the Otherworld.

The queen cleared her throat and James let out a heavy,

defeated sigh that echoed through the oddly quiet clearing. Charlotte nodded to James. Yes, it was time. With his lips pressed together so hard they went white, James pushed Charlotte's wheelchair forward until they stood in front of the arch where the queen was.

A tall and lanky man with a permanent leer also lurked nearby. A long knife dangled at his belt, the purple jewels on its hilt winking. The ritual knife. The one that had killed every mortal girl since the sacrifices began.

Still, Charlotte wasn't afraid. She gazed at the crowd, the Lake of Sorrows glimmering behind them. People jockeyed for position, children on their parents' shoulders, as they gathered around the arch. Even Ciarán, the dark king, had turned out with his band of ruffians. Air faeries filled the pink skies, and the silvery lake splashed as water faeries drew close to watch the ritual that meant they, their land, and their magic would continue on.

"Thank you, everyone," Charlotte told them. "Thank you for the parties and the presents, for giving a girl without the will to live a purpose." She turned to James. "And thank you, for loving me, for staying with me." The words *thank you* meant something in the Otherworld.

"You owe me no debt, Lottie love." James' face grew tight as his eyes filled with pain. He stood behind her, gripping her hand. Never would she have been able to do this without him.

"And as it has been, so will it be done—and her blood will spill on the ground, her Spark nourishing the magic." The queen flung out her hands in a dramatic gesture. The huntsman approached, unsheathing the knife.

Still, she wasn't afraid. After being abused by her uncle, suffering the harsh life at Findlay House where she'd met Noli, and enduring what had happened before James found her in that alley, Charlotte had nothing to fear from a mere knife or the ruffian in gold and purple who wielded it.

She held out her hand, and James helped her rise from the chair into a standing position. Her uncle may have taken away her ability to walk, but Charlotte wasn't about to sit as she was sacrificed. James understood this. His arms wrapped around her in protection, love, and support as she leaned heavily on him. They moved forward until she stood on the grass.

Tilting her head up, she kissed him one last time, savoring his sweetness. "Remember, James," she whispered. "The best way to remember me is to live your life—and make sure Noli lives hers as well. I don't want to be mourned."

"I'll keep my promise." His whisper broke.

"That's all I ask." With one last look at her love, at her dear friends Noli and V, Charlotte closed her eyes. The crowd hushed at the sound of heavy footsteps. James' arms tightened around her. She felt a prick at her throat and gasped, but it didn't hurt, and she didn't open her eyes. She knew that when her blood spilled to the ground, it would enable the people of the Otherworld to live for seven more years.

"I love you, Charlotte," James whispered. She felt him lower her to the grass as she grew dizzy and weak. "I love you so much."

That was all she needed to hear, and she drifted off into happy nothingness.

••••••••

Kevighn Silver slumped over the wooden table he occupied at a seedy air terminal bar. Where was he? Chicago? Atlanta? He wasn't even sure. Ever since he'd been exiled from the Otherworld, he'd drifted from place to place in the mortal realm, spending most of his time drunk, in an opium haze, or in the bed of yet another strange woman. Eventually he should get a job, since he was nearly out of money. He was a decent gunner. Those were always needed on airships, of both the respectable and the disreputable sort.

Raking his hand though his long, near-black hair, he picked up his glass of substandard rum and took a drink. Around him, the magic shifted with such force that rum sloshed over the side of the glass onto the scarred wooden table. A shift of this magnitude, at this point in time, could only mean one thing: the sacrifice was complete. Banishing him hadn't negated his abilities to sense this.

Hopefully the Spark ran strong enough in the girl who was the sacrifice to satiate the magic until the next cycle, so they wouldn't encounter all the problems they'd endured during this cycle. That redheaded girl had indeed glowed with the Spark—not as brightly as Magnolia did, but enough to cause the magic to stabilize.

Magnolia. Was she there, in the arms of V, her earth court prince, watching as the blood drained from her friend?

Yes, Magnolia would be there. Magnolia would cry.

Kevighn pounded his fist on the battered table and sighed. She should be with *him*, not that whelp of a prince.

At least she hadn't been the sacrifice.

Kevighn raised his glass of rum and drained it, toasting the memory of the redheaded girl who gave her life so Magnolia didn't have to.

And we fairies, that do run
By the triple Hecate's team,
From the presence of the sun,
Following darkness like a dream . . .
—William Shakespeare,
A MIDSUMMER NIGHT'S DREAM

ONE

Jeffrey Returns

Moving the basket to her elbow, Magnolia Braddock climbed up the trunk of the crooked oak tree in her backyard, the familiar bark rough under her hands. In a flurry of blue skirts, she hoisted herself, basket and all, into the tree house her father helped her and V build so long ago. It was no longer even big enough for her to stand in; her mother didn't like it that Noli, a nearly grown woman of seventeen, spent so much time there.

Most of the mishmash that composed the little house—cogs and gears, bits of discarded wood, pieces of brass, and other assorted things—she and her childhood playmates, Steven "V" Darrow and his brother James, had carted home. Each piece held a story. Noli's hand caressed a piece of brass that she and V had taken from an abandoned building in town.

But it was memories, especially of her father, that composed this place as much as all the random bits of things; nearly seven years ago, Henry Winston Braddock had disappeared in San Francisco. Noli still clung to the fragile hope that one day her father would return to Los Angeles, and they'd be a family again.

Charlotte's red braid, which Noli had carefully sectioned, wrapped in thread, and boiled, hung from a makeshift line inside the tree house. Here it could dry safely, away from her mother's eyes, and she wouldn't have to explain about Charlotte. Mama had no idea that the Otherworld and faeries existed, or that due to an ill-worded bargain Noli wasn't mortal anymore. She also had no idea that if Charlotte hadn't died, Noli would have. Nor did she know how much James was mourning.

Right now, her mother was toiling in the dress shop, dealing with the holiday rush. Edwina Braddock earned their keep by making gowns for the very people with whom she and Noli had once been social equals. They kept up appearances the best they could.

Ever since Noli had returned from her stay in the Otherworld, or, as her mother assumed, merely from Findlay House, the horrible "school" the authorities had sent her to after an incident with a flying auto, things had changed. Mama had decided that since Noli now *looked* the lady, her hoyden ways supposedly "cured" by Findlay House, she could actually become a lady. That meant a return to the parties, teas, and social events Noli had hated even when her family was moneyed and respected.

Fixing cars or working in the garden was *always* preferable to balls.

The now-dry skeins of Charlotte's hair went in the basket. She'd weave them into a watch chain for James. This way he could carry a piece of Charlotte wherever he went.

Let's prune the roses, the sprite suggested.

It was difficult not to sigh, even though she was used such comments by now. The faery queen, when she'd taken away Noli's mortality before allowing her to leave the Otherworld, had turned Noli into a sprite. Well, sort of. V and James had done something to prevent Noli from losing *all* of herself during the transformation; she'd gained the beauty and abilities of a sprite, and also had a sprite sharing the space in her head. Calling it "awkward" was an understatement.

The roses *did* need pruning, and the beautiful Los Angeles fall day called to her. But she couldn't.

Later, she told her sprite side. *We have other things to do before Mama returns from the shop.* Like washing dishes, fixing the upstairs shutters, and adjusting the steam-powered sewing machine she'd made for her mother.

The sprite mentally pouted. Really, Noli *would* rather prune roses than wash dishes. Every day it became increasingly difficult to keep the sprite from taking her over completely. Some days, resisting the sprite grew physically painful. Not to mention that being a sprite made some things harder—like thinking.

You think too much, the sprite piped up.

Ugh. Noli pushed the sprite back into her mental closet.

The last thing she wanted was for the sprite to take over—then she'd never get her chores done.

Across the yard, V's window in the Darrow residence next door remained dark. An entire day, and V still hadn't returned from the Otherworld. In the months since she'd returned from her misadventures, she and V had traveled back and forth to see James and Charlotte, but they'd usually gone together.

Also, his visit to the high palace to see Queen Tiana was hardly a social call. He owed the queen a favor—this was the price of the bargain that had freed Noli from the Otherworld, even after she'd eaten faery food. Hopefully V would fare well.

As Noli climbed down the bent oak, basket on her arm, the soft whir of a solar-powered hoverboard echoed behind her. "Very funny, James," she said over her shoulder.

As much as Noli loved to hoverboard, the crafts were one-person conveyances. Women couldn't legally fly them, since women needed a male companion when operating anything from airships to autos. Noli couldn't afford any more brushes with the law, so when V went off on his hoverboard, she stayed behind. Well, most of the time.

"Is James a suitor I need to rough up?" joked a very different, but still familiar, voice.

Noli hopped to the ground and turned just as her older brother's hoverboard touched down on the grass next to her tree. He pulled off his brass goggles, which were in need of a shine.

"Jeff!" Noli dropped the basket onto the grass and wrapped her arms around him.

A couple of years ago, her brother, Jeffrey, had left Los Angeles to seek his fortune as an aeronaut, flying cargo vessels. Although he'd never come to visit, he always wrote letters and sent money home. Despite the fact that they could barely pay the bills, her mother wouldn't touch these funds. It made no sense. Finally, V had told Noli the truth. Jeff wasn't an aeronaut, but an air pirate—which explained why her mother refused to use his money.

If there was such a thing as a good air pirate, Noli would like to think Jeff was one.

She looked up at him and grinned. Her brother seemed in good health and clean. "James isn't my suitor," she said.

"Look at you, all grown up." Jeff's goggles still dangled from his fingers; his tan trousers were covered with all sorts of loops and pockets, as was his leather vest. "Why does that dress look familiar?"

"Mama remade one of her old walking dresses. She's been trying out ideas on me." Noli smoothed the blue fabric of the bustled skirt; her mother loved bustles. Noli liked bustles well enough, but didn't love the color. She preferred the greens and browns V liked, but her mother often dressed her in blue because she said it brought out Noli's steel-colored eyes.

Jeff looked around the yard, concern etched on his face. "Is she here?"

"No, she's at the shop." Noli picked up her basket. "Would you like to come inside? I'll make some tea. I'm so excited to see you. What brings you back?"

Jeff tugged on her chestnut braid. "You, actually." He

gave her a boyish smile that reminded her of their father. "I also have some business here."

Translation: He was stealing or buying stolen goods. It was probably best not to ask.

A frown tugged at the corners of Jeff's lips as he glanced back at the house. "As much as I miss our mother, I doubt she'll want to see me. And I have some free time right now—may I take you someplace? Will anyone miss you?"

Noli shook her head. "I should be fixing the sewing machine, but that can wait."

"What's wrong with the sewing machine? I could take a look." Jeff rubbed his strong chin, which needed a shave.

"I built Mama a steam-powered sewing machine and she says it doesn't sew quite right. What's really the problem is that she doesn't like it nearly as much as her treadle one." Noli swung her basket back and forth.

"She's hopelessly stuck in the last century." Jeff tilted his head back and laughed. "She always has looked backward instead of forward." He glanced at the tree house and grinned. "You still use that? I should think a grown-up girl like you has better things to do."

"It reminds me of Papa," Noli replied. It was also a good place for talking with V where her mother couldn't overhear—and for kissing. Kissing V, and other such things, was definitely frowned upon in polite society. Even the idea of her and V alone in the tree house could cause a scandal. Noli might not care what society thought, but her mother did.

"Let me retrieve my hat and leave her a note." Noli entered the house and ran up the back stairs to her room.

She set the basket on her dresser, next to the magazine containing the pattern for the watch chain she was braiding, and frowned at her looking glass as she caught sight of her ears. They had a slight point—one of the physical side effects of becoming a sprite. Carefully, she fixed her chestnut waves to hide them. Part of her missed her curls, but waves were much less unwieldy. As long as they hid her ears. She really tried to keep them hidden, especially after Missy Sassafras had taken her aside at a tea and offered to give her the name of a doctor in Europe who could "fix that" for her.

Fix that indeed.

Hmm. Would this dress be suitable for walking out? She turned from side to side and smoothed the blue fabric.

Wear something else, something pretty, the sprite urged.

I don't want Jeff to wait. Besides, even Mama would agree this is a perfectly acceptable afternoon dress, Noli argued back. She took a dark blue bonnet and matching cape out of her wardrobe, the nice wool one with bows and ruffles, and put them on. Out came a pair of kidskin gloves from her dresser. As an afterthought, she grabbed her old lace parasol, then penned a note and galloped down the back stairs to leave the note on the kitchen table. Now that it was only herself and her mother, without even the lowliest servant, the kitchen had become the hub of the house.

"Noli, you have no food." Jeff stood in the kitchen, opening and closing the worn wooden cupboards, frowning deeply. His hoverboard stood propped against the kitchen door. "Where's Mrs. Diller? The house is a mess."

"Mama dismissed Mrs. Diller about a year after you left,

and I can only do so much," Noli huffed. "She still makes me go to school, and I can't clean up or fix things when she's around. And we do so have food." It just wasn't fancy, interesting, or tasty.

Jeff looked around the kitchen—at the breakfast dishes in the sink, clean laundry piled on one of the chairs, candle wax marring the surface of the table—and his forehead creased. "Why don't you have a staff? I send you money from every single job."

Noli sighed. "Mama won't use it. She hides it. Well. Believe me, I've looked *everywhere*. She says it's for my dowry. Between you and me, I think she's dipped into it to buy me things for when she attempts to force me upon society. Apparently, since I'm seventeen, I'm old enough to *stop this hoyden nonsense and get married*." Noli grimaced, not ready for marriage or willing to give up her dream of going to the university. "Mama's been talking about a trip to Boston to see everyone, which we can't afford unless she uses that money or asks Grandfather."

Jeff opened the empty breadbox and rubbed his chin. "What does *he* think of this situation?"

"He has no idea. You know how stubborn she is." Noli shrugged. "Mama tells him you support us. She's afraid that if he knew, he'd bring us back to Boston. If he does that, we won't be here when Papa returns." Grandfather Montgomery, their mother's father, was a very influential man in Boston, and as stubborn as their mother.

"Father's never..." Then Jeff shook his head and forced a smile. "Where would you like to go?"

Noli thought for a moment. "Could we go to the pier? Please? Like Papa used to take us? I haven't been there in ages."

Who knew if she would ever get the chance again? Noli knew that eventually, her life would take her away from Los Angeles. If she stayed with V, which she fully intended to do . . . well, he still held fast to his dream of eventually taking back his family's kingdom in the Otherworld.

"The pier? Don't you think that's a little far?" Jeff's eyebrows rose. He had dark brown hair, like their father. Actually, he looked a great deal like Henry Braddock, right down to the cleft in his chin. But he had their mother's startling blue eyes.

Noli raised her chin. "Not for a hoverboard."

Jeff laughed. "Hoverboards are one-person conveyances." His look grew sly. "Unless you happen to have one of your own?"

Noli's mouth spread into a smile. Of course she did, in the shed in the backyard. It was actually Jeff's old board, which she'd fixed up. But since flying it could land her in trouble, she had another—vaguely legal—solution.

"I know how to balance properly to ride tandem on one board," she assured him. "I ride with V sometimes." Although that had been an afternoon of laughing, bruises, and torn stockings.

"Is that even possible? Or legal?" Jeff asked.

"Of course it is, as long as a male is at the helm," Noli retorted. It was just that no one ever thought to try it, because of the small size of hoverboards—and the balance factor.

Jeff shook his head. "Flying tandem on a hoverboard? Only you."

"Is that a dare?" She laughed. If so, that would make it all the better.

"Yes. If you can fly tandem on my hoverboard all the way to the pier, then I'll buy you a sundae at the ice cream parlor." Jeff's eyes danced with delight. That look had gotten them into heaps of trouble as children.

Noli held out her gloved hand. "It's a deal."

They shook. Jeff cocked his head, a partially amused smile on his lips. "Since when do you wear gloves willingly?"

"It's proper to wear gloves." Noli's cheeks burned, both at the words that tumbled out of her mouth and at the fact that she'd unconsciously grabbed her gloves in the first place. This wasn't the first time; the sprite liked frippery and finery. Most of her newfound ladylike behavior, the very behavior her mother praised, was the sprite, not Noli herself.

And she hated herself for it, because she didn't *want* to be a proper lady—she wanted to be a botanist. Noli wanted to fix things, to save her family through hard work and a university education, not through marriage to a boring society lump.

But fighting her mother, society, and the sprite in order to hold on to herself and her beliefs tired her out, even more than homework and housework did. The sprite *liked* the idea of marriage, as long as it included parties and fancy gowns—which was precisely the type of marriage her mother sought for her.

"Noli?" Jeff touched her arm, bringing her out of her thoughts. His eyes brimmed with concern. "Are you feeling well?"

She shook it off. "I'm fine. Let's go before it gets too late."

....

The vast, unyielding blue-gray of the Pacific Ocean came into view as Noli and Jeff approached the pleasure pier on his hoverboard, the colorful cars of the Ferris wheel on the horizon. They touched down on the sand.

Jeff picked up his board and walked over to the wooden hoverboard rack alongside the pier. "I can't believe you stayed balanced the entire time."

Noli grinned as he put away the hoverboard. "You owe me a sundae."

"That I do." Jeff held out his arm. Noli opened her parasol against the afternoon sun and took it. Jeff eyed the parasol on her shoulder but didn't say anything as they walked up the wooden steps leading to the pier. It had two parts: a fishing pier and a pleasure pier filled with rides, games, shops, and—her favorite—the carousel.

They strolled past those fishing off the sides of the pier and made their way through the throng of carnival games. The air smelled of salt, fish, sugar, and funnel cakes. Carnies called out, asking Jeff if he wanted to test his strength or win her a bauble.

As they passed the candy floss vendor, Noli inhaled the sugary sweet scent, her mouth watering at the thought of the pink confection. "Do you remember how Papa always let us each have one game, one ride, and one treat?"

Jeff smiled. "Those were fun times. I'll tell you what, why don't we do the same? Your treat is your sundae."

"Really?" The thought of riding something made giddiness rise inside her. The sprite flitted around her head, bouncing off the sides like a pinball as she took the pier in. *I want to ride everything. Oh, that's shiny. Can we eat that?*

"Are you certain you're not too much of a lady to go on rides? You might get dirty..." Jeff flicked her parasol with his fingers.

"Would you like to be smacked with my parasol, sir?" Noli teased back, trying to damper the sprite's excitement before she grew out of control. "Besides, it's not improper to enjoy rides." A group of giggling girls in dresses finer than hers climbed into the Ferris wheel. "I'm going to ride the carousel."

Jeff cocked his head, looking the tiniest bit out of place in his flying gear and no hat. "The carousel? We're a little old for that, don't you think?"

Noli let go of his arm and strode toward the large wooden structure near the back of the pier that housed the carousel. "You might be, but I'm not."

Jeff held up his hands in surrender. "As you wish."

He opened the wooden door of the carousel house for her, and the sounds of organ music greeted them. Large, colorful wooden animals rose up and down to the music as the red-topped carousel whirled around and around. Nannies with prams and mothers speaking softly lined the walls. A young couple stood hand in hand, watching each other more than the carousel. Noli closed her parasol, remembering how their father had brought them here as a special treat before he'd left for San Francisco and disappeared forever.

Jeff bought two tickets. They leaned against the wooden barrier and watched as children and a few girls a little younger than herself streamed off the carousel.

Noli shot him a look that said *see, told you.*

The operator let them in. Hiking up her skirt with the hand not holding the parasol, Noli headed straight for her favorite—the white-and-pink horse. She climbed on, bustle and all.

Oh, pretty, the sprite whispered.

Isn't it? I always ride this one. For a split second, Noli could hear her father coming behind her, saying *up you go* as he boosted her onto the wooden horse.

Jeff climbed onto the blue horse next to her. He used to ride the red one up ahead, but a little boy had claimed it. Noli watched as the young couple took a seat on the sleigh, holding hands. Pangs of sadness pierced her heart. Hopefully V would return from the Otherworld soon.

The carousel lurched forward, music filling the air. She held on to the brass pole as the horse went up and down. Closing her eyes, Noli thought of happier times.

Of her father.

Too soon, the carousel slowed to a stop. Jeff jumped down from his horse and held out his hand to help her off. As they made their way outside, Noli turned and gave the carousel one last look, biting her lower lip. *Goodbye, carousel.*

"What should I win you?" Jeff asked as they strolled down the aisle of games, making their way through everyone out enjoying the pleasant fall day. "Unless you want to play?" As a child, Noli had usually let Jeff play for her, if she'd really wanted the prize.

They stopped in front of a Test of Strength. A doll with red curls and green eyes sat on a shelf watching her—she appeared to be *laughing.*

"Could you win this one?" Noli asked. She watched as a young man took a wooden mallet and struck a metal plate, trying to send a counterweight up to hit a bell. It didn't ring, and the carnie asked if he wished to try again. The young man shook his head and walked away.

Jeff studied the game, rubbing his chin. "I think so." He paid the carnie, took the mallet, and swung, ringing the bell on the first try. "What would you like?"

She pointed to the doll. "Her." The carnie handed her the doll. Getting up on her tiptoes, Noli gave Jeff a peck on the cheek. "On to the ice cream parlor?"

He linked his arm through hers. "On to the ice cream parlor."

At the ice cream parlor, which smelled of vanilla and sugar, they got a large sundae with extra whipped cream and two cherries and two spoons. They sat at a small table near the window, where they could watch people stroll by as they ate. The parlor itself was noisy, packed with sticky children enjoying a treat.

"Now, what's this about being thrust upon society?" Jeff asked between bites.

Noli poked at the ice cream with her spoon. "Mama has it in her head that the only way to save us financially is for me to marry well. She thinks that since we're still a family of fine breeding, I can attract a suitor even though we have no money. So, ever since I've returned from boarding school, she dresses me up and foists me off on *all the right people* so I can *meet a rich husband.*"

Jeff made a face of disgust. "How's that working for you?"

"It's not." Noli helped herself to the cherry on top. "Not that I thought it would. I don't think she did, either, hence the whole conversation about Boston. This is why I don't want go—they'll try to marry me off." Noli rolled her eyes. "Society boys are *so* boring."

"What *do* you want?" Jeff took another bite of ice cream.

"I want to go to the university and become a botanist." While being a sprite sometimes made it difficult to think, Noli felt lucky that at least she was an earth court sprite. Inventing things could be difficult, but understanding plants had grown *easier*.

Jeff nodded, waving his spoon in the air. "You always did love growing things. I believe in women being educated."

"There are universities only for women, good ones," Noli said. "I don't know why Mama thinks it's improper." She shook her head, absently spooning ice cream into her mouth.

"So, do you have any other suitors?" Jeff's eyebrows rose in a way that made her recall his earlier comment about roughing someone up.

"Well, there is one, and only one—V. Steven Darrow, you know, from next door." She suppressed a smile at the thought. "I'm quite happy with him. He believes in women being educated. We've even talked about attending the university together."

Jeff cocked his head. "Is he still scrawny, with his nose in a book? He's too young for marriage."

Why was she considered nearly too old, while V, who was *older,* was thought far too young?

"He's filling out, though he still often has his nose in a book." Noli's smile grew. "He's my best friend, Jeff. He's stood by me through *everything.* V understands me like no one else does." Sometimes even better than she understood herself. He kept her secrets, helped her fix things, and through the whole ordeal in the Otherworld and losing her humanity, V never lost hope.

Jeff's rough, tanned hand covered hers. "I wish I'd known earlier that things were so difficult for you. I never sought to abandon you and Mama or cause your social status to plummet. I simply needed to find my own way—and I knew it wasn't here in Los Angeles or among high society."

Noli nodded, focusing on her dessert and getting the perfect blend of ice cream, nuts, and chocolate onto her spoon. "I know. Do you like what you do?"

"You'd love my ship. She's a beauty. Raven-class." Jeff's eyes lit up like the sun. "I wish I was here longer—I'd show her to you."

"Are you ever going to get married?" Noli clamped her mouth shut and felt her cheeks warming. It was difficult, not being in full control of her own being. "I . . . I'm sorry." Her shoulders drooped. Technically, Jeff was rather young for marriage as well. Well, for a boy.

"Actually, I've met someone," Jeff told her. "But I'm having trouble convincing her to marry me. Not because she doesn't wish to be with me, but because she's like you, wanting to be her own person." He grinned. "Eventually, I'll convince Vix that she can be my wife and still be herself."

"I'd like to meet her." Noli took another bite, then dabbed her mouth with a napkin. Any woman who could capture Jeff's attention would have to be extraordinary. Vix. What a name.

"Noli, I'm worried about you." Jeff lowered his voice and leaned in, putting his elbows on the table. "Are you all right? James told me about the awful school they sent you to, and your letters have gotten odd. Sometimes it's as if they aren't even written by you."

Of course she wasn't all right. But it had nothing to do with Findlay House and its dreadful treatments. Not that she could tell Jeff about the Otherworld.

"I'm fine, Jeff." She plastered on a large, fake smile.

"Tell me what they did to you at that school. Please?" He took one of her hands in his.

Memories of the isolation box, water room, and private "lessons" cascaded down on Noli as fast and cold as the water that the horrible headmistress, Miss Gregory, had poured on her face as punishment. Noli wrapped her arms around herself, trying to push it all away.

She couldn't meet Jeff's eyes. "I . . . I'm fine."

He straightened in his seat, shaking his head ever so slightly. Reaching across the table, he laid a hand on her arm. “Come away with me. I’ll pick you up after my meeting tonight.”

Noli nearly dropped her spoon on the table. “What?”

“This could work.” Jeff’s face grew animated in a way that reminded her of their father. “We need an engineer on the airship. You’d get a cut of everything, like everyone else. You could save some money and then go to the university.” He smiled their father’s smile. “No balls, no gloves, no one trying to marry you off. You could be your own woman, make your own choices. Fulfill your dreams.”

The offer made Noli fidget in her chair. The sprite grumbled at the words “no balls.” Noli shook her head, as if shaking off the idea. “But Mama—”

Jeff held up a hand. “Let her go to Grandfather Montgomery. She loves Boston. I’m sure if—I mean *when*—Father comes back, he’ll look there. It’s his home too.” Jeff scraped the last of the ice cream out of the bowl. “Think about it, please?”

But that would mean leaving V. Noli grabbed her doll and parasol. “We should probably go back.”

They hoverboarded to the house, and Jeff walked her to the back door.

“I had a wonderful time, Jeff. I’m so glad you took the time to come see me.” Noli stretched up and kissed her brother on the cheek. “Keep writing, please? I love your letters.”

“I will—and please do consider coming with me.” He wrapped his arms around her.

"I... I don't think I'm suited to your airship. But I appreciate the offer." Noli looked up at him. "Have a safe trip. I worry about you."

"I really wish you'd come. I worry too." He waved as his hoverboard rose into the sky.

Jeff wanted her to be an air pirate. What a notion. Noli opened the back door and went inside. As tempting as saving for the university was, she wasn't about to leave V.

TWO

Ultimatums

Steven Darrow took a deep breath and crossed the threshold into his mother's tea room, wishing that Noli was at his side. Nerves coursed through him, and his green-and-brown velvet outfit, suitable for visiting the high palace, itched. Even though the high queen gave him no reason for her summons, he knew exactly what this meeting was about. After all, he had to uphold his end of the bargain that had released Noli from the Otherworld.

A bargain he regretted every single day, because of the pain it caused Noli.

"Stiofán, you're late." Queen Tiana sat at a small table near the window, taking a sip from a teacup shaped like a flower, her pinky up. LuLu, her silly mechanical lapdog, lounged on a purple pillow that was near the purple fire burning in the ostentatious gilt fireplace. Today, the queen's ridiculous dress looked as if it were made entirely of pink silk spheres, ribbons, and pieces of old clocks. A tiara of golden spires sat atop her blond coif, gleaming in the light streaming in from the window. Little mechanical roses decorated her hair, opening and closing, as if blooming over and over in an unending summer.

Steven sunk into the uncomfortable chair, belly full of lead, sword bumping at his side. "I'm sorry, Your Majesty."

"Never mind." His mother waved him off with her hand. "Please, have some tea."

A nameless servant in purple and gold poured him a cup of tea and brought him a plate of pink and green cakes. No mechanical walking teapot today? Then again, the queen saved her toys to impress people, and she hardly needed to impress him.

She took a sip of her tea and shot him an expectant look, the cup poised between her hands. "Stiofán, I have something I need you to do for me."

The words made him jolt back in his chair as if he'd been punched in the stomach, even though he knew this was coming. "You're calling in the favor I owe you?" Part of him twitched as he prayed to the Bright Lady that it *was* indeed that, and not some royal order. A direct order from the high queen was not to be disobeyed.

"Indeed." She sighed and leaned back in her chair, one head going to her forehead dramatically. "I'm bored, Stiofán. Bored, bored, bored." Her hand flung out. "Your quest is to find me an amusement. Something I've never seen before—something diverting, that I will adore."

This was the quest his mother wanted him to go on? Steven had to bite his tongue to keep from laughing. It seemed almost... anticlimactic, and a waste of a good favor. Perhaps she'd used some spell to keep herself young and it had addled her brain—or caused her bouts of childishness. After all, she hardly looked older than he.

Or perhaps Noli was right and his mother truly was insane.

"Of course, Your Majesty, if that is what you wish." He waited for her to add limitations, but he wasn't about to ask outright. The last thing he wanted was for her to set him up for failure, like requiring him to only walk backwards or perform the task blindfolded.

"Yes, it is what I wish. But Magnolia may not come with you on this quest—and you have one mortal month." Her blue eyes shone with joy as she took another sip of tea.

"As you wish." His stomach didn't unknot. There were both benefits and detriments to Noli not coming with him. Still, he worried about her being on her own, and what her mother—or his father—might do in his absence. His father had made it clear on multiple occasions that, in his opinion, sprites were as unacceptable as mortals were as consorts or wives for princes.

Steven took a bite of green cake. These were Noli's favorites. Perhaps he'd bring one back for her.

"Speaking of Magnolia, a sprite would make a dreadful queen." His mother's lips curved into a cruel smile as she cradled her teacup in her hands. "I'd hate for blind love to distract you from your goals." She set the cup on table. "Therefore,

I'm going to do you a favor, since I'm your mother and I love you."

The cake stuck in his throat, foreboding coating him like oil. "Truly, there's no need. Noli won't distract me from my goals, and besides, I'm not quite—"

"Oh, stuff it, Stiofán." She held up her hands and looked at the ceiling as if calling on the Bright Lady for help. "You're nearly a man, so act like it. I can't believe your father has permitted such dreadful habits. I never should have allowed you to go into the mortal realm with him in the first place. Before you begin your quest, you're to end this nonsense with Magnolia—and that includes breaking the stone in her sigil. Again, what was your father thinking?"

Terror rooted Steven to his chair. "Is that really necessary?"

Breaking the stone in Noli's sigil would break the magic that offered Noli the protection of his family—the House of Oak. Severing this magic would leave Noli unprotected, and physically hurt her as well. Not to mention that Steven had no interest in ending their relationship, which went far beyond the promise he'd made to her.

"Yes, and this is a direct and immediate order. Understood?" The high queen eyed him, probably hoping he would disobey so she could punish him.

"Of course, Your Majesty." Every fiber of Steven's being screamed in protest, and the words tasted foul in his mouth. It would be his death to disobey this order. "If that is all, I should be off." He stood, wanting to put as much distance between himself and this woman as possible.

She nodded. "Of course. Also, you are to say nothing about my order, or your quest, to Magnolia. Your brother isn't to speak to her about it either. Truly, son, it's better this way. She's a sprite, and a rather pretty one. I'm sure she'll find someone else to take care of her."

Bile rose in Steven's throat at the thought. "Yes, Your Majesty." With a small bow he left the room and made his way down the hall of the high palace, not watching where he was headed.

"Stiofán! My, have you grown," a male voice boomed behind him.

Steven's entire body went on alert as he turned around to face his uncle, resisting the urge to put his hand on the hilt of his sword in defense. "Uncle Brogan."

"Will you and James be staying here in the Otherworld with your mother, or are you returning to the mortal realm?" Uncle Brogan stood before him in green-and-brown finery, a crown of green-and-gold-enameled oak leaves on his head. A crown that should still grace Steven's father's head.

"I have obligations in the mortal realm. I haven't yet asked my brother about his plans." Steven tried to keep his voice neutral. One day, he'd take back his father's kingdom.

Uncle Brogan's eyebrows rose. "You and James are quite welcome to stay with me at the palace. Your father was exiled, not you two."

Brogan looked very much like Steven's father—the same broad-shouldered frame, regal nose, and strong chin. But he shared James' mop of curly, dark-blond hair.

"I appreciate the offer," Steven said. But he wouldn't take

it. The offer didn't extend to his uncle's green eyes. Brogan was far too much like Queen Tiana: self-serving, calculating. While Steven and James lived, they posed a threat to their uncle's throne. He gave his uncle a little bow. "If you'll excuse me."

Steven exited the high palace as quickly as he could without drawing notice. As soon as he reached the bridge that separated the palace from the wildwood, he took off in a run.

....

Steven kicked the ground with his shoe as he walked down the Los Angeles street toward his house, darkness falling around him. The order from his mother weighed down on him like an anvil. Of all the cruel things.

Queen Tiana thoroughly enjoyed being cruel.

"What do I do?" He kicked the ground again. Then there was the matter of his quest, which, as he considered it, wasn't going to be as easy as he first thought.

Raking a hand through his hair, trying to comb it into neatness from its usual mess, Steven trudged up the steps to Noli's house, next door to his own. Even with a fresh coat of paint and the repairs they'd tried to do, it still looked tired, and not as immaculate as the others on the block.

As he knocked on the door, his chest went so tight with anxiety he could hardly breathe. How would he tell her? Even if he couldn't say that his mother had ordered him to break off the relationship, Noli would understand this, wouldn't she?

She had to. After the quest, he'd figure out a way for them to be together again.

No one answered the door. Steven tried again. Nothing. He went through the gate at the side of the house into Noli's backyard; she was probably pruning the roses or fixing something. Empty.

He let himself into the back door of the house. "Noli! Noli, are you here?"

Something that didn't smell appetizing bubbled on the stove. She wasn't in the kitchen, but he could hear someone moving around in another room. He found Noli in her mother's sewing room, sitting on the floor in a rather fancy dress. With an engine on her lap and magnifying goggles over her eyes, she was attacking the hunk of metal with a screwdriver. Around her waist was that silly corset tool belt Charlotte had made her, with loops and pockets for her tools.

"Now what's wrong with it?" Steven couldn't help but smile as he leaned against the doorway. That steam-powered behemoth of a sewing machine had yet to work right. The small room held two sewing machines, several half-made dresses, heaps of fabric, baskets of buttons, and other such things.

"V!" Not mindful of the engine, goggles still over her eyes, Noli leapt up and wrapped her arms around him.

"Noli." His heart crashed as he remembered the reason behind his visit. Separating himself from her arms, Steven stroked her bound hair, his fingers lingering on her face.

"You're still in your court clothes, handsome." Noli kissed him on the lips, her sweet mouth probing his, her hands resting on his backside. He kissed her one more time, savoring her taste, the feel of her hair, the weight of her body against his.

She broke off the kiss, finally pulling up her goggles. "How did it go?"

"Could we talk in the tree house? Is your mother home yet?" Steven's very soul felt heavy at his impending announcement.

"Not yet, and of course." Noli took his hand and led him out the back door. "Race you." Laughing, her tanned hand released his as she took off across the yard, hiking up her skirts.

"I'll win." Steven ran off across the yard after her, making sure she got there first.

"Beat you." Beaming, she scrambled up the tree.

"Well, you're too fast for me." Steven took a seat in the tree house, which had always been their special place, and pulled her into his lap. He buried his face in her wavy chestnut hair, which, as usual, tried to escape from its long braid.

"That bad?" she whispered.

"Worse." His skin crawled with dread as he struggled to find the right words. "She's sending me on a quest, as expected. However, I can't tell you what it is or take you with me."

"Oh." Disappointment rang through Noli's voice as she leaned into him. "I didn't think I'd be able to go with you anyway. How would we explain me leaving for weeks? Mother gave me *another* lecture last night about the importance of maintaining propriety and not tarnishing my reputation by running off like we did when we were children. Because"—she pitched her voice to match her mother's—"we're not children anymore."

Steven put his arms around her as they sat on the wood and metal floor of the tree house. "Noli, darling, I—" His voice broke, so full of dread it threatened to burst right out of him. "I don't know how to say this so I'll … I'll just do it."

Turning her to face him, he pulled her necklace over her head. It bore the sigil he had given her: a medallion with the symbol of the House of Oak, a tree made of gold wire with roots and branches intertwined to form a never-ending circle. The green stone set in the tree's trunk symbolized its heart.

Noli's steel-colored eyes widened in horror. "V … V, what are you doing?"

"I'm so sorry. I love you so much." His gut wrenched as he reached for a hammer lying discarded on the tree house floor. Placing the sigil on the ground, he raised the hammer.

"Please, please, don't." Noli trembled, but she didn't physically attempt to stop him.

"I'm sorry. I'm so sorry." His voice broke as he brought the hammer down on the sigil, smashing the green stone in the center into tiny pieces.

A wail escaped Noli's lips, a sad, pained cry that broke his heart into as many pieces as the stone, now scattered across the uneven floor of the tree house.

They said that when the stone in a sigil was broken, the one who'd bonded with it felt physical pain. As Noli sobbed, Steven wrapped his arms around her. Judging from her cries, it *had* hurt her. He cursed his mother for it.

"I'm so sorry, darling. I still love you," he whispered over and over, hopelessness soaking into every pore.

"Why?" she sobbed, her body shaking in his arms. "Why?"

He stayed silent, wishing with all his might that he could explain.

Finally, her sobs slowed and she looked up at him with red-rimmed eyes. "Who made you do it—your mother or your father?"

A little relief flowed through him. At least she realized that it wasn't something he wanted to do.

"I'll wait for you," Noli said. "When you're an adult we can fix this."

Him being an adult wouldn't negate his mother's order, but hopefully he could find a loophole or something to bargain with.

"Don't let your mum marry you off." Steven gazed into her extraordinary steel eyes, which glistened with tears and pain, and cupped her face in his hands. "Unless… unless that's what you want." A wealthy mortal man wouldn't be able to take care of Noli the way she needed to be cared for—but his mother had had a point about her easily being able to find another faery who would willingly do so.

Kevighn Silver would take her in a moment, of course. The mere thought of that one made Steven's blood boil.

"No. I want only you," Noli said. "Besides, we still have to find a way to make me myself again." She hiccupped.

"Exactly." Steven wasn't nearly as concerned about Noli getting her humanity back as he was about her fully returning to her former personality.

He held her, and they sat in silence in the tree house until pink tinged the sky.

"I... I need to go. I need to get James and pack for my quest," he told her.

"You're taking James? Good." Noli's voice was muffled by his shirt, her face buried in his neck. "I worry about him with Charlotte gone."

Steven's fingers traced her cheekbone. "I worry about you." How badly would this damage her? The sprite might take over completely by the time he'd figured this mess out. Sprites didn't like being unhappy, preferring to live in the moment. He moved Noli off his lap, gazing at her one last time, memorizing her face. "I love you, Noli. Never doubt that."

"I love you too." Her voice broke and she didn't look at him. That made his soul ache.

He picked up the shards of the green stone and the sigil itself and shoved them into his pocket. Perhaps Quinn could repair it, so he'd have it when he and Noli were together again. If anyone could fix it, it would be his tutor.

Noli sat on the floor of the tree house, curled into a ball and sobbing into her knees. With one last look at her, Steven climbed down, his heart breaking with each of her pitiful cries. He crossed Noli's backyard and pushed past the loose board in the fence to enter his own yard. When he opened the back door of his house, he saw his father in the kitchen making a pot of tea. Great. Just what he needed.

"Finally." His father turned, blond eyebrows rising. The former king of the earth court, known in the mortal realm only as Donald Darrow, might be king no longer, but he still looked the part even in his mortal clothes—with regal features, neat blond hair, and green eyes that always seemed to see right into one's soul. Steven wasn't sure how long it had been since his father had held a sword, but he'd remained broad-shouldered and muscular.

"Her Majesty wished to speak with me," Steven mumbled. Really, he'd hoped to leave on the quest *without* seeing his father.

"Are you all right?" His father took two cups down and set them on the counter.

"I didn't realize you cared." Bitterness flowed through Steven's voice.

His father poured tea into one of the cups and handed it to him, then poured himself another, leaned against the counter, and drank.

"I may not be the best father, in any of the realms, but I do care... even if I have trouble showing it. She's calling in her favor isn't she?" Notes of *I told you so* rang through his voice, but Steven had to give him credit for not saying it.

Never bargain with the high queen. You'll lose.

Staring into the depths of his tea, Steven found himself unable to take a sip. "She's sending me on a quest," he said finally. "She also ... " He may as well tell, since he wasn't forbidden to tell his father things. "She ordered me to break the stone in Noli's sigil." He blurted it out, as if doing so would lessen the pain. A glance out the kitchen window told him Noli still wept in the tree house. "But ... " Emotion crushed

Steven's throat, making it difficult to form the words. "She wouldn't permit me to tell Noli it was on her orders."

"I see." His father took another sip of tea, his green eyes unreadable. "Will you be gone long? Should I manufacture a suitable tale to cover your absence?"

"Please? The quest can take no longer than a mortal month, but . . . " Steven took a deep breath; the quest seemed too easy. Also, who knew what orders might await him afterward?

His father made an empty gesture with his free hand. "You did bring this upon yourself, you know. You never should have gone after Noli in the first place."

Steven slammed his cup on the counter, tea sloshing over the sides. "You're going to be like that? Fine. I'm going to pack my things and leave."

"Wait." The single word rang out, with all the command of a king.

Steven stopped, eyes narrowing. "What?"

"If you're permitted, please take your brother with you. He won't come out of his room, and a bottle of good cognac is missing. I detest wallowing."

"I plan on it." Steven bit back a pert comment—his father detested wallowing? All the former king had done since they'd arrived in the mortal realm was wallow. "If that is all, I need to pack."

"Take whatever you require." His father remained there, leaning against the counter and holding his infernal teacup. But the offer was kind.

"I appreciate it, Father." Steven turned to walk up the back stairs.

"And Stiofán ... "

"Yes?" Steven huffed, glaring.

For a moment, his father looked at him with one of his unreadable expressions. "Don't die. Please?"

"I don't intend to." But the fact that his father cared enough to say it warmed him.

"You may not intend it—but she might." Mr. Darrow's voice remained mild. "I'm sure Her Majesty has realized by now that you're not going to be a malleable, perfect son. She's capable of a lot, and sending you on a quest that ends in your death is not beyond her."

"True."

For a moment, his father's gaze seemed far away. "Don't trust your uncle. While alive, you and your brother are threats to the one thing he values most in life: the throne."

A throne he stole from his own brother.

"I'll keep that in mind, Father." Steven went upstairs and straight to James' room.

James lay on the bed, fully dressed, his eyes closed. He reeked of liquor, and an empty bottle lay by the bed. Steven took the water pitcher from the bedside table and unceremoniously threw the contents on his brother.

Sputtering, James sat up and wiped his mouth with his hand, his curls sticking out every which way. "What was that for?"

"If I can't wallow, neither can you," Steven declared. "Get

packing. We're leaving on a quest." Before Noli's mother could come pounding on his door.

James rubbed his green eyes. "We're going questing?"

"Yes." Steven looked out the window, in time to see Mrs. Braddock walking up the front steps of her house, a basket on her arm. "We're leaving right now."

"Why?" James followed his brother's gaze to the window. "What happened?"

Steven's chest tightened, the memory still fresh and raw. "The high queen forced me to break the stone in Noli's sigil."

"Flying figs." James stood, grabbed the towel off the washstand, and wiped his face.

"Um, language, James. But, yes—and I wasn't permitted to explain it to Noli. And you can't explain it to her either." Steven sighed and raked a hand through his own messy blond hair.

"She'll understand. After all, this is Noli." As James padded to his wardrobe, Steven noticed that his younger brother had shot up in height yet again; at this moment, James was a scrap taller than he was. He also looked more like a man, having inherited their father's broad shoulders. But Steven had started to fill out a little lately, and he didn't feel nearly as gangly in comparison as he once did.

He stared out the window and fingered the remains of Noli's sigil in his pocket. "She might understand, but that doesn't make it hurt less. And it's one more thing I must undo."

James turned, empathy gleaming in his eyes. "At least she's still living."

Steven clapped his brother on the arm, remembering Charlotte and what the petite redhead had meant to James. "Indeed."

"So, where are we going?" James shook out a pair of trousers.

Steven gave the window one last look. Mrs. Braddock was now storming out the back door, a scowl on her face. She was probably looking for Noli, who was still hiding in the tree house.

"I don't know." Steven sighed again. "I need to speak with Quinn. Just pack. We don't have much time."

••••••••

Kevighn looked out the door of the sparrow-class schooner, his rucksack over his shoulder. He turned to the grizzled airship captain, grateful to have gotten this far. "Where are we?"

"Saint Louis. I wish I could take you farther, or hire you on permanently, but I can't afford it right now." The air pirate gave him a smile, teeth missing. "There are slim pickings here, but if you head toward Chicago or New York, you might have better luck."

"I appreciate it." After getting kicked out of that bar yesterday, Kevighn had had to go somewhere. Anywhere. Permanent employment wasn't his goal, but he needed to find jobs of some sort; the air community was small, and he could only win so much by cheating at cards before someone caught on.

Without another word, he disembarked the ship and

headed off into the Saint Louis Air Terminal, hoping the gambling was good, the opium was cheap, and the women were plentiful.

THREE

Leaving Los Angeles

Pain still reverberated within Noli as she sobbed into her knees. When V shattered the stone in her sigil, she'd felt it down to her very soul. It hurt nearly as much as the fact that someone had forced him to do it and he'd been unable to disobey.

"Noli?" her mother yelled from someplace, probably the back door. "Magnolia Montgomery Braddock, where are you?"

Noli ached inside too much to answer. It wouldn't take long for Mama to find her here.

"Are you up there?" her mother called from the base of the tree.

"Yes," Noli sobbed, not lifting her head.

"Get down here, now," she demanded.

Noli remained rooted to her spot on the tree house floor.

"Don't make me come up there," her mother threatened.

Sobs continued to roll uncontrollably from Noli's chest.

"Are ... are you crying?" Mama called, her voice softening. "Noli?"

After a moment, Noli heard the sound of someone climbing. Her mother appeared in the doorway—it had been nearly seven years since she'd last climbed the old oak.

"What's the matter?" Mama crouched in front of her, arranging her skirts about her.

"V ... he ... he ... broke ... " Noli couldn't force the foul and painful words out of her mouth.

Her mother drew in a sharp breath. "Oh dear. V broke it off? Did he tell you why? Should I speak with Mr. Darrow?"

Noli shook her head. "No, V's going away for a while," she finally choked out, trying to offer a half explanation. She didn't know which parent had ordered V to do it, but in either case, speaking to Mr. Darrow wouldn't make it better. Also, she could hardly tell her mother the truth.

Mama drew Noli to her chest. "I know V meant a lot to you—and you had high hopes for him—so I'm not even going to try to say anything to make you feel better, because it won't." She held Noli close as they sat in the tree house, Noli crying into her mother's burgundy work dress.

"Going to Boston won't help either," Noli finally whispered, face still hidden. "I ... I don't want to marry anyone else."

"Going to Boston was supposed to be a treat, since we've been through so much and haven't been back there in such long time. If you wish to then stay on in Boston for the season, I won't stop you, but none of it is an attempt to marry you off. I know you and V were sweet on each other. We'll wait. We don't have to go anywhere right now." Her mother stroked her hair.

Noli sniffed, taking a handkerchief out of her décolletage and using it to blow her nose, grateful for Mama's uncharacteristic understanding.

"You have a handkerchief. I'm so proud of you." Her mother patted her on the shoulder. "Why don't we go inside? This place is small. Whatever you were cooking has burned, but we'll find something else to eat."

Supper. Noli's hand went to her forehead. "I'm so sorry, Mama. I … I forgot."

"It's fine." The smile reached all the way to her mother's blue eyes.

They climbed down the oak's J-shaped trunk and Mama's arm snaked around Noli's waist as they made their way in the near-darkness to the house. Noli glanced over at V's house; lights were shining in both V and James' bedrooms. V was probably packing for the quest, and would undoubtedly take James with him. She'd miss them both.

A quest! It sounded like something from an Arthurian legend, but odds were that if the high queen was behind it, it would turn out to be as gruesome as a story by the Brothers Grimm. While the pain she felt from the stone shattering was subsiding, the mental anguish remained. V meant so much, was so many things to her.

"Noli, dearest—we are Montgomerys, and Montgomery women are survivors. We don't wither, we thrive." Mama stroked Noli's face with her pale, ladylike hand, then opened the back door.

She had a point. Noli wasn't about to be some vapid doll dependent on the males in her life to support her and direct her future. Eventually, she and V would find a way to be together, just like they'd find a way to turn her mortal again. Until then, she was determined to thrive—and avoid getting married off.

As her mother opened the kitchen door, she frowned at Noli. "I don't think that belt matches that particular dress."

Noli's hands went to her tool belt. Whoops. Usually she took it off before her mother came home. "I was working on your sewing machine, when—"

Mama laid a hand on Noli's arm. "Why don't you tidy up while I make tea?"

Noli put her tool belt in her room, washed her face, and returned to the kitchen to clean up the mess. There wasn't much to serve for supper unless she made soup—which would take too long. She could make griddle cakes, but there wasn't butter or syrup, only a little brown sugar.

Someone knocked on the front door.

Mama frowned. "Whoever could that be?"

As she bustled off to answer it, Noli followed behind. She peeked into the entryway, curious as to who'd come a-calling after dark. Not that anyone ever came a-calling.

"Papa, what are you doing here?" Unhappiness colored Mama's voice.

Noli poked her head out so she could see. Grandfather

Montgomery stood at their door—a shadowy figure in the low light, but it was him, nevertheless.

Panic whirled inside Noli like a dervish. If Jeff had noticed the state of the house, Grandfather certainly would. They'd always worked so hard to hide everything from him, so that he wouldn't make them return to Boston forever.

"Why are you answering the door, Edwina?" Grandfather said. "Are you expecting someone?" Disapproval at the impropriety of answering one's own door dripped from his cultured voice.

"No, Papa. It's ... it's only Noli and myself here. Please, come in. I've just made tea." Mama was cowering in front of him like a naughty little girl.

Theodore Montgomery strode through the door, looking ever the gentleman in an evening coat and top hat. He surveyed the dark entryway with critical eyes and frowned. "You're making your own tea and answering you own door? Why are there no lamps lit?" His nose wrinkled. "What is that smell—is something burning? Whatever are you wearing? For heaven's sake, what is going on?"

Her mother stood there, her face frozen in a look of total and utter terror.

"Good evening, Grandfather." Noli forced herself into the room in an attempt to deflect attention from her mother. "What brings you to Los Angeles?"

"Magnolia? My, have you grown." Her grandfather gave her a hug. "Well, I think you've grown—I can't see you properly in the dark. The new museum in Los Angeles opened last night. Some of my friends are behind it, and they invited me to their opening parties. Since my favorite girls live here, I thought I'd see the new art and *you.* It's been ages since I've visited."

"Oh, V was talking about the museum. Something about a collection of Dutch Golden Age paintings he'd like to see." Noli grinned. V had a mild obsession with Dutch painters.

Grandfather nodded. "There are some very nice paintings there, as well as some lovely antiquities. Although I could do without the exhibit on faeries." He made a face as if he'd eaten something bad. "Bah. Why must grown men believe in such things? There is a rather beautiful gem. It's such an extraordinary color, even if the tale that it once belonged to a faery queen is a complete fable."

"It's probably a story just to give a bit of pretty glass some value," Noli replied. Odds were, that's exactly what it was. Most artists and writers got the details about the fae folk wrong, just like many of the artifacts "proving" the existence of faeries were fabrications.

"Here, let me take your hat and coat, and I'll light a lamp in the parlor." Noli hung grandfather's garments on the seldom-used rack by the door. She walked into the parlor, which she always kept neat and mostly dust-free just in case. Like everything else in the house, it had seen better days. Noli lit the single gas lamp on the wall. Because of the cost, they mostly used candle lamps. Perhaps she'd start a fire in the seldom-used fireplace. Wait—they had no wood.

Grandfather Montgomery looked around the dimly lit parlor and frowned.

"Have a seat, Grandfather. I'll bring tea." Noli put a

hand on her mother's arm reassuringly. Having Grandfather arrive spontaneously and discover the situation they'd so carefully hidden from him must have devastated her mother.

"Perhaps you can play something for me later? I love hearing you play." He glanced toward the seldom-used piano.

Noli gulped. She'd stopped lessons ages ago, and, since the piano was out of tune, she'd managed to escape practicing now that she was back in polite society.

"Let me get some tea, Grandfather." Hoping the silver tea service wasn't too tarnished, she went to get it out, along with the good china. They had no cookies to go with the tea, but Noli poured the last of the milk and the brown sugar into the proper containers and arranged everything on the silver tray. Taking a deep breath, she carried the tray out to the sitting room, trying to smile like she was glad he'd come.

"Eady, please tell me your servants have the day off and my eyes are getting old." Grandfather's voice was kind, concerned. "I've heard the most dreadful tales—that you and Noli are living alone and in poverty, and that you've actually taken up a trade. But I hadn't believed it, or I would've come sooner."

Where would he hear such things? Then again, not everyone had the aversion to airships her mother did. Someone could have run into Grandfather at a party in Boston—or while he was traveling on business. It wasn't as if Los Angeles society didn't know of their situation.

Noli set the tray on the low table. "I … I'll leave so you may talk."

Her mother's hand caught her. She looked into Noli's

eyes; her expression said *stay.* Noli nodded and took a seat on the uncomfortable rose-covered settee, since her grandfather and mother were occupying the two matching chairs. Everything in the room smelled faintly of disuse.

Ever the lady, Mama poured the tea. In the lamplight she looked older; there were rings around her usually jolly eyes, and the faint wrinkles on her pale skin were more pronounced. She still looked beautiful, like a fine lady, but tonight even her chestnut waves looked duller in their simple coif.

Mama handed Grandfather a cup of tea. "Is it that dreadful for a woman to have her own business?"

"You're a lady, not a woman," Grandfather replied. "Also, owning it is one thing; actually engaging in the trade is something else." He went to add sugar to his tea, and frowned.

"I'm sorry, we're out of white sugar," Noli muttered, cheeks warming.

"Yes, I opened a shop. But it's doing well." Her mother added milk and sugar to her own tea. Noli gripped her dainty cup, not adding either.

Grandfather's dark eyebrows rose, his hair the same color as her mother's with only a touch of gray, which added elegance. "It's doing well? Eady, if your shop was doing well, you wouldn't be answering your own door in the dark and have no white sugar. How are you handling callers? Isn't Noli of that age?"

Her mother's cheeks pinked in two near-perfect circles, like on the doll that Jeff had won Noli that afternoon. "We're doing the best we can, and Noli's going out into society and such. Yesterday she attended a tea." Mama looked at Noli.

"Was Missy Sassafras there? You really do need to get her recipe for scones. Food *is* the way to a man's heart, you know."

What was it with Missy Sassafras and her ridiculously superior scones? Noli would rather dine with the high queen of the Otherworld than engage in willing conversation with that social-climbing dollymop.

"I thought Jeff was supporting you?" Grandfather prodded. "That's what you tell me every time I offer assistance."

"Mama's saving Jeff's money for my dowry and the season," Noli half-lied, clutching her tea. "We're planning on hiring a housekeeper. We just haven't yet. Good help truly is hard to find."

Her grandfather's eyes narrowed with an intensity that made Noli squirm. "Girls, don't lie to me," he said.

"I'm sorry, Papa." Mama drooped over her teacup. "We tried the best we could. I wanted to do things myself, and, well, I kept hoping…" Her eyes drifted to the photograph of Noli's father that hung on the blue-striped walls.

"I'm shocked—utterly shocked—that not only would you hide this from me, and outright lie, but that you would *allow* yourself to live like this. You are a Montgomery, Eady. Have you no pride?" Grandfather clucked his tongue in disappointment, and even Noli's cheeks burned with shame. Ironically, pride *was* why her mother had hidden this from him.

"And what of your daughter?" Grandfather continued. "How do you expect her to marry befitting her station?" He gave Mama a look that had her writhing in her chair. Then his expression softened. "Oh, I see. That was why you mentioned coming to visit. We would invite Noli to stay, she would accept, all would be well, and no one would be the wiser. Clever, clever girl." He patted Mama on the knee. "You and I are far too much alike. But truly, I don't appreciate you keeping things from me."

"I … I'm sorry, Papa," Mama sniffed, pulling out a lacy handkerchief and dabbing her eyes.

"Pack your bags. We're leaving in the morning." Grandfather sipped his tea and Noli could see that he was trying to not make a face as he swallowed. It wasn't very good tea—cheap and inferior.

"Papa, if I leave, then Henry won't know where to find me when he returns." Her mother's knuckles whitened as she clutched the delicate teacup so tightly that Noli feared it might break.

"Eady." Grandfather gave Mama a gentle look. "It's been nearly seven years. It's time."

Tears streamed down her mother's cheeks. "No. Henry's coming back. He is."

"He'll look for you in Boston, Mama," Noli soothed her, remembering Jeff's words and trying to be helpful. "It's his home too."

"Noli dear, is there any food in this place or do I need to get takeaway?" Grandfather asked. "Or I could take you out. How long has it been since you've had a nice supper?"

As appealing as a good meal sounded, Noli couldn't stomach the thought of putting on a fine dress and going out to places where people like her grandfather dined, and having to exchange pleasantries with all the fake people and gossips.

"There are a few places open this time of the evening for

takeaway," she said quickly. "I'll help Mama pack." It might be beneficial for her mother to return to Boston, to not have to worry so much.

"You should go pack your own things first." Grandfather gazed at her fondly. "If you forget anything, all you'll have to do is smile and your grandmamma will buy you whatever you wish."

Noli nearly dropped her teacup in her lap. "I'm to go as well? But I don't want to go to Boston."

"Papa, we're fine, truly," her mother insisted.

"Balderdash. We *are* going to Boston tomorrow, all three of us. Noli, I can't leave you here unchaperoned. This is not up for negotiation." Grandfather held up a hand. "I'll come up with a suitable story—no one needs to know about your situation."

Mama sniffed into her crumpled handkerchief. "I've worked so hard."

"Sometimes hard work and good intentions aren't enough," Grandfather said soothingly. "It is better for everyone this way, truly." He stood. "Now, I am going out to find something edible. You girls best get to packing."

....

Mama appeared in the doorway of Noli's room, a dark green dress in her arms. A dress meant for a Christmas ball that V was supposed to accompany her to.

"Noli, pack this dress. It's unfinished, but it will be gorgeous when I'm done."

"I'm not going to Boston." Noli flopped onto her bed. The room was only illuminated by the single candle lamp on her desk. "You said that we didn't have to go." It came out as more of a pout than an intelligent argument. She stared up at the ceiling.

Her mother laid the dress on the back of the desk chair and sat down on the bed. "I … I know. But what do you expect me to do, refuse?"

"Yes. You're a grown and married woman. Tell Grandfather we're staying here." Noli put her head on her mother's knee. Part of her wanted to believe that Boston wouldn't be so dreadful. Soon the holidays would be upon them, with parties and balls, then the season. Grandmother would certainly make sure that her entry into society was well-appointed; perhaps she'd even throw Noli a ball of her very own.

No. Noli shoved the thoughts of parties and gowns aside. *There's more to life than balls.*

Like what? the sprite argued. *I want a ball.*

"Noli, are you well?" Mama's brows furrowed. "You have that look on your face. I … " She eased Noli off her lap and stood, going to the trunk at the foot of the bed, which had barely been unpacked. It had *finally* returned from her misadventures at Findlay House.

Mama opened the trunk, making three efficient piles on the bed. Instead of helping, Noli just lay there, staring. Unless physically forced to, she would *not* go to Boston. Yet the possibility existed; many women needed to be sedated for airship travel, her mother included.

"As much as I adore your random bouts of ladylikeness

and how you've grown out of your awkward phase, you … " Her mother added a ball gown to a pile as her lips pursed in a way that meant she was forming her words carefully. "You haven't been quite right since returning from Findlay. There, I've said it." The piles grew as she sorted with rapid-fire quickness. "I know you're upset about V, and I'm not saying we should to go to Boston to find someone else for you. I'm saying that we should go to Boston for a fresh start. This isn't a new idea; we've spoken about this before. It might be good for both of us to begin anew." She turned to Noli's wardrobe, adding clothing to one of the piles.

Wait—could her mother *wish* to go back? Noli knew Mama had been missing Boston lately, but she hadn't given much thought to how their situation might wear on her mother. How she might wish to return home permanently, but hadn't wanted to give up on her shop and the possibility of her husband returning. To her mother, Grandfather's surprise visit might be a blessing in disguise.

Noli eyed Mama, who didn't appear to be too upset by the whole situation despite the small protests she'd made in the parlor. "True, a fresh start may not be a bad thing, but you know Grandmamma. She'll have me married off by Christmas."

Mama piled shoes in the bottom of the now-empty trunk. "She isn't that quick. It would take her at least to the end of the season. We'll tell her that the matchmaking needs to wait."

"What if … " If Noli didn't speak now, she'd wake up in her grandfather's house in Boston, her social calendar full for the next year.

"What is it?" Mama filled the trunk with the contents of her wardrobe and dresser—nightdresses, gloves, corsets, petticoats, handbags.

Noli drew her knees to her chest. "It's not that I don't wish to get married, because I do . . . eventually. But my dream is to attend the university and become a botanist. Not all men oppose women being educated. V and I talked about going to the university together. There are coeducational ones, and some where the men's and women's universities are next to each other."

"You what?" It didn't come out harshly, but surprised, as Mama held up one of Noli's gowns. She frowned, then placed it in a different pile on the bed. "When did you decide that?"

"When I was seven and Papa brought me to that lecture at the botanical gardens." Noli smiled, remembering that day and how grown-up she'd felt going with him. "I get good marks in my science classes. My botany teacher even offered to write me a letter. He thinks I could get a scholarship." Of course, he'd also mentioned she'd have a better chance if she excelled in *all* her classes, not just the ones she liked.

Mama nodded, examining a walking dress, then folding it and putting it in the trunk. "I remember you and your father discussing those plans in great depths when you were small, but I didn't realize that was what you still wanted."

Because her mother disapproved so heavily of higher education, after their father disappeared Noli had stopped talking about it. To everyone. Only recently, with V's support, had she talked to a few of her teachers about perhaps attending a university next year. At this point she wasn't picky—nearly any university that offered botany would do. V had his sights set on a good school, Ivy League even.

"I . . . I didn't know." Mama held up a dress from one of the piles and put it in the trunk. "I suppose we could look into it, but to what end? It's not as if a degree in botany will help you find a husband or manage a household. Can one even be a botanist and have a family?"

Noli glowered as her mother continued to stuff her trunk with finery. "I should think so."

Taking the unfinished dress, Mama laid it on the top of the packed clothes and closed the trunk's lid. "There, all packed. Let me gather a few hats." She looked at Noli and sighed. "Noli, if it's that important to you, we'll consider it. However, I'm not guaranteeing it will happen. A term or two would be better than none at all." She opened and closed hatboxes, placing a few on top of the trunk. "Maybe you'll meet someone of interest."

A term or two? Noli didn't want to go to a university for just a little while, or to meet a husband or any of that poppycock. That's exactly what would happen if she went to Boston, if she even managed to convince them to let her attend university in the first place. She scowled. "I don't want to go to Boston."

After all, she'd promised V she wouldn't let them marry her off, but if she wasn't here when he returned, he'd know where to look for her. Perhaps she'd leave him a note in the tree house. Yes, that's what she'd do.

"Don't be difficult." Her mother's tired eyes met hers. "Please. Just come without being argumentative and we'll figure it all out." Mama sat down on the bed and wrapped her arms around Noli. "I love you so much. This is all for the best. Truly."

"I love you too, Mama." Noli hugged her back. Her mother had the best of intentions, but Noli knew that the pressure she'd face to marry would be stifling. Not that it seemed like she had any choice. Like it or not, she was going to Boston.

....

Noli crept into the dark backyard in only her nightdress, a note clutched in her hand. The cool autumn air made her shiver as her bare feet padded across the cold dirt and grass. V's house was dark, and odds were that he and James had already left on their quest. She had full faith that they would accomplish the task. Those two could do anything.

Scrambling up the tree like she had a million times before, Noli put her letter to V in the hidey-hole they had for this very purpose. It said where she was, so he wouldn't worry. As she climbed down, she heard a soft whir behind her.

"Noli, why are you in the backyard in your nightdress? It's a little late to be out, isn't it?" Jeff whispered, landing his hoverboard nearby, dressed exactly as he had been earlier.

She looked over at him, surprised by his appearance. "Oh, I was leaving a note for V."

Jeff smirked, raking a hand through his short dark curls. Her eyes welled with tears as she thought of how much had happened since her brother had dropped her off earlier that day.

"What's wrong?" Jeff climbed off the hoverboard, put his goggles on top his head, and pulled her to him.

She softy and quickly told him everything—V ending their courtship, Grandfather arriving, the plans to depart for Boston in the morning. "I don't want to go to Boston," she hiccupped.

"Then don't." Jeff cupped her cold face with his warm hand. "Come with me. Work on the ship as our engineer, save money for university, and become a botanist. Let Mother go. She'll be taken care of and neither one of us will have to worry about her anymore."

Noli gazed at her dark house. If their mother was taken care of, and happy, then leaving wouldn't be so bad. As much as she didn't wish to become an air pirate, her desire to go to Boston was a thousand times less.

Resigned, she nodded, her belly clenching at the thought that she was actually going through with this mad notion. "I need to change my note. Good thing my trunk is already packed."

Jeff's eyebrows rose. "I can't carry you *and* a trunk on my hoverboard. The weight would crash us immediately."

Noli's cheeks warmed at her slip. "You're right. Could I bring a small valise? I think I can compensate for it, balance-wise."

"Pack light." He took out his pocket watch and checked the time. "Be fast."

Scrambling back up the tree, Noli fixed the note with a stub of pencil she'd stashed in a tin can in the corner. V would find her, and they'd take everything from there.

She returned to the house, her heart thumping so loudly she feared it might wake her mother. Was she truly doing this? Stealing off in the middle of the night with Jeff to go work on an airship? The thought made her so giddy her hands shook.

Pack light. That could be difficult, considering she was leaving forever.

Fortunately, she had a solution. Noli lit the candle lamp and dumped the contents of her valise on her bed. She'd packed it for the airship, with necessities and amusements. The necessities went back in, along with the new copy of *Nicomachean Ethics* V had given her, her parents' wedding picture, the botany book from her father, the doll, Charlotte's hair, and the magazine with the pattern.

She opened her trunk and threw some of her dresses into the valise along with other things—nightdresses, shoes, corsets, undergarments, even a few hats, sans boxes. The valise was magic, something she'd gotten in the Otherworld. The small bag could fit more than her trunk, and it weighed less than her parasol—which also went into the bag, along with the precious dresses she'd brought back from the Otherworld and hid. She tossed in her goggles, apron, cap, a couple of books, and work gloves. Things she'd need as a ship's engineer.

Anything else?

Noli scanned the room and added a few more things, including her tool belt, a leather bracelet Charlotte had made her, and a small knife from James. Opening her jewelry box, she withdrew an old brass key on a green ribbon. It was the key to the faery garden at Findlay House. She wasn't sure why she took it, but there was magic in that key—she could feel it even if V couldn't. If she didn't take it, she'd probably regret it at some point.

She changed into a blue dress her mother had made using a sketch from Charlotte. It was Noli's attempt to meld the comfort of her Otherworld dresses with the propriety of mortal fashion. The blue dress hung a little shorter, allowing for freedom of movement and preventing the need for a hoop skirt. Trim dangled from the bell sleeves, which could be kilted up when she had a task to tackle. Trimmed fabric swooped over each hip, and the waist was cinched with a belt reminiscent of the waist-cinchers and corsets worn on the *outside* of clothing in the Otherworld. It looked more like a belt than an undergarment on this dress. Often, she just used her tool belt instead.

Taking a scrap of paper, Noli scrawled a quick note to her mother:

> *Dear Mama,*
>
> *I love you. I love you so much. But I can't go to with you. I'm sorry.*
>
> *Go to Boston and start over. Don't worry about me, I'll be fine.*

None of this is your fault. I promise. You're the best mother a girl could want, and I hope to see you again someday. Give everyone in Boston my love.

Always,

Noli

A sense of finality coated her, clinging to her skin as she clutched her valise and gazed around her room one last time. This was it. Her mother would return to Boston and this would never be home again—not in the way it had been.

Wiping a tear from her eye, Noli blew out the candle lamp, put her good cape around her shoulders, and grabbed some black gloves and her dark blue bonnet. *Goodbye, room.* She crept down the hallway, boots in her hand, pausing in front of her mother's closed door. "I love you," she whispered.

Padding down the stairs, she grabbed her toolbox and her magnifying goggles from the sewing room and shoved them into her valise. She pulled on her boots and bonnet, tucked the small knife inside her boot, and turned in a circle in the kitchen, taking one last look. *Goodbye, house.* Sniffing, she walked out into the cold night.

Jeff stood outside the back door, stamping his feet and blowing on his hands. "It's about time." He tugged on her cape, the same one she'd worn earlier. "A little fancy for an airship."

"It keeps me warm." Not all places were as temperate as Los Angeles.

They climbed onto the hoverboard, Noli adjusting her

stance for the weight of the bag, her arms wrapped around her brother.

"You're doing the right thing," Jeff assured her as they rose into the sky.

Goodbye, Los Angeles. As bittersweet as this was, Noli felt excitement building within her. After all, she was running away with an air pirate.

FOUR

The Vixen's Revenge

As she and Jeff descended on his hoverboard, Noli gazed in awe at the many airships docked at the Los Angeles Air Terminal. The station housed everything from the tiny, birdlike, sparrow-class schooners held together with twine and rivets to luxury, eagle-class liners, sweeping pleasure boats like the one that would take her mother and grandfather to Boston.

Mama. A pang of sadness shot through her, but excitement pushed it away. Her mother would be fine.

They landed near the main building, the street in front bustling with carriages, motorcabs, hoverboards, flying cars, passengers, and aeronauts.

"Stay close." Jeff tucked his hoverboard under his arm, then offered her his free one. They strolled through the main building, with its ticket counters and baggage check, bars, restaurants, and shops. People were hurrying about even this late at night.

They left the passenger terminal and entered another terminal, this one dimmer, grimmer, and dingier. The floors were sticky, making Noli glad she'd put on a shorter dress. Her nose wrinkled at the ripe smell. Even the people here seemed . . . fiercer.

This place doesn't look fun, the sprite whispered.

No, it didn't. Maybe she should retrieve her parasol for self-defense.

"This is the terminal for cargo vessels. There's also one for private pleasure craft," Jeff explained.

Ah, the cargo vessel terminal. Many cargo vessels were reputable, but most folks who worked on them weren't people Grandfather Montgomery would ever invite over for tea.

Jeff glared at a man with one arm and a scar on his face, who'd stalked past them with a scowl that caused Noli to inch closer to her brother. "Whenever we're in port, stay with me," Jeff said. "Even passenger terminals aren't safe for a lady alone." He pulled her to him.

They passed a drinking establishment, lively with noise and packed with bodies. Two men unceremoniously threw another out the door, onto the ground right at their feet. Jeff pulled Noli out of the way. They went through a doorway marked *Docks*, navigated several flights of rickety stairs, and went out another door.

The cool night air kissed Noli's face. The sight of the moored airships greeted them as they walked out onto the wooden pier, the ground far below. Noli's eyes widened as she took everything in under the light from the dim gas lamps. It had been some time since she'd seen so many airships up close. Most of them were fairly small, raven or falcon-class and a few little sparrows, often looking like a cross between birds and pirate ships. Balloons filled with helium or hydrogen bobbed alongside the wood-and-metal bodies of the vessels. One or two of the airships looked like repurposed military ships, gunmetal gray rather than dark wood and gleaming brass, and containing only a tiny cabin and one large balloon.

Noli frowned as they walked past a sparrow, a small wooden schooner more birdlike than boatlike. One gas-filled balloon held it aloft, and an outboard engine sat on each side of the wooden body. Its hull was riddled with bullet holes, and two men dressed similarly to Jeff stood on ladders, working to repair it by gas lamp.

Jeff raised an arm in greeting. "Encounter some trouble, Finn?"

One of the men waved back from his perch on a ladder. "Blasted MoBatts nearly shot us out of the sky over Deseret. Don't know what's going on, but steer clear if you can. Those MoBatts are sons of—" He blushed and tipped his floppy cap at Noli. "My apologies, miss."

"No offense taken." She bobbed her head in greeting. What was a MoBatt?

Jeff shook his head and pushed her past the men, giving them a wave goodbye. "Noli, let me show you my ship."

Finn eyed them curiously, but waved back as they moved down the docks.

Noli stayed close to her brother. The high wooden dock

didn't have nets or fences like the ones she'd been on before, and it was a long way to the ground below.

Can we throw something off and see what happens? the sprite asked.

Maybe later. She and Jeff had done that as children. "Who's Finn?" she asked.

"A good friend of mine. He flies decoy. I didn't introduce you because, on second thought, he's not someone you should be acquainted with." He grimaced. "I'm starting to think this wasn't the best idea."

Noli's jaw gritted as she shifted her valise on her shoulder. "If you force me to go to Boston, I'll run away."

"I wouldn't do that to you." Jeff squeezed her arm. They passed more beautiful airships, of all shapes and sizes.

"What's a MoBatt?" She made a face as she tried to think of what it could be.

"Deseret Territory's private security force. They can't have their own army, but the U.S. has no problem with them having private security, especially ones that like to chase air pirates."

"Deseret?" Noli blinked. "We studied them in school. What an odd little territory." Deseret was located between Nevada and Colorado. "Do you think they'll ever become a state?"

"I think that as long as they pay taxes, use U.S. currency, obey the law, and don't deny settlers, the government will leave them be. Did you know that drinking and gambling are illegal there?" Jeff made a face as if this was a terrible, horrible thing.

Noli laughed at his expression. "I suppose opium and joy-houses are illegal as well? What a completely inhospitable place."

His lips pursed in a way that meant he didn't find her joke nearly as amusing as she did. "They mean business. Those MoBatts are a nasty lot. Well . . . " He shot her a lopsided smile. "If you're on the wrong side of the law, that is. That's why certain types of ships utilize decoys when we need to travel through Deseret. MoBatts are even worse than the air patrol."

Noli's stomach sank to the toes of her black boots as she realized she was about to cross over to the wrong side of the law. There was a big difference between air piracy and crashing an unregistered flying auto while lacking an operator's permit.

"Decoy? Well, that's one use for a sparrow-class ship," Noli observed. She knew that the only good thing about the little ships was that they could be jerry-rigged to outfly anything in the sky.

They stopped in front of a raven-class ship. Two oblong, gas-filled balloons held by woven nets floated above it, the crow's nest in between. This type of vessel always reminded Noli of flying pirate ships. Wood and brass fashioned the body, and it had a central engine that was partly inside and partly outside—not entirely outboard, as on a sparrow—and two smaller engines, one on each side of the main engine. Unlike on falcon-class ships, nearly everything took place inside the vessel, although a brass wheel sat up top for emergencies. A flag waved from the crow's nest, burgundy with a blue stripe—a cargo ship for hire.

Clearly, someone took pride in this airship. Its wood was polished, its paint was fresh, and if it had ever been shot up, the damage had been carefully repaired and concealed. The brass railings gleamed in the moonlight. The gangplank was down.

"Here she is—the Vixen's Revenge." Jeff beamed as he gestured at the shining vessel.

"There's no name on the hull." Or picture. Many of the vessels Noli had seen in the past had pictures of scantily clad women, mermaids, or other mascots painted on the side, along with the ship's name.

Jeff shook his head. "Makes you easier to find. Also, that's more of a pleasure-craft convention than a commercial one. Though the boats *you* usually fly on probably have them."

"What boats?" Noli laughed. "Mama doesn't like airships, remember? When we went to San Francisco, she forced me to *take a train*. A train! Why plod across the ground when you can race through the air?" She made a noise of disdain. "This is your ship? She's lovely."

Jeff patted the wooden hull. "She's a good ship."

"Jeff, is that you?" called a female voice with a hint of a southern accent. "Where have you been? As soon as Asa and Thad return, we need to be off."

A woman strode down the gangplank. Well, if the voice belonged to this person, she must be a woman, but Noli had never seen a woman like *this* before. She stood nearly as tall as Jeff and had a thin body devoid of any of the curves that women usually had. Her boyishly short, near-black hair—

a lock of it dyed *blue*—hung over her big, brown, slightly slanted eyes.

"Vix, come here, there's someone I want you to meet." Jeff waved her down.

Wait. Vix. *This* was the woman Jeff was sweet on?

Noli had seen women in trousers before—one of Queen Tiana's handmaidens often wore them—but they were always feminine trousers that showed off the wearer's figure. This woman wore an outfit similar to Jeff's, as if she *wanted* to be mistaken for a boy.

Leaping onto the dock with the grace of a cat, Vix looked Noli up and down and shook her head, dark strands flying. "We don't take passengers."

"She's not a passenger, she's our new engineer—I hope." Jeff gave Vix a charming smile, the sort men give women when trying to get their way. "Vix, meet my younger sister, Magnolia Braddock. Noli, meet Captain Vix. This is her ship."

"Captain." Noli curtsied. A female captain who wore trousers! "I thought this was your ship, Jeff?"

Jeff laughed. "I'm just the pilot. Vix tells me where to go."

Women couldn't legally pilot airships, only co-pilot. But there was no law against female captains. What adventures she must have!

Vix furrowed her dark brows in a way that made Noli's stomach twist. "This is the little sister? The one who fixes things?"

"We need an engineer, and she needs work. It could be mutually beneficial," Jeff replied.

Vix scowled. "This isn't a place for just anyone."

"This isn't just anyone, this is my sister. Give her a chance, please?" Jeff's look became pleading.

Noli's chest tightened as she smoothed her blue skirts. She hadn't given any thought to the idea that someone on the ship might not want her.

"Please, Captain?" she asked, her voice soft. "I'll pull my weight, I promise." Noli wasn't sure what she'd need to do besides keep the ship running and in good repair, but whatever it was, she could handle it, surely.

"Find yourself on the wrong side of the law again?" Vix didn't quite sneer, but her expression wasn't kind, either.

She knew? Mortification crept through Noli. How much had Jeff told her of her previous exploits?

"If I allow them take her to Boston, they'll have her married off to some society dirtbag three times her age before Christmas." Jeff gave Vix another beseeching glance. "Noli wants to attend university. She'll stay with us for a while, save up, and then I'll get her settled in."

"No favors. She pulls her weight like everyone else." Vix turned to Noli. "On my ship, we don't make allowances based on gender—women do the same tasks men do. Or"—she grinned at Jeff—"men do the same jobs as women. You maintain the ship, you keep the engine room tidy, and you make sure we have what we need to make repairs. Also, we share jobs onboard; you'll have assignments like everyone else." Standing toe-to-toe with Noli, Vix looked her right in the eyes. "Understood?"

“Yes, ma’am.” Noli felt as if she should salute or something.

“It’s *sir.*” But Vix didn’t snap or say it rudely. Although the captain’s accent wasn’t quite the same as Charlotte’s, it still made a pang of sadness shoot though Noli. A southern, female captain. What would dear Lottie have made of that?

“I don’t suppose you can use a pistol—or defend yourself?” the captain added.

“I can use a sword a little.” Noli tried not to fidget under the scrutiny.

Vix scoffed, her rough, tanned hand combing through her short hair. “A sword? That’s not going to help.”

“She’s an engineer, not a fieldhand or a gunner. She doesn’t need to know how to shoot.” Jeff kept his voice calm and quiet.

Fieldhand. Gunners. Pistols. One more indication that this wasn’t a respectable cargo vessel. The pistol at Vix’s waist only added to this impression. Did Jeff have a pistol as well?

Vix shook her head, then looked to Jeff. “Go put her someplace where she won’t cause any trouble, then get to the bridge. They’ll be here any moment and we can’t afford to dally.”

“Of course, Captain.” Jeff didn’t kiss her or put an arm around her, but the look he gave her told Noli that yes, this was the woman. And he loved her. A lot.

Jeff offered Noli his arm. “Noli?”

She remembered something from the days of visiting airships with her father. “Permission to come aboard, Captain?”

"Granted. Welcome to the Vixen's Revenge." Vix almost cracked a smile. Almost.

Jeff and Noli walked up the gangplank to the top interior deck of the ship. It looked as if they were in some sort of lounge or common area. Jeff set his hoverboard in a rack, then they went down another flight of stairs. The inside of the ship seemed as neat and tidy as the outside.

"I'll give you a tour later, but I need to get to the bridge. Let me show you to your little domain." Jeff gave her a shy smile. "Also, Vix will warm up to you. She didn't get where she is by being a pushover."

Noli smiled back, not entirely believing him. "If you love her, then I'm sure I will too."

They went down a hallway toward the stern of the airship. Jeff pushed open a door marked *Engine Room.* He turned on a lamp hanging on the wall inside near the door. "Here it is, the heart of Vixen's Revenge."

The engines, bigger than Noli, greeted them, motionless and silent. The brass gleamed in the dim lamplight.

"She's beautiful." And cleaner than the kitchen back home. Closing her eyes, Noli put her hands on the still main engine, getting a feel for it. *Hello there.* Metal came from the earth, and sometimes working with metal came easier when she remembered this fact, overcoming the sprite's insistence that thinking was hard.

Thinking is hard, the sprite piped up. *Oh, that's shiny.*

It's shiny, indeed, Noli replied.

Jeff chuckled in the background and her eyes snapped

open, her cheeks burning. The last thing she wanted was for anyone to think her eccentric, or even worse, mad.

"Engineers are *so* strange," Jeff teased, picking up a lamp. "The parts closet is over there." He gestured to a wardrobe in the corner of the room. "Now, I want to show you something." A little door marked the far wall. "This was also a closet. A previous engineer, long before Vix got the ship, made this one into a workroom. Since an engineer on a ship like this is also chief inventor, tinker, and handyman, it makes sense."

He opened the door. Inside was a workbench covered in tools that took up most of the back wall. Boxes of parts and such filled the little room. If Noli stood in the middle and stretched out her arms, she could probably touch all the walls. The only light came from the lamp in Jeff's hand.

"This room and everything in it are yours to use. Also ..." He gestured to the cluttered space, lighting the corners with the lamp. "I think it would be best for you to sleep here. I don't want you with the rest of the crew. Hopefully, you can fit all this stuff into the parts closet, though you can build some shelves if you need them. I'll get you a hammock and a locker for your things." Jeff looked at her bag and frowned. "Believe it or not, Vix is very good at shopping. Eventually we'll have time for you to get a few things. I'm sorry you couldn't bring your trunk."

"I've got everything I need." Noli patted her bag and peered into the little room. "This is really where I'll sleep?" Once she moved the boxes out, it should suffice.

Jeff nodded. "It's safest. Right now we're running light.

There's Vix, Thad, Asa, Winky, myself—and now you. But we'll need to bring on at least one more person, perhaps two, and, well, crew quarters aren't the place for a lady."

The corners of Noli's lips twitched. "Do you share the captain's quarters?"

Jeff blushed to the roots of his dark and messy hair. "I have a hammock in crew quarters, like everyone else."

"Of course." She laughed. "It would be improper not to."

Jeff squeezed her shoulder, which was still covered by her good cape. "There's not a lot of 'proper' on an airship like this—or in what we do."

"I know." Noli looked up at him in earnest. "What did you steal? That's what you're waiting for, right? Asa and Thad stole something and you're leaving as soon as they return?"

His dark eyebrows rose. "You're smart."

The door to the engine room opened. "Jeff, what are you doing in here?" a gravelly voice asked from behind them.

"Hi Winky, readying the engines?" Jeff smiled at an older man who was short and a little chubby, with a white beard and a red-striped stocking cap over his too-long white hair. He was dressed similarly to Jeff.

Winky nodded. "Captain's orders. You should get to the bridge." When he looked at Noli, the man's eyes widened in surprise. "Captain didn't say nuffin' about passengers."

Jeff pushed her toward Winky. "This is Noli, my sister—she's our new engineer. Noli, Winky came with the ship. He can tell you everything you want to know about her."

Very useful. Noli curtseyed. "It's a pleasure to meet you… Winky. I look forward to getting to know this ship."

He doffed his cap. "My pleasure. No one knows this ship like me. But never have I met a lady engineer."

Jeff made an annoyed noise. "Hayden's Follies has a female engineer. So does the Laughing Mermaid."

"Female, yes, but never a *lady*." Winky nodded so vigorously Noli thought his head might fall off. At the very least, his striped cap.

Making a face, Jeff glanced at his pocket watch. "I need to get up to the bridge. You make sense of your little place here and get settled in. Winky's going to ready the engines, which is usually something the engineer does. You should watch and take notes." Jeff bent down to give her a kiss on the cheek. "I'll check in on you later."

Noli took the lamp. "I'm glad I'm here."

"Me too." Jeff left, going back the way he came.

Noli looked to Winky. "Mr. Winky, would you kindly introduce me to the engines?"

His brown eyes lit up and he inclined his head. "Why, Miss Noli, it would be my pleasure."

....

Despite the late hour, Noli was buzzing with too much excitement to sleep. Once the airship was aloft, Winky had returned to his duties below, after first giving Noli an overview of the engines and the ship's quirks. Then she'd concentrated on getting the workroom in enough order to sleep in. Her hat and cape hung on hooks on the door, and she noted that other hooks, on the walls, sat at about the right level for a hammock. She would tackle the rest in the morning.

Jeff hadn't returned, but maybe he was still needed on the bridge. Noli yawned. Perhaps it was time to find the necessary and peek in on Jeff. If he told her where they stored the hammocks, she could get one herself. She'd never slept a hammock before, but it sounded better than sleeping on the floor.

All ships of this class had the same basic layout, so Noli had no problem finding the stairs to the bridge. The common area had a room at one end—probably the captain's quarters—and a kitchen area at the other end, with a sitting room in the center. The bridge should lie on the far side of the kitchen, right at the bow of the ship. Voices came from that direction.

"What were you thinking, Jeff?" Nearly tangible exasperation dripped from Vix's voice.

"We need an engineer. We're courting disaster every day we fly without one," Jeff replied. "There's only so much Winky can do. Noli has decent general knowledge of airships and she's an ace at fixing things. She *rebuilt* that deathtrap of a flying car my father had. And she rebuilt the hoverboard *I'd* given up on. She even built my mother a steam-powered sewing machine out of junk lying around the house."

"From all your stories, I never realized she was so… dainty." Vix sounded as if she considered this a detriment.

Noli stood in the dining area where she could hear but not see them. *Dainty?* That wasn't a word usually used to describe her. Part of her preened at the idea. She knew it would make her mother proud. What would Mama think of Vix? Noli took a deep breath and tried to squish those thoughts away.

"Just look at her—she's dressed for a party." It sounded as if Vix was pacing the bridge as they spoke.

"As long as she can work in it, what does it matter?" Jeff replied

"This isn't the place for a lady. You always painted her as a hoyden, but . . . "

"They did something to her." Jeff sighed. "I don't know if it was the school or something that happened when she was kidnapped, but something's not quite right. If I let our mother take her to Boston, who knows what will happen. The last thing I want is for her to be taken advantage of or even worse, institutionalized."

Noli's blood went cold at the thought of being sent to an asylum. The words *something's not quite right* made her stomach churn. True, something wasn't quite right, but until her mother and Jeff had mentioned it, she hadn't realized anyone had noticed. She worked so hard to hide it.

"You don't know for sure she was actually kidnapped," Vix retorted.

"True. She never said in her letters exactly what happened, but she seemed to have gone missing from that school for a while."

Well, Kevighn hadn't *exactly* kidnapped her. But she'd been held in the Otherworld against her will.

"In any case, things happened to her—and you know what those schools are like," Jeff added. "She'll be an asset, and she won't get in the way of our work. If she can hoverboard and fix flying cars in a dress, then she can be an airship engineer in one."

"That's against everything the women's equality movement works for," Vix muttered.

"No, it's not," Jeff soothed her. "You work for women to have choices. This means they should have any and all options—not just the ability to wear trousers and take on men's jobs, but the right to wear skirts and stay home with the children if they so choose. The point is that they have a *choice.* After all, if all women eschew staying home and raising children, the human race will end, right?"

Vix made an annoyed noise. "Your logic makes my head hurt. She still has to pull her weight. I'm not making exceptions."

Before Noli could stop herself, the sprite took over and she strode to the doorway of the bridge. She watched in horror, fighting to regain control of her body but unable to, as the sprite spoke.

"I'll do my share. I promise. I can be helpful even in a dress." She twirled a little as she spoke. The sprite liked being helpful nearly as much as she liked being pretty—or happy. "Jeff said you're good at shopping. I can't wait—that'll be so much fun." A giggle punctuated the statement. Mortification crept through Noli as she saw the look on Vix's face.

Shush, she told the sprite, trying to regain control. *If she doesn't like us, she'll throw us off the ship.* It was disconcerting, when this happened, to observe her words and actions while being unable to do anything about them.

Then we'll go to Boston and wear pretty dresses and go to

parties? I want to go to parties. Will there be cute boys? And dancing? I like dancing.

Flying figs. The last thing she needed was the sprite *trying* to get them kicked off. *No, we don't want to go to Boston, we want to stay on the ship*, she told the sprite firmly. *It'll be so much fun if we stay—more fun even than pretty dresses and parties.*

Oh, it will? The sprite perked up. *I like to have fun.*

Noli used this distraction to regain control of her body and lock the sprite away, wincing at the pain it caused.

"Noli! Noli, is everything all right?" Jeff's face creased in a frown.

"I'm fine." She brushed it off. "I . . . I didn't mean to intrude on your private conversation. I came to ask you where the hammocks are kept, so I could set one up and go to sleep." She yawned for emphasis, though it was a legitimate yawn as sleep pressed down on her. "I know you're probably busy. I'm perfectly capable of getting one if you tell me where they are." Noli turned to Vix, hoping to salvage the situation. Blasted sprite. "I can do everything in a dress. Give me a chance. Please, Captain?" She didn't understand why it mattered what she wore as long as she got the job done.

Vix nodded, brow furrowed. "I believe in giving people chances—and you don't *have* to wear a dress."

"I like dresses." The words slipped out and Noli put her hand to her mouth. "I . . . I . . . " She looked at her feet. "I've always worn a dress or a skirt, even when hoverboarding."

"What Vix is trying to articulate is that you have a *choice*," Jeff said. "If you wish to wear a dress, you may, but if you want to wear trousers, that's perfectly acceptable. Whatever you're comfortable in. We don't really give a gear what you wear."

Noli nodded, not wanting to offend anyone. She couldn't envision herself wearing trousers, but options were useful. At least here, no one would think her indecent if she wore a dress without sleeves when she worked on the engines. "I . . . I appreciate that."

"Vix, if you would kindly take the helm for a few moments, I'll get Noli set up." Jeff gave Vix a wheedling smile.

Vix shook her head and waved them off. "Go ahead."

"Are you part of the women's equality movement?" Noli asked Vix shyly. "I . . . I hope they make it legal for women to operate conveyances solo. I happen to like hoverboarding."

"Me too." Vix exchanged knowing glances with Jeff. If she dressed like a boy, she could probably get away with hoverboarding far more easily than Noli could.

Jeff pushed on Noli's shoulder. "Let's get you to bed. It's been quite the day."

"Too much excitement running away from home?" Vix snipped as she took the helm.

Noli watched her, fascinated. The bridge had a panoramic view of the sky. There was also a periscope, which projected what was happening behind them onto a small screen, and all sorts of lights, switches, and system monitors. A large lever controlled the speed of the engine and another released barrels of water from the hull, lightening the ship to make it go faster.

"Vix, please?" Jeff put an arm around Noli.

Vix huffed. "Good night, Noli."

"Good night, Captain." Noli nodded, nearly bobbing a curtsey out of habit.

Jeff led her down the stairs. "Go back to your room, I'll be right there."

"You don't want me to see the crew quarters?" Noli grinned.

"No." This came out sharp.

"I'll meet you there." Noli returned to her little room and took a few things out of her bag, such as her nightdress. She frowned as she held up a soft knitted blanket made of many different shades of green, with fringe and tassels. Charlotte had made it for her, but she didn't remember putting it in the bag, nor the little embroidered pillow. Sometimes that happened—not remembering things. Hazards of the sprite occupying her body. The sprite didn't remember much, since she preferred to live in the present.

There was a rap on the door. "Noli, it's me."

"Come in." She turned the little pillow over in her hands. It was blue, with brightly colored, inexpertly embroidered flowers on it. A gift from Elise, the little sister of James and V.

A small footlocker filled Jeff's arms, and he sat it down on the ground in an area she'd cleared. "Here you go; a blanket and hammock are inside. Sorry I couldn't find a pillow."

She held up hers. "I have one—it's small, but it'll work."

Jeff's eyebrows rose. "You had one little bag to fill and you brought a *pillow*?"

How would she explain all her things? Using the magic valise had seemed like a good idea at the time. She shrugged. "Um, my valise is bigger than it looks."

"Is it new?" Jeff studied the valise on the workbench.

"It was gift from my friend Charlotte." Noli sniffed a little. Generous, sweet Charlotte had given her so much—including her life. "I miss her."

"Charlotte?" Jeff's face contorted in thought. "She's your school friend and from the south somewhere, right? When we head south, perhaps you could visit her."

Noli shook her head, busying herself by opening the trunk and taking out the hammock so she didn't have to look at him. "She passed on recently."

"Oh, I'm sorry to hear that. What happened?"

"It's . . . complicated." She wasn't ready to speak of it.

"All right, then." His voice softened. "Here, allow me." Jeff hung the hammock for her, turning the right wall of the little workroom into a sleeping area with the footlocker underneath. "You'll find this surprisingly comfortable."

"I appreciate it." She gave Jeff a big smile. "I'll try hard, I promise."

"I know. I meant it when I said you're an ace at fixing things. This will work out for the best, you'll see." Jeff pulled her to him. "We'll take everything one day at a time."

She laid her head against his shoulder. "I've not gone round the bend, I promise."

No, she just had some other girl in her head, one who sometimes took over. Not that she could say it out loud, since that *did* sound as if she were barking mad.

Jeff stroked her hair. "No, you haven't gone mad. You've simply been through a lot."

"V will find a way to fix everything." To fix her, for them

to be together. Noli had total and utter faith that it would happen eventually, and until then, she'd persevere. At least she was with Jeff, who accepted her as she was and didn't try to change her to conform to society.

Jeff pressed his lips to the top of her head in a way that reminded her of their mother. Then he held her at arm's length. "One day at a time, little sister. Now go to bed."

"Good night, Jeff." She yawned. Her brother left, and Noli pulled on her white ruffled nightdress, slippers, and cap. Exhaustion filled her. She draped her dress over the workbench and turned out the light. Grabbing her pillow and blanket, she crawled into the hammock, closed her eyes, and went to sleep, listening to the hum of the ship's engine.

FIVE

A Questing We Will Go

With a heavy sigh, Steven signaled for their sprite waitress. Again. She'd forgotten to bring them their supper. Again.

"Couldn't we have left in the morning?" James whined, head in his hands, elbows on the rough wooden table.

"We needed to get out of the house before . . . " Before Noli's mother knocked on the door. Before his heart broke in half at the thought of Noli being whisked off to Boston and paraded before potential suitors. Before his father told him one more time that he'd brought all this upon himself.

"Before Jeff beats the stuffing out of you for making Noli cry?" James lifted his head up.

"Jeff?" Steven cocked his head, his hair falling in his eyes. It never did like to lie flat.

James nodded, rubbing his temples, one elbow still on the table. "I saw him land his hoverboard in their backyard today. He must have come to visit her. Ugh, my head hurts *so much.*"

"Overindulging will do that to you." Steven took a notebook and a pencil from his rucksack. "I didn't realize Jeff was in town. Are you certain?"

Noli hadn't mentioned it to him. Then again, there'd been more urgent matters to discuss. Steven knew she'd been in contact with her brother since returning from the Otherworld, but he couldn't remember Jeff ever visiting since he'd left to become an "aeronaut."

"That, or it's the twin brother he doesn't have." James moaned and laid his head right on the table.

"Sit up, you brute." Steven kicked him. Indulgence brought out the worst in his little brother.

The noise of this place was overwhelming. The small pub and boarding house, which catered to the Otherworldly, was alive with a cacophony of sounds and a symphony of smells. The non-mortals of Los Angeles ate, drank, and were noisily merry. Quinn had recommended they start here, and spend the evening coming up with a strategy. He'd agreed they had to leave the house as soon as possible.

Not to mention, it was a quest—heroes were *supposed* to dash off immediately, not wait for their younger brothers to sleep off their grief-induced hangovers.

The serving girl set steaming plates of boiled meat and potatoes in front of them. Finally.

"We need to figure out what *sort* of amusement we plan to acquire for the high queen." Steven moved his notebook to the side so that he could eat and write at the same time.

"You've spent the most time with Tiana. Has she mentioned wanting anything in particular?"

James squinted at his plate. "I'm not sure I can eat." He picked up his fork and stabbed the mutton. "Now that I think of it, she's mentioned wanting a mechanical peacock more than once. Also, no one has a mechanical unicorn. We could do that. Or a flying horse . . . what are they called?" He took absent bites of meat and vegetables as he spoke.

He must be hungry after all.

"Pegasus? You think we should seek out a unique animal for her menagerie? I think that should be amusing enough." Steven rubbed his chin. "Where do we even start?" He poked at his own food. They'd ordered mutton, but his tasted like chicken—whether it was the fault of the cook or the serving girl, he was unsure.

"We go where they make the best clockwork toys in this realm." James continued making unconscious inroads in his food.

Steven made a face, fork paused halfway to his mouth as he tried to recall where that might be. "Switzerland?"

"New Bern, North Carolina."

Steven's eyebrows rose. "And you know this, because?"

"Father ordered toys from there for Elise. When she wanted that little bird, remember?" James downed his drink. "I can't remember which shop, but it shouldn't be difficult—unless you *want* to go to Switzerland. I'm sure the toys there are nice too."

"North Carolina is closer." Steven made a few notes. *Peacock. Pegasus. New Bern.*

While this sounded easy, he had a feeling there was much more to it. There always was with Tiana. As much as he wanted to dismiss what his father had said about both his mother and his uncle wishing him dead, he needed to heed it. After all, these were the people who'd conspired to oust their own family from the throne, and exile them.

"How will we get there?" he added.

James made a rude noise over the rim of his glass. "It's called an *airship*. Maybe you should spend more time paying attention in school and less time reading philosophy books under your desk. I don't suppose you brought any money?"

"Money?" Steven had his sword, which currently looked like a pen, in his shirt pocket. Books, maps, and a few items for bribes occupied his rucksack. But money? He hadn't thought to ask his father for that. He reached into his trouser pocket. "I have some, but it's not enough for us to take an airship across the United States. I suppose we could cut through the Otherworld."

Apprehension crept through him at the idea. Given that there was a chance someone was hoping to kill them, staying in the mortal realm could be safer. Then again, it might not be.

James shook his head, scraping bits of meat off his plate with his fork. "The queen's going to have spies everywhere. I can't shake the feeling we've walked into a trap. We should avoid the Otherworld. Even now she's probably told everyone that you're on a quest, and you know how *everyone* loves a quester." He rolled his eyes. "She'll have a guaranteed stream of gossip on our progress."

"Yes, everyone does love a quester," Steven replied dryly.

"Love" was a relative term. Where some people liked to aid questers, plenty liked to toy with them, which was perfectly permissible as long as you didn't actually impede them. "Impede" was also relative.

"Also, we should try not to request aid, since that's just begging for gossip." James polished off the rest of his food, then took a forkful of meat from Steven's plate.

"True, but how do we do things, then? Should we return to the house and get some money?" Not asking for quest aid meant avoiding the people who might assist them with things like airship travel.

James shrugged. "We'll do the same thing any boys our age do when they want to go somewhere and don't have the coin. We gamble or work our way there."

"I think we should work for our passage." Steven scooted his plate out of James' reach. The idea of James gambling made him queasy. James couldn't beat Charlotte at cribbage—even when he used magic.

The serving girl refilled their drinks. "You're the young princes, right? The ones on the quest?" She shot them a winsome smile and giggled.

And so it began. Steven had hoped they'd have at least some time before the Otherworld gossip mill started moving.

"No, that's not us," James lied blithely. "I *wish* I was a prince."

"Oh." Her face fell. She took their dishes and left.

"Smart. If people do figure us out, we should say we're headed back to the Otherworld." Steven lowered his voice. "I can't shake the feeling we're missing something… it doesn't make sense. Out of all the things she could have me do, this seems ludicrous. Especially if she wanted it to lead to my death." A quest couldn't be designed to end in certain death, but plenty of people accidently perished while questing.

"*She* doesn't make sense." James lowered his voice, his words bordering on treason. "I have to say, sometimes I wonder if Noli's right."

Of course, if Queen Tiana was insane, she'd have to be a mad genius, since everything she did was so cold and calculating despite her preoccupation with amusements. She wasn't a very good queen—the mishaps with the sacrifices were only two of many instances compounding the matter. Instances no one dared mention if they valued their life. Still, even if no one would say it out loud, Tiana wasn't a fraction of the queen her sister had been.

"Well, we should return to the Otherworld before we're missed." James said this loudly, as Steven left some coins on the table.

"Yes, we should," Steven mumbled. He wasn't very good at play-acting. Anything was better than mentioning their actual unspoken destination, the Los Angeles Air Terminal. They would stay far away from Jeff's airship. It wasn't as if he could explain everything to Jeff, and, well, as much as it pained him to admit it, unless they had swords, Jeff probably *could* kick the stuffing out of him.

....

"I can take you boys as far as Chicago," a grizzled man with a medium-sized commercial passenger ship told them. "From Chicago, you can get to North Carolina much easier than you can from here. We leave in the morning. I can't pay you, but you can have a place to sleep and three meals a day in exchange for being our kitchen boys."

"We appreciate that, Captain," Steven replied. It was the lowest position to be had on a ship like this, but it should only take a couple of days to get to Chicago.

The captain held out his chubby hand. "It's a deal then. Welcome aboard."

SIX

All in a Day's Work

"Get out of here." A burly man picked Kevighn up by the scruff of his coat and unceremoniously tossed him out into the early morning light. Kevighn felt the air whoosh out of his chest as he hit the cold pavement.

He'd forgotten exactly why they were throwing him out in the cold. Perhaps it was because he was out of money; the gambling hadn't been as good as he'd hoped.

He brushed himself off and skulked back toward the Saint Louis Air Terminal. A new day brought new ships. If there were no positions to be had here, perhaps he could work his way toward a larger city. Chicago and New York were both good options. Los Angeles and San Francisco were also ideas, but those cities made him think of Magnolia. Denver and Atlanta were gateways to smaller stations that could also suffice.

Kevighn stumbled into a seedy bar in the cargo terminal—the perfect place to find employment. Even though he had no coin and it was dawn, he ordered a mug of ale. That was what everyone drank.

"Looking for anything else, sailor?" The mortal serving woman had seen *much* better days, with age lining her face, breasts sagging in her low-cut blouse.

"I'm looking for employment. I'm a fair gunner, and have some experience in fieldwork. If not a job, then passage to someplace where I might find one." Kevighn downed the bitter beverage, trying not to make a face. *Fieldwork* was air pirate slang for securing a "take" and protecting it while it was delivered to the customer. Did he even have his pistol in his rucksack?

The server, realizing he wasn't looking for companionship, left. A short while later, a young, spindly man with an eye patch sat down across from him.

"Hear yer looking for a job, stranger." The man drummed his fingers on the table. "I know of a few ships looking for crew, but none of them are in port here."

Kevighn looked at the man and took a drink as if to say, *then why are you here?*

"I can offer a lift to Chicago, if you assist me and my crew by guarding some cargo we aim to take on here." The man cocked his head. "You pull a fast one and you'll be tossed over the side of the ship."

"Fair enough. If you're sure there's work in Chicago."

Air pirates had rules—simple rules, but rules nevertheless. In this industry, a man was considered true to his word until proven otherwise, which generally resulted in said man being tossed off the side of an airship, midflight.

The man shrugged. "Can't promise, of course. Depends on who's in port. But in Chicago I'll give you the names of the ships I heard are looking for crew—especially gunners. It's easy to lose good gunners to the Pineapple Rebellion."

"That war is *still* going on?" Kevighn took an absent sip of bad ale. Last time he'd been trolling the skies, Hawaii had been battling for their freedom. The United States had decided to annex the country, but luckily for the island nation, a group of air pirates helped the Hawaiians out, birthing the Pineapple Rebellion.

"Hawaii won, a couple of years back. But the U.S. keeps nipping at their borders, since the natives kicked us off their land." The man grinned, revealing a gold tooth. "Guess the powers that be hope this second attack will force them to become part of America. But the islanders keep a well-stocked air force and treat their gunners well. It might be a big hunk of dirt, but I hear it's a pretty hunk of dirt, with some even prettier women."

Kevighn raised his glass in a mock toast. "To pretty women."

The captain raised his. "Hear, hear. The name's Red. Let's discuss what I need from you."

• • • • • • • •

"Noli. Noli, are you awake?" Jeff whispered.

"Mmm." Noli rolled over in her hammock. She didn't open her eyes.

"I need your help. Please?"

Noli's eyes cracked open as she turned toward the voice. "Wha . . . ?"

Jeff was standing in the doorway of her little room, desperation etched on every inch of his face. "It's my turn to cook. Only I think I broke breakfast."

"Broke breakfast? You mean you burned it?" She stretched, trying to make sense of her brother's words.

"Nooo. I didn't burn it, but it's not turning out right. Will you fix it? Please? If we have a nasty breakfast again, they'll toss my boots into the head." This meant, into the necessary. His look was so earnest she couldn't not help him.

Noli swung her slippered feet down to the floor. "Let me dress and I'll take a look and see how we can save breakfast."

"Air pirates don't wear ruffled nightdresses." Jeff flicked the ruffles on her collar.

Noli shoved him out the door. Recalling Vix's comments about her clothing, she donned one of the simple green gowns she'd brought back from the Otherworld. The design was feminine, but it was easy to move in and do things such as climb on the roof and build sewing machines.

Once dressed, Noli rebraided her hair, slipped on her boots, and made her way upstairs. She yawned as she entered the kitchen area, or the "galley," as Jeff called it. More sleep sounded divine, but odds were Vix wasn't one for lie-ins and the last thing Noli wanted was to garner more disapproval from the captain.

"Now, what exactly is wrong with breakfast?" She didn't smell anything burning.

"How can oatmeal be lumpy and runny at the same time?" Jeff stood over the cast-iron stove, stirring a giant copper pot with a long wooden spoon. A bucket of sand sat nearby.

Noli peered into the pot and frowned. Whatever he'd made, it wouldn't be oatmeal unless they started over. As at home, wasting food probably wasn't an option. However…

She opened cabinets, taking stock of what they had. "Is anything off-limits?"

"Only if it has someone's name on it." Jeff leaned against the counter. "We stocked up in port, but go easy on what you use."

"Of course." Noli eyed the spices and selected a few with no one's name on them. Jeff probably didn't realize how good she'd gotten at making meals using as little as possible. Flour, sugar, baking soda, and a bottle of oil took their place on the counter. A sad-looking pouch of dried fruit—sound, but hard as a rock—got emptied into a pot of boiling water on the other burner. She turned to Jeff. "I need a frying pan, a colander, and a mixing bowl. A colander is a pot with holes in it that you use to drain things."

Jeff rummaged through an upper cabinet, then held up a strainer. "You mean this?"

"That'll do." Noli strained the oatmeal. One thing she

didn't see was an icebox or any place to keep food cold. "Do you have any eggs?"

Jeff shook his head as he took a bowl and a frying pan out of another cabinet. "We don't keep many perishables onboard; when we do, we usually cook them up right away."

Pouring the congealed lumps into a bowl, Noli mixed in some flour, soda, spices, and a dash of sugar. A splash of water from the pot with the fruit helped smooth out the batter. The now-soft fruit went in as well.

While the oil heated, she formed little cakes and tossed them into the sizzling pan. The fruit water continued to boil, and she added sugar and vanilla to make a simple syrup. Someone has purchased good spices. Not what she'd expect from a group of air pirates.

"Oatmeal pancakes?" Jeff washed the dirty pot in a little sink next to the stove. *Where does the water come from*, Noli wondered. *Where does it drain?*

"Beats whatever you made." She flipped the cakes over with a fork so they'd cook evenly on both sides. The soda made them puff up slightly, and hopefully would lighten them into something edible. The thickening syrup bubbled, and she stirred it so it wouldn't burn.

Jeff made coffee and she finished breakfast, pouring the hot syrup into a little pitcher and placing the steaming cakes on a plate. She covered them with a clean dishcloth to keep them warm. The pitcher and cakes went on the table, where Jeff had already stacked mismatched plates, forks, mugs, and napkins.

"I suppose you have no milk for the coffee?" Noli preferred tea, and she definitely couldn't choke coffee down without milk.

"I suppose you drink tea?" Vix stood in the doorway between the bridge and the galley, dressed in black trousers and a black shirt. That blue lock of hair still hung in her eyes.

Noli set the table properly. "Mostly. My mother never was one for coffee, even if it is fashionable."

"There's nothing wrong with tea." Jeff rang a metal bell that hung on the wall, and the loud clanging made Noli wince. "We have powdered milk; it's not bad in coffee." He took a bowl from one of the cupboards and set it on the uncovered table next to the sugar.

Thunderous footsteps followed as two large men bounded up the stairs. Both were the epitome of nefarious, from their wrinkled pocketed vests and trousers, to their tattooed biceps and scars, to their *very* large frames. One had an eye patch, scruffy brown hair, and an equally scruffy beard; the other was darker than anyone she'd ever seen before.

"Asa, Thad, this is Noli," Jeff said.

"Nice to meet you. I'm Asa." The dark man had a British accent. His dark eyes gleamed nearly as much as his bald head.

"Thad." The man with the eye patch had a guttural voice. He jerked his head in greeting.

"Nice to meet you," Noli squeaked, unsure what to do. She'd never been around men much—especially giant men of dubious nature.

Vix took a seat at the head of the rectangular table.

Thad looked at breakfast and nodded, taking a sip from a flask at his belt. "We hired a ship keeper? Finally, decent food and someone to darn my socks."

"Noli, my *little sister*, is the ship's new engineer, not a ship keeper. But she's a better cook than I am." Jeff put a protective arm around Noli's waist.

"Oh, that's too bad. I have a lot of socks that need to be darned." Thad plopped down on a long bench at the table and poured himself a cup of coffee, emptying the golden contents of the flask into the steaming liquid.

Winky meandered up the stairs and into the galley, sniffing the air like a rabbit. His striped hat was askew, and his round wire glasses were sliding down his nose. "Jeff made this?"

Noli laughed at his surprised expression. "I may have helped."

"Miss Noli," Winky bobbed his head. "Now, I don't mean to generalize, however, you wouldn't by chance be able to manage buttons, would you? I can't see the holes to sew them back on the way I used to."

"Maybe you could make a trade?" Jeff pulled out a chair for her and she sat down. "We all have chores we do every day around the ship, from making breakfast to cleaning the head. Often we'll swap. I reckon darning socks and sewing on buttons could be worth something, don't you?" He looked at the other men and grinned.

"I might be up for it." Noli would much rather darn socks than clean the head.

The captain helped herself to breakfast, then passed the plate on. Noli watched, and noted that everyone waited for the captain to start eating before taking their first bite.

"Who's flying the ship?" she asked Jeff as she stirred sugar and powdered milk into her coffee and took a tentative sip. They had *white* sugar.

"It's on autopilot, but I keep an eye on it." Jeff stood, taking his plate with him.

Thad took a bite of oatcake and made happy noises. "Now this isn't bad at all. Much better than anything Jeff makes."

Noli added more sugar to her coffee and took another sip. Ah, much better.

"This is a very good breakfast," Asa added, his manners slightly more refined than Thad's. "So we've got ourselves a new engineer. We still looking for a gunner? Denver might be a good place to find someone."

Vix nodded. "Preferably someone with fieldwork experience. Noli won't be leaving the ship much, and certainly her duties are confined to the engine room."

The firmness to her voice gave Noli the feeling that she was talking about more than the duties of stealing, or whatever it was they did.

"Noli's my *little sister*, did I mention that?" Jeff stopped in the doorway between the galley and the bridge, arms crossed over his chest, eyes narrowing.

"Little sister will be fine," Asa boomed. "I have little sisters back in England. You're about sixteen?"

"I recently turned seventeen." Noli took a bite of oatcake.

"I wish we'd hire a ship keeper." Thad licked syrup off his fingers.

"Keep wishing, Thad. We're not a pleasure boat," Vix retorted. "We clean our own ship, do our own washing, and fix our own meals."

It was nice that Vix sniped at people other than her.

"Speaking of pleasure, are we stopping in Denver?" Thad's eyebrows waggled.

"Yes—and don't cause any trouble, Thaddeus. We may stop off at a few places along the way, but not for long." Vix took another pancake, pouring on some syrup. She met Noli's eyes and gave a nod of approval.

Noli's insides warmed at the affirmative gesture. She'd done something right.

"What makes a girl like you join a ship like this?" Thad gulped down the rest of his coffee in big slurps.

"If Jeff's onboard, it can't be that bad." She smiled.

"It'll be nice to have a lady around," Winky added shyly. "Appreciate the nice breakfast you made here, Miss Noli."

"Anytime." She dabbed her mouth with a napkin. "I don't mind cooking—or sewing—but I can do far more than that," she added, so Vix wouldn't comment.

"I officially vote for little sister to cook on Jeff's days," Thad offered.

"Hear, hear." Asa raised his mug and grinned at Jeff.

Jeff waved his hand in a rude gesture, then blushed. "Umm … excuse me, Noli."

Vix made an annoyed noise as she eyed them over her mug of coffee. "She's a woman, not a lady. Though honestly, I wouldn't mind if you decided to use better manners."

"Yes, Captain," everyone muttered as they finished eating.

The captain stood and put her dish in the sink. "Personally, I think you should always trade with Jeff, so yes, you cook meals when it's his turn." Vix gave him a sly look. "However, I'd name your price high. Very high."

Jeff snaked his foot out as if he was going to trip her.

She shoved him playfully in return. "As you *were*, Mr. Braddox," she laughed.

Noli chuckled. Perhaps Jeff was right and Vix wasn't so bad after all. She gathered the remaining dishes. "I think if I cook, then Jeff should still have to wash up, right?" Looking at Vix, she smiled, hoping she wasn't crossing a line by teasing back.

"Winky, why don't you ensure Noli knows everything she needs to about the ship." Vix picked up her coffee mug and shoved it in Jeff's hands. "Jeff will wash up. I'll take the helm." She strode onto the bridge with as much poise as Queen Tiana.

"And that is our beloved ship's captain." The corners of Thad's lips twitched as he tipped back on his chair, his unpatched eye gleaming.

Jeff shook his head, smiling to himself, as he began to wash up.

Noli brought him the stack of plates. "You sure know how to pick them."

He laughed. "Oh, Noli, you have no idea."

SEVEN

Detour

"If I never see another potato, it'll be too soon," James moaned as they disembarked the passenger ship in Chicago, their rucksacks slung over their shoulders.

"Considering we're not in North Carolina yet, you'll probably see plenty," Steven replied, tired of his brother's complaining. "Let's see if we can talk our way onto a ship to Atlanta, then a connection to Raleigh. The cook told me we could definitely get there from Atlanta."

They had a belly full of food, a meal for the road, and, even though the captain had said it wouldn't pay, they'd gotten a couple of coins for their work.

"Can't we go directly to Raleigh?" James grumbled as they made their way toward the main part of the terminal. People from all walks of life passed by—from ladies with maids and steam trunks to lowly kitchen boys shuffling along.

Steven studied the large board hanging in the main lobby, which displayed arrivals and departures. "I don't see any direct flights to Raleigh today *or* tomorrow—not that I was expecting one." He frowned at the listings. "It looks as if there are a few ships going to Atlanta, and one might be in port right now. Should we see if we can gain passage?"

James' face scrunched in disgust. "Can't we try cargo ships? Maybe someone's going by Raleigh? Could we simply stop someplace and *ask*? I just want to get there."

Steven glanced at his pocket watch, then looked back at the board. Checking cargo ships meant they'd probably miss the first airship to Atlanta. But there was another later today and one tomorrow. Never would he have pegged Chicago to Atlanta as a popular route.

"All right, we'll check, but don't get your hopes up. If nothing surfaces, we're heading to Atlanta with no complaints." What he wanted was for James to stop whining, which he'd been doing constantly since they'd left Los Angeles.

"Deal. Let's see what we can find." James led them through the terminal until they found a smoky pub, filled with ship workers drinking and eating even at this early hour.

The stench of sour ale, stale food, and unwashed bodies made Steven's nose wrinkle. This wasn't a place where first-class passengers or captains of luxury ships dined. No, this establishment catered to lower workers, cargo haulers, and aeronautical entrepreneurs—those people otherwise known as air pirates.

As if he was perfectly comfortable with places such as this, James strode in, took a stool at the bar, and ordered coffee for both of them from a one-eyed man. The man didn't even wear a patch—there was just an empty socket, and it was difficult not to stare.

"Coffee? I'd rather have tea." Steven's nose wrinkled in disgust as he slid onto the none-too-clean stool next to his brother.

James snorted in disdain. "Tea? We're not at one of your silly social events. Really, we should be drinking beer."

Beer? Steven wiped the bar with his handkerchief, trying not to show the blatant repugnance he felt about this substandard establishment. His spine prickled—there were people from the Otherworld here. He should have guessed. Many of their kind who chose to linger in the mortal realm involved themselves with persons of the lowest common denominator. He and his brother would have to avoid contact so they wouldn't be recognized. The last thing he wanted was for the queen to know where they were headed.

The one-eyed bartender plunked two chipped mugs in front of them, filled with something resembling engine grease. "What are you doing here? Shouldn't you be on your quest?"

Steven's heart tumbled. Of course James would lead them to a shady establishment run by one of the fae. He wanted to smack himself in the forehead.

James leaned forward, looked both ways, and lowered his voice. "We're trying to get to Raleigh. Know anyone headed that way?"

Warning bells clanged in Steven's head. What was James doing? Did he want *everyone* to know their destination?

Maybe it was his sorrow—usually James was more careful than this.

"No, we're not going to Raleigh, remember?" Steven hissed. "We're going to . . . San Francisco." It was the first city that popped into his head. "Yes, we need to get there as soon as possible—and we're not the princes. I hear we resemble them a little. Is that true?"

James scowled over his cup of coffee. "I'd *rather* go to Raleigh or Atlanta."

The bartender scanned the room, squinting with his good eye. "Wherever you're going, I'm sure someone would be willing to assist you." His one eye winked. "Even if you're not the princes."

Steven's heart skipped a beat. Had his mother been circulating images of them, or did they resemble her or their father so greatly that there was no question? Whatever the reason, they'd have to tread carefully, lest anyone's "help" be malicious—on their mother's orders or otherwise.

The bartender waved at someone. A man with dark hair and a long black coat—who, disconcertingly, reminded him of Kevighn Silver—sauntered over. He looked cleaner than most of the pub's current patrons, but disingenuous nevertheless.

"Yes?" The man put one hand on the bar, his middle finger glinting with a black ring.

The bartender smirked. "The boys need passage; make sure they get there in one piece."

The man nodded, giving them a once-over that made Steven want to squirm. He leapt to his feet, the need to flee overwhelming, and flung a coin on the counter. "While I appreciate your kind offer, my brother and I must head out now." He looked at James, jerking his chin toward the door. "Right?"

"I really don't want to peel more potatoes." James seemed oblivious to the ominous undercurrents of their situation.

Several other large men joined the first, all with sneers and leers plastered on their rough faces. They crowded around James and Steven, preventing their escape.

"Oh, don't worry." The first man cracked his knuckles. "There won't be any potatoes."

....

"Let us out! What do you want from us?" Steven shook the bars of the airship prison they'd been forced into. There were no chairs in the cell and things of dubious origin covered the floor. The stench of the human condition surrounded him, making his eyes water.

The dark-haired man appeared on the other side of the bars. "We're helping you." Mischievousness dripped from his voice. "You'll be there in no time."

"Where?" James eyed him from his spot in the corner.

"You'll see soon enough." The man winked and left.

Steven hit his forehead against the bars in despair. "This is exactly why I wanted to avoid anyone from the Otherworld, James. Why I wanted to stick to reputable ships." Frustration leaked into every syllable. "We only have a mortal month, and who knows how much time we'll be in here—or where they'll leave us? They could hurt us, or worse."

James peered through his fingers and blinked. "Do you really think they'd do that?"

"Just look at them." Sighing, Steven leaned against the bars, which looked cleaner than the wall. Desperation rooted him to the floor, making him wish it were cleaner so he could sink to it.

"This is my fault. I'm sorry." James put his face back in his hands.

"I hope this ends well. Because if it doesn't ... " Steven glared at his brother, hoping that despite James' poor choices, he'd live to see Noli again.

• • • • • • • •

Kevighn sauntered into a pub in the Chicago Air Terminal and took a seat at the bar, hoping he'd still be welcome in an establishment run by those from the Otherworld. His exile included such locations, to an extent, but the man running this bar played by different rules.

How those rules applied to him, he wasn't yet sure.

"Silver, it's about damn time you blew into town." Roderick turned around, giving Kevighn a smile that made his stomach unclench.

He smiled back at the old one-eyed bartender. "Is it because you have work for me? I'm a little down on my luck."

"I've got a message for you." Roderick handed him a mug of ale.

"I can't pay for this." Kevighn wasn't about to cheat the likes of Roderick. Those of the dark court played for keeps.

Roderick leaned an elbow on the bar. "You've done enough for me in the past that I can spare you a pint of ale. As for that message, Ciarán says you need to stop moping and go find him. He's got work for you."

Kevighn's eyebrows rose, and he took a swig of ale. "How old is this message? Are you certain he wants to see me?"

Roderick cleaned the bar surface with a bit of dirty rag. "I think His Majesty misses you. He's doing some business in this realm, and unless you went soft working for the high queen, a man with your skills could be an asset."

Relief swept over Kevighn. The dark court was the one place he could be welcome in the Otherworld. He and Ciarán, the king of the dark court, went back a very long way, but he didn't dare make assumptions. His stint as the high queen's huntsman hadn't made him many friends. Queen Tiana and those who did her bidding weren't well-liked in the circles he used to run in.

"What sort of business?" Kevighn took another long drink. Since when had Ciarán been interested in the mortal realm? Then again, an increasing number of his people were coming into this realm for diversion, business, or to escape the mess the high queen was making.

"I'll let the boss tell you himself." Roderick grinned.

Kevighn shook his head at his friend's ambiguity. Roderick enjoyed being infuriating. "Where can I find him?"

"He's been spending a lot of time out west—especially

San Francisco." Roderick gave him a knowing smile. "Apparently there's this opium den there … "

Once, San Francisco had been among Kevighn's favorite places, home to a particularly pleasant opium den. Then he'd met a beautiful, clever mortal girl named Magnolia—and the whole world he'd carefully created, to shield his heart from the pain of losing his sister Creideamh, had tumbled down like a building during an earthquake.

Could he bear returning to San Fran? Then again, what choice did he have? He couldn't keep wandering around the United States, getting kicked out of air terminal pubs and opium dens. Kevighn polished off his ale.

"Have you heard about the museum robberies happening all over the country?" Roderick added. "They're not stealing paintings, but odd things." He gave Kevighn a meaningful look.

Odd things. Kevighn knew Roderick was trying to tell him something, but he was in no mood for riddles. He simply nodded and pushed his mug forward.

"Oh!" Roderick's eye lit up with delight as he refilled Kevighn's mug. "Have you heard? The high queen's sons are *questing.*"

"Her Majesty's sons?" Questing? Interesting. Was she trying to get rid of them? "Was a girl with them?"

"No girl. However, Her Majesty has made it clear that we're to be as *helpful* as possible." Roderick rubbed his hands together with glee.

"I hope by *helpful* you mean dropping them off the side of an airship." Kevighn had no love or sympathy for either of the spoiled princes. Especially Stiofán. And if they were questing, where was Magnolia? Odds were they'd left her safe in Los Angeles with her mother.

Hmm. Perhaps he should visit her.

Roderick grinned so wide it practically spilled off his face. "The queen made it clear that she didn't want them to be coddled, and that, well, she understands that . . . mishaps happen."

She *was* trying to get rid of them. Clever. The news made happiness bubble inside him. The Otherworld would be better off with fewer earth court brats.

"Well, I wouldn't want them to *struggle*." Kevighn grinned back.

"In fact, they came through here. You just missed them," Roderick said. "But don't worry, they're with Igan and his crew. They'll take good care of them." His one eye winked.

"You let them go with Igan?" Kevighn nearly snorted ale out his nose. "He'll probably leave them someplace desolate, naked and free of everything they brought with them."

"Wouldn't you?" Roderick laughed.

"Of course. Nothing's too good for the young princes." He'd leave them in a lion pit wearing only a necklace made of meat.

Roderick leaned in farther and lowered his voice. "I know their whereabouts, if you're interested in *helping* . . ."

"Not today, old friend. I don't suppose you know anyone going west?"

Roderick surveyed the pub, his eyes narrowing. He nodded and snapped his fingers. "I can get you as far as Denver."

"I'd appreciate that." The idea of the dark king wanting

to see him pleased Kevighn. Still, he wasn't quite ready to abandon his sulking. Maybe he'd see if he could find any of the ships Red told him needed employees and see where the wind—and the Bright Lady—took him. If it took him to Ciarán, that would be good.

If it took him to Magnolia, that would be even better.

EIGHT

The Lives and Times of Air Pirates

Noli crept toward the bridge, list in hand, and popped her head through the doorway. "Captain?"

Vix turned around in her chair and scowled. "No, you may not disembark in Santa Fe. We're only stopping briefly, and there's no time to buy hair ribbons or other fripperies. And remember, I meant it when I said you may only leave the ship with either Jeff or myself."

Hair ribbons? Why did wearing dresses make Vix think she was a vapid doll?

Wait, I want some ribbons, the sprite interjected. *Pink ones with flowers on them.*

"I only wanted to give you the inventory and supply list you requested." Ignoring the sprite, Noli thrust the piece of paper at Vix as if it were a shield between them.

"Oh, thank you." Vix took the list from her.

Noli took a moment to admire the panoramic view from the small bridge, gazing at the blue sky and the white clouds. "It's so pretty up here."

Jeff nodded from his place at the helm. His eyes fell to her waist-cincher tool belt. "Oh, now that's a good idea. I can see a few people wanting one of those."

Noli smoothed the brown leather. "It's useful. My friend made it. Mama hates it." A pang of sadness shot through her. No, her mother was better off in Boston without her. She thought for a moment. "I don't need ribbons, but if you have the time, I forgot my toothbrush. Also, I'd like a plant, if you please. A little one is fine."

"A *plant*?" Vix scoffed as she tucked away the list. She eyed Noli's tool belt. "I can see Hittie and Hattie wanting matching ones," she said to Jeff.

More female air pirates?

Noli met Vix's eyes, not about to be made to feel embarrassed for her request. "I miss being around plants and trees."

"Perhaps Noli could design a shipboard garden, like the one they have on the Vertragus?" Jeff suggested. "It would be nice to have fresh food."

Vix tilted her head, the lock of blue hair nearly covering her eyes. "Perhaps. Conditions up top can be tempestuous, so it would need to be sturdy."

"I can design something along the lines of a greenhouse . . ." Noli could almost see the structure in her mind: light, durable, and making good use of space.

Jeff grinned. "I know you'll come up with something. You're an ace engineer."

Noli rocked on the heels of her boots. "I need to spend some quality time with the engines and do a complete diagnostic, which means the engines will be out of commission for at least a day, possibly two. Will we be stopping someplace for long, soon?"

"What's wrong with the engines?" Vix frowned, one hand on her hip as if she was unsure whether Noli was fabricating this.

"I... I don't quite know. Something feels—and sounds—off." Noli clasped her hands behind her back and tried not to fidget, since her explanation sounded rather ridiculous. Winky kept assuring her that nothing was the matter. "I want to head off any problems at the pass. Also, depending on what it is, I may need parts—or have to make parts, so it might be beneficial to be in a place where at least I have access to items I can re-engineer or repurpose."

"We don't have time for you to muck around with the engine simply *because*," Vix huffed from her captain's chair. "Is there a problem or not?"

"That is why I need to run the diagnostics, Captain," Noli responded, trying to stay calm. "In order to accomplish that, I need to take the engines apart."

"What are your suspicions?" Jeff asked as he steered the ship into port.

"Engines in raven-class ships are notorious for overheating. I'll start there. It could be as simple as a motor being out on the multi-fan cooling system."

"That's easy enough to fix, right?" Vix's look dared her to say anything but "yes."

"Of course it is, Captain." It was indeed an easy fix. In all honestly, Noli didn't think that was the problem, but she had to tell them something other than it "felt" wrong.

Vix waved her hand in dismissal. "After Santa Fe we're headed to Denver, and you can do your diagnostics then. As you were."

"Yes, Captain." Noli returned to her quarters. Now that she'd attended to all her assigned tasks, perhaps she'd finally have time to make her little room more comfortable and darn a small mountain of socks.

Yes, darning socks was infinitely better than cleaning the head.

....

"Might I be of assistance, Miss Noli?" Winky appeared with a crate under his arm, hat askew, glasses halfway down his nose. Noli had just finished attaching a wooden box to the door of her little room. There were now two boxes, next to each other: one said *in* and the other said *out.*

"I'm almost finished, though I appreciate the offer. These are sewing boxes," she explained. "The *in* box, the one on the top, is for things you need me to fix. The *out* box is for things I've finished. That way, no one needs bring their mending to supper." She grinned at Winky as she tightened the last screw holding the box to the door. At supper last night, the captain had not been amused when Thad brought a bag of socks to the table.

Winky nodded and held up the crate. "Smart idea, Miss Noli. I found a few things on the ship that might be of use to you."

"You did?" She tucked the screwdriver into the loop on her tool belt and peered into the crate, which seemed to hold a mound of burgundy fabric.

"These were left by one of the previous occupants. Yer a bit more… refined, but I thought you might appreciate them."

Noli took the offered crate. "It's very nice of you to think of me."

Winky blushed to the roots of his white hair. "Just trying to make this place feel a little more like home. It's probably not what yer used to."

No, it wasn't. "I'm getting adjusted."

"The previous owner used the fabric as curtains. I thought you could drape it around the walls to make it look… fancy." He blushed again.

"What exactly did the previous owner do on the ship?" Noli's lips pursed, trying to think of why someone might need curtains on an airship.

Winky looked at the ground and stammered, "Why, this was before Captain Vix took the helm, but this ship has held a soiled dove or two in its time."

Soiled dove? Winky turned so red that Noli was afraid that if she asked for an explanation, he might explode. Besides, she could guess what a "soiled dove" might be.

"I'll help you … if you'd like" Winky added.

Already she could imagine how much nicer her little room would look with the fabric on the walls. Decorating also made the sprite happy. "Why, Mr. Winky, that sounds like an excellent idea. Let's get started, shall we?"

....

Noli sat at the workbench in her room, frowning at the open magazine. A large wire spool sitting on the worktable served as a base, since she needed something round with a hole in the center in order to weave the watch chain, and she had no hatbox to sacrifice. She put her finger on the red strands she was plaiting together and re-read the previous step in the article.

Ah, that's what was wrong. She undid the last row, redid it, and continued on.

Weaving the watch chain out of Charlotte's hair was taking longer than expected. Fortunately, the sprite adored this craft and Noli used it as a bribe to keep her in check, especially since she detested thinking or getting dirty—which was pretty much everything an engineer did. The last thing Noli needed was the sprite attempting a takeover while she was trying to make repairs.

Someone knocked on the door. "Noli?"

"Come in, Jeff." She continued weaving the red hair into the intricate pattern. "How did everything go?" The ship had gone aloft a while ago, presumably now headed for Denver.

"Very well." Jeff strode in and surveyed her handiwork, his hands behind his back. "It's amazing what you've done to this place. Where did the fabric come from?"

The burgundy fabric, only a little faded and dusty, was draped about the walls along with the accompanying swags and ribbons. The effect was quite fancy, like living in a spice box.

Noli looked up at Jeff as she wove. "Is a 'soiled dove' what I think it is?"

Jeff's lips puckered. "Where did you hear that term?"

"Winky brought me a box of things that belonged to a soiled dove who once lived aboard ship. That's a woman of ill repute, right?" She marked her place with a cog so she wouldn't lose her spot in her intricate weaving.

"Um, yes." Jeff squirmed in place, obviously uncomfortable with the topic. "And I should talk to Winky," he muttered under his breath.

"I thought it was sweet. It was only a few baubles, the fabric, some black net gloves, a hair brush … " Some *very* risqué novels she wouldn't mention. "I'm not actually sure what this is." Noli held up a cylindrical object about a foot long made of smooth, hard material.

Jeff snatched it out of her hand. "I'll take that."

Noli blinked. "But what is it? I've never seen anything like it before."

A look of terror spread across Jeff's face as he tucked it in one of his vest pockets. "Um, I'll let Vix explain that to you."

Like she'd ever ask her. Her brother's discomfort at the plain object seemed odd. What could it be?

"You like the room, then?" Noli changed the subject. The sprite preened, quite happy with her decorating. Her books, tools, and a few toilette articles shared shelf space with books and tools left by the previous engineers. Clothing had been stowed in her footlocker. The doll Jeff won her sat on her hammock, along with her pillow and blanket.

Jeff took everything in, one hand rubbing his chin, which was in need of a shave. The other hand stayed behind his back. "How much *did* you manage to fit in that bag? A pillow and blanket, several dresses, books, hats… is that father's toolbox?"

Whoops. "I… I told you, my bag is bigger than it looks." She should have realized he'd notice.

"I brought you a present." Jeff held out his other hand and presented her with a pot of tiny pink roses, each bloom a minuscule replica of what grew in her garden in Los Angeles.

"For me?" Noli took the pot and inhaled their sweet scent. "Oh, Jeff, I appreciate this so much. When I asked you to bring me a plant, I didn't think you'd bring me *roses.* I've never seen ones this small before. They look like doll roses."

They are darling, the sprite gushed. *Even the high queen doesn't have tiny roses in her gardens.*

Jeff beamed at her praise. "I knew you'd like them. I bought them off a merchant docked in Santa Fe. The windows of his ship were full of them."

Window boxes on an airship? What an excellent idea.

"They're wonderful." She sat them on the workbench next to her weaving.

"What are you making?" Jeff squinted at her project.

Noli repositioned the roses. So, so pretty. "I'm making watch chain for James."

"Oh, is that what it is?" He made a face as if he'd never

seen hair weaving before—which, being a boy, he may not have. "Supper's about ready. Asa isn't a bad cook, he just prepares strange meals."

She stood, smoothing the wrinkles from her dress. "I'm still wearing my work dress. Should I change?"

Her cheeks warmed. How idiotic she sounded.

Jeff made a concerned face that was becoming all too familiar. "No, Noli, you don't have to dress for supper here."

"Of course, how silly of me." Part of her wanted to. The sprite had slipped a couple of nicer gowns into the bag.

Jeff offered her his arm. "Let's see what strange concoction Asa made tonight."

They strolled into the engine room. Noli frowned and went over to the hybrid engines, the ones that were part inside and part outside the ship. The off-kilter hum filled her ears.

"Can't you hear it, Jeff?" She put her hands out, not quite touching the large one in the center. "Something sounds *wrong.*"

Jeff shook his head. "I'm a pilot, not an engineer. If you think something's wrong, I'll make sure you get enough time in Denver to perform your diagnostics."

"That would be helpful," she replied as they left the engine room. "I'd hate for something to go wrong with the engines when we need them most."

....

"And some for little sister." Asa put a spoonful of yellow stew on Noli's plate, then passed the bowl on to Thad. Thad's face screwed up in distaste, but he plopped several spoonfuls on his plate anyway.

"What is it?" Noli took a piece of flatbread off another plate, then passed it to Jeff.

Asa smiled at her, dunking his bread in his food. "Just try."

She tentatively took a bite of the thick stew. The strange spices exploded across her tongue, and she nodded. "This is delicious. Not like anything I've tried before, but very good."

Everyone talked about their plans for Denver. For Noli, the first order of business would be figuring out why the engines were unhappy.

After supper, Thad brought out a bowl full of apples.

Vix eyed them dubiously, then took one. "Did hell freeze over?"

"I just thought I'd share. Got them in port." He offered the bowl to Noli. "Little sister?"

Noli took one of the shiny red apples. "I appreciate your generosity, Thad."

He passed the bowl around. Winky took his and retreated into the bowels of the ship where he spent most of his time. The captain bit into hers. Noli withdrew her knife from her boot, cut a piece of apple, and popped it into her mouth, savoring the sensation of the sweet, crisp flesh.

"Mmm, these are so sweet." She cut off another piece and ate it. Everyone stared at her, and she squirmed. "Did I do something wrong?"

"You cut your fruit with a knife before eating it?" Vix sneered.

"Of course." Noli didn't see the problem, though she should be using a fork as well.

"She can cut her apple with a knife if she likes." Jeff squeezed Noli's shoulder. "Every time I bite into a piece of fruit I can hear my mother lecturing me in my head."

Noli chuckled, imagining her mother snapping, *Jeffery Cornelius Braddock, what sort of gentleman are you?* from across the table.

"That's an exquisite knife. Where did you get it?" Jeff peered at the little knife. Green stones formed a pattern on the golden hilt.

"It belonged to Charlotte." Noli sliced off another piece of apple.

"That *is* quite fancy," Asa said as he cleared the table.

"Eh, it's a girl's knife. So little and sparkly." Thad took a swig from his flask. "Couldn't even clean your nails with such a bitty thing. No good for nothing but playing darts and slicing apples."

Noli examined the bejeweled, filigreed knife about as big as her index finger. "Well, Charlotte *was* a girl, though she preferred cribbage to darts."

After Charlotte died, James had gifted it to her, saying Charlotte had wanted her to have it. Noli loved it because it was Charlotte's. The sprite liked it because it was shiny.

Also, wouldn't an air pirate have a boot knife?

"We should teach her how to throw knives," Asa suggested. "So she can defend herself."

Thad nodded. "And win money in air terminal pubs."

How did one do *that?* Not that she planned to ever be in an air terminal pub.

"Please? I *would* like to learn to defend myself," she told them. Then perhaps Vix wouldn't think her quite so useless.

"You will do no such thing," Jeff snapped. His brow furrowed and he sighed. "Noli, did you see Charlotte after you both left the school? Did you run away to go to her?"

"Yes... and no." Noli busied herself with slicing off more of the apple. "It's complicated, but yes, I saw her in between leaving the school and her passing on."

"Where? Did you go to Georgia?" Jeff pried, taking another bite.

Ugh. How did she get out of this?

"No, James took her back to the big house and stayed with her there until it was time." The words poured out as the sprite spoke for her.

"The big house?" Jeff made a face.

"Where V and James lived before they moved to Los Angeles." Noli wrestled with the sprite for control before she could say something really incriminating.

Jeff blinked in confusion. "What?"

The sprite wouldn't budge. "James is really sad now that Charlotte's gone, so he went with V on his errand for their mother."

Jeff paused, apple halfway to his mouth. "I thought their mom was *dead*."

Noli shoved the sprite back into her mental closet and sighed, trying to ignore the stab of pain slicing through her mind as she retook her body. "It was easier to tell people their mother was dead than the truth—that she abandoned them," she explained, truthfully. "It's not a happy story. Anyway, James and V recently made contact with her. She doesn't like me much. I think that's why he broke it off with me—because she forced him to. After he returns, we'll figure out how be together again." *Somehow.*

The more she thought about it, the more V's behavior smacked of Queen Tiana. Mr. Darrow preferred subtlety.

"And we're not trying to find a way to be together simply because I have some societal need for a man," she added when Vix frowned in disapproval. "I can make my way in the world without a husband just fine. But I enjoy being with V."

Jeff's eyebrows knitted. "Noli, I'm very confused. When did you meet Steven's mother? Is she in Los Angeles? And, well, if she abandoned them, why would he listen to her? I could see how Mr. Darrow might take issue with you and Steven courting—"

"Wait, that's why you're here?" Vix's face contorted in dismay; she was weighing her apple in her palm as if she were about to throw it. "You're fleeing Los Angeles because some boy broke it off with you because his mother made him?"

"It's complicated." It wasn't as if Noli could tell them that V could never disobey an order from the high queen, or that he was fae, or that the big house was V's home in the Otherworld and he was actually a prince of the earth court.

Or that she was no longer mortal.

"I . . . I'm sure it is," Vix said.

"Well, I need to return to the bridge and fly this tub before we crash. Perhaps you'll sit and explain all this to me?" Jeff gave Noli a pleading look. "You could start with when you left the school. I'm still not precisely sure what occurred when you went missing."

That definitely wasn't a story she could share with Jeff and Vix. "It's *fine*, Jeff." Noli finished her apple and tucked her knife into her boot. "Eventually V and I will figure it out. I'm sure as soon and he and James finish their errand he'll get in touch with me. That's why I left the note—so he can find me when he returns."

"Noli, if a boy won't stand up to his parents in order to be with you, then he's not worth it." Vix shook her head, dark strands flying. "It doesn't matter how handsome or wealthy he is. If he truly loves you, he'll be *with you*. He's not coming back. He's not going to fix this." Her voice wasn't harsh, but Noli still bristled as their eyes met.

"Yes, he is." She shot up out of her seat and threw away the apple core. "You don't know him the way I do." V valued his honor, his word.

"Noli ..." Jeff put a hand on her sleeve, cautioning her.

She looked into his eyes, and what she saw made her knees shake under her skirts. "Wait—you don't believe it either? But you *know* V."

"I knew him once, but you aren't children anymore. Marriage and courting are complicated—especially among families like ours, and with Mother's situation being what it is ..."

Noli's jaw dropped. "I can't believe you're telling me this. He'll come back." Her throat swelled. "He will."

Without waiting for an answer, she ran down the stairs and into her little room. Clutching the little pot of roses, she curled into her hammock, not quite crying but upset nevertheless.

Sometime later, there was a knock on the door. "May I come in?"

"No, you may not," Noli sniffed, not wanting to speak to Vix of all people. Whatever she meant about men not being worth it if they wouldn't stand up to their parents didn't apply to V, since his parents weren't mortal.

"Please? I promised your brother, and he gets cranky when he doesn't get his way," Vix said.

A sigh died on Noli's lips. Vix did say "please," and she hadn't spouted anything about this being her ship. Truly, since she was the captain, Noli should say "yes."

"Well, we don't want to make Jeff cranky, because then he'll become insufferable and make everyone around him miserable." She sat up in the hammock, still holding the pot of roses. "You may enter."

Vix strode in. She closed the door and took a seat on the workbench. "They say you never truly get over your first love… and it can be very difficult when things don't go the way you planned." She held up a hand. "I'm not saying this to be mean… I'm saying this because when you spoke, all I could hear was myself when I was about your age. I don't want you to go through what I did."

Noli crossed her arms over her chest. "I'm not you."

Vix laughed. "No, not unless you snuck into his barn, stole his prize horse, let the rest of the horses go, then lit the barn on fire."

Noli's jaw dropped. "You actually did that?" She scrunched her nose. "But who still keeps horses? You're not that old."

Vix's lips pursed as if she was holding in her gut reaction. "Plenty of people still use and raise horses. Some people like them for recreation or sport—these were race horses, and very *expensive.* If I'd realized exactly how much race horses were worth, I would have stolen more."

She'd stolen horses?

"So, he didn't stand up against his parents?" Noli's voice softened.

"No, he didn't." For a moment Vix looked far away. "In all honesty, it was the best thing that ever happened. It started a chain of events that changed my life. Otherwise, I'd never have become a captain, gotten my own ship, or … " She smiled in a way that seemed almost school-girlish. "Or met your brother. You know Jeff and I are … "

"He told me. And, well, now that I've met you, I can see why." Noli smiled back. Jeff had never liked proper girls, any more than Noli liked being a proper girl. And Jeff loved things that flew more than anything. Any girl who could capture his attention would have to share that passion.

Vix's smile grew wry. "I hope that's a good thing."

"Usually."

On the bench, Vix squirmed a little. "Noli, there's no chance you might … be in a delicate condition, is there? No one will be angry, no one will blame you, but since you're on my ship, I need to know."

It took a moment for Vix's words to penetrate Noli's

brain. Then her jaw dropped. "No . . . that's not why at all . . . how . . ."

"It happens. More than you think, even among society girls." Vix's shoulders relaxed, her expression returning to her usual cool one.

"No . . . no, that wasn't it at all." Noli felt anger well up inside her. "First of all, V would never do that. Second of all . . ." Embarrassment replaced her fury. "We never . . ." They'd never done *that*, for this precise reason.

For a moment, Noli thought Vix might sneer at her lack of experience, or worse, think she was lying or that she was some dollymop who irresponsibly did *things* with boys.

Instead, Vix nodded, face devoid of judgment. "I needed to ask."

"It might be difficult to fix engines if I was in the family way." Noli tried to smile.

"In the time that you . . . disappeared . . . did anyone . . . hurt you?" Vix didn't sound completely sure of herself, but she didn't avert her glance as if embarrassed. "We don't know what happened to you, and, well, Jeff is worried."

Noli bristled, remembering the conversation she'd overheard her first night on the ship. "No one hurt me." Not in any way that left marks on her body. Some of the punishments at Findlay House had left marks on her soul. The feeling of water pouring down on her face still made her heart race and caused her to gasp for breath.

"Where did you *go*? Jeff thinks you were kidnapped." A familiar note of disbelief tinged Vix's voice.

Noli sighed. How could she explain making a wish, falling into the Otherworld, and Kevighn trying to get the magic to bind her as the sacrifice? She couldn't. Not to her mother. Not to Jeff. Certainly not to Vix. Speaking about the fae and the Otherworld would cause them to think she *had* gone round the bend . . . and if she wound up in an asylum . . .

It was difficult not to shudder.

Vix gazed at her expectantly. Noli groaned inwardly. There was only one way to get out of this, since it looked as if the captain required an answer. She tried to plaster her face with an expression both spoiled and wounded. "I . . . I don't want to talk about it." The rawness in her voice was surprisingly real as her eyes met Vix's.

However, it *was* the truth, in so many ways. Not only couldn't she tell anyone here what had happened, but the events—from the wish, to her losing her mortality, to Charlotte's death—tore at her soul. The very memory made her regret everything she'd done since April, especially the joyride in the flying auto which had put everything in motion.

No, she couldn't bear to *think* about much that had happened, let alone talk about it. Even V didn't truly understand her pain and regret—or how hard she struggled every day to maintain the sliver of self that remained. V. Noli clutched her roses and sniffed. Where were he and James? What were they doing? Oh, how she missed them . . . missed him.

A sigh hissed from Vix's lips. "You don't want to talk about it? You were missing for months and you *don't want to talk about it*?"

"No, Captain. I'm sorry, but I don't." As she exhaled, her entire body shuddered.

Vix shot out of her chair, her persona of Irritated Ship's Captain fully returning. "I don't know what to make of you." Making an exasperated noise, she marched out of Noli's room, closing the door behind her without so much as a backward glance.

Noli couldn't expect her to understand. No one understood—except V and James and Charlotte. And they were gone. All of them. Leaving Noli all alone.

She changed into her nightdress and slippers. Braiding her hair, she covered it with a cap, not caring that air pirates didn't sleep in bonnets. Her arms wrapped around her pot of roses, she climbed into her hammock, pulled her blanket close, closed her eyes, and fell asleep to the off-kilter song of the engines, wishing everything had happened differently.

NINE

New York City

The air pirate who'd abducted them—Igan or something—sneered at Steven and James from the other side of the bars. "End of the line, you two."

Steven's pocket watch said that only about twelve hours had passed. Still, he had a sinking feeling that they'd gone twelve hours in the opposite direction of North Carolina.

"Thank goodness, I'm starving." James shot up off the floor.

Steven rubbed his arms against the chill, his stomach growling in protest. "Where are we?" He prayed to the Bright Lady that they weren't in the middle of nowhere.

Igan's eyebrows arched, a smirk playing on his crooked lips. "If you were left on an island with only one item—any item in the world—what would it be?"

Steven's heart lurched. An island? However, he couldn't think of any island twelve hours from Chicago via airship.

Igan reached through the bars and smacked Steven. "Answer me."

"My pen," Steven replied, not really thinking, his face stinging.

James eyed Igan. "My trousers."

Igan pointed a pistol at them. "Strip, the both of you. Shoes too."

Neither brother moved.

The sound of a pistol cocking ricocheted through the hold.

"I said strip. I might not be able to kill you princes—but that doesn't mean I can't relieve you of some body parts." Igan gave them a mad grin, eyes gleaming, as his pistol focused on a region Steven wanted to keep free of bullet holes.

After removing their clothes, shoes, and socks, Steven and James were tied up by the rest of the unsavory crew and frog-marched at gunpoint down to the cargo bay. Steven's heart pounded and his belly clenched with apprehension.

One of the unwashed air pirates opened the hatch. Steven couldn't see what loomed on the other side, but frigid air blast through onto all his bare bits.

"Out you go." Igan cut their bonds, then unceremoniously shoved them through the hatch.

Gritting his teeth, Steven prayed to the Bright Lady this would end well. A second later he hit the ground hard, scraping his bare flesh. He looked up and saw the airship hovering above them, the sound of wind and engines roaring in his ears.

Igan waved at them from the ship's hull, his eyes dancing with mad delight. "Have a good quest!" He threw something at them. "Here's your pen."

Steven watched as his pen skittered across the strange triangular surface they'd landed on. He took in his surrounds in a three-hundred-and-sixty degree turn, and saw nothing but darkness. Wind whipped at his hair. Where were they?

"Hey, you said one thing! Where are my trousers?" James yelled up at the ship.

"These?" Igan dangled James' trousers out the hatch, then tossed them into the wind. The crew laughed maniacally as they flew out of reach and disappeared over an edge. The hatch snapped shut and the ship departed.

Steven stood, bracing himself in the still-present wind. He sucked in a sharp breath as he peered down at the lights of a city below—far below—which was still busy even in the dark of night.

"Flying figs." James stood beside him. "We're in New York City. I'd know this skyline anywhere."

"Language, James," Steven snapped. They'd been dropped on top of the tallest building in sight. The winter wind nipped at him, making goose flesh break out like a rash across his exposed skin. He picked up his pen, which could become a sword but was of little help to them currently, and peered around the dark roof. "Any sign of your trousers?"

James shook his head sadly. "Let's get off this roof."

Good idea. However ...

"Um, James, we're naked," Steven said.

James rolled his eyes. "Yes, we are, genius. Which is why

we're turning into icicles. We need to get *off* the roof before the air patrol comes to investigate, get ourselves some clothes, and figure out what to do next."

"So you propose we simply *walk* into this building stark naked." Shivering, Steven wrapped his arms around himself. It *was* nice to see the old James returning, but part of him would rather turn into an icicle than be found naked by passersby.

James shrugged and held out his hands in an empty gesture. "You have a better idea? Because I don't know about you, but I'm turning blue."

Try as he might, a better idea didn't come to him. He couldn't believe they were going to walk into a building in New York City in the nude.

James had a point—they needed to get off the roof before they were found by the New York City air patrol. That would probably end in jail and aethergraphs to Quinn. They also had no money, identification, shoes, or clothing.

Steven surveyed the skies, looking for hovercops. None yet. He thanked the Bright Lady that the door into the building was unlocked, and thanked her again that the slightly warmer stairwell also stood empty. He braced for discovery at any time.

James opened the door leading out onto a floor.

"What are you doing?" Steven hissed, clutching his pen and glancing around as if someone might appear out of thin air and drag them to the police.

"It's late. I'm sure everyone's gone home. Might as well start on the top floor." Without even poking his head out the door first to look both ways, James strode into the hall as if he were wearing a suit of the finest clothing instead of… nothing.

Steven hurried to keep up with him.

"Look for clothes. Money, too." James disappeared into an office.

In the darkness of the empty hallway, Steven just stood there, blinking. If only he could be as free as James. Also, the idea of *stealing* made him uneasy. However, they needed clothes. What choice did they have?

He crept toward the big double doors at the end of the hall, his heart thumping so loudly James could probably hear it. Gulping, he tried the knob. Locked. Sending out a tendril of magic, he saw a flash of green and heard the lock click. He tried again. This time it opened easily.

Being earth court had its privileges. His gifts ran more toward plants and trees than metal-working, but this was easy enough. Noli seemed to do well with both. Then again, she always had.

Giving his eyes a moment to adjust to the darkness because he was afraid to turn on the lamps, Steven surveyed the room. No, there didn't appear to be anything useful, other than the candies in a crystal bowl on the desk. Wait—the coat rack in the corner held an overcoat, a top hat, and a walking stick. Perfect. Nevertheless, they would likely look silly walking down the streets of New York with no trousers.

Strangely shaped offices lurked behind the waiting area. Steven poked through them one by one, noting mentally that one held a morning coat and another, galoshes. He walked into another office. On the desk was a neatly folded suit. Shoes sat on the floor.

Had the Bright Lady answered his prayers? She did work in mysterious ways.

Next to the suit sat a note. *Jillian, 6 p.m. Don't forget the ring.* Underneath the note was an address. Just his luck that the person had brought a nicer suit of clothes to work, to change into for his evening on the town with his lady. Hopefully he had remembered the ring.

Mentally apologizing to the man who was meeting Jillian, Steven pulled on the trousers, shirt, vest, tie, and coat, feeling a little strange wearing someone else's clothes. They were meant for daytime; the waist was a little big and the sleeves were long. This man also had a larger neck, but wearing his suit was infinitely better than going naked. The shoes weren't a bad fit, even if there were no socks.

The last office, which had a pointed end, offered a spectacular view of the city but only held an overcoat—a fine wool one. Steven shrugged it on. The pockets contained a few coins and a book of matches. On his way out he grabbed the galoshes for James, making mental notes of the offices he'd taken things from. Somehow he'd find a way to replace them. Back in the reception area, he shoved a few candies in his pocket and put on the top hat. A look in the mirror told him he hadn't done too badly. He took the other overcoat from the rack and returned to the hallway.

"Well, aren't we fancy." James appeared wearing a rough worker's uniform, a satchel over his arm. "Find anything for me?"

Steven held up the overcoat and galoshes. "Should we keep looking?"

James pulled on the galoshes. "Trade me shoes?"

"No." He didn't feel guilty, either, since James was responsible for them being in this mess in the first place. If they'd just avoided their kind, as he'd wanted…

James pulled a few coins from the coat pocket. "I've got eleven cents. You?"

"Forty-three." Steven dug into the suit-jacket pocket and found seven more. "Sixty-one cents total. We're rich."

"I've got some more, though it's not much." James indicated the satchel.

That wouldn't get them passage to Raleigh but it could get them to the air terminal, where they could hopefully find work on a ship headed in that direction.

James slung the satchel over his shoulder, wiggling his galoshed feet comically. They crept down the stairs.

"I'm taking the elevator," James huffed after several flights.

"There won't be an operator this time of night. We'll have to walk," Steven snapped, though he secretly wished they could take one. The building must have had at least twenty stories.

All the way down, James moaned and groaned. Steven's fingers fisted and unfisted, itching to smack him. Finally, sweaty and exhausted, they made it to the ground floor and slipped out the back door into the throng of people coming and going from a restaurant in the basement. His stomach growled; now that they had some money, supper would not be unwelcome.

Their breath formed little frozen puffs as they emerged onto the street. Steven was grateful to have a warm coat. James studied the street signs and started walking.

"Where are we going?" Steven trotted to keep up.

"We need to catch a streetcar or whatever they call them here." James kept moving. "Unless you think we have enough for a motorcab."

Steven blinked. "Where are we going?"

"To someone who can help us." James looked comical in his workpants, galoshes, and the fine coat.

Steven glanced around the still-bustling street. Honking motorcabs crowded the roads. Hoverboards and flying cars streaked the skies, their lamps lit so they were visible in the dark. People milling about filled every other inch. How could so many people be out so late?

"Have you even been here before?" Steven asked.

"Yep. When I was searching for Jeff. Got some help from one of Quinn's friends. If we can figure out how to get to him, I know he'll help us."

The words "he'll help us" made Steven groan inwardly. They were here in New York *because* of fae help. "A friend of Quinn's? How did you run into him?"

James shrugged, a half step in front of him. "What, you think that when you ran pell-mell into the Otherworld to find Noli, I just took off to find Jeff without a plan? I went home, and Quinn helped me figure out the most logical places to look. Told me who I could trust and such."

"Oh." The idea of more fae help made Steven's belly

churn, the stink of the airship still in his nose. But if this man knew Quinn …

"One more thing." James grinned as he looked around the busy streets. "On our way we have to find a fluffy cat."

TEN

Mathias' Place

"Are you sure this is the place?" Steven eyed the building dubiously. Men dressed in fine clothes drifted in and out, and the place had the feel of a gentleman's supper club. Yet despite its fashionable address, uniformed doorkeeper, and elegant appearance, he got the impression that this place might be something less … reputable. The sign read simply, *Mathias' Place.*

"I'm sure." James strode up to the doorkeeper, a large man in a burgundy uniform with gold epaulettes and a hat.

It didn't help that his brother's jacket now *squirmed.* Steven, not wanting to march down the street with the kitten they'd found, had told James that he had to hide the cat in *his* coat. He still wasn't sure what the cat was for … or even if he wanted to know.

The doorman narrowed his eyes at them. "Do you have a reservation? I'm certain you're not members."

"Yes." James' eyes twinkled. "Under the name Gentry."

Steven bit back a groan. "The Gentry" was one of the many silly things mortals called his people. Some of their stories were downright ridiculous.

The doorman stepped toward them as if preparing to toss them out. "You're not dressed properly."

"That's a long story. We're here to see Mathias," James wheedled. "It's important."

The doorman didn't move, blocking their entrance like a wall. He scowled at them. "We have a door charge for non-members."

A door charge? Did they even have enough?

"Maybe we should go elsewhere—find someone else to help us," Steven suggested. Someone who didn't require a *cat* as a present.

"It's fine." James pulled some coins out of his bag and held them out.

The doorman squinted, lips pursing. "I have my eye on you."

They paid, and the doorman let them inside. The reception room reminded Steven of the inside of a cigar box: plush red walls, a few settees and tables, a podium. Several women—well, girls, since they were around the same age as him and James—surrounded the podium, giggling.

Beyond them, men dined in a restaurant. Tantalizing smells made Steven's belly want more than the snack they'd bought from a street vendor on the way. A velvet curtain hung behind the podium.

"Two for supper?" A blond girl approached, menu in her hand. Too much face-paint accentuated mortal features that didn't need to be made up. Her red dress revealed more arms and décolletage than was proper in polite society. The ruffled, bustled skirt, if one could even call it that, stopped just past her derrière, showing stockings and red garters. As in the popular Otherworld style, she wore her underbust corset *over* her dress instead of underneath like mortal girls did.

"We have a reservation under Gentry," James told her. "Also, we need to see Mathias."

"Mathias? What do the likes of you want with him?" Another girl in a red dress emerged from the other side of the curtain, her black hair swishing as she appraised them. This girl—who was *not* mortal—nodded at Steven as if he'd passed her unspoken test, but she frowned when she saw James' workpants and galoshes.

James ran a hand through his mop of curls. "We need his help. Could you seat us and let him know?" He winked, patting his squirming coat. "We even brought him a gift."

Steven stared at his feet. James dealt with girls so easily. The only girl he'd ever been truly comfortable with was Noli.

The girl's black eyebrows arched. "Mathias has no patience for time wasters."

"We won't waste his time. Please?" James turned his puppy eyes on her.

Steven hoped he didn't tell her who they were or what

they were doing. If Mathias didn't assist them the way they needed…

Perhaps he should have gone on the quest solo.

Then the front door opened and an exuberant group of well-dressed young men burst in. The blond girl scuttled over to the new group, greeting them and taking their coats.

The dark-haired girl's gray eyes narrowed at James. "Next time, be properly dressed. I'll allow you to keep your coats. This way." Brusquely, she hustled them through the red velvet curtain, down a hallway, then past a second curtain and another doorman. Lively music greeted them as they entered.

Steven stood rooted to the ground. The place was *much* larger than he'd assumed from the modest storefront, especially when taking into account the restaurant. The room they were now in resembled a cross between a dancing hall and an opera house. Around them, sloped like in a theater, were tables of men drinking and watching the show. Wall boxes with red curtains held tables for the more elegantly dressed men. Giant chandeliers illuminated the place.

"Stop gawking. It's a burlesque hall, not a bawdy house." James smirked. "Although some of the girls do make *personal visits.*"

Steven's jaw dropped. "You've brought us *where*?"

James laughed and turned to their dark-haired guide. "You'll have to excuse my brother, he's a prude."

This from the man with the cat in his coat?

She laughed and swished her hips, showing off red drawers under her many ruffled, far-too-brief skirts. "This way, *boys.*"

The girl brought them to a table in the corner. Steven shrugged off his overcoat, though James left his on. On stage, girls pranced to music, wearing what resembled corsets, drawers, and garters. Some had bustles with feathers, and more feathers in their hair, making them look like deranged, colorful birds. They kicked their legs high, arms wrapped around each other. Some danced on platforms both on stage and around the hall, wearing longer ruffled skirts that they held up and swished around, revealing even more leg and garters.

He looked away, uninterested.

James ordered drinks from an exotic-looking girl in a blue dress. She had a blue flower in her dark hair and blew James a kiss as she left.

"You are such a fussy old bodger," James teased.

"So what if I am?" Sure, in the Otherworld women wore less and acted freer than their mortal counterparts, but it wasn't quite like ... all this. At least not in his experience.

"This is a perfectly legitimate gentleman's club," James replied. "They pay taxes and follow all the rules. The girls—mortal and not—are here of their own free will and are compensated."

"Well, that's a plus." Even in this day and age, girls sometimes were stolen or lured from their homes, then forced to work in bawdy houses or places such as this.

A fluffy black head peeked out of the top of James' coat. He gently tucked the kitten back underneath. "You get back in there."

With a sigh, Steven shook his head in resignation.

The girl in blue returned, setting two drinks on the table,

winking again at James before she flounced off to the next table.

Absently, Steven took a sip of amber liquid. He nearly spit it out as it burned his mouth and throat. "What is this?"

"Whiskey." James' eyes twinkled. The kitten had worked its way up to the top of his coat again.

Steven's forehead furrowed. "How exactly are we going to pay for whiskey?"

James shrugged, tucking the kitten back into the coat and taking a drink. "You know what your problem is? You worry too much."

James' problem was that he didn't often worry at all.

The music, provided by a live band of scantily clad women, changed. The colorful-bird girls wandered among the rows of tables, taking men by the hand and escorting them onto the floor to dance. Hopefully Mathias would come soon.

A girl with blond hair, wearing a yellow outfit that made her look like a busty canary, headed toward them. Suddenly, Steven's cup became *very* interesting.

"Dance with me." She grabbed his hand and pulled him up.

Startled by her forwardness, he stood. The only girls he'd ever been around who'd demand to be danced with were Noli, his little sister, and sprites. This girl was no sprite. She was mortal, but plenty of fae lurked in this place.

"Come on." She smiled at him, her hips swaying to the music, making the feathers on her bottom shake.

"I . . . " He got a good look at exactly how little she was

wearing. Yes, she was probably Noli's age, if that. "I don't know how to dance."

"Balderdash," James snorted. "My brother's an accomplished dancer."

"Not that kind," he sputtered. If James didn't watch out…

She tugged on his hand again. "It's easy."

James laughed. "Have fun."

Not wanting to be rude, Steven allowed the girl to lead him to the floor. She put his hands on her and talked him through the most scandalous version of the waltz he'd ever seen. His insides squirmed as her hands kept… roving, and he saw quite enough of her garters, milky white thighs, and yellow drawers. When she pressed him to her in a highly inappropriate way, he jumped back as if burned.

"What's wrong?" she laughed, tossing her blond hair over her shoulder. It wasn't nearly as pretty as Noli's hair.

"I… I should return to my brother." He couldn't even look at her. It didn't feel right.

She got very close to him, her décolletage practically in his face. "Awww, stay with me." Her lower lip jutted out in a fake pout. "We could go someplace more private if you wish."

James' mention of "personal visits" came back to him. Steven retreated hastily, bumping right into another couple. "Sorry," he muttered. "I… appreciate the dance, miss, but I need to go." He turned and hurried away, shame burning inside him.

When he got back to their table, he found James chatting with an elegant man. He had blond hair nearly as pale as Quinn's, and piercing blue eyes the color of the sky after a rain. James said something and the two of them laughed. The man was holding the kitten in his arms.

Steven gritted his teeth. Of course James thought this was all fun and games—it wasn't *his* quest. He could return to Los Angeles any time he wished.

"Did you enjoy yourself?" James grinned.

Without a reply, Steven sank into his chair, seething.

"Mathias, this is my brother, Stiofán." James seemed oblivious to Steven's anger. "V, this is Mathias. He owns the place. He's helped me a lot, and he's known Quinn for a long time."

Steven had trouble believing that this elegant man in the expensive suit, who was affiliated with an establishment full of mostly naked girls, would be friends with the studious Quinn.

"Stiofán, it's a pleasure to meet you. Not only has Séamus spoken highly of you, but Quinn has as well." Mathias' smile reached all the way to his eyes.

If Quinn truly *had* told this man about him, how could he be rude? Steven pushed back his anger and returned the smile. "The pleasure is mine. This establishment is yours?"

The music changed again. Girls with longer skirts danced around the main floor like mad tops, kicking and spinning, showing off their legs, garters, and drawers.

If only the music weren't so loud.

"Yes, this place is mine. Are you hungry?" Mathias signaled the girl in blue.

Steven eyed the kitten. "Do I want to know what happens to the cat?" There were some denizens of the Otherworld who'd eat such a thing.

Mathias grinned. "Perhaps it's a snack for my hound."

The only hounds Steven knew of that would snack on a cat were the huge hunting beasts favored by the wild hunt and many of the royals.

"Wait—I thought those sorts of hounds aren't allowed in the mortal realm." How bitter he sounded. But his father had made him leave his hound at the palace when they'd been exiled.

Mathias leaned toward him and lowered his voice, his eyes twinkling. "They're not."

The cat purred and stretched out on Mathias' lap, unaware of her fate. If that was even it. For all he knew, Mathias was fabricating the entire thing.

"Séamus tells me it's your turn to go questing. It's my pleasure to assist, and I don't mean that in any sort of devious way. I promise." Mathias' fisted hand went to his heart.

Steven raised his eyebrows at his brother. He'd heard a little about James' escapades after his brother had left Findlay House to search for Jeff, before he returned to the Otherworld, but most of this had involved Charlotte. Exactly what other adventures had James had? And calling it a *quest*? It hadn't been a true quest, but he wasn't about to call his brother out, even if he was vexed with him.

Mathias' promise *did* make Steven's belly unknot a little. But only a little.

The exotic serving girl in the blue dress took their order. James requested grouse. Steven hesitated, scanning the menu with its multi-course meals featuring dishes like pigeon pie, scalloped chicken, and veal. They couldn't pay these prices, and one paid one's checks at establishments owned by the fae.

"Get whatever you'd like," Mathias whispered, petting the kitten's head as she purred.

Steven ordered, the girl hustled away, and he realized that Mathias was still waiting for his answer regarding how he could help with the quest.

"Tell him," James urged. "He's safe. He'll help—really help, not like those air pirates."

Steven clutched his glass as if he could gain strength from it, but didn't drink. "We're trying to get to Raleigh, but some air pirates decided to 'help' us in Chicago by relieving us of our clothes and belongings and leaving us on top of a building here in New York City."

Mathias nodded, steepling his fingers on the table in a thoughtful gesture. "Her Majesty has told everyone in both realms to be as *helpful* as possible."

His stomach heaved. No good could come of this.

"Exactly what are you seeking?" Mathias took a drink, the facets of the lead crystal catching in the light, sending little rainbows dancing across the white linen tablecloth.

Steven paused, toying with his glass, still not ready to completely trust this man.

"We're looking for a mechanical peacock… or any unusual mechanical toy," James said when Steven didn't speak. "We thought we might find one in New Bern, since the best mechanical toys come from there. Perhaps you know of someplace closer?"

Steven suppressed a groan. Of course James had to go and

tell him. But the thoughtful look on Mathias' face caused Steven's anger to ebb.

"Unusual mechanical toys?" Mathias rubbed his bare chin. "Must it be an animal?"

"No, just an amusement," Steven replied. "An incredibly *unique* amusement."

Mathias' forehead furrowed in thought. "Have you considered an automaton?"

"An automaton? Are those even a reality yet?" Steven had been reading about the possibility of intelligent mechanical beings for years, but had yet to actually hear of a truly successful creation. Then again, LuLu, his mother's little dog, seemed fairly intelligent for something made of metal. However, who knew how much of that was magic?

"It all depends on who you ask and what you consider to be an automaton." Mathias' eyes gleamed. "There's a scientist upstate who is rumored to have created *actual* automatons—as in mechanical people with a small level of intelligence."

James whistled. "Flying figs. Truly?"

"I don't have time to chase rumors," Steven snapped, sounding more frustrated than he'd intended. A true automaton—all mechanics, no magic? The scholar in him was intrigued. However, the implications of rational, intelligent machines appalled his inner philosopher a little.

But only a little.

Mathias leaned in farther and lowered his voice. "It's not a rumor. Some people are... unhappy about the scientific ramifications of such creations. But if you're looking for something unique, something no one else has, well, he's your man."

"An automaton would be *much* better than a peacock," James added.

"True." Steven mulled the idea over for a moment. An automaton. The queen had nothing even close to that, other than LuLu and a tiny mechanical dancer.

The girl in the blue dress brought their food.

Mathias nodded, the cat now asleep on his lap. Polishing off his drink, he handed his cup to the girl for a refill. "Eat, then we'll discuss maps, provisions, and transportation."

"That's quite generous of you." Steven took a bite of meat, trying to understand this enigma of a man.

"Quinn helped me considerably over the years, and you two mean quite a lot to him," Mathias replied. "Truly, it's my pleasure."

Steven prayed to the Bright Lady that this wasn't too good to be true. An automaton. Yes, that could be exactly what they needed—and much better than a mechanical peacock.

ELEVEN

Surprises

Why, oh why wouldn't the engine tell her its secrets? Noli sighed as she repaired one of the fans in the engine's cooling system.

The door opened and Thad entered, an impish look etched on his weathered face. Right now they were the only ones onboard. Thad had, literally, drawn the short straw, which meant he had to stay on the ship with her.

"Your socks are in the out box." Noli tightened a screw, securing the replacement blade.

"Thanks." Thad strode over to the far wall and tacked something to it. "Don't mind me."

Not even looking up, Noli tightened another screw. The cooling system was what prevented the engine from overheating. Should she replace all the fans while she had the chance? It would be a good preventative measure. But she still hadn't figured out the underlying problem with the engine. If she had time, she'd replace the fans. Yes, that's what she'd do.

What we should do is cover it with flowers. Then it will be prettier, the sprite suggested perkily.

We will do no such thing, Noli sighed.

The sound of something going *thunk* drew her from her ruminations. Looking up, she saw a knife sail through the air and land in the center of a paper target.

Noli sat back on her heels. "What are you doing?"

"Oh, nothing." Thad's good eye gleamed as he threw two more knives, each shot smooth and perfect. He walked over to the target and plucked them from the wall.

"I thought knives spin when you throw them. I saw knife throwers once when my father took us to the circus," she said.

"Do I look like circus folk?" Thad threw the knives again.

Noli fingered the little knife in her boot. "Do you think you could teach me? It could be useful." Even if she still didn't know what knife throwing had to do with air terminal pubs.

"Your brother said no." Nonplussed, Thad removed the knives again.

Noli snorted. "Since when did you do anything that wasn't an order?"

"True." Shrugging, he eyed her. "Since you can't even clean your teeth with that bitty girly knife, I might as well teach you to throw it. Then you can at least gamble with it."

Pulling her knife out of her boot, Noli examined the double-edged blade in the dim light of the engine room. "I can use a sword a little. Is using a knife the same?"

Thad shrugged. "That's an Asa question. But I suppose I could teach you how to do a little bit." He grinned. "Just in case you get in a fight at a tea party."

"Society events can be violent affairs." Well, only in the sense that she often wanted to throttle Missy Sassafras. "I won't tell Jeff, promise." Since she was on a ship with air pirates she might as well learn a few things about fighting. Perhaps Jeff would teach her to shoot. No, he didn't even want her to use a knife. She should ask Vix.

Thad nodded. "All right, little sister, we'll do some throwing, then I'll teach you a few moves. First off, before you throw a knife, you've got to learn the different kinds of grips and figure out what kind you like best..."

••••••••

Bitter cold whipped around Steven and James, tugging at their clothes and hair and impeding their progress as they slogged down the empty, muddy road.

Not a person, auto, or hoverboard was in sight. Steven didn't even see any airships flying high in the clouds. Given how the cold chilled to the bone, even *without* the wind, and the road was filled with muddy snow, Steven was hardly surprised. Too bad they couldn't be in front of a fire with a nice cup of tea. He'd give nearly anything for a hot cup of good tea right now—or a hoverboard.

"Are we there yet?" James whined.

"Hopefully we'll arrive soon." Steven glanced up at the

darkening sky, which threatened to add fresh powder to the soggy mess surrounding them.

"Let me see." James tugged at the map in his hand.

Steven handed it to him. "Here. It's exactly the same as it was five minutes ago."

Mathias had given them a map, clothes, and provisions. Steven still wondered why he'd been so nice, trying to see the trap, even while James insisted repeatedly that there was none.

Frowning, James squinted at the map, then looked up. "It should be over that ridge."

That's what they'd thought the last several times they'd checked the directions. With a shiver, Steven pulled his coat closer, his trouser legs heavy with mud and snow. No conveyance had been available at the tiny train station they'd arrived at, someplace in upstate New York. Walking was their only option.

Tiny snowflakes fell from the sky, their dance making him miss the wood faeries at his family's home in the Otherworld. Noli loved those silly little things. They loved her, too.

"Flying figs," James muttered, pulling his jacket closer against the flurry.

It was too cold to scold James for his language. Something loomed in the distance as they walked up the ridge. *Please, please, please let it be the house.* Steven's legs and hands felt like blocks of ice. Snowflakes fell, larger and faster by the moment.

James grinned so wide it nearly slid off his face. He broke into a schoolyard lope. "It's a house, it's a house."

Steven quickened his step, which was difficult in this

slush, his rucksack bumping across his back. "Hopefully it's the house we want," he muttered to the snow, since James had dashed out of earshot.

Surely, no one would turn them away in this weather, miles from civilization. Then again, he'd never thought anyone would leave them naked atop a building in New York City.

"Hurry up, V," James called as he neared the steps of a house.

Steven shivered as he followed James up the wooden steps, stamping the snow off his boots in the process. The three-story house seemed in good repair, with big windows and spindly turrets. A swing hung from the snow-covered tree in the front yard. The window boxes probably held flowers in summertime. Not what he'd expected from a mad scientist.

James thumped on the door with the huge brass knocker. Steven joined him as the door opened. A uniformed maid, probably not much older than Noli, peered out with big blue eyes, her blond curls poking out of her neat white cap.

"May I help you?" she asked, her accent heavy. German, perhaps?

Steven took off his hat and bowed. "Good afternoon. We're here to see Dr. Heinz."

A frown creased her winsome face. "Is the doctor expecting you?"

"No, he's not, but it's a very important matter. I'm Steven Darrow and this is my brother James." He had to see the scientist—he just had to. Behind them, the snow fell in white sheets as the wind howled in a way that sent shivers up his spine.

"We're willing to wait." James shot her his wheedling smile. "We've traveled all the way from Los Angeles to see him."

"Los Angeles?" The maid's eyes brightened and the door fell open, revealing her attractive body. "I hope to go there next year and be an actress in the moving pictures."

Her and every other pretty girl in the world.

James' smile became snow-melting. "Oh, I think you'd do well."

Her hand went to her lips, to hide her grin. "You think so?"

"Oh, I do." James winked.

"Could you see if Dr. Heinz is available, please?" Steven interrupted, tiring of James' shameless flirting. His brother's wild moods were disorienting. Everyone coped differently, but perhaps he really should have left James behind in Los Angeles to drink away his sorrows.

The maid bobbed and stepped back, gesturing to the open door. "Please, come in, it's too cold to wait outside."

"We appreciate this greatly," Steven replied as she showed them to a comfortable parlor. A fire roared invitingly. He took a seat in one of the brown chairs, but James stood in front of the hearth warming his red hands.

"Captain Scott, is that you? Do you have word?" an accented male voice called from the hallway. A tall, thin man with spectacles and blond hair entered the room. Magnifying goggles were perched on his head. A leather apron, the sort Noli preferred, covered his clothing. This mortal mad scientist glowed with the Spark—as much as Noli had. More.

Looking them up and down, Dr. Heinz frowned. "You are not Police Captain Scott."

Steven stood. "No, Dr. Heinz, sir. I'm Steven Darrow, and this is my brother James. We've traveled a very long way to meet you. We hope you can help us."

Dr. Heinz's face fell. "Help you? I don't have time to help."

The maid bustled in with a tea tray.

"Bridgid," he barked, "I thought I told you not to bother me unless it was the police."

"I couldn't turn them away in the snow, sir." Bridgid set the tray on the table and poured three cups of tea, then left after giving James a saucy wink. Dr. Heinz just stood there, scowling.

"Mathias, in New York City, sends his regards—and a bottle of whisky. He says it's your favorite." Steven took the bottle out of the rucksack and held it out toward Dr. Heinz.

"Mathias sent you?" Dr. Heinz eyed the bottle, then took it, examining it carefully. "He does have good taste in wine, women, and song."

"That he does." James plopped down in a chair, grabbing a cup of tea.

Dr. Heinz took a seat on the settee between the brothers, setting the bottle on the low table by the tea tray. He let out a sigh that trembled through his entire being.

"I apologize," he told them. "I'm Dr. Maximilian Heinz, inventor. Usually, I adore guests. However, I'm currently in the middle of something…delicate. I may not have time to assist you. Given the weather, and the fact that you probably walked from town, I'll hear you out."

"I appreciate that, sir." Steven took a cup of tea from the tray on the table in front of them. "I'm looking for an automaton. Nothing specific, just very unique. Something no one has ever seen. It's..."

"It's a gift for our mother. She loves amusements no one else has," James supplied.

Steven glared at his brother over his teacup. "Anyway, Mathias says that when it comes to automatons, you are the best."

"*True* automatons are impossible." Dr. Heinz laughed a little too hard and fast. "However, I do have some mechanical beings and creatures, if you wish to take a look. Perhaps you'll find something you like."

Steven's belly unknotted, warmed by the fire, tea, and good news. "Now that would be splendid."

....

As he appraised the assortment of toys and animals in Dr. Heinz's basement laboratory, Steven thought how Noli would love this place, so crowded with gadgets and do-dads.

A mechanical bird zipped around the room, perching on the good doctor's wrist at his whistle. It was much like one Tiana already had. As nice as Dr. Heinz's inventions were, none of them were extraordinary enough to satisfy the high queen of the Otherworld.

"Do any of these seem interesting, young gentleman?"

Dr. Heinz put the bird back in its cage, looking expectant. Through all his demonstrations, he'd seemed … dispassionate. No, more like distracted, as if his mind was straying far from them and his inventions.

"Where do you keep the good stuff?" James asked. "This is nice, but we're looking for something more … sophisticated."

Dr. Heinz pushed his glasses up, which had slid down the bridge of his very straight nose. His lips pursed into a hard line. "Mathias told you about Helga." Unhappiness dripped from his voice as he shoved his hands deep into his trouser pockets. "Helga is not for sale."

James opened his mouth and Steven elbowed him in the ribs.

"Could we … see Helga? Please?" Steven ignored James' scowl.

The doctor crossed his arms over his apron-covered chest. "I will never sell her."

"This means you've created a true automaton—one with intelligence?" Sparks of hope zipped through him. Even if Helga wasn't for sale, that meant the doctor could create something for them.

Dr. Heinz huffed, as if trying, and failing, to find the words he sought. "I'll show you. She is … she is unlike anything you have ever seen. Helga? Helga, come here, please."

Silence blanketed the lab as Dr. Heinz expectantly watched the doorway to the other room.

Clink. Clink. Clink.

Metallic footsteps sliced through the silence like scythes.

A figure made of brass appeared in doorway. Not all the pieces matched, making her look like a well-made quilt of metal. Most definitely female, or at least formed in the shape of one, she stood about the height and girth of a grown woman.

She stopped in front of Dr. Heinz but didn't say anything. Dr. Heinz motioned to her. "This, young gentlemen, is Helga. She's my laboratory assistant. I have programmed her with twenty-seven routine tasks."

"She's marvelous," Steven breathed, taking Helga—and the concept behind her—in.

"Does she speak?" James' eyes were alight with boyish curiosity.

"No, but she responds to simple voice commands that correspond with her programmed tasks, as well as directions like *come here* and *stop.*" Dr. Heinz puffed up with pride and gave the automaton a fond look.

Steven moved closer to get a better look at the automaton. Twenty-seven task and voice commands? Wondrous. Helga's back was as smooth as her front, with the exception of a windup key. "She's clockwork?"

"Partially. She also runs on an analog system ..." Dr. Heinz continued, but Steven didn't understand a word past "system."

"She truly is amazing," he finally said, trying to get the good doctor to cease speaking about things he didn't have time to understand. If only Noli were here. She'd probably have Dr. Heinz telling her all his industrial secrets in moments.

Dr. Heinz shook his head. "She's not for sale."

"Of course, you need her for your work," Steven said reassuringly. Having often worked beside Noli, he could understand the benefits of someone who obeyed orders perfectly and didn't offer their own opinions.

"Is she intelligent?" James squinted at the automaton.

"Intelligence is relative," Dr. Heinz replied. "She can perform up to three tasks in a series, but cannot look at something and decide which tasks to do on her own. Not yet, anyhow." He twitched. "There are . . . . there are people who would as soon *never* see such a thing."

"True. Not everyone has embraced the progress of the American Renaissance," Steven agreed. Such as Noli's mother. Though she simply didn't *use* the new inventions; some sought to keep others from using advanced technology, or even from creating it.

"Could you make something like Helga, but make her tasks more feminine?" James grinned cheekily. "I think my mother would like something that responds to her orders."

"That she would," Steven added dryly. Especially something that couldn't think for itself.

Dr. Heinz rubbed his chin. "Yes, I could. But it would take time. Months."

"Oh." Steven's heart fell all the way to the floor and lay at his feet, gaping like a fish on land. "We need it in about two weeks." This would give them about a week's buffer to get it back to the Otherworld, just in case they encountered more helpers.

"I . . . " The scientist went quiet for a long moment, then walked into the other room, gesturing for them to follow.

When they joined him in what seemed like a half storeroom, half junkyard, Dr. Heinz pulled back a curtain. "This is Hilde. She's unfinished. She's being programmed to play games, tell stories, and sing songs. She, too, will respond to voice commands, but cannot speak directly."

Hilde was smaller than Helga, a child instead of a woman, with a molded dress and hair.

"Could you have her ready in a week?" Steven asked. Hilde would be *perfect.*

Dr. Heinz's mouth clamped shut and his eyes narrowed. "If you want Hilde, not just another one like her, it will be expensive, but yes, I could have her ready in a week for the right price."

"Oh. Right." Something else Steven had forgotten—Mathias had given them supplies, but not money to purchase the item. That was his responsibility.

Dr. Heinz stiffened. "I think it would be best for you to go. Return when you have the money and we'll talk."

"Is there something we can trade, or do for you?" James asked.

"Not unless you can bring back my daughter." Dr. Heinz stomped back into his main lab. Steven and James followed.

"Daughter?" Steven asked softly. "Wait, was Hilde for her?" An automaton that played games, told stories, and sang would be ideal for a small child.

Dr. Heinz nodded. "She doesn't know about Hilde, hence my willingness to sell her for the right price and create another when I get my daughter back. The police keep promising to find her. But they haven't." His cheeks flushed with anger and his hands fisted. "If I could, I'd go after her myself."

"Wait—she's been taken?" For a moment, Steven had thought that his daughter had died.

"My Rahel is only five. She's all I have left." Pain swept through Dr. Heinz's face, causing it to contort. "She was taken several days ago. I fear the traffickers got her."

"Traffickers?" The very word soured in Steven's mouth. They stole children and young people, often selling them into nefarious industries.

"I hope not, but who else would steal a child from her own yard? They *were* reported in the area." He sighed. "They're probably halfway across the States by now."

"What if we brought her back?" James piped. "If we bring back Rahel in two weeks or less, could we have a fully functioning Hilde for no charge?"

"James, what are you doing?" Steven hissed, his eyes bulging. As terrible as the doctor's plight was, he didn't know how to find a stolen child. He'd barely found Noli in the Otherworld when he could track her by her sigil.

James shook his head and hissed, "Trust me."

Dr. Heinz looked at the both of them, so much pain in his face that Steven took a step back. "Young gentleman, bring back my sweet Rahel and you may have whatever you wish."

....

As soon as the storm passed, the doctor gave them a ride to town and they caught the train back to New York City.

Unlike Noli, Steven didn't mind trains, but he couldn't enjoy the ride. He put his head in his hands.

"I can't believe you promised him we'd find his little girl. '*Nay, if our wits run the wild-goose chase, I am done*,'" he quoted. That's what this felt like: a wild-goose chase.

"Ease up," James shot back from the seat next to him. "And stop quoting Chaucer."

"It's Shakespeare, you heathen," Steven corrected.

James waved him off. "Whoever. I can't believe you borrowed a *book* from him." He nodded at the book on Steven's lap. "Boring."

Steven narrowed his eyes at his brother. "Machiavelli's *The Prince* is not boring."

"Sure," James scoffed. "You know, if we pull this off, then we'll have the best automaton ever and the doctor gets back his little girl. Everyone wins. Besides, the idea of children being stolen makes me ill."

"Me too. But time is slipping away. How are we going to find the traffickers?" Steven picked up the book, grateful he had something to block out his brother with.

James shoved a little doll under his nose.

"What?" Steven sat up.

"This was Rahel's. I can use it for a tracking spell." James' chest puffed up with pride.

Steven blinked at his brother's words. "You know a tracking spell? *I* don't even know a proper tracking spell."

James smirked. "Finding Noli would have been much easier if you had. Um … " His cheeks flushed. "After you two left, I had to do something in the Otherworld when

Charlotte was busy, so I started working with a magic tutor from the Academe. It was either that or join mother's royal guard, and you know I'd rather muck stalls than do that."

"You voluntarily learned spells?" Steven gaped at his brother in disbelief. Usually James had to be bribed with swordplay to learn spells.

"I told you, I had to do something." James shrugged it off as if it were nothing.

What had they gotten themselves into? Part of Steven wanted to rage at his brother for leading them into *another* idiotic mess. Yet at the same time, if they succeeded, then not only would they have what they sought, but they'd have done something good for someone else in the process.

Steven sighed, wishing he could exhale all his problems. "We might as well."

Certainly they didn't have more to lose.

TWELVE

Denver

Kevighn skulked into yet another pub at the Denver Air Terminal. Hopefully this time the Bright Lady would smile upon him and he'd find *someone* who was hiring—or going toward San Francisco. He sat at a table with a good view of the bar and ordered a glass of rum from the buxom serving woman.

"Anything else?" She gave him a saucy wink as she set his drink in front of him.

"You wouldn't by chance know if Snowball's Chance or Ardentia Nare is in port?" Kevighn added an extra coin to her palm along with the cost of the rum. Roderick had introduced him to some very bad gamblers back in Chicago.

She shot him a sly smile, pocketing the coin. "Perhaps." He handed her another coin, groaning inwardly. "You looking for work, or you got a job for them?" she asked, letting her breasts waggle in his face.

"Work."

Nodding, she cast a glance around the pub. "Snowball's Chance is here—captain's over in the corner." She jerked her head to indicate a larger, balding man with a hat who could have stepped right out of a penny dreadful. "Also, you can ask over at the Vixen's Revenge. I hear they're looking for someone."

"To do what?" Not that it mattered at this point.

"Not sure. But I think they're having engineering issues." She giggled.

Did he have enough coin to find a harbor to drop his anchor in?

"They've been in port a couple days, and their captain's getting testy. Though that captain's always testy." She chuckled. "The first mate and some of the crew are at that table over there." She jerked her head toward a table near the window with two *very* large men, one of them dark. The third man, with a mop of chestnut curls, threw back his head and laughed, revealing big, steel-colored eyes.

Kevighn studied the man a little ... could it be? These eyes were bluer. Still, there was quite the resemblance, and her brother *was* an air pirate.

Did he dare? It might be nice to have a connection to Magnolia, if this was, in fact, the person he thought it was.

"The one with the curly hair—is his name Jeff?" he asked.

She nodded vigorously. "He's first mate. Mighty fine pilot."

Yes, the Bright Lady was smiling upon him indeed.

Kevighn handed the serving woman another coin. "Buy

him another glass of whatever he's drinking, with my compliments."

She hustled off. Kevighn drank his weak rum and sighed, praying everything would work out for the best. He peered at his fellow patrons—this bar wasn't the dingiest or dirtiest he'd been to since he was exiled.

Magnolia. By the Bright Lady, he missed her. Who would have thought a slip of a mortal girl could have gotten under his skin the way she had?

A while later, Jeff wandered by. "I hear you're looking for a job."

Kevighn nodded, gesturing to the free stool at the small table. "The name's Kevighn—Kevighn Silver. I'm a fair gunner, have experience with fieldwork and safekeeping, and can pilot a bit. I even know a small amount about engines. I hear you're having engineering issues?"

Jeff's eyes flashed in a way that reminded Kevighn of his fair blossom. "We're fine," he replied with a hint of tension. "You know engineers. *I need to do a diagnostic* is code for *I want to do things to the engines that you won't approve of and may not actually work.*"

Kevighn laughed at his summation. "True."

Jeff visibly relaxed and took a seat. "The name's Jeff Braddox. First mate on the Vixen's Revenge."

Braddox? Not Braddock? Then again, he could be trying to protect his family's good name.

"Got any references?" Jeff looked him over in a way that was, again, reminiscent of Noli. As if he were trying to weigh his soul and read his mind in a single glance.

Kevighn rattled off the fake references Roderick had given him in Chicago.

Jeff rubbed his chin, nodding. "We'll try it out, and if it doesn't work we'll leave you in a large port, one where you can find other work. However ... you don't have any issues working with women, do you? And I mean women crew members, not soiled doves or the like."

"No, none at all," Kevighn replied. The promise of being left in a port where he could find work if it didn't work out smacked of an honorable respectability he didn't usually encounter among air pirates.

Then again, he knew Magnolia was wellborn.

"Good. Captain's a woman." Jeff looked around, then motioned to someone.

A very tall boy strode over. It took Kevighn a moment to realize it was actually a woman in boy's clothing. A lock of blue hair hung in her dark eyes.

"Captain Vix, I think I found our new crew member. His name's Kevighn Silver," Jeff told her. "He's quite qualified and has excellent references."

Vix's eyes narrowed as she took him in. "I don't welcome troublemakers." She had an accent better suited to a joy-girl than a captain. "You don't bother my crew, you don't cause problems on ship, you don't cause problems in port, and you don't cause problems when we're on a job. You follow orders—*my* orders. Everyone pitches in onboard, including with the cooking. You get food, a place to sleep, and a percentage of the take. Understood?"

Cooking? Well, Magnolia had never complained about his cooking. "Sounds good, Captain."

A woman captain. Why not?

She and Jeff exchanged looks, then she extended her hand. "We agree to a trial, then?"

"Agreed." They shook.

"Welcome to the Vixen's Revenge. Be onboard by sundown tonight. Oh—" Her eyes met his, so intense they burned into him. "Stay out of the engine room. That's an order."

How strange. Perhaps they hid cargo in there. "Yes, sir."

"Good." She left. Jeff followed, throwing Kevighn a friendly smile over his shoulder as they walked out of the pub. Magnolia's smile.

Sundown tonight. He had more than half the day. Now… how to spend it?

••••••••

Hmmm. Noli cocked her head, a wayward strand of hair falling in her eyes. Pushing it back, she added some pink. Yes, that was it. Now for more yellow… such a cheerful color. Oh, and green—the very best color of them all.

"What are you doing?" Jeff's voice startled her, and Noli jumped. She was standing in front of the center engine, a paintbrush and palette in her hand. Tiny flowers festooned the gleaming brass, and she was surrounded by the parts she'd taken *out* of the engine and should be putting back in. Pain shot through her head, and she rubbed her temples with one paint-covered hand.

Wait. *Paint-covered?*

Her heart skipped a beat. The paintbrush fell to the floor as panic rippled through her.

"Shhh, it's all right, Noli, it's all right. It's me." Jeff came up behind her, voice soft.

"I . . ." The sprite had taken over and she *hadn't even noticed.* Her knees buckled.

Jeff's hand brushed her face, cupping it. "Vix is on her way down. Put on your gloves and goggles and make like you're getting the engines back together. I'll put this away. Tell her that you're almost finished and then we'll get you out of here."

She nodded, gulping. Her throat stayed swelled shut and she gulped again, her body shaking. Closing her eyes, she tried to remember what had happened. Nothing. Given the number of flowers decorating the engine, she'd been at this for a while.

Jeff picked up the paintbrush and took the palette out of her hand. "You can't let her see you like this. She won't understand."

No, she wouldn't. Gloves. Where were they?

The work gloves lay discarded on the floor. Noli tugged them over her paint-spattered hands, flipping her leather apron over to the side without paint. Footsteps echoed in the distance. The heat in the engine room was stifling, so she'd worn one of her sleeveless work gowns that she'd brought from the Otherworld, and pink paint streaked her right arm. Hopefully Vix wouldn't notice.

Noli's heart raced as if she were a naughty child scrambling to hide her actions before her mother came into the room. She grabbed her magnifying goggles and flung herself onto the floor of the engine room among the parts, her arms shaking. Vix strode in just as she picked up a gear.

Her heart continued to pound. Flying figs—she couldn't remember if she'd done anything with the engine while the sprite was in charge.

Vix's eyes narrowed at the state of the room. "I need those engines working by sundown. We've been here too long."

Gulping, Noli nodded. "Yes, Captain. The fan on the starboard engine was malfunctioning, causing the engine to overheat and making the other fans overcompensate. I've fixed that. Also, there were a number of parts that looked like they'd been spot-fixed, to be replaced at another time. Since we had those parts on hand, and the time, I made those changes and a few other preventative repairs. The last thing we want is something to break when we're on the run."

While she wasn't certain what the precise problem had been, the engines certainly seemed happier. She may have also made a few … improvements as well. This was why the engine hadn't been put together yet.

"Oh, very good." Vix's eyes filled with surprise, as if she hadn't expected there to have actually been a problem or that Noli would be capable of fixing it.

Noli realized that the captain was gazing at her expectantly. Her cheeks burned. "I'll get the engine put back together—it shouldn't take me long."

In theory.

"Hurry up or you won't get to go off ship. Everyone needs to be onboard by sundown." Vix looked around, and Noli prayed she wouldn't notice the flowers on the engine.

Distraction time.

"Will you teach me how to shoot, Captain? Please?" she asked quickly. "I... I was considering what you said about defending myself." Noli didn't know if pistols worked in the Otherworld, but who knew when she might return there? Knife fighting would probably help her in both worlds.

Vix's dark eyebrows rose. "Have you asked Jeff?"

"I figured you were a better shot." Noli grinned at her.

Vix shook her head, her mouth twitching. "I do have to say, I think that dress is quite practical. It can get hot and stuffy down here." Vix craned her neck. "Where *is* that brother of yours?"

As if on cue, Jeff sauntered out of the workroom, their father's battered toolbox in his hand. "Noli, I have no idea what part you're talking about, so I just brought your entire toolbox."

"You're the best, Jeff." Noli took it from him. Toolbox. Good call. She'd been using the ship's tools, since most of them were specific to fixing airships. But she could have something special in her own toolbox; Vix wouldn't know.

"I'll help, if you like." Jeff pulled on a spare set of goggles. "I know a little about engines."

"Well, I suppose. I hear you had an excellent teacher." Noli laughed; their father had taught the both of them. After he'd disappeared, Jeff had continued to help her build and invent.

Vix rolled her eyes, her lips still twitching. "I'll leave you to your repairs. Remember, Noli, you can't disembark without Jeff."

"I know." She took a deep breath in attempt to slow her racing heart.

"We've already got plans." Jeff smiled at Vix and waggled his eyebrows. "If you're a good captain, perhaps we'll bring you back something."

Laughter bubbled from Vix's lips. "You two are very strange. Oh." Her laughter stopped. "Noli, you should know that we brought on a new crew member for a trial. While he could be perfectly fine, I don't trust him yet, so steer clear."

Noli blinked, trying to understand what this meant.

"Asa, Thad, even Winky—I trust them with my life, and I know they won't lay a hand on you. But him ... " Vix shook her head. "Be careful around him."

"Yes, sir." A new crew member?

"That's all. As you were." She left.

As soon as the door closed, a sigh of relief shuddered through Noli. That was close. *What did you do?* she shouted mentally at the sprite. *Do you understand how much trouble we could have been in?*

But this is so *boring*, the sprite whined. *We've been doing this for days. I did a good job. The engine is so pretty. The pink ribbons add a nice touch.*

Ribbons? Sure enough, pink ribbons festooned the engines.

Do you want to get thrown off the ship—or worse, sent to

an asylum? Noli yelled. *Do you know what those places are like? They make Findlay House look like a seaside resort!*

The sprite wouldn't know—or care—about the dreadful Findlay House, since she didn't like unpleasant things.

But Noli remembered. Suddenly, she was back there, strapped to the table, water pouring over her face, choking her.

"Noli, Noli, look at me." Jeff's voice sliced through her panic as he crouched in front of her, both hands cupping her face. "Shhh, it's all right."

"I … I can't breathe." Her lungs screamed for air, but water filled her mouth and nose.

He pulled her to his chest. "Yes, you can. Just take a deep breath. In, out, in, out."

"The water, the water is choking me." Over and over, all she could see, all she could feel, was the deluge of ice-cold water.

"No, it's not," Jeff soothed. "There's no water here. Just me and you in the engine room aboard the Vixen's Revenge. It's all right." He whispered to her over and over, until she was able to remember that she wasn't at Findlay.

"That's my girl." He smiled at her, but it was a worried smile.

"They tried to break me." Noli's voice cracked. "They tried to take away everything that was me until I was nothing but a vapid pile of mush." The memories of Findlay made her tremble. "If … if … " Her mouth clamped shut. She couldn't tell him about the wish she'd made to escape, or about the Otherworld.

Jeff's eyes bore into her. "My word, what did they do to you?"

She looked away, shame consuming her.

And this is why I don't think about unpleasant things, the sprite said.

Jeff's hand grazed her cheek, and for a moment he reminded her so much of their father her heart ached.

"There's grease on your cheek," he told her, wiping it off with his fingers.

"Hazards of the job." She flashed him a weak grin.

He held up a gear shaft. "Let's get this engine put back together. Then I'll take you off ship. What would you like to do?"

"I want to go to a park." The words slipped out, but she wanted to see trees, feel bark under her hands, play in the dirt. Her roses were nice but not enough. "We could go on a picnic," she added, trying to cover her odd request. "Like we used to with Mama." Before their father disappeared, they'd gone on a picnic in the park nearly every Sunday that the weather was pleasant. Actually, it did sound like a good idea.

"Noli, we're in Denver, and it's *cold.* There's snow on the ground. But—" He gave her a gentle smile, his eyes still brimming with concern. "I understand wanting to go outside. It can be a little much being cooped up, especially at first. I never thought to ask if you wanted me to take you up top—sorry."

"It's all right." She smiled back, then held up a wrench. "Now let's see how much you remember."

....

The engine had been reassembled, the pink ribbons had been put away; the painted flowers, however, hadn't seemed to want to come off. But Noli felt excitement bubbling inside her at the thought of being off ship, back among plants and trees.

She changed into the blue bustle dress she'd worn to the pier and positioned her derby hat, the one with the bird on it, on her head, smoothing down her hair to cover the spritely points on her ears. Then she pulled on her cape and the net gloves she'd gotten from the box. They were rather striking.

Perhaps she could find a clip for the watch chain while they were out. Progress on it was slow, but the pattern was turning out beautifully.

Voices came from the bridge as she approached it to find Jeff. Didn't they realize how far their voices carried? The ship was quiet; everyone but Vix and Jeff was already in port.

"I don't know if I like this," Vix said. "But I trust you."

"Everything will be fine," Jeff replied.

"I hope so. Do I even *want* to know what happened in the engine room?" Vix's tone made Noli squirm in her dainty black boots.

"No, you don't," Jeff replied. "But we got everything put back together and cleaned up, mostly."

"Is this going to become a *problem*? Yes, she's your sister, and I understand that she's been through who knows what. Still, I must maintain order aboard my ship, and if she's going to put us in danger—"

"Give her a chance. I'm her older brother—it's my job to take care of her. You know exactly what will happen if we send her to Boston." Frustration tinged Jeff's voice.

"She wants to go to university, so perhaps we should help her with that sooner rather than later." It sounded as if Vix was pacing on the small bridge. Again.

"Not yet," Jeff replied. "If something happens, who's going to take care of her? They *hurt* her at that school, and it was a place for ladies of gentle breeding. I can't stomach the idea of someone sending her to someplace even worse."

"This is an airship, not a finishing school," Vix snapped.

A finishing school for air pirates. What a notion! Noli swallowed her laugh, not wanting them to think she was spying. Again.

Jeff sighed. "Let's take this one day at a time. She truly is an ace engineer."

"Perhaps. But what if we need her help in a crisis? Not only is her job important, but it's creepy when she's just… gone like that," Vix replied.

It was even creepier when it happened *to* you. The fact that Vix noticed made fear swirl inside her. All the captain needed to do was make it an order and Noli would be gone—even if Jeff didn't wish it. Where would she go?

Wait. She wasn't some sniveling society girl. If it came down to it, she could return to the Otherworld and wait at the big house for V to finish his quest. Yes, that would be a splendid backup plan. She could get there by herself… most likely.

"If she's going to stay aboard, someone should teach

her to defend herself, if not fight and shoot," Vix added. "For her own personal protection. Though the idea of her with a pistol frightens me."

"My sister is a *lady*. Ladies don't shoot pistols or fight," Jeff grumbled.

Vix made a rude noise. Noli made a production of bumping into the table in the galley in order to alert them to her presence.

"That sounds like my cue," Jeff replied.

Noli arrived in the doorway just in time to see Jeff plant a kiss on Vix's cheek.

"Sorry," Noli muttered. It was the first time she'd seen them be outright affectionate, and heat rose to her cheeks.

Jeff laughed. He wasn't wearing his usual pirate gear, but a gentleman's suit and hat. "Noli, let's get off this tub."

They disembarked and Noli wrapped her cape around her, the cold biting through the wool and ribbons. Snow crunched under their feet on the wood docks and her breath came out in frozen puffs. It didn't get *this* cold in Los Angeles.

Jeff led her into the passenger terminal, where they stopped at a small shop that made takeaway meals for people to bring on their journeys. They also had a blanket to sit on so they could have a proper picnic.

Noli swung the sack as she skipped down the street, following Jeff. Skipping kept her warm. Also, she couldn't contain her joy at being *off* ship. Autos puffed down the road, a few hoverboards streaked the skies, and airships took off and landed in the distance.

"Have you heard from Mama? Is she well?" Noli asked. "Should we send word to her?"

"I sent her an aethergraph when we first arrived. She's in Boston and quite happy. She's worried about you." Jeff squeezed her arm. "I assured her that you were safe here with me."

Noli squirmed. "Did I dishonor our good family name?"

Jeff made an ungentlemanly sound. "No, and you know Grandfather has probably engineered some story—you're off on a well-chaperoned tour of the United States with a group of young ladies of good breeding, or some other ridiculousness."

"I... I'm trying hard, truly, I am," she whispered, remembering his conversation with Vix. "I appreciate you defending me."

He pulled her a little closer, his body warm against the cold chill. "You're my little sister. Please, keep trying as hard as you can. I can only do so much."

Noli gulped. "I... I promise." *Got that?* she scolded the sprite.

I want to go back to the Otherworld. You said this would be fun, the sprite pouted.

"Noli?" Jeff brought her out of her inner conversation. He touched her face. "You've got to stop this. Vix has noticed your strange behavior—especially when you sort of... go blank. It can't become an issue."

Vix had a point. What if the sprite took over in the middle of something important?

Jeff led her to a public garden. The sign on the wrought-iron gate read *Closed.*

"Oh, it's not open." Noli didn't hide her disappointment.

"This way." With a sly grin, Jeff led her along the fence until they came to an out-of-the-way place near a greenhouse. "Up you go."

"Wait—we're breaking into the garden?" Noli grinned, the idea dangerous yet appealing. It was something she, James, and V might have done. Once.

Jeff boosted her up and then hopped over the fence himself. Noli looked around the frozen garden. It was probably breathtaking in summertime.

"This way." Jeff led her to an unlocked greenhouse and they walked inside. "How's this?" He gestured to the seedlings and blooms that filled the glass and metal structure. The air was fragrant with perfume.

"It's perfect." It felt illicit to be here, yet the need to be among the plants pressed on Noli with such weight that tears pricked her eyes.

Jeff spread a blanket on the floor of the greenhouse, right between rows of exotic blooms. Noli unpacked their picnic. They took a seat on the blanket and ate the hearty sandwiches they'd purchased along with dainty scones, which, in Noli's opinion, were twenty times better than anything made by blasted Missy Sassafras.

"Noli, what really happened to you? Will you tell me? Please? If I understand, I may be able to help you better." Jeff laid a hand on her arm, grease under his nails.

"I . . . I don't want to talk about it." The bite of sandwich stuck in her throat and she took a sip of lemonade to clear it. The thought of the sprite taking over like that still made her tremble. This could be problematic.

"Noli, you're safe on our ship. No one will hurt you, and I'm going to do whatever I can to protect you," Jeff reassured her.

She nodded, wishing V were here. They had to find a way to stop this from happening. They just had to—and if V couldn't, well, she'd do it herself. Somehow.

"I know they hurt you at the school," Jeff murmured. "I know Mother has no idea what that place was, or that you went missing from it. But what I *don't* know about is what happened to you while you were gone. Did you run away? Or were you kidnapped?"

Noli sat up, straightening her hat as it went askew. How could she explain any of this? "I … I went missing."

"We know that." Jeff's voice was gentle, his forehead furrowed with worry. "But were you actually kidnapped? You're a pretty girl, and of a very good age for … things … and there was that opium den and bawdy house next door … "

"What?" She tried to make sense of his vague words.

"Vix calls it 'human trafficking'—girls and boys who are kidnapped, lured, or tricked, then forced to work in factories or unseemly places." Jeff grimaced as if the words tasted bitter.

Unseemly places. Noli's hand went to her mouth in horror. "You mean the girls in those places are there *against their will?* How could anyone let such atrocities happen in this day and age? It's the twentieth century."

"Some of them, not all. There's more of a demand for joy-girls than a supply of willing ones." Jeff's cheeks pinked as if the subject embarrassed him. "Vix can tell you all about it. She's quite against it. It might be illegal, but it occurs often enough—even in 1901—and no one does much to prevent it."

"That's… that's horrible." Revulsion made Noli throw up a little in her mouth. "That didn't happen to me."

No, they just wanted to kill her.

Jeff's eyes met hers. "What *did* happen?"

Her mind raced to compose a suitable story. "I was taken away from the school. They wouldn't let me return to Los Angeles. But V rescued me and together we found a way home."

There. No Otherworld. No faeries. No sacrifice. No mention of her no longer being mortal.

Jeff's eyebrows arched. "How did Steven know you were missing and where to go?"

"I don't want to talk about this." Noli sighed. The pain of the memories pricked her like the pins in one of her mother's unfinished dresses. "No one hurt me. I promise."

Well, except for the high queen and Miss Gregory.

Jeff nodded slowly. "When you're ready to talk, I'm here. I'm so worried—especially today. Walking in on you was frightening… it was as if you were someone else entirely." Pain filled his eyes. "Like another person was inside you, using your body, like something out of a penny dreadful or a moving picture."

That's exactly what had happened. Noli scrunched her nose. "Do they *actually* have moving pictures about those sorts of things?"

Jeff laughed. "Well, perhaps not. But it would make a good one, don't you think? Now, why don't we finish our lunch? I still have someplace to show you."

....

"We're going to a museum?" Noli gazed at stone building in front of them, which said *Museum of Art* over the large doors. "Since when do you like museums?" She didn't mind going to museums, but they generally weren't at the top of her list of things to see in a new city. Jeff had never been fond of museums before, mainly because touching the exhibits was frowned upon.

He gave her a lopsided smile as he held open the door. "I *have* grown up a little."

"No, I don't see it," she teased as she walked inside, the warm air greeting her and wrapping around her like a blanket. They hung up their wraps and walked into the first exhibit area. Noli took in the paintings by Rubens. The museum wasn't empty, but it wasn't packed.

"Fat naked women were never a subject I found interesting," Jeff whispered, taking her arm and leading her out of the room just as a group of uniformed schoolgirls came through with their portly, faded teacher, listening listlessly to the dowdy old schoolmarm prattle on about the virtues of Rubens.

Noli laughed softly; yes, he was still her Jeff. Still, curiosity rose inside her as to what was so extraordinary that he'd brought her here.

The next room held a collection by Dutch artists. Noli

strolled among the paintings, trying to remember which artists were featured so she could tell V about them. Most of the paintings displayed were scenes portraying everyday life—V's favorite.

This is boring, the sprite huffed. *I want to go back to the greenhouse.*

Me too, Noli replied. *Though this isn't that boring. Besides, Jeff wants to show us something.*

Oh, I wonder what it is, she said. *These are dumb. My flowers are better.*

Noli ignored the comment and continued perusing. When Jeff made impatient noises, she slowed down in order to annoy him further.

"Are you enjoying the paintings, dear?" An older man in a plaid vest and polka-dot bow tie toddled over to her. "I'm Mr. Jenkins, the museum curator."

Noli turned to him and nodded. "Pleased to meet you, sir. Your collection of Dutch paintings is splendid. Do you have any by Jan Steen?"

"You are a fan of Dutch painters?" Mr. Jenkins' eyebrows, which resembled two woolly caterpillars, leapt in surprise. "No, we don't have any of Mr. Steen's work here. But they're quite lovely, aren't they? My favorite of his works is *The Feast of Saint Nicholas.*"

Noli tried to remember if she'd ever seen that one in V's book. "I like *The Dancing Lesson* because of its playful celebration of childhood."

Actually, that was V's favorite. When it came to Dutch

painters, Noli preferred woodland scenes. Not that a painting of children teaching a cat to dance wasn't amusing.

Jeff cleared his throat. "Noli, we don't have much time."

"Sorry, my brother's being impatient," Noli told the curator. "I'm still not sure what he wants me to see so badly."

"If you only have a short time, you absolutely must see the antiquities room," Mr. Jenkins suggested. "We just got a few new additions."

"Oh, that sounds lovely." Not really. Antiquities? She'd rather see something interesting, like tools—she loved examining tools used throughout the ages.

"Why don't I show you?" Mr. Jenkins' brown eyes lit up through his spectacles.

Noli glanced at Jeff. Allowing him to guide them *would* be the polite thing to do.

"Trying to avoid the school group?" Jeff laughed.

Mr. Jenkins looked around and lowered his voice. "Their instructor, actually."

Noli put a gloved hand to her mouth and chuckled. "Please, lead the way."

They followed the doddering curator through the small museum. It wasn't as grand as the one she'd once been to in Boston. The antiquities room stood on the second floor; afternoon light streamed through the picture windows and the domed skylight in the center of the ceiling.

A collection of metal masks on the wall drew her over. She studied the intricate expressions. It was almost as if the faces of people had been frozen, removed, and bronzed for posterity. Gruesome, really.

"Everything in this room is Iron Age and before," Mr. Jenkins told her.

"Iron Age? What a remarkable collection." She hadn't been expecting to see things that ancient.

"We're quite lucky. You must see these statues." He showed her headless statues and old coins, even a sword, the entire time engaging in a rather uninteresting banter that reminded her too much of school. She smiled and nodded, making the appropriate noises and asking the occasional questions. Jeff wandered off to examine the other end of the room, probably bored by Mr. Jenkins' commentary. Not that she blamed him. One thing she didn't miss about Los Angeles was attending school.

"Mr. Jenkins?" A young man with red hair and a smattering of freckles poked his head into the room. "The schoolgirls are waiting to hear your lecture on Baroque painters."

"And here I'd hoped they'd forget me," he whispered to Noli, giving her a droll wink. "Of course, Mr. Williams, I'll be right down."

Mr. Williams nodded. "Yes, but please hurry. Mrs. Carlson doesn't like to be kept waiting." He disappeared.

Mr. Jenkins made a face, as if he were forcing himself to swallow something distasteful. "Well, dear, it's been a pleasure. I now have to go bore some schoolgirls."

Noli laughed, since she could imagine just that. "I appreciate you taking the time to tell me about the antiquities."

"Please, continue to look—there are some baubles of feminine interest in the corner." He gave her a fond smile and, with a bob of his head, tottered off.

"Finally. He was *so* boring," Jeff whispered. He closed his eyes and pretended to snore.

Noli elbowed him in the ribs. "It *was* awfully nice of him."

"Come, look at these." Jeff led her to some glass cases against the wall filled with pottery, daggers, bracelets, and such. "Isn't the crown pretty?" He pointed to a brass crown decorated with intricate knots. It probably once belonged to a Celtic princess.

"It is." Noli's gaze fell on the design carved on another piece of metal. Frowning, she leaned over the case, wishing Mr. Jenkins were here so she could ask him to unlock it. The scrap might look like a bit of junk, but it was the carvings that interested her.

"What do you see, Noli?" Jeff asked from beside her.

"I … I've seen those carvings before." She frowned, trying to place it. The incompleteness of the design made it difficult to recall not only what it looked like whole, but where she'd seen it.

Then it hit her, and her knees buckled. Yes, she'd seen the design many times. When complete, it was a bloom made of five entwined circles—the symbol of the high court of the Otherworld.

How had it ended up in a mortal museum?

Jeff made a face. "Perhaps you've actually started paying attention in history?"

A nervous laugh leaked from Noli's lips. "Yes, that must be it."

The reason why this artifact was in the museum wasn't

her concern, after all. It was just a scrap. She'd mention it to V later.

Jeff offered her his arm. "Are you ready? We have to be onboard before sunset—and we promised to bring Vix back something. I think we passed a sweet shop."

"Oh, I could use a pastry—and a cup of actual tea." Noli grinned at Jeff, since he had to listen to her whine about no tea every single morning.

He took her arm, schooling his expression into their mother's favorite and mimicking her with a pained sigh. "I suppose."

Noli shook her head as they left the room and walked back down the stairs. "Wait!" she exclaimed, stopping. "What was it that you wanted me to see?" She looked around the gallery of Rubens; the schoolgirls were gone.

Jeff laughed. "Me? What do I care about art? I just wanted to go someplace warm, and the museum is *free*."

Noli elbowed him in the ribs. Hard. "Grown up, indeed. Now come along. I think you owe me a cup of tea."

THIRTEEN

Shipman Silver

Pink streaked the sky as Kevighn wandered through the cargo ship docking area toward the Vixen's Revenge. The gangplank of the ship was down, but no one seemed to be around.

"Shipman Silver requests permission to come aboard?" he called, stamping his feet on the wooden planks to keep warm, hoping to garner someone's attention before he froze.

"Oh, it's you." Captain Vix appeared, looking up and down the sparsely occupied docks as if expecting someone else. "Permission granted. Stow your things below, in crew quarters. Supper will be soon, in the galley, and remember—" Her brown eyes narrowed. "Stay out of the engine room."

"Yes sir." Curious how she kept saying that. Now he wanted a peek even more.

Kevighn stepped inside the tidiest airship he'd ever seen. In the galley a very large man with an eye patch was cooking something. Oh, right, they all took turns cooking. It didn't smell half bad.

The wooden stairs led down below. He turned and found himself at a door marked *Engine Room.* Hmm…

He glanced around the small hallway, then slipped inside the engine room. The first thing he noticed was how clean the room—and the engines—were. The second was the little painted flowers festooning the engine. Interesting. He wouldn't have pegged the captain for such things. She probably didn't even like men.

Toward the back stood another door with two boxes hanging on it, one of them filled with socks. Odd. Airship folk got strange sometimes.

He peeked inside this door, which was partially open, his curiosity propelling him. Deep red fabric swathed a tiny room. A doll, a needlepoint pillow, and a blanket lay draped on a hammock in the corner. Ladies' hats hung on the back of the door. Very, very interesting. A toolbox sat on the desk, and books on engineering, along with a few others, filled the shelves.

"What do you think yer doing?" a male voice demanded from behind him.

Kevighn turned and found himself looking at a short, pudgy man with glasses, white hair, and a striped hat, who had dirt streaking his cheek. "I'm the new crew member," he explained. "I was looking for crew quarters."

The older man's eyes narrowed as if he didn't quite believe him. "This way. You best be leaving her alone."

"Who?" Was the engineer a woman? Or was there a joy-girl in the only available space on the ship?

"Our engineer," the man replied.

Kevighn nodded as he followed the man out of the engine room. "Of course." She was probably the captain's *lady friend.* Yes, that made perfect sense, given the captain's warnings.

"The name's Winky, and *these* are the crew quarters." Winky opened a door that led to a *very* small, lightless room with six hammocks and footlockers. "Those two are both unoccupied. Take yer pick."

Kevighn chose the top hammock. Winky watched as he stowed his things in the footlocker, as if waiting for him to do something wrong.

"Chore list is in the galley. Changes every day." Winky turned to leave. "Come along or you'll miss supper."

As they climbed the stairs, the sound of the captain scolding someone echoed down the stairwell. Her voice certainly carried, especially in close quarters.

"I told you to be back before sundown," she chided.

"Sorry," a man replied bashfully. "It's just sundown now."

She made an annoyed noise. "Go eat, both of you—and thank you for the cake."

"We thought you'd like it," a female voice said shyly. It reminded him of Magnolia, but lately everyone seemed to remind him of her.

Meeting the crew would be interesting. Hopefully, they'd be more like Jeff and less like Winky and the captain. As if hearing his thoughts, Winky narrowed his eyes at him as they crossed what looked like a common area and entered the galley.

A young woman, hair long and loose under a hat with a little bird on it, was setting the table with mismatched dishes. The hat hid her face, and her bustled gown looked rather fancy for this sort of airship.

Jeff held up a hand in greeting. "Ah, Kevighn, you made it."

"Kevighn?" The young woman whirled around, nearly dropping the dish in her hand. Steel-colored eyes stared at him. A familiar jaw dropped.

His heart pounded. "Magnolia? What are you doing here?"

Was the Bright Lady continuing to smile upon him, or playing tricks?

The woman engineer was his fair blossom. No wonder the crew was so protective. Their first mate's little sister—a young girl—not to mention that Magnolia inspired protectiveness. The fact she didn't like being protected would make this even more fun.

Jeff did a double take. "Wait—you two know each other?"

Kevighn's chest tightened. How exactly could he explain knowing Magnolia in a way that wouldn't get him pushed off the ship?

"He knows V and James." Magnolia continued to set the table without missing a beat. But she bit her lower lip as she did so.

"Does he?" Jeff focused on him.

The intensity in the air made Kevighn want to squirm. Instead, he shrugged, wishing she'd chosen a better explanation. "I wasn't always an air pirate."

Jeff harumphed.

That probably wasn't the best answer either. But it wasn't as if he was *friends* with these rapscallions. Kevighn studied Magnolia out of the corner of his eye. She looked even more beautiful than the last time he'd seen her, before he'd been exiled.

Then he sucked in a sharp breath as he realized something. Magnolia was no longer mortal. When had *that* happened?

And *why?*

The captain took the seat at the head of the wooden table. Kevighn tried to sit next to Magnolia, not that he could speak with her so publicly, but she ended up in between Jeff and the large dark man he'd seen earlier in the pub.

Supper was uncomfortable. Every time he even looked in Magnolia's direction, someone got his attention and pelted him with questions.

The message was clear. If he was going to speak with her, he'd have to be very discreet, otherwise they might make a detour over the Grand Canyon.

••••••••

Noli put away the dress she'd had laundered off ship. The clever laundress had even managed to get the grease out, but she could hardly feel pleased about this at the moment. The newest member of their crew could pose a problem.

Kevighn. On this ship. Flying figs.

He'd been exiled from the Otherworld, just like V's family was. That meant he had to make it on his own in the mortal realm and take up an occupation. She knew Kevighn had been a pilot before, and he'd even owned his own airship once. It wasn't as if exile would make him respectable all of a sudden.

Why couldn't he have simply gone to work in an opium den? Certainly he'd spent enough time in them.

Kevighn wished to speak with her—she could see it in his eyes. But Noli didn't want to have a discussion about how she came to be here and why she was no longer mortal. No, it still hurt too much, and Kevighn . . .

Well, as a man of opportunity, he would consider V breaking the stone in her sigil as a chance to court her. However, no matter how handsome or attractively dangerous he might be, Noli wasn't about to be pursued by the likes of him again. Ever. Fortunately, Jeff and the crew were doing an excellent job of deflecting him.

Someone rapped on her bedroom door. Noli's insides knotted as she closed the latch on her footlocker.

"Who's there?" She prayed it wasn't Kevighn.

"It's me." Captain Vix.

"Come in, Captain." Noli placed her new plant, a pot of mint, on her worktable next to the roses.

Vix popped her head in. "The new crew member isn't bothering you, is he? Winky said he was poking around."

"No. Though I have to admit, him being here surprised me." Noli sat on her hammock, toying with the curls of her redheaded doll.

"If he bothers you, let me know. I'm not completely certain about him." Vix's face twisted a little. "I'm actually here because I want to know if during your repairs you by chance did anything to make the engines faster." The gleam in her eyes told Noli that she hoped the answer was yes.

Noli grinned, glad she'd taken the time to make those adjustments. "I may have tweaked a few things. Why do you ask?"

"Good. Stand by in case there's a problem. We're leaving."

"Right now?" Noli threw her leather apron over her good dress she'd yet to change out of and stuffed her work gloves in her pocket.

"We're going to chase some *real* baddies." Vix's eyes danced with delight, like she was a child opening an enormous bag of sweets. "We've been after them for months, but it always seems like they never have cargo when we're in a position do anything. Since the federal government won't do anything about it, we—me and a few other ships—do. We try, at least."

The conversation she'd had with Jeff came back to Noli as she grabbed her toolbox. "Human trafficking, right? You mean these girls are transported by air?"

Vix nodded. "It's less regulated than sea or rail. Now stand by. If we're going to catch these sons of dogs, we're going to have to give it all we've got."

....

As if nothing was wrong, Noli sat at her worktable weaving her watch chain. Not that anything was truly amiss ... the entire crew, sans Winky and Jeff, was currently boarding the ship of the bad air pirates—the traffickers. Since Noli couldn't use a pistol, she apparently had no value.

What she needed to do was check the engines; also, the hull was going to need repairs, as was whatever else the baddies had shot up when the Vixen's Revenge attacked them.

But no—Noli had been ordered to stay in her room like a naughty child *so she wouldn't get in the way*. Perhaps she couldn't use a pistol or fight, but surely she could do something more useful than work on her watch chain ... or practice throwing her knife into the door, which she'd done until the sprite threatened to take over. Thad had said she had a knack for knife throwing, which was good because she didn't seem as adept at knife fighting.

I like making the watch chain. It's much more fun than playing with the knife. James is going to love it so much. See how the beads sparkle? the sprite pattered as Noli wove the tiny silver beads she'd bought today into the pattern.

They are pretty, she replied. This would be part of the alternating sections of the watch chain, which would be made of five separate sections united with the silver clasps she'd also bought. Ideally, it should only be three longer sections, but Charlotte's hair wasn't long enough for that, and a shorter piece was easier to start and stop anyway.

She'd just finished off a section when someone knocked on the door.

"Noli?" Captain Vix asked.

"Come in." She took the weights off the finished section, glad she hadn't been practicing knife throwing. The last thing she wanted was Thad to get in trouble.

Vix cocked her head. "What are you doing?"

"Making a watch chain. What can I help you with? May I check the engines now? Do you need me to go up top to make repairs?"

"We're going to have to limp along until we reach San Fran. Especially now that we're heavy with their supplies and cargo. Whatever you did to the engines worked perfectly. Hopefully, Hayden's Follies will get here to fly decoy before we cross MoBatt territory, since the quickest way to San Fran is through Deseret. Right now I need you down below."

Noli followed, skirts rustling, as Vix led her down to the main cargo hold.

"There's no place else, so we've put them in the hold. But I'm no good with small children," Vix told her. "I know you're an engineer, not a nursemaid, but perhaps you could help with them? They're afraid of the men—and rightfully so."

Noli nodded, imagining what horrible things they'd been through. "They'll warm up to Winky soon enough."

"I think they will." Vix gave her the slightest of smiles and opened the door. "I'll have him bring down some supper."

Six little girls peered at her with wide eyes. Some had cuts and bruises, one was naked, and the others wore everything from rags to ripped party dresses. The eldest-looking girl was as dark as Asa. Another had almond eyes and yellowish skin.

A tiny blonde with giant blue eyes toddled over to Noli and wrapped her arms around her leg. "Are you taking me home to my popi?"

Noli ran her fingers through the girl's tangled hair and looked to Vix for the answer.

"We're taking you someplace safe; the ladies there will help get you back to your mommies and daddies." Vix used a baby voice, bending down with her hands on her knees. Noli bit her tongue to keep from laughing at such ridiculousness.

"What should I do?" She surveyed the group, the torn dresses and bruised faces.

"See if anyone has any major injuries. Also, could you just stay with them for a little while? Please? I need to return to the bridge." Vix shifted her weight from foot to foot.

"Go ahead. We'll be fine, right?" Noli looked down at the little blond girl.

The little girl nodded. "I'm hungry."

Other heads bobbed in agreement.

"Winky will bring down some food." Vix left.

"Hi, I'm Noli." She smiled at the small, scared girls. "Is anyone hurt?" None of the girls had injuries besides cuts and bruises, and she did what she could to tend to them.

Suddenly, Noli felt herself shoved out of her body as the sprite took control. "Why don't we get you all cleaned up so we can have supper?"

Noli watched as the sprite paraded them up to the engine room, where she'd secretly rigged a way for the heat of the engines to warm a barrel of water that was *supposed* to be used as a ballast, which she'd snuck up from the hold. She'd meant it to be for her bath later; ballast water didn't need to be clean to be useful, and there'd been no time in Denver for a hot bath. She would return the barrel to its rightful place when she'd finished with it.

"I only have one bar of soap, but we'll make six wash cloths," she told the children. The sprite used her little knife to cut rags into pieces and gave one to each girl. "We have some nice warm water, so let's get everyone clean." She helped the girls wash up, then dressed them, deftly using the fabric from her walls and hair ribbons. Actually, it wasn't half bad. Still . . .

Let me back in, I can do this. Noli tried to shove the sprite aside.

I'm a much better hair-braider, the sprite shot back as she sat everyone down in a long hair-brushing chain. Noli hadn't even realized she owned that many combs and brushes, let alone brought them with her.

It's my turn, Noli demanded after everyone's hair had been combed and braided.

No, it's always your turn. No fair, the sprite retorted. "Let's see if Mr. Winky has your supper," she told the girls.

"Miss Noli, are you and the girls in there?" Winky asked from the other side of the engine room door.

"We're coming right now!" She led the girls back down the stairs, into the cargo hold, and sat them on crates. The sprite peered at the tray Winky carried. "What *is* that?"

Winky bobbed his head. "Oatmeal, Miss Noli. We weren't planning on taking passengers."

"Oh."

Noli wanted to smack the sprite. *Tell him he did a good job.*

Why?

Because it's nice, and he's nice. Otherwise you'll hurt his feelings.

Oh. The sprite didn't like to hurt anyone's feelings. She gave him a huge smile. "It was nice of you to make this, Mr. Winky. I'm sure it's delicious."

"I try my best, Miss Noli." He gave her a little bob of the head as he helped her dish out six bowls of surprisingly unlumpy oatmeal.

"Could you try to find some spare blankets?" the sprite added.

"Of course, Miss Noli." Winky left.

Noli watched in a combination of horror and boredom as the sprite fussed over the girls, made a bed for them out of blankets, and told strange stories that made no sense to Noli but had the girls rollicking with unladylike laughter.

Every time Noli fought for control, she lost. Fear consumed her. What if she couldn't regain possession of the body? What if she never did and eventually her real self faded away, leaving only the sprite? No one would ever know that something else had resided in her body, that she wasn't truly like this.

You worry too much, the sprite scolded as she stroked the

little blond girl's hair. The child's eyes were heavy with sleep as the sprite hummed an unfamiliar tune.

Finally, the little girl fell asleep. All six girls slept, a redhead snoring softly in the corner. Noli knew that girls her own age could often be found in joy houses, but girls this young? The tiny blonde was five; the eldest of the lot was only ten. She would have liked to convince herself that they were destined for factories. Unfortunately, factories weren't much nicer, and probably weren't where they'd been headed.

The sprite yawned. *I think it's time for us to go to sleep.*

Too bad we used all the water. Noli tried not to sound sour.

But I only used one barrel. The other is for us. I was just trying to be nice. Hurt leaked into the sprite's voice.

There were two barrels? When did she get two? This was getting to be too much. Noli sighed inwardly. *Being nice is good, especially to these hurt little girls. Yes, let's take a bath and go to bed.*

Perhaps in the morning she could wrest control of her own body back from the sprite.

••••••••

Desperation to speak with Magnolia chased Kevighn like the air patrol pursued air pirates. He crept into the engine room; his eyes fell on the flowers painted on the engine as he snuck past. It reminded him of Creideamh—his sister would do something like that, though she'd been a more accomplished painter.

The door to the workroom wasn't closed all the way, and he pushed it open. "Magnolia?"

The only light came from the engine room; it illuminated the sleeping Noli, sweetly cradled in the hammock. Her ears poked out slightly from her sleep cap, and a doll was cradled in her arms. She looked so... vulnerable when she slept.

"Magnolia? It's Kevighn." He stepped inside her tiny room, so that his presence wouldn't be obvious if anyone entered the engine room, and closed the door behind him.

Her eyes flickered open. "I know you."

Kevighn took a step backward, nearly crashing into the wall. What an odd thing to say. "Um, yes, you do."

She sat up, her green blanket slipping to reveal a white ruffled nightdress. "You're fun. I like to have fun. It's boring here."

Magnolia flashed him a flirtatious smile—which was something *very* un-Magnolia-like. Kevighn's stomach churned, and the hairs on his arms stood up. Something wasn't right. This wasn't his little blossom.

"Who are you?" He peered into her steel eyes, which didn't quite seem like hers. No. It was like someone else was looking *out* of her eyes.

"I'm Noli," she giggled, tossing her head a little.

That wasn't her laugh. It reminded him more of those vapid courtiers the high queen kept. Magnolia never tossed her head like that, either.

"Where's Noli?" he demanded. This girl who looked like Magnolia wasn't a changeling or simulacrum—but she wasn't quite Magnolia either.

"I'm Noli." She giggled again. "Oh, you mean the other Noli? The boring one? She's sleeping." Magnolia made an exasperated noise. "Finally."

"What do you mean, *the other Noli*?" His heart sped as he leaned against the closed door. Something was amiss.

"She lives here too." She tapped her head with her index finger. "She's so bossy. She *never* lets me have a turn."

His heart seized. "There are two of you in one body? How did *that* happen?"

"Queen Tiana. One day I was just *here*, in this body—but the other Noli wouldn't leave. She was supposed to leave." She huffed, blowing a wayward piece of hair out of her face. "How am I supposed to have fun if I have to share with *her*?"

Queen Tiana? How and why would she do *this?*

"What are you?" he asked. Although it wasn't difficult to guess—the pointed ears, the beautiful body, the not-so-bright-but-chipper occupant.

"I'm a sprite, of course." She giggled again.

Things started to make a sense. But only a little.

"Will you take me to the Otherworld? It's so boring here." She batted her eyelashes at him.

"I don't think Stiofán would like that very much." Kevighn kept his voice guarded as he tried to make sense of what was happening.

"Why?" She cocked her head, eyes widening. "He broke the stone. It hurt. The other Noli's no fun because she hurts so much."

"Wait—Stiofán broke her sigil?" His jaw dropped as his

heart did a dance of joy. If Stiofán had broken it off with Magnolia, that meant he still had a chance.

She nodded. "The other Noli thinks someone made him."

That sounded like his little blossom. Poor girl.

"You said the other Noli is sleeping? Could you wake her for me? Please?" He gave her his most charming smile.

"No. If I wake her up, she won't let me have the body back." Her lower lip jutted out. "I *never* get a turn."

"Please?" he pleaded, wondering if he had anything shiny in his rucksack to offer her. "I *really* need to speak with her. I'll tell her that you should have more turns."

"You will?" Her whole being brightened with such intensity he winced. Not being mortal anymore, she no longer had the Spark, but she certainly possessed *something*.

"Of course." Kevighn added another smile for good measure. The sprite wouldn't have the answers he sought, and, well, she wasn't his Magnolia. Magnolia and a sprite in the same body—a very attractive fae body—who could imagine?

"I suppose I could." She sighed a little, as if it were a huge imposition. "Let me see if I can wake her."

For a moment she was . . . *gone*, eyes blank, body still. It was nearly as strange as the other girl speaking out of Magnolia's pink lips.

Her eyes blinked and widened. "Kevighn, what are you doing here? Do you know how much trouble you'll get in if they catch you?" she hissed.

Now *that* was his Magnolia. "Noli, why aren't you mortal anymore?" he blurted, not knowing how else to say it.

She looked away, her face darkening. "I don't want to talk about it—and I never gave you permission to call me Noli."

True. However, everyone on the ship called her that, as did her friends—and that whelp of a prince.

He brushed her shoulder in an overly familiar gesture, the white cloth of her ruffled nightdress soft under his fingers. "Please? It involves the queen, doesn't it?"

"Never bargain with the high queen." Magnolia's voice was a whisper. She clutched the doll to her chest like a shield, her expression contorting into one of pain.

Kevighn kept his hand on her shoulder, since she didn't glare at it or brush it away. "Why would you bargain with her?"

"I had to get home somehow." Her voice cracked with pain.

"Oh, right." He'd been the one to inform her that eating faery food had bound her to the Otherworld—and that the high queen possessed the power to send her home.

Her eyes brimmed with pain as she looked up at him. "It wears me out trying to keep the sprite in check." She straightened with resolve. "But we'll fix it and I'll be me again."

"Of course." He still didn't understand what had happened, but there wasn't any way he knew of to get her humanity back. Getting rid of the sprite, well, that seemed more feasible. Maybe.

Then again, Magnolia Braddock was the most determined girl he'd ever met, even more so than his sister.

"Why are you on this ship?" Her eyes met his in her old, refreshingly direct manner.

“I was looking for a job. You?” Kevighn leaned back against the door again, since she hadn’t invited him to sit. Not that there was a place to, other than a little bench or her hammock. If she invited him to her hammock, he’d want to do more than sit and talk.

“It’s better than Boston.” She hugged the doll to her chest. “I miss V.”

V, who was off questing—if Igan and his crew hadn’t accidently killed him. Kevighn prayed to the Bright Lady that they had.

“I’m here.” He gave her a reassuring smile but didn’t touch her. Yes, that was the right card to play. Slow and steady. “When you’re ready to talk, I’m here.” His smile grew lopsided. “If your brother doesn’t toss me off the ship while it’s moving.”

Magnolia laughed *her* laugh, which was like bubbles popping in a glass of champagne. “I won’t let him torture you too much.” Her laughter stopped abruptly. “If he knew you were involved with my disappearance…”

“I won’t tell… will you?” He gave her a searching glance.

She swallowed and shook her head. “No. I won’t tell.”

Taking her hand, the one not holding the doll, Kevighn looked into her eyes. “I’ll help you in any way I can.” He kissed her hand. “Good night.”

“Good night, Kevighn.” Her big eyes stared up at him, a mixture of too many emotions to read. He most definitely had her off balance. Good.

He left, closing the door behind him, praying he wouldn’t run into Winky.

Magnolia wasn't mortal. Stiofán had left her. Things were just getting better and better, and he gave his thanks to the Bright Lady.

Then again, Kevighn was a huntsman, and he always got what he wanted in the end.

FOURTEEN

MoBatts

"I can't believe we missed them again." Steven wanted to bang his head on the wooden table of the dingy air terminal bar in Denver. "This is the most problematic tracking spell I've ever seen." It made tracking with a sigil seem simplistic.

"At least I know one," James huffed, signaling a serving girl. They placed their order.

Steven gave his brother a smile, trying to keep his frustrations at bay. "I... I'm glad you do. I don't know what I'd do without you."

"Really?" James brightened.

"Really." For every problem James had instigated, he'd also offered solutions. Certainly this quest had been more interesting, albeit frustrating, with his younger brother in tow. Also, he was grateful for the company and assistance.

Although he *could* do without the sulkiness and odd moods.

The serving girl brought their food and left, but not without giving them both winsome smiles. Many a girl in pubs like this also made... personal visits.

"How *are* we going to find the ship she's on?" Steven raked a hand through his hair.

James rolled his eyes and chewed his overly large bite of meat pie. "Um, *ask* if anyone knows where Barrel of Monkeys is headed? What sort of ship name is that, anyhow?"

"The name isn't important. Finding them *is*." Days had been wasted chasing this blasted vessel across the country. But if they found little Rahel and returned her to Dr. Heinz, it would be worth it. If they failed... well, he didn't have the luxury of even entertaining the notion.

"What do you know of the Barrel of Monkeys?" a female voice demanded, a click of a pistol punctuating the question. Two blond women, well, girls really, most likely sisters, stood in front of them. One was broad and brawny with short hair, the other daintier. Her long hair was pinned up in a braid.

The smaller of the two held a pistol at them. No one in the pub even looked up from their conversations, as if such things were usual occurrences in this place.

"Please, don't shoot." Steven put his hands up. "We're just trying to find it."

"Why?" The one with the pistol didn't lower her weapon or gaze. Both wore *trousers*. Trousers!

James shrugged. "They have something we want."

"What?" she snapped.

"An acquaintance has contracted us to retrieve his child," Steven stammered, hoping these were friends, not foes. At least they were mortal.

She lowered her pistol. "Oh. We're on the same side, then. I'm Hattie Hayden and this is my sister, Hittie. And we happen to know where those sons of dogs are."

Steven perked. "You do?"

"You part of the children's liberation front, or just for hire?" Hittie asked, her eyes narrowing. She seemed to be the elder of the two. The smaller one, Hattie, didn't look much older than James.

"We're just the hired help." James gave her a disarming smile.

Hattie shrugged. "Everyone's got to make a living. Anyway, our friends are hopefully boarding that ship and stealing Barrel of Monkeys' cargo right now. We're meeting up with them soon."

"Wait—they're boarding the ship of air pirates and stealing their cargo?" Steven blinked. Who in their right mind would rob an air pirate?

Hittie bristled, her broad shoulders squaring. "It's for the greater good. Children shouldn't be stolen and forced into slavery."

"True. But what do they do with the children afterward?" he asked.

"We take them to a safe house and try to return them to their families," Hattie replied. "Here's the deal. We just lost a crew member. You help us, and when we meet up with our friends, we'll make sure you get the girl you're looking for. If the safe house contacts her parents first, you won't get paid for finding her."

True. The last thing Steven wanted to do was waste more time.

"How can we help you?" James took a casual sip of beer, as if discussing the weather or something equally inane.

"You do what we tell you," Hittie snapped, taking a step toward them. "We're an all-female crew and we don't tolerate no disrespect. We don't usually take on men."

James' face brightened. "Wait—you're Hayden's Follies! I've heard of you."

"Good things, I hope." Hattie preened.

An all-female band of... well, he had a feeling they were air pirates. Steven rubbed his chin, taking this all in. "If women can't legally fly airships, how can you operate?"

Hittie wrinkled her turned-up nose in disdain. "Do you think we care?"

"No, of course not." Well, that was one way to look at the law.

Hattie checked her pocket watch and tapped the toe of her manly boots. "Are you in?"

Steven and James exchanged glances. It beat their other options. Standing, Steven offered his hand. "We're in."

Hattie shook his hand, her grip stronger than he expected for a small woman, and jerked her pointed chin toward the door of the pub. "Good. Let's go rescue some little girls."

....

"Hope you're well-rested, because the next twenty hours are going to be *hell*," Hittie sneered as she showed them around the microscopic ship.

"Why?" Steven had taken an instant dislike to Hittie, the older sister. A sparrow-class ship only held three people comfortably; Hattie was the pilot and captain, Hittie the engineer. They'd lost their gunner, which James had been assigned to. The ladies had deemed Steven useless and told him to stay out of the way.

Useless? Him? Then again, Steven never had felt the need to learn to shoot. "*Because your own strength is unequal to the task, do not assume that it is beyond the powers of man . . .*" He quoted Marcus Aurelius under his breath.

"As soon as we meet up with Vix, we're going to be flying decoy. The fastest way to San Fran is through Deseret Territory—MoBatt country." Hittie looked at James. "Which is why we need a good gunner."

None of this meant anything to Steven, and he didn't want to sound stupid or anger her by asking. All he knew from Noli was that sparrow-class ships were fairly useless except for the fact that they could go *very* fast.

"Wait—Vix, as in Captain Vix?" James asked.

Hittie's blond eyebrows rose. "You know her?"

"I met her a few months ago when I was looking for her first mate. We know his sister." James turned to Steven, his eyes alight. "This is good—really good."

Steven's brows knitted. "Sorry, I'm not following."

"The Vixen's Revenge is Jeff's ship. I remember from when I went looking for him, back when you went after Noli.

They'll be far more likely to hand Rahel over to us." James' forehead wrinkled. "Well, you should let me do the asking. He probably wants to kick the stuffing out of you."

It took a moment for this to sink in. "Jeff's ship. As in Noli's Jeff?" Steven made a face trying to assimilate this information. The Bright Lady played tricks, surely. "Is the air pirate community *truly* that small?"

"Pretty much—which is why we're the ones stealing the children," Hittie retorted. "The men don't have the gall to break the rules and the government doesn't give a gear." Her lips formed a smirk. "Why does Jeff want to beat the stuffing out of you?"

"Um ..." Steven's cheeks warmed. "I want to marry his sister." James' eyebrows rose. "What?" he retorted. "I'll find some way to be with her, no matter what people say."

He had to. Not just because he'd promised, but because Noli made his life better—him better—in so many ways.

"Good. I like Noli. She keeps you from being insufferable." James shoved his hands into his pockets. "You should still let me do the talking, just in case."

Hittie held up her stubby, rough hands. "Enough chatter. We should be meeting up with the ship any moment. Then it's time to hold on."

••••••••

The sound of another airship's engines woke Noli. Sparrow-class, judging by the sound.

"Noli?" Jeff whispered from outside her door.

"Come in." She sat up and yawned. "Trouble?"

"No, our decoy is here, in case we encounter MoBatts. After we get to San Fran, I'll introduce you to them." Jeff shook his head as he stood in the doorway. "It's crazy, I tell you. Not only are we limping from that battle with the traffickers, but we're about to limp through Deseret. The sooner we get those kids to San Fran the better." Circles hung under his eyes. Dark shadows colored his chin. Shaving didn't seem to be a priority. Neither did sleep.

"So, this decoy... they're air pirates worthy of my acquaintance?" Noli smiled, remembering Jeff's reluctance to introduce her to his friends back in Los Angeles. How long ago that seemed.

Jeff grinned and leaned against the door frame. "An all-female crew. They're part of Vix's women's equality movement and the Children's Liberation Front. Female air pirates who work to stop human trafficking. It's their engineer I think you'd like."

"I'd like to meet a female engineer." Noli had never met another girl who liked to fix things.

"Well, anyway, the reason I'm waking you up is that we need you to be on hand," Jeff told her. "Being chased by MoBatts is... interesting. We need the girls to stay with you up here in case they become scared. We can't risk having you away from the engines."

Noli crossed her arms over her chest. "I should have been given time for repairs. How *are* we flying with holes in our hull?"

"We patched them the best we could—believe me," he replied. "This is a *very* risky venture."

"Oh." Noli nodded, understanding. "Because the law won't see what we're doing as a good deed. We're as guilty as those who stole the children in the first place."

"Exactly. And the authorities will probably know where we're headed as soon as they find the traffickers' ship, so we need to beat them to San Fran. If there are no children onboard when they search us, they can't do anything." His smile grew lopsided. "Sometimes there are perks to the holes in legislation."

....

"I'm scared, Noli." The little blond girl, Rahel, wrapped her arms around Noli's leg as she attempted to tighten a loose screw on the fan of the starboard engine. It was always the starboard side. At least the ship was holding up. But she was worried that the fans weren't. If they didn't, the ship could overheat.

Gunfire rang in the distance. Making sure the screw was tight, Noli tucked her screwdriver into its loop on her tool belt and embraced tiny Rahel. The other girls slept soundly in the corner of the engine room. Fear of being caught—or shot down—balled in the pit of her belly, so she could hardly blame the little girl for being afraid.

"Everything will be fine," Noli soothed her, running her fingers through Rahel's long blond hair as a loud noise boomed behind them, followed by the *rat-a-tat-tat* of a

Gatling gun. "Why don't you go to sleep? When you wake, everything should be over."

She hoped.

"I want my bed," Rahel sobbed. "And my popi." Fat tears streamed down her little face.

"Would you like to sleep in my bed?" Noli took her by the hand and led her to her room, trying to think of a way to make her happy and quiet before she woke up the other girls. Again. "Look, you may sleep in my hammock."

Rahel peered into the dim room and made a face. "You sleep *there*?"

"It's actually quite comfortable." Noli helped the little girl into the hammock. "Here's a pillow and blanket." She tucked the small pillow under Rahel's head and covered her with the green blanket. "You may even hold my doll."

Rahel took the offered doll and fingered her red curls. "What's her name?"

"Charlotte," Noli replied without a thought. The ship shook and the engines made a noise of protest. "You go to sleep. I'll return to check on you."

Rahel closed her eyes and nodded. Noli caressed the little girl's cheek, then ran back into the engine room just as something boomed in the distance.

•••••••

Steven gripped the bolted-down table in the tiny common area as Hayden's Follies rolled, the entire ship tilting to one side as everything not secured slid around, creating a merry mess. A slew of gunfire punctuated the evasive maneuver, every *rat-a-tat-tat* of the patrol's Gatling gun sounding as if it would pierce the hull and hit him.

Perhaps this hadn't been such a good idea. Apparently "flying decoy" meant that they drew the patrols away from the ship they were chasing. They were flying through "MoBatt territory," although to be honest he wasn't exactly sure what that meant.

The ship rolled in the opposite direction, and things continued to fall. Steven's knuckles whitened as he held on, not wanting to join the loose objects. A large boom radiated from the back of the ship and they took a nosedive, which threw him forward. He stopped when his body hit the wall, the breath knocked out of him.

"Pull up, pull up," James was shouting from the bridge, gunfire continuing to be exchanged.

"I'm trying, but we're going to crash!" Hattie yelled back.

Rubbing his head, Steven gulped. Being caught by the air patrol was bad. The kind of "bad" that meant jails and aethergraphs to Quinn.

"Hold on," Hattie yelled. "We're about to kiss the ground."

Something between a boom, a screech, and a wail filled the air as the entire craft shook. Steven was thrust forward again. This time he put his arms out in front of him. Pain shot through his left wrist.

"Everyone keep still," Hattie ordered when the craft stopped shaking.

An eerie silence blanketed the ship as the engine went quiet. They could hear the engines of the other ships. It was so quiet they could probably hear the thunder of his own frantic heart. Steven crept toward the bridge, where Hattie looked like she was literally holding her breath. Finally, the sound of the other ships disappeared. He breathed a sigh of relief that made his entire body shudder.

"What now?" he whispered from the doorway.

"Being downed air pirates in Deseret isn't a good thing," Hattie whispered back. "We get out, survey the damage, and pray we get ourselves back in the sky as soon as possible."

"What about the Vixen's Revenge?" James asked from the gunning station, a trickle of blood leaking from his lower lip.

Hattie shook her head slowly. "We pray they got away."

....

They stood in front of the small craft, the sun rising above them. Certainly the wilds of Deseret Territory were beautiful, with snow-crested rocks and mountains. Never had Steven seen such colors, at least not in the mortal realm.

"What's the damage?" Hattie asked Hittie.

The corners of Hittie's lips turned down, her deep and disturbing frown seeming to permeate through her entire wiry form. "Fortuna smiled on us... sort of. It's purely structural. They missed the engines. But how in Hades are we going to fix a broken tail and the breaches in the hull? If we can even find the tail."

The schooner was made of wood and metal. Hmmm...

Ignoring everyone, Steven placed his hands on the bullet-riddled hull. Yes... that could work. What about the tail?

Moving over to the tail section, he examined it. If they could find the rest, he just might be able to reattach it.

"Captain, if we repair the tail and the holes in the ship, could we still get to San Francisco?" A plan formed in Steven's mind. Getting to Rahel before the safe house alerted Dr. Heinz was still priority—and they couldn't do that when grounded in enemy territory.

"We could… in theory," Hattie replied slowly, nodding as if doing so made the words true. Certainly they wouldn't last long if they couldn't get airborne.

"Good," Steven replied. "Why don't you two find the rest of the tail? James and I will start on the repairs."

The sisters stood there, blinking as if he'd spoken in tongues. Hittie's arms crossed over her ample chest. Skepticism was etched in every inch of her face. "You mean *you* can repair the ship?"

"I think so." Steven looked at James. "Right, James?"

James' forehead furrowed; he clearly didn't understand what Steven meant. "Um, sure."

"That gives me so much confidence," Hittie huffed.

"Jeff's sister is an ace engineer, and I've been her chief assistant since we were children," Steven stated. "I've learned a few things over the years." Hopefully that would be explanation enough. "I can't make any promises, but we have just as much reason to get back up in the air as you."

Hattie toyed with the ends of her braid, which had come unpinned at some point. "True…" She looked to her sister. "We don't have anything to lose."

"You wreck my ship, I wreck your face," Hittie spat.

"Let's see if we can find the tail." The two sisters retreated in the direction they'd fled from.

James came up beside him, his eyes dancing with amusement. "What exactly is your plan?"

Despite the bone-chilling cold, Steven rolled up his sleeves so he could work. "We're *earth court.* The ship is made of *wood.*"

"Are you mad?" James hissed, eyes wide. "We're not supposed to use magic unsupervised in this realm."

Steven laughed. *Now* James wanted to be sensible? "Right, like you've ever paid attention to that. We've been using a *tracking spell,* remember?"

"That's different. You want to use *magic* to repair *a mortal's ship?* While they're *here?*" His voice rose in pitch, cracking a little, and his cheeks flushed.

"James, if we don't get there when the Vixen's Revenge does, we won't get Rahel, which means we won't get the automaton, which means we're back at square one and we're running out of time." Steven met his brother's eyes. "If you have a better idea, I'd love to hear it."

"You look and sound so much like father right now." A smile tugged at James' lips.

Terror seized Steven's chest and his hand went to his forehead. "I do? I'm *so* sorry."

James chuckled and shook his head. "Better you than me. All right, let's see what we can do … I'm not really good at this sort of magic."

Steven put his hands over the nearest breach in the hull. "Let's give it a go."

"Sure. I'll take the other side, you take this one?" James jerked his head toward the other side of the little ship.

"Sounds good." Steven's attentions returned to the hull in front of him. The bullet holes were mostly superficial. It was the breaches in the hull that he needed to repair so they could get airborne. Time to survey the damage. Magic tingled through his fingertips as he probed the first breach and gently manipulated the wood to close the fissures. It was a slow, tedious process. He kept needing to stop, stamping to warm himself and blowing on his hands. Finally, the breach closed and he breathed an icy sigh of relief. *One down, one more to go*... on this side. Then the tail.

When he'd finished both, he found James peering at him, his cheeks red from the cold. James whistled. "That's nice work. Too nice."

"What do you mean, *too nice*?" Steven's fingers traced the breach as he scowled at his brother. "You can't even tell."

"Exactly. They won't believe we plugged it if it looks perfect. Here, look at mine." James grabbed his arm and led him to the other side of the ship. Obvious repair lines marked where he'd merged the wood.

"I didn't mean it to look this way, but then, I'm not as good as you."

"It's patience you lack, not talent," Steven replied. "But I see what you're saying. It's a good idea." The idea of marring his beautiful handiwork still made his belly churn.

"Really?" James brightened so much that Steven wanted to put out his hands to warm them.

"Yes. Let me fix mine. Why don't you see how many

bullets you can pull out of the hull, and repair what you need to. Hopefully the women will return soon—with the tail." They'd have to find some way to get the Hattie and Hittie out of eyeshot so that they could repair the tail, which would be a similar process.

Steven returned to his side of the hull and carefully, artfully, made his perfect work look marred—like James', but more deliberate. He'd just finished when he heard the sound of female voices and something being dragged.

His heart leapt. If they could get up in the air soon, they might still be able to arrive in San Francisco near the same time the Vixen's Revenge did—and get Rahel.

"Need some help?" he called, running to join them, James on his heels.

"Titties on a fish it's cold out here," Hittie called, her breath coming out frozen.

They joined the women, took the heavy tail section from them, and dragged it back to the ship. The battered tail piece was worse for the wear, part of it broken, but it was still better than nothing.

"You two did this?" Hittie stared at the hull in disbelief, her jaw hanging open as if she didn't quite understand what she was looking at.

"You have to admit, they did an ace job." Hattie flashed James a comely look.

James gave her a large grin. "We do what we can. You have to admit, it *is* cold enough to freeze the balls off a brass monkey out here."

Steven scowled at James' vulgar language.

His brother ignored him. "I know being women doesn't mean you automatically know how to cook—but we can't cook *at all.* Steven burns water. Anyway, maybe you could make us all some coffee and we'll get this fixed so we can get back up in the sky?"

"You don't have to ask me twice." Hittie stamped and blew on her hands. She turned to her sister. "Coming, Hattie?"

Hattie shot James another long look, this one through veiled lashes. "Are you sure we can't be of assistance?"

"We're fine—something warm to drink would be the best help of all," James replied.

The way James said that sounded almost . . . naughty, and Steven looked away.

"Suit yourself. We'll return." With a final wistful look, Hattie followed Hittie into the little ship.

Well, that was elegant. Steven knew he'd never get away with saying anything like that. Hittie would probably smack him. Hard. With a loaded pistol.

"Will you help me?" he asked his brother. "This is a two-man job. One to hold, one to fix."

"I'll hold," James volunteered.

"Good."

James held the tail and Steven worked to fuse it to the back of the ship. This proved much harder than repairing the breaches, and the end result wasn't nearly as neat as his earlier work—but again, the imperfections were probably for the better. The ship being sound mattered more than its appearance, anyhow.

Above them, an automobile engine sputtered.

Hittie and Hattie ran out of the ship, pistols drawn, as the shadow of a flying auto passed over them. Unlike Noli's bat-winged, bugged-eyed Pixy, this flying car looked like a beast. Giant leather wings, twice the size of the Pixy's and shaped like dragon wings, flapped steadily. The loud sound sliced through the cold, quiet air. The car, a Dragon model by the looks of it, was an odd shade of green; the shape of the hood was reminiscent of a dragon's head, with large headlamps for eyes.

"Do we signal them for help?" James hissed.

"We don't know if they're friend or foe," Hattie warned, her pistol still drawn.

Something felt wrong. Deseret was large, its sparse population clustered together, which left vast stretches of open land. They'd taken care to avoid civilization.

Then the *rat-a-tat-tat* of a Gatling gun had everyone ducking behind the ship for cover.

"Hells bells," Hattie hissed, firing her pistol at the Dragon.

"That's not a patrol ship. No one—not the MoBatts, not the air patrol, not the military—uses flying autos as attack vehicles." Hattie fired again, using the tail of the ship as a blind.

James ducked behind the airship for cover as the flying car buzzed them, sending out another spew of metal bullets that clanked against rocks, dirt, and the hull of the ship they'd just repaired.

"I say, you'd think they were trying to kill us," James hissed.

Gulping, Steven looked up at the three leering men in the Dragon, which was careening through the sky like a drunken wood faery. The men all reminded him of Igan—ruffians who liked hassling others for sport.

"I can't tell from here, but they could be," he muttered to his brother as the sisters continued to fire at their assailants.

"Wait—what are you talking about?" James paled.

"I think we've got ourselves more helpers. Who did you think they were?" Steven winced as another stream of bullets flew past. At this moment he didn't dare use magic. Not yet.

"Come out, come out, wherever you are," one of the men called.

James' eyes widened. "Flying figs, you mean they actually want to *kill* us? But outright killing us is against quest rules."

"Since when has she ever played by the rules?" The words tasted bitter in Steven's mouth.

"Why aren't you leaving?" Hattie cried, firing more. "Oh hells bells, I'm out." Her empty pistol made clicking noises.

"Dance for us," one man leered.

"Could we go back inside and take off?" Steven called to the ladies. An airship was faster than a flying car… right?

"I think we should try to get back onto the ship, if at least to use our Gatling gun," Hittie called back.

James huddled closer to him. "I think we need to use magic to crash it," he whispered. "Do you know a spell to make the engine seize?"

"Why would I know that?" Steven found it difficult not to roll his eyes in annoyance.

"Um, because you always help Noli."

"I *never* used magic to help her fix things, not even once." He was quite proud of that—learning to blend in seamlessly with the mortals, not using his magic unless it was part of his lessons or at his father's or Quinn's direction.

James made a face of disgust. "There's no time to be a fussy old bodger. We need to do something. Are you going to do it or am I?"

"I'll do it," Steven huffed as the spray of bullets crept closer. Of all the idiotic things. Then again, what choice did they have? Not that he knew what to do.

Closing his eyes, he muttered a few choice words under his breath. Magic tingled up his hand as he felt the air around him charge, making the hairs on his arms stand on end.

Taking a deep breath, he opened his eyes, releasing the pent-up pure magic at the flying car. The invisible bolt of magical energy zipped through the air, searing the Dragon in half as easily as one might cut a loaf of bread. Screams from the vehicle bounced off the rocks as the front half and back half fell toward the ground, in different directions.

"Let's get out of here," Steven called as the Dragon crashed. The screams and curses of the men curdled the air, which still prickled with lingering magic.

Hattie stood there, frozen, her mouth hanging open.

"Good one, Captain Subtle," James hissed.

He hadn't known what else to do.

"You're right." Hittie gritted her jaw. "Come on, Hattie, let's get out of here." She looked back at the wreckage and shook her head. "I don't want to be here when those men get to us."

If they'd survived.

Fear gripped Steven, rooting him to the spot. He could have killed the men. But they'd been trying to kill him. Also, hopefully they were fae, not mortal.

Either way, he couldn't let them hurt Hittie and Hattie.

"Think later." James shoved him toward the airship.

They got inside. Hittie fired up the engines and Hattie took off into the sky, leaving their assailants behind.

"What happened back there?" Hattie's voice went soft, her eyes on the currently empty sky.

Steven's heart sank as he crowded onto the tiny bridge. How did he explain what he'd done? "Deseret has pockets of aether. Aether has been known to do strange things."

Yes, that worked. Aether could cause all sorts of problems, from disappearances to war and creativity. But what the mortals called "aether" was actually magic leaking from the Otherworld.

"I . . . I suppose so." Hattie looked pale, her hands gripping the controls so tightly her knuckles were white.

"Whatever it was, I'm glad we're out of there," Hittie said. "I hope the ship holds."

"Me too," Steven replied.

"Were they after you?" Hittie's eyebrows rose as she looked him up and down, as if trying to figure out who would want to kill him—and why.

Steven gulped. "I think they were."

"Who'd want to kill you?" Hattie's hands relaxed a little.

"Well, it's either our mother or our uncle," James replied, chipper as usual.

Hittie nodded, in some gesture halfway between approval and acceptance. “Some family. Now, let’s see if we can make our way to San Fran without any more problems.”

Their lack of probing questions was like a weight lifting from his shoulders. Steven smiled. “Yes, that’s an excellent idea.”

FIFTEEN

Taking Chances

As far as Kevighn knew they were out of Deseret, but he wasn't sure. The bridge of the Vixen's Revenge was no less tense as they sped toward their destination. He manned the front guns and Asa and Thad took turns operating the back guns, which were up top.

"I have a feeling they got Hayden's Follies." Jeff's voice was quiet, his eyes on the horizon while he steered the ship.

Captain Vix's lips pressed together until they went white. She bowed her head and closed her eyes as if praying to whomever mortal air pirates worshiped.

"Should we look for them?" Kevighn asked from his gunner's post.

"No," the captain replied. "We can't risk it. But if they don't appear in San Fran soon after we do, we'll send out a search."

Jeff gave Vix a long look. "Hittie and Hattie are the most resilient people we know. They'll be fine."

Someone stirred in the doorway. "Are we out of Deseret yet?"

Magnolia leaned against the door frame. The last time Kevighn had seen her in that green-and-brown dress had been back in the Otherworld, when she told him she'd chosen that whelp of a prince over him. This time her hair was bound—not free and wild as he remembered. Grease streaked her pale cheek and she held a wrench in her hand.

Though no longer mortal, she was still his Magnolia.

"Noli, you should be below," Vix scolded from her captain's chair.

"The girls are asleep, and I was feeling trapped. I'll go below again in a moment. I just—"

"It's quiet right now, Captain," Jeff reassured them, surveying the horizon again.

Kevighn tried to think of a reason to keep Magnolia up here, even for a few moments. "Would you like to learn how to gun? There's no one around right now, and it might prove helpful one day," he added when Vix and Jeff frowned.

"I was always taught that you had to learn how to call first," Vix replied. "Usually someone calls the targets and then the front gunner knows where to aim," she explained. "You use the numbers of a clock. If something is at two o'clock, he would fire there." Her hand gestured toward the panoramic window.

"What about if it's behind us?" Magnolia asked.

"That's what back gunners are for," Jeff told her. "Noli, if you want to help, you could make us all some coffee. You're getting pretty good at it." He smiled. "Then I suppose I can teach you to call targets if you truly are interested in learning."

"Coffee?" Her nose scrunched up in one of her cute faces. "I suppose I could do that." She went into the galley.

Kevighn caught Jeff giving her a concerned look. "Is she all right?" he asked softly, remembering his very odd encounter with the other Magnolia. Did they know? Probably not.

"My sister is none of your concern, Mr. Silver," Jeff snapped, his eyes flashing. "I'm unsure exactly what your relationship is with—"

Kevighn held up a hand, hoping to stave off any conflict. "The last thing I'd ever do is hurt her. I promise. She told me all about you."

Jeff's eyes narrowed. "Did she?"

"She did—which is why I sought you out over anyone else when I needed a job. Magnolia is one of the most honorable people I know, and she idolizes you." Kevighn figured he might as well tell Jeff the truth. "I didn't know she was here, honest. I figured she was with your mother."

Jeff shot him a look that rivaled the high queen's angry face. "If I ever find out differently…"

"Of course." Kevighn understood where Jeff was coming from. "I had a sister once too." He looked away. One day he would find that earth court bastard and make him pay.

……………

Kevighn walked into the galley and Magnolia handed him a cup of coffee.

"I appreciate it." He took the steaming mug from her. She'd already brought Vix and Jeff their cups, and he wanted to escape their scrutiny.

"Who hurt Creideamh? You never told me." Magnolia took a sip of her coffee as she leaned against the wooden table.

"Just some earth court whelp." Kevighn brushed it off, not quite ready to say his name out loud. To remember. After all, he'd said they were friends. He'd *promised* to take care of her. Lies. All lies.

Steel eyes gazed up at him and Magnolia's hands wrapped around the mug like she wished to steal its warmth. "It wasn't V's father, right?"

"No. It's complicated, but it wasn't him." Though they, too, had a score to settle. One day.

She sipped her coffee, clutching the cup with both hands. "Will you kill him one day?"

"One day." He couldn't help but smile at the sweet thought of revenge. And the Otherworldly bloodthirstiness in Magnolia's voice made Kevighn warm with happiness. Yes, she could easily fit into his world—even if he decided to join the dark court. In fact, Ciarán was probably the one person who could help her with her little sprite problem.

"Jeff," Vix yelped from the bridge. "Are those air patrol cannon ships?"

"I think so," Jeff replied after a long silence. "Our decoy is nowhere in sight, so we should presume we're on our own."

Kevighn's insides froze. Just because they were out of

Deseret didn't mean they were out of danger. Cannon ships were the fear of all air pirates. A few well-placed cannonballs could sink this ship in seconds, and no one onboard could do anything about it.

Well, magic could, in theory.

"Should we try to outrun them?" Jeff added.

"What else can we do? Noli, go down below. Now," Vix yelled. "I need you on the engines. Kevighn, get back in here."

If they were hit by a cannonball, they were finished. Kevighn's eyes fixated on Magnolia as she downed her coffee, grimacing the entire time.

"Captain, should I go up top, relieve Asa, and send him down here to gun?" Kevighn didn't want to shoot at ships in the cold with a Gatling gun, but a half-baked plan was forming in his mind.

"Make it quick," she called.

He put his mug in the sink, then jogged to intercept Magnolia who was heading toward the engine rooms.

"Do you have earth magic?" he whispered, praying to the Bright Lady she did.

Magnolia's eyes widened and she looked around, her face growing frantic.

"Cannon ships are a death sentence—especially since we can't go very fast," Kevighn hissed. "But if you can control metal, you can save us all."

Gulping, Magnolia looked at her boots. "I'm not good at it."

"This isn't complex. I need you to come up top and deflect cannonballs. I'll defend you with the Gatling gun so you can work." Impatience stirred within him—they had to move. Now.

"I . . ." She shook her head and swallowed hard. "Let me ask Winky to watch the engines and I'll be right up."

"Hurry," he hissed.

When he emerged up top, the biting cold sliced through his shirt, chilling him to the bone. It was too late to get a coat. He'd have to make do with what he had on, and hope he wouldn't freeze before they were done with the battle.

Holding on to the icy rails, Kevighn made his way to the rear guns. "Asa, I'll take over—you go man the front guns."

With a grateful nod, the large man undid the belt and rope that anchored him to the ship and unceremoniously gestured to the large gun mounted on a tripod and affixed to the stern. "Thanks."

As Asa disappeared into the ship without another word, Kevighn spied Winky up in the crow's nest with a spyglass.

"Winky!" Kevighn cupped his hands, hoping his voice carried. "Noli needs your help with the engines."

Winky scrambled down the pole with surprising agility for an old man. Straightening his striped hat, he peered at Kevighn through his spectacles. "Did you say Noli needs help?"

Kevighn nodded. "Down below. She's looking for you."

"Of course." He scurried below, leaving Kevighn alone.

Two cannon ships loomed in the distance, their air patrol flags flying high. These were simple brown military vessels, not much more than tiny cabins, with cannons on all sides, hanging from a singular hydrogen-filled balloon. They were meant for two things—chasing air pirate ships and shooting them down. The less weight they carried, the faster they could be in a chase.

Soon they'd be in firing range. Kevighn blew on his gloveless fingers to warm them, praying Magnolia would come up soon. When she emerged, she was wearing a fancy cape, a bonnet, and gloves. Her fine clothing looked out of place, although it was probably warm. It also didn't go well with her goggles—which were a good idea, considering the wind.

"I don't know what to do." Her gaze fixated on the cannon ships.

"Cannonballs are metal. What you need to do is deflect them." Kevighn readied the gun, filling the clip with bullets from a nearby trunk of ammo; the trunk was bolted to the deck for that specific purpose.

Her face screwed up in confusion. "How?"

Kevighn fingered a long, smooth bullet, then dropped it in the clip. "Tell it to move, deflect it with magic, do whatever you need to do. You could even send it back to hit *their* ship. You just have to keep them from hitting us or we're all dead."

"Dead?" she squeaked, paling until she matched her dainty white gloves.

"Dead." He hated to scare her, but it was the truth. There'd be time to comfort her later.

For a moment, Magnolia's expression was blank and she went eerily still, like a breathing statue. Her eyes blinked, and he wondered which girl would speak.

"I think we can do it." His Magnolia gazed at the looming crafts with fearful eyes.

A warning shot boomed from one of the two ships. "Stand wherever you need to and tie yourself to the rail." He handed her the rope. "Hurry."

Magnolia took the rope and tied herself to the rail on the starboard side.

Kevighn finished loading the gun, prepared to provide cover for her. A Gatling gun was no match for a cannon, but by the Bright Lady, he'd do what he needed to do—even if it meant setting fire to the cannon ships. If only he were better at fireballs.

••••••••

Shivering from the biting cold as the wind whipped at her cape and hair, Noli tied herself to the railing.

What do we have to do again? the sprite asked.

They'll shoot a metal ball at us. We can't let it hit our ship. Internally, Noli shook as the full weight of what she needed to do pressed down on her—especially since she would have to rely on the sprite.

But what do we do with it?

Noli remembered what Kevighn had said. *We can send it away or back to them.*

Oh, like Mintonette! The sprite rippled with excitement.

What? Noli made sure the knot was good and tight, her fingers stiff with cold through her gloves. The sun was up, but it wasn't warm.

When we play Mintonette with Breena and Nissa, we lob the ball over the net and we can't use our hands, only magic, and the ball can't touch our side of the ground. Only this time the net is invisible and there's no ground, just ships. Yes, I can do this. I'm good at Mintonette.

Noli was about to protest when she realized that the sprite *was* good at Mintonette. So good she'd let her play the idiotic court game with the high queen's sprite courtiers in her stead whenever they visited Charlotte and James at the palace.

Please let me have the body. I can do this, the sprite insisted. *You're supposed to let me have more turns anyway. I'll give it back, promise.*

Despite the sprite's prowess, Noli had reservations about letting her take over. It was getting increasingly difficult to wrest her body back. *The metal balls can't hit the ship*, she repeated. *If they do, we're dead—which means no more balls, parties, or fun, ever.*

I get points if I hit their ship, right?

Of course, Noli said, inventing on the fly. *One point for every time you make the ball hit them instead of us. Ten points if you blow up their ship.*

Ten points? The sprite squealed in delight.

Yes. But you have to give the body back when we're done. Understood?

I promise. I'll win. I'm so good at this.

Noli relinquished her body as an air patrol ship released its first cannonball at them with a deafening boom. *Now*, she commanded.

The sprite held out their hand and frowned in concentration, making the ball veer to the right. It missed them, but didn't return to strike the air patrol ship.

Oh, I missed, the sprite pouted.

As long as it misses us, we're fine, Noli reassured her, her heart racing. So much rested on the sprite, who wasn't always reliable.

But I wanted a point.

Two more cannonballs streaked across the sky, one from each cannon, the booms from the discharge so loud they seemed to rattle her down to her very core. *You have two more tries right now,* Noli said.

The spite lobbed the first ball back at the cannon ship, barely missing their deck, but the second one nearly hit the Vixen's Revenge.

Good job, keep focused, you nearly hit one, you'll get that point next time I'm sure. Noli knew from experience that scolding would only frustrate the sprite, and a frustrated sprite wouldn't get the job done. The cannon ships fired two more.

Take that, the sprite yelled as she lobbed the first cannonball back in an arc that hit one of the ships squarely in the balloon, causing it to dissolve into a ball of fire. *Ten points,* she squealed, dancing a little. *Ten points!*

Don't miss this one, Noli cried as another cannonball careened right at them.

Oh no! The spite deflected it, again just barely.

Careful. Noli watched the first ship sink toward the ground in a ball of fire, parachutes popping open as the crew bailed out. The other ship threw ropes and deployed men on hoverboards to help their fallen comrades.

Another cannonball hurled toward them.

I got it, I got it, the sprite cried. In a perfect volley, the cannonball arched back toward the cannon ship, hitting its gas-filled balloon. As soon as it made impact, the hydrogen exploded, that ship joining the other in defeat as it careened to the ground. More parachutes deployed. *Ten points!* the sprite all but crowed aloud.

And that was why helium should be used instead of hydrogen.

Flying figs, they'd done it! Knees giving out, Noli sank to the ground in relief and realized that she had control of the body. *You did such an amazing job,* she praised the sprite. *Twenty points for you, none for them. You win.*

The sprite preened. *What do I win?*

"Noli, what are you doing up here?" Captain Vix's shout roused Noli out of her internal conversation.

"I... I was just helping," she stammered, fear pushing the elation at their success aside.

"I gave you an order and you disobeyed it—that's treason." Vix's voice rose in pitch as her face contorted in anger.

"I... I'm so sorry, Captain." Noli stared at her feet. Had Vix seen? There was no way she could explain what she'd done. But Kevighn had been correct—there was no alternative.

"Go to your room, now, and stay there. I'll deal with you later. First we have to get out of here." Vix was scolding her like a naughty child.

But she was right. Noli had disobeyed a direct order to stay below and tend the engines.

"Yes, Captain." She untied the rope from her waist and tried to keep the tears out of her eyes, since Vix wouldn't be moved—or amused. "I'm sorry, Captain."

"You'd better be." Vix turned to shout at Kevighn.

Noli went below, her heart heavy.

Why is she mad? We won the game, right? the sprite asked.

Never mind. You won. Do you want to weave now, or sleep? Sleep pressed down on her, but she should reward the sprite. Noli still couldn't believe how well she'd done.

Sleep. But we can weave later? We're close to finishing.

Noli yawned as she trudged to her room, every footfall heavy. *Of course.*

When she reached the workroom, she saw that Rahel was sleeping soundly in her hammock. Oh well. Not even bothering to pull on her nightdress, Noli climbed into the hammock, wrapping her arms around the little girl and the doll, and drifted off into a dreamless sleep.

....

"Noli, wakey, wakey," Rahel whispered.

Noli's eyes fluttered open in time to see Rahel making the doll dance. On her chest.

"Winky brought you something to eat. Are you in trouble?" Rahel frowned in concern.

The early morning's events rained down on her with the force of a thunderstorm as Noli sat up and rested her still-shod feet on the floor. "Only a little. Why do you ask?"

"Winky's been checking on you and we're supposed to let you sleep, and the grumpy man-lady has been yelling a lot." Rahel made the doll dance on the hammock.

Noli wasn't sure how all this related to her being in trouble. "We should be in San Francisco soon—then we'll try to find your papa."

Rahel danced around the tiny room, holding the doll tightly in her arms. "Oh, I'll have to give you back your dolly. Thank you for sharing."

One look at Rahel was all Noli needed. "You may keep Charlotte. I'll make Jeff win me a new dolly."

"Truly?" A giant smile broke out across Rahel's face.

Noli couldn't help but grin at the little moppet. "Truly."

••••••••

The moment Kevighn slunk up the stairs to get some coffee in the galley, he could hear arguing on the bridge. At least if they were fighting, Vix wouldn't see him. He feared if she did, they might toss him off the moving ship instead of just booting him when they arrived in San Francisco.

Actually, getting off in San Fran, as he'd originally planned, wasn't a bad idea. He could find Ciarán. But that would mean leaving Magnolia. If he could get anywhere near her, he'd ask her to come with him. Unfortunately, Vix had Asa guarding the door to the engine room.

Kevighn was certain that Vix had seen Magnolia in action. Actually, his fair blossom had been quite something, lobbing those cannonballs as if playing that idiotic game Tiana's ladies enjoyed, the one with the nets and the golden balls.

Of course, to a mortal, the sight of sweet Magnolia in

her cape and bonnet using magic to send cannonballs *back* to their ship might be terrifying.

"I don't like this idea at all," Vix was saying. "I don't think this is the right place for your sister."

"Will you at least tell me what you saw?" Jeff asked.

Kevighn quietly helped himself to a cup of coffee as he eavesdropped.

"Will you tell *me* why you want her on the drop? Kyran is particular," Vix retorted.

Kyran? Kevighn's ears pricked. *Kyran* was one of Ciarán's aliases.

Wait—were they doing business with Ciarán? Why?

"I think Noli knows... about their kind," Jeff said. "I've seen the design on her knife before... on one of their knives. Her valise *has* to be magic—there's no explanation as to how she could have brought *all those dresses* in a regular one."

"But how would she know?" Vix insisted.

"I think this Charlotte friend of hers must have been one of them, since she received the knife and the valise from her. For all we know, they could have been the ones who kidnapped her."

Kevighn nearly dropped his mug. How close they were to the truth. Well, about the kidnapping, not about Charlotte.

"Even if she does know of them, what good will bringing her with you do?" Vix asked.

"I... I just think I need to bring her. Also, she had a reaction to the artifact, the one we stole from the museum in Denver. She noticed it in the case when I was inspecting the museum during open hours. I know there's more to what Kyran is telling us." Jeff sighed.

"We're thieves," Vix hissed. "It doesn't matter why someone wants something or if their stories line up. All that matters is that they pay us."

Wait. *Artifacts. Museum thefts. Roderick's message about a job Ciarán needed him to do.* What exactly *was* his old friend up to?

Well, he was about to find out. There was no way Vix would allow him to accompany Jeff and Noli on the drop, and he wasn't about to reveal to them that he was fae. Not yet. So, when Jeff and Noli went to meet Ciarán, Kevighn would follow—if nothing else than to follow up on Roderick's message that Ciarán had work for him.

SIXTEEN

The Drop

Noli hunched over the watch chain as she wove, the project nearing completion. Still trapped in her room like a disobedient child, she had to do something to keep from going mad. Rahel seemed to be the only one allowed to come and go freely, and they'd played "dolly tea party" more times than she cared to count. The sprite *liked* dolly tea party. Noli wasn't actually sure where the little girl had currently gone off to. Perhaps she was playing with the other children.

Was Thad was guarding her? If she asked, he'd probably show her more knife throwing.

"Noli?" Jeff rapped on the closed door.

"Come in." Noli secured her spot in the elaborate weave with a cog. She was almost done.

Jeff popped his head in. "We're going to be arriving in San Francisco soon."

"May I go with Vix to deliver the girls?" She returned to her weaving, anxious to finish. "I'll miss them."

Jeff's eyebrows rose. "They haven't been onboard that long."

"Still, I'll still miss them, especially Rahel." She kept weaving. Just a few rows to go.

Jeff sat on her hammock. "You do understand that what you did was wrong?"

"Yes, Jeff." Her voice went bland as she completed another row. She'd replayed the scenario in her head. Every time, she'd chosen to do what she'd done. Constantly being protected and coddled was tiresome. She wasn't some vapid pile of mush.

"Mr. Silver won't be coming with us when we leave port again. It's not working out." Jeff looked as if he were truly fascinated by the needlework pillow on the hammock.

Noli finished the final row of the section. "What you mean is that Vix blames him for me disobeying orders."

Jeff's jaw clenched. "Mr. Silver isn't suited for this ship."

"And I am?" she snapped. It wasn't Kevighn's fault. The sprite had saved them all. But it wasn't like she could tell anyone that. Noli finished off the section and added it to the others. Using her little knife, she trimmed all the ends neatly. Now to assemble the five pieces into a chain.

Jeff's hand lay on her shoulder. "You're still learning. Besides, I need your help right now."

"Did you burn the food?" She scrunched her nose at the thought. Cooking would get her out of this miniscule space.

"Actually, I need you to help me with something even more important. I need you to accompany me on a drop."

"A drop?" Noli attached the silver clasps and joined the sections into a single chain. "That's a delivery, right?"

"Yes. We've been collecting items for a client," he explained. "Now it's time to make the exchange—the goods for the money."

"You want *me* to accompany you?" Noli's fingers traced the complex design of the watch chain as she pondered Jeff's words. The little beads and clips she'd bought to accent her work sparked in the dim light.

Jeff nodded. "This client is quite refined and doesn't like Vix much. We always do drops in pairs, and you're far less suspicious than Asa or Thad. Why don't you get ready? Wear something pretty."

"What sort of pretty?" Noli clamped her mouth shut, frustrated.

"Like something you might wear when visiting someone in the morning?" Jeff's face contorted in puzzlement.

"I'm sure I have something," she replied. She still couldn't believe that her brother wanted her to go with him on his air pirate business... and that Vix had permitted it.

Wait. Findlay House was in San Francisco. A chill enveloped Noli's entire body and she shuddered in spite of herself.

Jeff frowned as he stood. "What's wrong?"

"Please, don't send me back to Findlay." Tears pricked Noli's eyes at the thought of that dreadful place, and the watch chain fell through her fingers onto the worktable. "Send me to Boston, but not Findlay."

Jeff's arms enveloped her. "I'm not sending you anywhere. You, with your fine manners and pretty dresses, are going to help me deliver some items to a very genteel man who appreciates such things. Then we'll have tea. How does that sound?"

Tea sounded quite nice, actually.

And cake, the sprite added. *Could that be my prize?*

Yes, that sounds perfect.

"All right, then. But I want cake." She looked up at Jeff, and he wiped a tear off her cheek with his thumb. "Will you send in Rahel?"

Jeff smiled as he smoothed her hair. "Of course."

....

"Which one?" Noli held up two hats: the bonnet that matched the cape, and the blue derby with a little bird on it.

Rahel looked from one to the other and back again. "The bird one."

Noli put the derby on, making sure, as usual, that her hair covered the points of her ears. "This always has been my favorite."

"I may really keep Charlotte? Forevers?" Rahel was clutching the doll to her chest.

"Yes. Forevers. Just promise me you'll take good care of her." Noli stowed the bonnet and donned her cape. She'd decided to wear her blue dress with the slightly shorter skirt and the bell sleeves. One probably needed freedom of movement when on a drop, and even her mother had deemed it perfectly proper for daywear.

"Oh, I will. I promise." Rahel looked up at her with large, solemn eyes. "Will I ever see you again?"

Noli sniffed, she'd already grown so fond of the little girl. "You're going to be reunited with your papa. That's the most important thing of all."

Jeff stood at the door, looking ever the dapper gentleman and carrying a black attaché case in one hand. He held out his arm to her. "Shall we?"

Noli grabbed her parasol and planted a kiss on Rahel's blond head. "Be good."

Rahel gave her a wave, sniffing into her sleeve. "Bye bye."

Noli dabbed her eyes with her handkerchief as they walked up the stairs. Thankfully, Jeff didn't say anything, just patted her shoulder.

He led her through the bustling San Francisco Air Terminal. They caught a motorcab to a very posh part of town filled will elegant buildings and homes—all newly built after the earthquake nearly seven years before, and truly modern with plenty of brass and glass.

How could Jeff move so easily through the city that had stolen their father? Unbeknownst to most, the earthquake had opened up rifts to the Otherworld. Some simply let aether—magic—escape into the mortal realm, but other rifts were large enough for people to fall through. Kevighn had insisted that her father must be long gone, but Noli held fast to the idea that he still might be alive, someplace in the Otherworld.

"Who are we calling on?" Noli asked as they walked down streets crowded with people, streetcars, and autos. A few flying cars and hoverboards swooped overhead. She pulled her cape closer to ward off the chill. At least no snow lay on the ground.

"We are meeting a gentleman named Kyran. He asked us to... collect... some artifacts," Jeff replied, holding the attaché case tightly.

Collect? He meant *steal*, of course. The man paid Vix's crew to steal things. Noli nodded toward the attaché case. "A painting wouldn't fit in there."

Jeff laughed. "It would if rolled. But no, he asked for... other things."

Noli stopped in her tracks. "Museums. You stole things from museums, didn't you? Like the one we went to in Denver—and Los Angeles! Did you take something from there as well?"

"Shhh," Jeff soothed her. "You can't have hysterics right here on the sidewalk."

Noli turned to face him, her eyes narrowing as she held up her parasol. "For your information, Jeffrey Cornelius Braddock, I don't 'have hysterics.' However, I do have a parasol and I know how to use it."

Jeff's hands flew up in surrender. "Point taken. Don't worry, they're just random bits of things. If they weren't so old, they'd be junk." He gestured to the elegant restaurant in front of them. "Let's meet Kyran and get our money."

They entered the place, which reminded her of the establishments they'd gone to with their parents, once. Places where men made business deals and women chatted with their friends over cups of tea or coffee. White-linen-covered tables dotted the room, which was filled with well-dressed people eating a late breakfast.

"That's Kyran over there." Jeff gestured to a man with regal stature and a mop of dark-blond curls who was sitting at one of the tables, reading the newspaper.

"Him?" Noli studied the man from a distance as she smoothed her skirt. "He looks familiar."

The man looked up from his paper, but not directly at them. Noli caught a glimpse of his eyes, green like oak leaves. V's eyes. She sucked in a sharp breath. "*That's* who we're meeting?"

"Do you know him?" The corners of Jeff's lips turned down.

Noli gulped. She didn't *know* him, but she knew exactly who he was. "His name isn't Kyran. It's Brogan."

As in Uncle Brogan, V and James' uncle, the current king of the earth court. Her chest tightened. Why was her brother consorting with the likes of *him*?

"I hardly expected him to use his real name," Jeff whispered. "Wait—how do you know this? Was he the one who kidnapped you?"

"We *can't* do business with him. We can't," Noli hissed, snatching the attaché case out of Jeff's hand. She ran out of the restaurant, onto the street.

And right into someone.

"Slow down." Kevighn's arms wrapped around her.

"Kevighn, what are you doing here?" Noli made a face as she stared up into his piercing, gold-flecked eyes, then struggled out of his grasp.

"Following you. What are you doing?" he asked.

Kevighn was *following* her? That didn't actually surprise her, since he hadn't gotten to say farewell aboard the ship. Also, he was the one person who might be able to assist her with her current predicament.

Noli held up the attaché case. "Jeff is doing business with King Brogan."

"What?" Kevighn dragged her into a space between two buildings where they were out of the way of those going about their day.

"He calls himself Kyran, but he's not—he's King Brogan, and he's been having Jeff steal things from museums." Noli examined the outside of the attaché case. "What do you suppose they stole?"

"Jeff's doing business with Brogan ... and Brogan's calling himself Kyran?" Kevighn rubbed his chin, the sun glinting off his black hair, which hung loose instead of in its usual tail. "This is serious."

Tucking her parasol her arm, Noli flipped the latch on the attaché case and opened it. "Oh, Kevighn, look." She held up a small scrap of golden metal. The sun caught on it and she could make out the partial design, which caused her to suck in a sharp breath. "This is the piece from the museum in Denver. I saw it there! This is the high court sigil, isn't it?"

Kevighn leaned in to examine it, standing far too close for polite comfort. Then again, he always did take any liberty he could.

"Yes, it is." He stroked the piece with his finger. "What

is Brogan up to, and why is he using the name Kyran? The real Kyran won't like that very much at all."

"We can't give this to him." Closing her eyes, Noli held the piece in her hand. "There is so much magic in this." Her voice shook as the power from it coursed through her. *Tell me your secrets*, she begged. All she felt was the hum of magic under her skin.

"Noli?" Kevighn sorted through the other objects in the attaché case. "I think I know what's going on. It's incomplete, but you're right. We can't give this to Brogan."

"What's incomplete?" Whatever was going on, it couldn't be anything good—not if Brogan was involved.

"These are all pieces of an artifact that's been missing from the Otherworld so long it's presumed to be only myth and legend," Kevighn breathed. "If half the stories are true, it's probably best if this object remained out of the hands of people like Brogan."

Noli's belly twisted. No, not good at all.

"What do you think you're doing, Noli? This is no time for antics." Jeff appeared in front of them, a deep frown on his face. He did a double take. "Mr. Silver, why are you here?"

"Magnolia, it appears Jeff has been doing business with Otherworld folk," Kevighn announced. "Though I'm certain he has no idea who Brogan is or what this is."

All the air left Noli's body, making her feel as if she would suffocate. Could Jeff *know* about the Otherworld? How? Why? Her eyes widened as she looked up at her brother, suddenly feeling betrayed even though she was just as guilty.

"My word. You *do* know about the Otherworld," Jeff said, staring at her. His jaw dropped.

"Um, yes, I … I do … and we can't give this to Kyran. We can't. Do you *know* who and what he is?" She waved her parasol at him. It didn't matter to her what the legendary artifact was—it was the principle of the matter. She didn't approve of doing business with anyone who betrayed their own family for power.

"It's just a business transaction," Jeff insisted, taking a step back to avoid being hit by her parasol. "What he does with it is of little importance."

"Yes, it is important, because he's up to no good." Kevighn held up another piece from the case and examined it in the sunlight streaming between the two buildings.

"The Otherworld is none of my concern. I'm just in it for the money—and if I don't give it to him, we don't get our money. No money means an unhappy crew." Jeff gave Noli a firm look, as if she were still a little girl and had taken his hammer without permission.

Her arms fell to her side, the piece with the sigil still clutched in her hand. "The Otherworld *is* your concern, Jeff. Don't you know it's symbiotic? If something happens there, it affects our world as well."

Jeff chuckled. "And I suppose next you're going to tell me that aether is really faery magic."

"But it is." Noli just stared at her brother. How could he think this was all just business? Or a game. The Otherworld played for keeps.

"Oh, you're serious." Jeff deflated. "Wait—isn't this a

fairly odd development? You knowing Kyran … and Mr. Silver showing up and getting involved at this particular moment?"

Kevighn glanced at Noli in a way that seemed far too intimate, all things considered. "Everything is the will of the Bright Lady."

Jeff's hand went to his face. "Good lord. You're one of them as well?"

"Kyran, whose name is actually Brogan, can't get his hands on this," Kevighn continued, ignoring Jeff's statement. "There's a reason it was broken up and hidden throughout the mortal realm. Just the fact that he's paying people to track down the pieces is troublesome." His eyes flashed with passion.

What *was* the artifact? But now wasn't the time to ask, and there were more pressing matters at hand.

"Do you think he's doing it by himself, or do you think he's in a partnership?" Noli couldn't suggest out loud that Brogan and Tiana were in this together, but it made sense.

"I don't know." Kevighn turned to Jeff. "Let me have this and I'll get you your money."

"Who are you going to sell it to?" Noli asked, remembering his exile status.

"No one. I'm going to dispose of these pieces. Thank the Bright Lady they're not all here, but who knows how many he already has. As for the money, I know someone who would gladly pay to ensure that this artifact remains out of the wrong hands." He returned the pieces to the attaché case.

"Who?" Jeff eyed Kevighn and the case as if at any moment he might snatch it away from him.

"The real Kyran." Kevighn snapped the attaché case shut. "He wouldn't want Brogan to have these—he could use it to destroy the very fabric of the Otherworld."

"Are you trying to tell me that this is some powerful faery artifact, one that could start a war?" Jeff's eyes brightened. "So it's worth a lot of money?"

Kevighn nodded. "Quite a bit."

"Will you truly bring us this money?" Noli asked. "Because if you won't, I can't allow you to take the case." Sliding the sigil piece into her left glove, she strode over to Kevighn and poked him in the chest with her parasol. "I'm not powerless, Mr. Silver." She recalled what the sprite had done and knew she could do it again herself.

A wounded look crossed Kevighn's face. "Do you honestly think I'd double-cross you? You, of all people?"

She shook her head. "No, of course not." Kevighn had done a lot of things, but he'd never double-crossed her.

Jeff put a hand on her arm, his body still blocking Kevighn's path back to the street. "Noli, we can't just give him the artifacts. He's never going to pay us. Since it's so valuable, perhaps we should bring it to Kyran—Brogan—whatever he calls himself—and request double the price."

"No." Noli's voice sharpened and both men looked at her, startled. "Jeff, you have no idea what Brogan is. Kevighn, you have one hour. Meet us at Miss Molly's Tea House with the money." She met his eyes and narrowed her own, holding her parasol menacingly. "You cannot hide from me. If you betray me, I will hunt you down."

A smile twitched at the corners of Kevighn's lips. "You dare to challenge a huntsman, little blossom?"

His smile, along with that pet name, made ire rise within her. "Oh, I do. Do you have a problem with that?" A dare dripped from her voice, and she kept her parasol poised.

"You may hunt me all you wish, I don't mind." Kevighn's eyes danced.

Jeff cleared his throat. "The money, Silver. All I care about is the money."

"Two hours. I need two hours, and then I'll meet you at Miss Molly's Tea House. I promise." Putting a fist over his heart, Kevighn bowed.

Jeff drew his pistol and aimed it at him. "I'm only letting you go with my take because my sister seems to trust you. If you don't come back with my money, so help me, what I will do to you will make shooting seem like mercy."

"Point taken." Kevighn extended his hand to Noli. "Come with me. That way you may ensure that I get your money."

This *would* be the prudent choice. However, the last time she'd followed Kevighn she'd ended up at his cabin and nearly succumbed to his advances. Noli knew better now than to fall for his charms, but still, who knew where he'd lead her?

"No." Jeff's voice cut through her reverie. "Noli is going nowhere with you, Silver."

"She's quite able to answer for herself, Braddock," Kevighn snapped. "Magnolia?"

Both men looked at her expectantly.

Being put in the middle made Noli seethe. "If you don't

mind, gentleman, I'm going to get some tea. Kevighn, you have one hour."

Without waiting for either, she brushed past them and headed down the streets of San Francisco. She'd go to Miss Molly's Tea House on her own. As she walked, she slid the piece of the artifact from her glove into her dress pocket. There was no good reason for keeping it, really—if she'd thought Kevighn would double-cross her, she never would have let him leave with the rest of the pieces. After all, she hardly needed Kevighn. Quinn would know what to do about Brogan—V's tutor *always* had an answer. If anyone had a dusty old book about a missing artifact, it would be Quinn.

"Noli! Noli, wait," Jeff called from behind her.

Noli didn't stop or slow down. Jeff finally caught up with her, his cheeks pinked with exertion, his chestnut curls messy.

"What did you do?" Jeff asked, his eyes searching her face as he kept pace with her.

"We can trust Kevighn," Noli assured him. In some ways, she thought of Kevighn as a friend. Either way, he understood exactly why Brogan couldn't possess *anything* that would give him more power than he already had.

Jeff shook his head. "There's no trusting a man like that."

Noli wasn't going to grace that statement with a reply.

"Did the faeries kidnap you?" Jeff's voice went soft.

"Yes." She looked ahead as she walked, slowing slightly.

"And Charlotte—the one who gave you the knife—she's a faery?"

"Charlotte? No, she was mortal."

"But why did they kidnap you?" Jeff said this in all seriousness, as if he truly wanted to understand.

She might as well tell him the truth. "Because they wanted to kill me."

Jeff stopped in his tracks. "They *what*?"

For a moment, Noli studied his familiar face. He'd changed so much since they were children. His words in the alley about money and doing business certainly proved that.

"Do you know anything about their culture?" Pain colored her voice as she thought of sweet Charlotte. Of how much James had loved her. "Every seven years, they find a mortal girl with something they call the Spark. It's that something special that some people have—you often see it in great painters, musicians, inventors, and such. They lure the chosen girl into their realm, ply her with beautiful things and attention; sometimes she's even seduced. Then, they kill her to feed the land, which is the very magic that composes their world. If they don't do this, the Otherworld, and all those who call it home, will perish."

"My word, they wanted to kill you?" Jeff's face contorted into a look of sheer terror. "The realm of Faerie lives off the blood of girls?"

"It does. And they would have sacrificed me, had Charlotte not volunteered to take my place." Tears pricked her eyes and she dabbed them with her handkerchief. "It's hard to talk about this."

He pulled her close to him. "Noli, none of this makes sense."

"It's the truth. I regret all of my dealings with them."

All except for those that involved V. "You have no idea what you've gotten yourself into with these business dealings." She flinched, hearing the pain in her voice.

"Who *is* Brogan?" Jeff asked.

"Someone who conspired to exile his own brother in order to take over the throne of the earth court." Noli didn't hide her bitterness.

Jeff blinked. "He's the king?"

"*A* king, the earth court king." For some reason his ignorance angered her. "If you don't know anything about the fae, you shouldn't be doing business with them."

"So what, exactly, is Kevighn?" Jeff said Kevighn's name as if it tasted bad, completely ignoring her scolding.

Revealing Kevighn's role in everything that had happened wouldn't be prudent. "Nothing special. Kevighn's naught but an exile—granted, a crafty and resourceful one. But really, why are you doing business with the Otherworld?"

"I'm sorry, Noli, but I can't tell you." Not a sliver of regret tinged Jeff's voice or shone in his eyes. "Why don't we go have that tea and you can explain all this. For one thing, if Kevighn is in exile, how can you be sure he'll bring us the money?"

Noli looked at her brother, crestfallen. "The money? You can't tell me why you're stealing dangerous artifacts and selling them to an unscrupulous king, and all you want to know about is the *money*?" She waved her parasol at him. "No, I'm not going anyplace with you. Not until you explain."

Picking up her skirts, she ran, not stopping until she'd lost Jeff. When she had, she leaned against a wall and caught her breath, refusing to cry or allow her knees to buckle. No, she had no time for this. Right now, she needed to go to the tea house and meet with Kevighn before Jeff did. That way, her brother wouldn't actually get his money unless he gave her some answers. If he refused to tell her, she'd go to Vix.

Yes. If Jeff was stealing things for faeries, odds were that the ship's captain knew all about it.

•••••••••

Valise in hand, Kevighn hummed a merry tune, his step light as he traipsed down the street. Jeff and his mortal crew hadn't had any idea of what they'd been about to do. And Magnolia—the fact that she trusted him enough to give him the attaché case made his heart soar.

Now, to find Ciarán.

If the king wanted to be found, a simple finding spell should do the trick. Kevighn followed the spell through the city. A grin spread across his face when he saw where it led, and he remembered what Roderick had said about a particular opium den.

Ah, how he'd whiled away many a day, here at the Red Pearl.

As he strolled through the front gates, he glanced at the yellow house beside it and shuddered. Soulless place, that Findlay House.

Mr. Chun, the owner of the Red Pearl, opened the door. A puzzled expression crossed his face as he peered at Kevighn. "May I help you?"

"Mr. Chun, it's Kevighn Silver. I'm here to meet someone; I believe he's already here. He goes by Kyran or Ciarán." Kevighn couldn't help but feel the tiniest bit wounded that Mr. Chun didn't recognize him, considering all the time and money he'd spent here.

Then again, he'd always dressed impeccably on his visits. Today, he looked like an air pirate in need of a bath. How did Magnolia always manage to stay so neat and clean? Especially given her position on the ship?

"Ah, Mr. Silver, it's been some time." Mr. Chun looked him up and down in a way that made Kevighn think he might not be allowed in. Finally, Mr. Chun stepped aside. "He is in the garden, and expecting you."

"I appreciate it." Kevighn walked through the house, into the lavish back gardens filled with nooks and grottos. Even in winter, the gardens remained green and beautiful. Through the fence, in the yard behind the school, he spied two girls in gray hanging laundry on a line—as he had once before. Neither laughed nor smiled. What a waste.

Kevighn felt someone standing behind him.

"Do you know what that place is?" Kevighn indicated the school beyond the fence. "It's a place where they *beat* the Spark out of young girls in their prime. Literally."

"There's also a wild portal in their back garden. Someone should take care of that," the mild and familiar voice replied.

Oh yes, he'd forgotten about that. The portal in the faery tree was what had enabled Magnolia's innocent Midsummer's wish for escape to bring her to the Otherworld in the first place.

"I meant to send someone to check on it, but with all the activities surrounding ... well, surrounding everything, I forgot." Kevighn still didn't turn around, apprehension building inside him. While he hoped Ciarán would welcome him back with open arms, there was the chance that he wouldn't.

Long ago, Ciarán had brought Kevighn and his sister into his fold, to protect them from the wrath of the fire court that arose in reaction to Creideamh's throwback earth talent. The fire court and the earth court were foils to one another, bitter enemies; not to mention that his sister's abilities broke certain laws. But after Creideamh's death, Kevighn had turned his back on the dark court, easing his pain about Creideamh by taking the position of the high queen's huntsman.

"I've been expecting you, Kevighn Silver-Tongue," Ciarán stated. "Though I *was* expecting you sooner."

Kevighn finally turned to face the man behind him. The smile Ciarán offered wasn't cool, predatory, or fake, which gave him some relief—but only some. Dark hair hung in Ciarán's amber eyes, and when he dressed as a gentleman, as he did now, it was difficult to tell exactly how ruthless he was. Which was probably the point. For once, the dark king wasn't flanked by his henchman, though that didn't mean they didn't lurk nearby. Ciarán was only a little older than Kevighn, but he was young for a dark king; it was a dangerous job for a dangerous man.

Kevighn got down on one knee in the soft grass. So many emotions warred inside of him. He hadn't expected that seeing Ciarán again after such a long time would impact him so.

"I'm sorry, Your Majesty. You . . . " His voice lowered, as did his eyes. "You were right."

A chuckle, albeit not a vicious one, reached his ears. "I usually am." Ciarán held out a hand and pulled Kevighn up. "You've known, ever since Tiana took the throne, that your days as huntsman were numbered." He shook his head. "That one's not right."

Only Ciarán, as Tiana's opposite, could make a comment like that out loud. Even though most everyone knew that Tiana wasn't nearly as good a queen—or as mentally stable—as her older sister had been.

"I . . . I hear you have something for me to do?" Kevighn's chest didn't untighten, though he was grateful for his old friend's welcome.

"I might." The corners of Ciarán's lips twitched.

"Perhaps it involves some artifacts?" Kevighn had just remembered that he didn't have much time. "I have something that might be of interest to you." He handed the attaché case to him. "King Brogan hired some mortals to steal these. How he knew where they were, I don't know. Also, he's using the alias 'Kyran.' I have a feeling you might be interested in this information."

Ciarán sat down on a nearby bench and opened the case. "Oh my. So Brogan's the one who's been after my quarry? I've been wondering who had similar business interests as me. Though it makes sense."

"So, I was right in thinking this shouldn't be in Brogan's hands—and that you might find it useful?" Kevighn continued to stand, hope taking seed within him.

"Indeed." Ciarán looked up at him. "These are for me?"

"If you are willing to pay for them. I only ask because the mortals I took them from were depending on payment from Brogan."

Kevighn had never intended to dispose of the pieces, as he'd told Noli. No, they were far too valuable. But unlike Brogan, Ciarán would use these remnants of the legendary artifact for the good of the Otherworld. But first, he needed to think about getting the money; he didn't want to disappoint Magnolia, even if he was double-crossing her in his own way.

This was for the greater good.

Ciarán's eyebrows rose. "You care about mortals? Has exile made you compassionate?"

He cared about Magnolia. "The woman I took them from is one of us. However, she doesn't know what this is." Very few knew of the artifact, and even fewer would recognize it in its current state.

"Why doesn't it surprise me that a woman is at the center of this?" Ciarán chuckled. "If I get you your money, will you finally come home where you belong?"

Kevighn bowed his head, focusing on the grass. "I never should have left."

"Your cabin is still there. So is the grove. I know how much they mean to you. And you know you're always welcome to stay with me." His voice grew tentative.

"That was your work?" Kevighn suspected it had been. His cabin and the grove around it should have disappeared when the queen exiled him. Very few possessed the power to prevent something like that.

Ciarán nodded. "Of course. The grove is Creideamh's. Also, the cabin wasn't Tiana's to take."

"I am grateful for it, Your Majesty." Kevighn bowed in thanks. Ciarán's gift would have strings, but not the way a similar gift from Queen Tiana would. "May I ask, why?"

"How could I not forgive you?" Ciarán said. "Besides . . . " He grinned slyly. "As I've said before, I'm in need of someone with your skills." He closed the attaché case.

"Which skills would those be?" By the Bright Lady, he'd missed Ciarán.

"You'll see." The dark king's look grew devilish. "I'm glad you're back. Things are brewing in the Otherworld, and I need you by my side."

"You're really allowing me back?" Relief washed over Kevighn. Friendship aside, he hadn't been sure what Ciarán would decide. Accepting a banished high court huntsman wasn't a light decision.

"With one condition." Ciarán held up a finger.

Kevighn's stomach tightened again. "Of course, Your Majesty."

"Don't leave again. Next time, come to me with your difficulties, and I'll help you." For a moment, Ciarán's eyes flashed with pain.

Kevighn exhaled, his chest catching. "I promise."

"Good." Ciarán stood and embraced him. "Let me get you the money. Do you have time for a drink, so that I may tell you what has happened and what I need you to do for me?"

"I actually need to deliver the money to the mortals first—after that, your wish is my command." Kevighn bowed, grateful that Ciarán forgave him. Could he convince Magnolia to come back with him to the Otherworld? She was wasted on that ship, as much as she was with that whelp of an earth court prince.

Ciarán clapped him on the shoulder. "Anything for you, Kevighn. Anything for you."

SEVENTEEN

Getting Down to Business

Elation increased with every step Steven took as he made his way down the wooden dock of the San Francisco Air Terminal with James, Hittie, and Hattie. They'd arrived in one piece. The Vixen's Revenge was said to be in port. The end of this blasted quest lay in sight. Finally.

"What now?" Hattie asked James. The young airship captain seemed to have a soft spot for his younger brother. For some reason, the ladies always seemed to like James.

"We get Rahel and take her home," Steven replied. And, in return, get their automaton from Dr. Heinz. Then people would stop trying to help them, kill them, or kill them by helping them. Hopefully.

They stopped in front of a ship that was bigger than Hayden's Follies but smaller than the large passenger ships. It had gleaming brass, several balloons to keep it aloft, and a crow's nest that peeked out between the balloons. A very large dark man stood on a ladder, making repairs to the hull.

"Run into trouble, Asa?" Hittie called.

"You should have seen the other guy." The dark man waved. "Hittie, Hattie, you made it. The captain will be happy to see you. We were all worried."

"We're fine, as always," Hattie replied. "Takes more than MoBatts to keep us down."

Asa laughed. "That it does. Captain!" he bellowed. "Look who blew into town."

A boy appeared on the top of the airship. He was in need of a haircut, a lock of blue hanging in his eyes. His face broke out into a wide grin. "You're here!"

It took Steven a moment to realize that the boy was actually a woman. She slid down a ladder and landed gracefully on the dock, then embraced Hattie and Hittie.

"Vix, how can we help?" Hittie asked.

Captain Vix smiled. "Don't you have your own repairs to do? I hope they didn't get you too badly."

"Surprisingly enough, our passengers helped." Hittie gave Steven and James a less-than-tart look. "We still have work to do, but we can always lend a hand for your ship."

"You have passengers?" Vix focused on him and James in a way that made Steven feel like he was in trouble.

"Bounty hunters," Hattie replied. "Hired to find one of the little girls you took from those nasty rascals. Are they still onboard?"

By the Bright Lady, he hoped so.

"Actually, they are; I was waiting for Jeff to get back before I took them over to the safe house. But if you're willing to help, I'd appreciate it. I don't like having them onboard longer than necessary," Vix replied.

Jeff wasn't onboard? Relief shuddered through him.

"Always happy to help," Hattie said. "Which girl are you here for?" she asked Steven.

"Rahel Heinz. She's small, blond, and five. Her father, Dr. Heinz, contracted us to bring her home," he added for Vix's benefit.

"Rahel?" Vix's brow furrowed. "I know who she is." Then her eyes rested on James and she squinted in the sun. "Have we met?"

"Captain, it's a pleasure to see you again. I'm James Darrow. We met a few months ago." James gave a little bow. "I'd been looking for Jeff. May I introduce you to my brother, Steven?"

"Steven Darrow?" Vix's eyes narrowed. Without warning, her fist shot out and hit Steven squarely on the jaw.

His hand went to his mouth as he stared up at the very tall woman. For a girl, she could punch pretty well.

"I guess Jeff told her all about you," James said softly, his expression halfway between compassion and amusement.

Vix's hands went to her hips. "I'll give you the little girl if you depart immediately. You should feel lucky that Jeff isn't here right now. Breaking his sister's heart like that. He's likely to break your head."

Steven didn't wish to see Jeff anyway. His jaw throbbed.

"I'd be grateful if you'd give us Rahel. We have far to go and need to be on our way."

"You stay here," Vix told them. "Hittie, Hattie, will you help?"

The sisters smiled. "Of course," Hattie replied.

A few moments later, Hattie reappeared with a little blond girl wearing an odd red dress, a doll clutched to her chest.

"Rahel, this is Steven and James. They're taking you home to your daddy," Hattie explained.

Her lower lip quivered. "You're bringing me to my popi?"

"We are. He misses you so much." Steven gazed at the cute little blonde, with her curls and big blue eyes.

A smile broke out on her face and she did a little dance right there on the dock. "I'm going home, I'm going home."

Vix frowned at them. "You should go. Now."

She seemed to be in a hurry. Not that he wanted to see Jeff.

Hattie gave James a long look. "How do you plan on getting back ... where are you going?"

"Upstate New York," James replied. "And I'm not actually sure."

Hattie looked at the little girl and then back at them. "Let me see if I can find you a ride." She glanced around at the ships. "In fact, let's all go. Believe me, you don't want to be here when Jeff returns. Did you really break his sister's heart?"

Steven sighed heavily, a piece of his own heart breaking. "Unfortunately, I did. I'll fix it as soon as I can. I promise."

Oh, Noli. He hoped she wasn't holed up in her tree

house, refusing to come out like she had after her father disappeared.

Hattie's eyes met his. "You should do that. Soon."

If only it were that easy. First things first. He put an arm around Rahel. "Let's get you home."

....

By some stroke of luck, Hattie got Steven, James, and Rahel aboard the Indefatigable, an eagle-class streamliner headed to New York City. After that, they would be on their own. But this would be a huge help, considering they were currently on the opposite side of the United States and Steven didn't dare cut through the Otherworld with an innocent little girl in tow.

Both he and James would have to work for their passage on the Indefatigable, but they had their own tiny cabin and food. Most of the women aboard seemed absolutely enchanted by little Rahel; Steven and James said she was their cousin, and that they were accompanying her home after a visit to see relatives.

In the corner of the cabin, Rahel played with her redheaded dolly and the rag doll they'd used to track her.

Steven sat on the bed, reading the book Dr. Heinz had lent him so that he could return it. Bright Lady bless, he was grateful that Vix had handed Rahel over without a problem. His hand went to his jaw, which still ached. It could have been worse.

"Rahel, what's your dolly's name?" James flopped down on the bed beside her.

"Charlotte, Charlotte, Charlotte," Rahel sang.

All the color drained from James' face as he sat straight up. "Charlotte? Your doll's name is Charlotte?" His voice shook. "Which doll?"

She held up the redheaded one, the one she'd been carrying when they took her off Vix's ship.

"Relax, James. It's a coincidence," Steven soothed him, looking up from the pages of *The Prince*.

"But Charlotte is her name. Noli said so," Rahel pouted, her lower lip quivering as she clutched both dolls to her chest.

"Noli?" Steven nearly dropped the book.

Rahel nodded. "Noli gave me the dolly. She told me her name is Charlotte. I miss her." The last part came out as a baby wail and her face scrunched up.

"Wait—Noli was aboard the ship?" The news felt like a blow to his chest.

"Noli's my friend," Rahel replied. "She took care of me."

It all made sense. Vix didn't know about him only through Jeff—she knew about him because after he'd left Noli heartbroken in Los Angeles, Jeff had taken Noli aboard his airship.

"Noli's on the ship." The words shook as they left Steven's lips. "She's not in Los Angeles. She's on Jeff's ship."

When they'd gotten Rahel, Noli must have been out with Jeff. *That* was why Vix had been in such a hurry for them to depart. She hadn't wanted Noli to know—or for him to see her.

"Flying figs," James muttered, now upside down on the bed.

"Language, James. But I can't believe Noli's on the ship," Steven repeated. And he hadn't known.

Jeff punched him in the arm. "Focus, V. Noli couldn't have come with us. And now we know where she is. We take Rahel home, we get the automaton, we take it to Tiana, and *then* we find Noli."

"Yes, that would be prudent." Steven put the book on his lap and looked over at Rahel and the doll. Of course Noli would name a redheaded doll Charlotte.

Rahel looked up at him, both dolls clutched to her chest. "Do you know Noli?"

Steven smiled. "I do, and I miss her quite a bit."

"You should tell her that. She's sad a lot." Rahel made the dolls dance.

The idea of Noli being upset because of *him* hurt his heart. Steven picked his book back up. "I will do just that, very, very soon."

••••••••

Noli sat in a plump floral chair, sipping hot tea from a dainty teacup and eating chocolate cake in Miss Molly's Tea House. It was a bit like taking tea in a giant dollhouse, but pleasant nevertheless. She'd only known about the place because when she was at Findlay House, Miss Gregory came here every Thursday to meet with friends, leaving the girls with extra chores and lessons to keep them busy.

Too bad we didn't bring the key to the faery garden, the sprite mused. *I want to visit the wood faeries.*

Right. The secret faery garden at Findlay. The brass key was with her things on the ship.

We're not going to Findlay. It's a dreadful place, she told the sprite. Just the thought of it made her shudder, though she sometimes did miss that wondrous garden. Hopefully it had stayed locked, and no other girls had fallen through the wild portal in the old oak.

With a bit of luck, Kevighn would arrive soon with the money from Ciarán; she didn't actually have money to pay for her tea and cake. Oh, it was nice to have real tea. Perhaps she'd bring some back with her.

And more cake, the sprite piped.

Just then, Kevighn sauntered through the door holding the black attaché case. Noli waved. He wove his way through the tables filled with ladies and joined her.

"I trust you brought it." She took another sip of tea.

"You doubt me?" Kevighn's eyebrows rose as he set the case next to her. "You may check it if you like."

Placing her teacup in the matching saucer, Noli picked up the case and opened it. It brimmed with green bills. Closing it quickly, she moved it to the ground next to her feet.

"I trust you—and I'm trusting that the money is real,

because I don't know how to check." Pity that Jeff wasn't there; he'd know.

Actually, the fact that he wasn't there saddened her. However, her having the money first *did* gain her leverage. Vix would make Jeff explain things.

"You'll dispose of the pieces?" Noli's eyes met his.

"I'll make sure they don't end up in Brogan's hands," Kevighn assured her.

She sighed with relief. "Good, because Brogan doesn't need any more power."

"No good can come from Brogan having it. Also, he'd need all the pieces for it to work properly." Kevighn helped himself to her pot of tea and Noli picked up her teacup.

Her free hand went to her pocket, where the piece with the sigil still hid. "Then he won't ever have it."

"Come with me." Kevighn's voice became a caress as he gazed at her over his teacup, his eyes compelling. "I'm returning to the Otherworld now, and I want you to come with me. I can take care of you so much better than Jeff."

"The Otherworld." Tea sloshed out of Noli's cup onto the pristine white tablecloth. "But you were exiled."

"From the five main courts, yes," Kevighn replied. "I don't think Tiana realized that once, long ago, I was affiliated with the dark court, and they have welcomed me back." He took a sip of tea.

Noli sucked in a breath. "Yes, they would." She remembered seeing Ciarán and his ruffians a few times when she'd gone back to the Otherworld to visit Charlotte.

"Are you insulting me?" Kevighn recoiled as if slapped.

"Not at all. I met Ciarán once. He seems more … your kind of people … than the high court." She'd learned quite a bit about the high court from Charlotte and wondered how someone like Kevighn had stood it.

Kevighn took a sip of tea and nodded, visibly relaxing. "Yes, they are far more my people—and they could be yours. They loved Creideamh, and they'll love you. If anyone could reverse what the queen did to you, it would be Ciarán."

Noli hadn't thought of that. But as tempting as getting her old self back might be …

"I can't go with you." She met his eyes as she said it. "You're still not good for me, and you never will be."

Reaching across the table, Kevighn tilted up her chin with a rough finger. "Yes, I can be. That earth court rogue hurt you—and he'll continue to hurt you. You deserve better."

She flinched as if his words burned. "V is more man that you'll ever be."

Kevighn stood. Taking her hand, he kissed it, his lips lingering a little too long. "You sound so much like Creideamh, it hurts my heart. I only hope that it doesn't take your death to show you the error of your ways. If you ever need me, leave word at the Thirsty Pooka. It's a tavern in the Blackwoods." His hand lingered on hers. "I will always be there for you, Noli. Always."

With one more kiss to her black-gloved hand, Kevighn strode out of the tea house.

Well, that was interesting, the sprite observed. *Now let's order more cake.*

....

Noli returned to the air terminal alone, attaché case clutched tightly in one gloved hand, a paper sack in the other, parasol under her arm. Where could Jeff be? Was he angry with her? Her chest tightened. He must be. Otherwise he would have found Miss Molly's.

Vix stood on a ladder, carefully sanding the ship's hull. Jeff was nowhere in sight.

"Captain, may I speak with you?" Noli's heart thumped in her ears.

Vix glanced over at her from her perch on the ladder. "Where's Jeff?"

Noli sighed, disappointed he hadn't returned. "I don't know. Please, may we go inside and talk?" This wasn't the place to discuss King Brogan—or the attaché case full of money.

"Of course." Vix climbed down the ladder, her usually annoyed expression replaced with one of concern. "The girls are gone, by the way."

"They are?" It was like a knife in the heart, and her hand went to her chest.

She's gone? the sprite cried.

Yes, she is, Noli sniffed.

"Rahel is on an airship to New York, to be reunited with her father," Vix assured her, herding Noli onto the ship. "She'll be home soon."

"I'm glad." Noli dabbed at her eyes. She looked around

the quiet common area of the ship. "Where could we speak privately?"

Vix gestured to the table in the galley. "We could sit here. No one's onboard but Winky, and he's below."

"Let me make some tea," Noli suggested. "Do you drink tea? I bought some." With some of the money from the attaché case. After all, she had to make sure it could be spent. She busied herself with boiling some water in a pot, since they had no kettle.

Vix sat at the head of the table, looking at Noli with something halfway between concern and amusement. "I do drink tea sometimes; I'm not a complete heathen. But don't go telling everyone that," she added conspiratorially.

"I brought you cake." Noli set a bag from the tea shop on the table in front of Vix. She had another, and an extra piece for the sprite.

Captain Vix eyed her slice of cake. "Do you often do this? Use food to solve problems?"

Noli made a face as she found a clean fork and handed it to Vix. "I . . . I know so little about you. All I know is that my brother loves you, you return stolen children to their families, and you like chocolate cake."

"Oh, we haven't actually gotten to talk much, have we?" Vix took a bite of cake as Noli prepared the tea. "Where is Jeff? Did he go on the drop alone?" Then she froze. "There wasn't a problem with the drop, was there?" Her dark eyes narrowed at Noli.

Setting the cups of tea on the table, Noli took a seat,

making sure the attaché case was by her feet. "How long have you been doing business with the fae?"

Vix nearly spit out her tea. "Jeff was right."

"How exactly did he suspect I knew?" She'd wondered about that.

"Something about a magic valise?" Vix shoveled another bite of cake into her mouth. "This is very good cake."

Noli's hand went to her face. Of course it was the magic valise. "But why are you doing business with them?" she repeated.

"I'm not sure I feel comfortable sharing that with you," Vix replied.

Although Vix had said this politely, not snappishly, anger welled inside Noli at her refusal. She slapped the attaché case onto the table, just out of Vix's reach. "This is your money from the drop. I get my answers, you get your money."

"Where's Jeff?" Vix's eyes became frantic, and she looked about the room as if Jeff might magically appear.

"I don't know. He was... unhappy with my business decisions and left me on my own. But I don't think you know these people like I do." Noli moved the case closer as Vix snatched for it.

"Vix! Vix, have you seen Noli?" Jeff's voice called, from out of sight. He sounded anxious.

"What *is* going on here?" Vix stood, her hands on the table.

Noli grabbed the case and held it to her chest.

Jeff strode in and came straight over to Noli. "Please

tell me you have the money. Do you have any idea what you've done? I tried to find your tea house, but I couldn't. Is it even real?"

Standing, Noli smacked Jeff with the attaché case. Hard. "Of course the tea house is real. Kevighn had no problem finding it. Do you still have no idea of what you were about to do?" She smacked him with the case again and again, pouring her frustrations into it. "I will never allow you to sell things to King Brogan, especially if he intends to use them to hurt more people."

When it came time for V to kill his uncle, she'd gladly stand by his side. Maybe she'd even help.

"I have your money, but I'm not giving it to you until someone tells me what is going on here," she finally said. Quiet anger tinged Noli's voice as she gripped the case to her chest again, stepping away from the both of them.

"Jeff, go get the bottle of whiskey." Vix still stood at the head of the table, pale. "I don't know about you, but I need a drink."

Jeff looked from Vix to Noli and back again. "Are we actually going to tell her?"

"We want our money, don't we?" Vix's look to Jeff was matter-of-fact.

Finally, she'd get some answers.

With a shake of his head, Jeff left. Noli sat down and took another sip of tea.

Jeff retuned and poured himself and Vix a drink, not offering any to Noli, not that she liked spirits much.

"When I first left home, I was befriended by a man," Vix began. She took a swig. "Unsavory sort, yet fairly honest, all things considered. He helped me out a fair bit and I did a number of jobs for him. Eventually I discovered he wasn't mortal, and that there were plenty more of his kind. Others like him asked me to do a job here and there. They've always been just jobs—business transactions. I don't ask questions, and I don't get involved with them or their politics. "

"How long have you worked with Brogan?" Noli polished off her tea and went to the stove for more.

"Who's Brogan?" Vix took another pull from her cup.

"Kyran. Only he's not the real Kyran. Whomever that might be." She refilled her teacup, leaning against the counter, holding it in her hands.

"The man *we* know as Kyran is a new client. We met him through someone else we sometimes do work for. Kyran—Brogan—needed us to collect some artifacts for him. He gave us a list of where and what to get." Vix finished her drink and poured herself another. "I didn't ask questions. That's not my job. But something did seem off about him."

Jeff, still standing, made a face. "It's because he doesn't like you much."

If looks could kill, Jeff would be dead.

"No, that's not it." Vix turned to Noli. "So, yes, we do jobs for Otherworld folk sometimes, but it's just work."

That didn't seem wise. "You've never been to the Otherworld?" Noli asked.

Vix's eyes widened. "No. Have you?"

"Enough to know that you don't just 'do business' with King Brogan any more than you bargain with the high queen." Oh, flying figs. She'd left the case of money on the table within their reach.

"You didn't give the artifacts to him like you were supposed to?" A look of fear crossed Vix's face.

"No, she didn't," Jeff retorted. "She gave them to Kevighn Silver, who apparently is one of them as well."

Ugh, why was Jeff acting like this? Perhaps he needed to be beaten more; her parasol would be less awkward than the case.

"I have your money." Noli scowled as she gestured to the attaché case on the table. "Count it. Kevighn knows what the pieces are, and he knows King Brogan. He promised to make sure the pieces are lost again, as they should be. This artifact cannot be assembled and put into the wrong hands." She still didn't know why, or what it was, but she completely believed that giving it to Brogan or Tiana would be disastrous.

Vix took the case and counted the money. "Can we trust Kevighn?"

"Not a chance," Jeff said at the same time that Noli replied, "I do."

"There's a lot of money here." Vix divided the money into piles. "More than we were promised. But I dislike the idea of selling it to someone else. It makes us look bad—and I value my reputation. Also, I got the idea that our client was . . . powerful."

Why didn't they comprehend the severity of the situation? "He's the earth court king—of course he's powerful," Noli retorted. "And yes, he's bound to get angry. But nevertheless, he's trying to piece together a lost artifact of great power. We can't let him do that."

"Why do you care so much about them?" Jeff wondered aloud. He took a drink directly from the bottle.

Vix's lips pursed, and for a long moment the only sound was that of her counting the money into piles. "Are you even Noli?" she suddenly asked. "You're one of them, aren't you? Disguised as Noli. What are they called—changelings?"

Noli felt all the breath leave her, and her hands shook. "I'm not a changeling. I'm Noli."

Usually.

Vix didn't look up. "I saw what you did with those cannonballs. I've seen them work magic before—not often, but enough to know you were using magic. "

She *had* seen. Noli's knees went weak.

"You have *magic*?" Jeff's eyes widened.

Noli looked into the depths of her half-drunk teacup. "Just a little. I only did that for the good of the ship, because we couldn't survive a cannon attack. It wasn't Kevighn's fault."

We have a lot of magic. I just never feel like using it much other than to play games, the sprite offered.

How much is a lot? As much as V? Noli asked.

I don't know.

"You're doing it again." Jeff stood in front of her, a hand on her shoulder.

Noli closed her eyes and gulped, not relishing the thought of telling this story. "I'm not right, Jeff." Her voice shook. "Some of it is Findlay and some of it is what happened when I fell into the Otherworld."

"Will you tell me?" Jeff pulled her to him

"I haven't gone round the bend. Honest." Her voice broke as she leaned her head on his chest.

"Of course you haven't." His arms wrapped around her. "Vix, I still don't know what to do about Kyran—Brogan—whoever he is. He's not very happy with us."

"Well, we wouldn't be the first to sell something collected for one client to a higher bidder. We should lay low and hope this blows over." Vix kept counting the money. "What's the last place anyone would look for us?"

Jeff thought for a moment. "Do you think we could make it to Boston by Thanksgiving?"

"Boston?" Noli and Vix said in unison.

"The last place anyone would look for us is Boston. And … well, Vix, don't you think it's time you met my mother?" Jeff's voice went shy.

"I—" Vix's eyes widened as she paused, money in her hand.

Boston? It might be nice to see her mother.

"As long as you don't leave me there," Noli put in, looking up at her brother.

Jeff shook his head and patted her shoulder. "No, I won't leave you there. Promise."

"You're not going to stop until you've made an honest

woman of me, are you?" Vix looked stricken, her hand hovering over one of the piles of money.

"Would being my wife truly be so bad?" Jeff let go of Noli and walked over to Vix, taking her hand. "It won't mean giving up your ship or being captain, or our work."

Noli dropped her gaze and leaned against the counter, not wanting to intrude on such a private moment.

"Promise?" The way Vix looked at Jeff seemed more like a threat than anything.

Jeff kissed her. "Promise."

"All right then, I'll say *yes*. At the very least so you'll stop asking." Vix continued counting and gave Jeff a sharp look over the bills. "But I'm *not* going to settle down."

He toyed with her short hair. "I wouldn't have it any other way. It's settled, then. As soon as everyone's onboard, we'll go to Boston for Thanksgiving."

The idea of seeing her mother made Noli's heart leap with joy. At the same time, part of her feared that Jeff and Vix would sneak out in the dead of night, leaving her to be someone else's problem.

"Congratulations," she told them. Her brother was getting married! That made her *and* the sprite happy. "What's everyone else going to do while we're at Grandfather's?"

Jeff gave her a wide, mischievous grin. "Grandfather does have a very large house."

Noli laughed. Jeff was going to bring his trouser-wearing wife-to-be and a bunch of air pirates to Grandfather Montgomery's for Thanksgiving? "Boston's never going to be the same, is it?"

"Probably not," Jeff chuckled, giving Vix a fond look. "Probably not."

"Rogue or not, this is very generous." Vix packed the piles of money into the attaché case. "We'll have payday later. Let me put this in the safe for now." She and the case disappeared into her quarters.

Noli turned to Jeff. "I can't wait to see Mama."

"Captain Vix! I need to speak to you right now," a voice boomed from outside, sending shivers down Noli's spine.

EIGHTEEN

Visitors

"Come out, come out, Captain Vix," the man shouted again.

Jeff's arm shot out in warning as his other hand fumbled for his pistol. "Noli, stand back."

Vix barreled into the galley, her pistol drawn, just as King Brogan appeared in the common area, still in his morning coat and top hat.

"Why are you on my ship, Kyran—or should I say, *Brogan*?" Vix kept her pistol focused on the earth court king.

"Ah, what's in a name, *Victoria*?" King Brogan raised his hands in an empty gesture.

Noli craned her neck, trying to see if anyone lurked behind Brogan. One thing she'd learned was that Otherworldly monarchs liked entourages.

"I contracted you for something, and I expect it to be

delivered. Promptly." Brogan tapped his walking stick on the floor for emphasis.

"You gave us no payment in advance. We aren't bound to sell it to you." Vix held her ground. "Perhaps we found a higher bidder . . ."

"Kevighn Silver stole it from us," Jeff blurted out, still blocking Noli with his body. "He masqueraded as a crew member and then stole it. I think he works for someone also named Kyran."

"Kevighn Silver took it? And he's working for another Kyran?" For a split second, worry crossed Brogan's face. "We can't have a rogue like him with an artifact like that."

"No, we can't, but we just don't have the resources to find him," Jeff apologized.

Noli looked on in horror as Jeff blamed this entire debacle on Kevighn. "How could you?" she hissed at her brother, taking a step forward. "Kevighn—"

Jeff put a hand over her mouth as if she were a naughty child. "You'll have to forgive Noli. She's not feeling well."

How dare he? She struggled against her brother.

King Brogan focused on her. His eyes might look like V's, but they lacked V's soul and insight.

"An earth sprite, on an airship?" he cackled. "Whose ingenious idea was that? Kevighn didn't have to *steal* my artifacts. He probably traded her something shiny for them."

Noli's heart fell and she stopped struggling. She wasn't yet ready to reveal that particular detail about herself to Jeff and Vix.

Did he give us something shiny? I want something shiny, the sprite whined.

Shush, Noli retorted. "I'm not an earth sprite," she declared, getting free of Jeff's grasp. "You, sir, must be mistaken."

"Is that any way to speak to your king?" Brogan took several menacing steps toward her.

"You aren't my king," Noli spat, her heart pounding. She was treading on dangerous ground. The high queen would kill someone for speaking to her like that.

"Stay away from my sister." Jeff fixed his pistol on Brogan, using his body to shield her.

King Brogan's eyes unfocused, then refocused, his lips curving into a deep frown. "You aren't part of my court, yet you aren't dark court, nor high court—how did *that* happen? Who do you belong to? You look familiar ..."

Taking a deep breath, Noli gathered every ounce of courage she possessed and looked right into his eyes. "I belong to no one."

"What's going on? You need to get away from her," Jeff yelled, taking a step toward Brogan.

Vix grabbed his arm. "Jeff, wait."

"You are very much out of your element, little courtless earth sprite." King Brogan smirked. "It's not good to be out of your element."

What did that mean? She'd never heard that before.

"You need to get off my ship, Brogan. Now. We don't have your artifacts." Vix kept her pistol focused on him.

All these pistols and Brogan didn't seem fazed.

"Your weapon won't hurt me." He shrugged. "What if your little sprite gives me the piece that's in her pocket, and I don't kill you all? I think that would be more than a fair trade. What exactly does a sprite *do* on an airship? They're not very good at practical things."

Noli's hand went to her pocket. How did he know?

Don't give it to him, please, a female voice echoed in her mind.

It wasn't the sprite. Unless she was truly going mad, it could only be the Bright Lady herself. Noli didn't know who else it might be.

"I won't." Her jaw set. She wasn't about to defy the Bright Lady.

"Noli, you have a piece?" Jeff's brow furrowed, and he didn't put down his pistol.

Her hand reached into her pocket and wrapped around it. "You can't have it."

"Guards, seize the sprite," King Brogan called. Two large men, clad in gentlemen's clothes, entered the room and stormed toward her.

"Leave her alone." Jeff charged at them. One of the large men tossed him aside like a doll.

"Jeff!" Vix ran to him.

"Leave my brother alone." Noli looked around for something she could control.

Just push them, the sprite told her. *Like they're a ball.*

Holding out her hand, Noli *pushed* with her mind, like the sprite had done when volleying the cannonballs. One of the guards stumbled backward into a wooden table.

"Do you dare use magic against me?" Brogan roared, holding out his hand and sending her flying into the wall. The air whooshed out of her body as she smacked against it.

"Noli!" Jeff stumbled up from the floor.

"Wait," Vix hissed, holding out her arm.

One of the guards peered at Noli. "Your Grace, do you know who this is?"

"Who?" Brogan looked down his nose at Noli as she lay crumpled against the wall, her ribs smarting though nothing felt broken.

"She's Stiofán's. I remember her from the House of Oak."

The guard looked familiar. Noli sucked in a breath, which hurt, as she remembered. "You worked at the big house. You're a spy!"

Brogan's hands clapped his chin. "Stiofán's little mortal—well, not so mortal anymore. Tiana's work, I'm sure. What should we do with her? Bait? Or perhaps we should just kill her. After all, she's not wearing his sigil anymore, which could only mean—"

"Leave. Me. Alone." From her spot on the floor, Noli sent out another blast, this one aimed directly at Brogan.

He sidestepped it, strode over, and grabbed her by the throat. "You are *very* much out of your element, little sprite, and lacking a protector. You best watch your step. Also, are you sure you're well? Your color looks off."

Noli's throat grew warm and tingly and, for the briefest second, his hand shimmered as she struggled for breath.

Wait—she had her knife. Kicking up her foot, she fumbled for it.

"Now give me that piece," Brogan demanded.

Don't give in, the other voice told her, as her hand wrapped around the knife handle.

"No." The word barely escaped Noli's lips as the earth court king choked the air out of her. Grasping the knife, she jabbed it in his hand, praying it would force him to release her.

His face contorted in pain. "Why, you little—"

"Leave my sister alone," she heard Jeff roar. *Pop. Pop. Pop.* Jeff fired his pistol several times into Brogan's leg.

Again, Noli jabbed him. *Take that.* His grip lessened, and she dropped to the floor with a jarring thud, knife falling to the ground. She quickly put the knife back in her boot, then found the piece in her pocket. She must keep it safe.

Several other pistol clicks echoed through the room. Brogan didn't look up, keeping a hand over his bleeding leg.

"No one messes with little sister." Thad aimed his pistol at Brogan, his uncovered eye fierce. Asa and two women wearing trousers also held pistols.

"Brogan, you need to get off my ship. You're bleeding everywhere." Vix's voice remained calm, her pistol still focused on the earth court king.

"I only want what's mine." The hand not staunching his wounds extended, as if Brogan expected Noli to hand the artifact over.

"You didn't pay for it, so it's not yours," Vix retorted. "Asa, Thad, escort these men off my ship."

"I think we should go," the guard who'd spied on her and V said, guiding Brogan toward the exit. "I'll send men after Kevighn Silver for the other pieces."

"You'll pay for this!" Brogan yelled as he limped off the airship leaving a trail of blood, guns still focused on him. "Stiofán too. Oh yes, you will all pay."

A heavy silence filled the air. Noli gasped for breath and stayed crouched on the floor, feeling lightheaded. The piece cut into her hand. She'd done it—she'd even used her knife to protect herself. At least Brogan hadn't hurt Jeff.

She'd never forgive herself if he had.

The new voice in her head stayed silent. That was probably for the best; her head was crowded enough without adding a goddess.

"Are you all right, Captain? Who was that?" Thad tucked his pistol away and took a drink from his flask.

"Business gone bad. Thank you for that." Vix put her pistol away as well.

"Noli, are you well?" Jeff crouched next to her.

"I can't catch my breath." Clammy heat spread across her skin as she rasped for air.

Jeff pulled her into a sitting position so she could lean against him. "Asa, could you please get Noli some water? It's all right. They're gone."

"Who's Stiofán?" Vix joined them, concern in her eyes.

"V. Steven." Noli took the cup of water from Asa but

didn't feel like drinking. It was still difficult to breathe, and her neck ached where Brogan had grabbed her.

"We'll talk about this later, the three of us, while we're en route to Boston," Jeff said quietly. "Vix and I are engaged—we're all going to Boston for Thanksgiving to tell my family," he explained to the others.

Various congratulations came from those in the room. Noli had no idea who the women were. She closed her eyes and leaned on Jeff.

"If we're going to Boston, we best be leaving," Asa finally boomed.

"Noli, you don't look good." Jeff smoothed her hair. "Vix, she's warm."

"Take her downstairs, have Winky ready the engines. Hittie, Hattie, thank you so much. Until next time?" Vix called.

Jeff scooped Noli up in his arms. She should protest. But the words just didn't come out.

"Will little sister be all right?" Thad asked.

"She'll be fine." Jeff carried her down to the little workroom.

Noli kept clutching the piece in her pocket. "I didn't give it to him."

"I still don't understand why it's so important."

"It just is," she insisted.

Jeff put her in her hammock and covered her with the blanket. "We need to talk—you, Vix, and me. I'm not sure precisely what I saw and heard back there."

Noli closed her eyes. "Brogan is V's uncle."

“V’s one of them as well? Don’t they have their own realm?” Exasperation colored Jeff’s voice as he tucked her in.

“V and his family are exiles, forced to live in our realm because of Brogan and Queen Tiana.” Noli ached all over and just felt … wrong. “V broke it off with me because his mother is the high queen and she ordered him to. May I have my roses?”

“Um, sure.” Jeff retrieved her pot of roses from the worktable. Noli wrapped her arms around the tiny pot as if it were a doll. Much better.

“I don’t feel good,” she murmured, trying to get comfortable in her hammock.

I don’t feel good either, the sprite whimpered.

“You sleep. We’ll figure this all out later.” Jeff’s fingers traced her cheek. “We’ll figure this all out later. I promise.”

••••••••

Kevighn stepped through the swinging wooden doors into the Thirsty Pooka, deep within the Blackwoods of the Otherworld. Once, it had been his favorite watering hole. Despite the shady characters who frequented it, the tavern was actually quite safe. Safe enough to bring Creideamh. Or so he’d thought.

People stopped drinking and throwing knives to stare at him. The brownies screeching naughty songs at the piano stopped as well.

"What are you doing here, huntsman?" a large ogre sneered, cleaning his teeth with his dagger as he sat at a table filled with other ugly, smelly, large ogres.

"Yeah, your kind isn't welcome here," a goblin added. They were smaller than the ogres, but just as strong and twice as ugly.

Kevighn's heart sank as others in the bar echoed the sentiments. They'd begin throwing things at him any moment.

"Stop." A cloaked figure at the wooden bar stood up. He was barely taller than Kevighn, but imposing nevertheless. Immediately, the pub fell silent.

Ciarán had spoken.

"Kevighn, did everything go as expected?" The dark king's hood fell back. He gestured to the barstool next to him. "Sit."

Everyone returned to their business. Kevighn took a seat, and Ciarán signaled the bartender, a rather comely lady leprechaun, for two drinks.

"Yes. Everything went as expected." Kevighn tried to forget his suspicion that Magnolia still had possession of that one piece. *That won't be a problem*, he told himself. It would be safe with her, and when they needed it, he could get it.

Ciarán accepted the clay mug from the bartender, who stood on a box in order to see them. She handed a drink to Kevighn.

"Brogan has been collecting them?" Kevighn took a sip of decent ale, dark and cool. Ciarán made it himself.

"Indeed. He's contracted others to collect the pieces as well, from museums, private collectors, and even archeological digs all over the world. Though I don't appreciate him using my name." Ciarán's eyes twinkled. "He knows where many of the pieces are—but not all. I'm not entirely surprised he learned of its existence."

All who knew of the legendary artifact must have gotten their information from one source—the man who'd spent years researching it, then put that research aside when he realized the artifact was much more than a scrap of legend. It was something that would change the face of the Otherworld when reassembled.

"Are you planning to rebuild it, or merely to keep the pieces out of harm's way?" Kevighn asked. Either option would be less self-serving than what Brogan would do.

Ciarán shrugged. "What do you expect? The time has come to rebuild the Staff of Eris. We both know that this is the only way. Only I shall be successful. A rebellion is brewing."

"Rebellion?" Kevighn breathed. Even thinking the word could be treason. Being dark court didn't make them immune to spies or the high queen's wrath.

"Yes. Tiana isn't good for the Otherworld. She cares naught for it or her subjects." Ciarán shook his head. "Pity. But no one can stop her except me."

Well, conceivably the Bright Lady herself or the magic could stop the queen, but there was only one time in memory when that had happened. It was when the Bright Lady first broke apart the Staff of Eris, scattering its pieces to the ends of the mortal realm. Without the staff, the land had to rely on the blood of mortal girls for nourishment.

Most of that era had been forgotten—especially by the monarchs. Even the stories told to children to explain the sacrifice forgot that small detail.

"We still need a queen," Kevighn murmured. There had always been a high queen, one who possessed a rather peculiar set of gifts—the ability to use all four elements.

Ciarán's hands wrapped around his mug. "I think most have forgotten about Tiana's daughter. She lives in the mortal realm with her father."

"Did she inherit her mother's abilities?" Then Kevighn did a double take. "Wait—are you planning on killing the girl?"

Ciarán's face contorted into a look of disgust. "Do you honestly think I'd do that? No, we'll raise the girl here, with us. We'll continue collecting the pieces of the staff, and when we're ready, we'll have our revolution. Tiana will be overthrown, and the girl will be the new high queen."

There were many, many holes in Ciarán's plan, but it wasn't Kevighn's place to question him. "How will you get the girl in the first place?"

"That is where you, my dear friend, come in." Ciarán clapped him on the arm. "I need you to do what you do best—get me the girl."

"You want me to go to Los Angeles and steal the girl away

from the former king of the earth court?" Kevighn couldn't quite believe his ears.

"You do know who her chief tutor and companion is, right?" Ciarán's smile grew sly as he swirled the drink in his glass. "I don't think anyone will mourn if you killed Quinn the Fair in the course of your task."

Kevighn drew in a sharp breath. "You're offering me the chance to kill him?"

Ciarán nodded. "If it had been my sister he'd done that to, I would have killed the bastard straight out."

"You could have . . . I couldn't. It would have caused a war."

Ciarán grinned over the rim of his glass. "It won't cause a war now."

For reasons unknown, Quinn had joined his former king in exile. But then he always was an odd sort. That was partly why his sister had been drawn to him.

"I'll do it." Maybe Stiofán would be there and give him a reason to kill him as well . . . or he'd have a chance to settle his score with the former king himself.

"Good." Ciarán raised his glass in a toast. "To brotherhood."

Kevighn raised his. "To brotherhood."

They drank. Putting down his glass, Ciarán gestured to the pub. "Welcome home. It's about damn time."

Kevighn looked around at the various dark court folk—brownies, goblins, ogres, the banished, the generally unscrupulous; the real "monsters" behind the stories used to scare mortal children. Perhaps the high court looked down on these folks, but the dark court followed a code one never found anyplace else, especially at the high court. They were welcoming him back as if he'd never left.

He clapped his old friend on the arm. "It's good to be home."

Ciarán was right; it was about damn time.

NINETEEN

Ill

Noli's mouth felt like it was stuffed with cotton. She hurt too much to even consider moving. The door opened, but she kept her eyes closed.

"I brought you coffee. How's the patient?" Vix whispered, the door closing behind her.

"Her fever's not breaking," Jeff murmured. "I'm worried."

"We'll be in Chicago soon to refuel. I think we should get her to a doctor," Vix replied.

"No, I think our best chance is to refuel, press on to Boston, and bring her to Grandfather's."

Right. She was unwell. Her skin blazed and she wanted to drink a barrel of water—which, unfortunately, required sitting up.

"Jeff… do you actually think your family will welcome us?" Vix blurted out. "It's so sweet and old-fashioned that you want me to meet them, but what if they turn us away? At least in Chicago we can find a doctor. She's so pale and still."

"Grandfather Montgomery is a lot of things—but he won't turn us away on Thanksgiving, especially when I'm trying to do what's right," Jeff returned. "Also, if Noli's unwell, it's a non-issue. Mother would never allow Grandfather to turn us away."

Right now, all Noli wanted was her mother. Mama always knew how to make tea just right, and when coddled eggs would be better than toast. Real sheets, cool ones that smelled nice, would feel so much better on her too-warm skin than hammock strings.

"Are you certain? It just feels so ... risky."

"We need to take her to Boston," Jeff insisted.

Noli struggled to sit up. "I want to see Mama." The words felt as thick as badly knitted socks, but if she didn't speak up, they might stop in Chicago instead.

"Easy." Jeff helped her sit, the hammock rocking with her movement. "How do you feel?"

"Warm." She shrugged off her blanket. "And thirsty."

Jeff handed her a cup of lukewarm weak tea, which she drained in two gulps and returned to him. He placed it on the worktable, sat on her workbench, and picked up his own mug. Dark rings circled his eyes and stubble dotted his chin. Vix didn't look any better as she leaned against the closed door. The three of them took up all the space, crowding the miniscule room.

Taking a handkerchief, Jeff dipped it in some water and

handed it to her. Noli wiped her face with it. Her entire body throbbed and the tea did little to slake her thirst.

"Where are my roses?" She looked around.

Jeff gestured to the worktable. The wilted roses drooped, their tiny leaves and petals raining onto the floor. "Would you like your pot of mint?"

"Please?" She just wanted to be near something green and growing.

"There you go." He tucked the pot of mint in her arms and put the fallen blanket back on her lap. "Could I get you something to eat?"

"I don't feel like eating." Really, she just wanted to drink some water and go back to sleep. "I'd like some more tea or water, please."

"I'll get some." Vix left.

"I want to see Mama," Noli said again. She just didn't want to be left behind in Boston. "I feel horrid." Even her hair hurt. Though someone had removed her boots, she noticed that she still wore her blue dress and corset.

Jeff squeezed her shoulder. "We're going to Boston. Grandfather will summon a doctor, and Mother will have the kitchen make you coddled eggs and tea."

"And Mama and Grandmother will have your and Vix's wedding all planned before we even finish Thanksgiving dinner." Noli smiled weakly. "Better you than me."

Throwing back his head, Jeff laughed. "True. You'll help Vix out, won't you?"

"Help me with what?" Vix returned with a cup in her hand, which she gave to Noli.

"I appreciate it." Noli took a tentative gulp of the water, wishing it were cooler.

"Why do you never actually say 'thank you'?" Vix leaned against the door frame.

"Those words mean something to them." Noli took another gulp of water. "I'll help you with the legions of female relations who'll spend all of Thanksgiving arguing as to whether we should serve quail or pheasant at your wedding."

A look of sheer and utter terror crossed Vix's face. "We're not getting married *at* Thanksgiving, are we?"

"I don't think even Grandmamma can plan a wedding that quickly," Noli joked as she finished her water. "Though she might try."

"Noli, since you're feeling a little better, could you *please* explain what's going on here? I don't understand—about you having magic, about that man calling you a sprite, about Steven Darrow being fae." Jeff squeezed her knee.

"Must I?" She looked away, her stomach churning at the idea of talking about everything again.

"Would you like me to leave?" Vix asked.

Noli shook her head. "It's the idea of telling the story that bothers me—not you hearing it." She lay back down in the hammock, clutching the pot of mint, not truly wanting to talk about all this. "In order for it to all make sense, I have to start at the very beginning. The day I regret with all my being. That was the day when everything changed. I'd finally managed to fix Papa's old Hestin-Dervish Pixy and V and I took it out for a test flight..."

....

"No, stop, Miss Gregory, stop," Noli screamed as Miss Gregory poured cold water over her face again and again, not stopping for more than a second. Her lungs burned and she gasped and sputtered for breath.

"Noli, Noli, calm down," Jeff soothed, rubbing a damp cloth over her forehead. "You're not at school; you're safe on the ship with me."

Noli felt torn between the two events, not knowing which was real. "Stop," she sobbed.

"We've docked in Chicago to refuel," Vix said from the doorway. "Are you certain we shouldn't find a doctor … or other help?"

Noli just wanted Miss Gregory to stop. If she didn't get a good breath in soon she'd suffocate. Her lungs screamed for air.

"Other help?" Jeff stroked her face. "Shhh, everything is going to be just fine, Noli."

"It's a bit of a coincidence she fell ill immediately after that Brogan fellow threatened her. I swear I saw his hands … do something," Vix said. "Honestly, Jeff, I think that maybe, especially after hearing Noli's entire tale, we should stop doing business with them."

Noli's breathing eased, but she shivered … and thirst parched her throat.

"You think he did this?" Jeff asked.

"You heard what he did to his own family," Vix replied.

"And he kept talking about Noli being out of her element—I'm certain we're missing something here."

"If it were as simple as finding Steven, perhaps. Those two always have been the best of friends. But I wouldn't know where to even start looking for him. I wouldn't trust anyone else—not even, no, *especially* not Kevighn." Jeff sighed, his head in his hands. "I can't believe our neighbors are *faeries.*"

"I miss V," Noli squeaked. She remembered a little now about what she'd told them, and how she'd left Kevighn's role out of the story as much as she could.

Jeff stroked her cheek, and even that touch hurt. "You're too warm."

"I'm *cold.*" Noli shivered, wincing at the pain it caused. "May I have another blanket?"

"We should get a doctor before it's too late." Vix pressed a cup into Noli's hand. "Here, drink this." She helped Noli take sips of water.

"I still say we need to get her to Boston—they'll know what to do," Jeff insisted. "Perhaps someone can pick up some broth for her. She hasn't eaten much."

Noli didn't feel like eating, but it took too much effort to tell them that. She closed her eyes again, praying she didn't have more nightmares about Miss Gregory—or Queen Tiana.

"Are you sure, Jeff?" Vix's voice broke.

"I'm certain. We should send Winky to get her a new plant—both of hers have died, and she sleeps better with one in her arms." He stroked Noli's hair. "Just go back to sleep, Noli. We'll get you to Boston soon."

Noli nodded and drifted off to sleep.

....

She ran through the wildwood, a legion of pink croquet mallets nipping at her heels. Breena and Nissa, the high queen's handmaidens, lobbed purple and gold cannonballs at her, laughing at Noli's attempts at escape.

"I just want to go home," Noli sobbed as she tripped over a root and sprawled on the ground of the wildwood, croquet mallets marching closer. "I just want to go home."

"Noli, you're dreaming again." Jeff shook her. "Vix, did you summon a motorcab?"

"Are you certain this is a good idea?" Vix asked, trepidation lurking in her voice.

All Noli wanted was to not be caught by the croquet mallets.

"Up you go, Noli." Jeff lifted her. "I'm taking you to Mama; she'll know what to do."

"And if she doesn't?" Vix goaded him.

Noli leaned her head against Jeff's chest, her eyes closed.

"She's our mother. She always knows what to do," Jeff replied.

Noli felt herself being carried as they talked about her. Again. They were going to Mama. Would she see V as well? It would be nice to see that fussy old bodger. A drink would also be welcome. Her throat felt like it was made of sandpaper, and she was sweltering in her dress.

For a long time Vix and Jeff stayed silent, but she was no longer being chased by mallets or purple cannonballs, so she leaned into Jeff, enjoying the respite.

"We're on the way to Grandfather's," Jeff whispered, stroking her hair over and over. "Vix, everything will be fine—they'll love you."

"I'm worried more about her," Vix muttered.

A few moments later, Noli heard Vix suck in a sharp breath. "Is this your house?"

"Grandfather's house, not ours," Jeff replied. "Noli, we're here. Let's find Mama."

Noli's eyes fluttered open, they felt so heavy, so she let them close again. Cold air hit her face. Ah, that felt divine on her overheated skin.

There was a rapping sound and Noli realized someone knocked on a door. Her eyes cracked open. Jeff seemed to be holding her as Vix knocked.

The door opened. "May I help you?" an old voice creaked.

"Jameson? Is that you?" Jeff asked. "It's Jeffrey Braddock, Edwina's son. I need to speak with Mother, or Grandfather, quickly. It's Noli—she's ill."

She was ill? Was that why she felt as if her skin burned with a million steam engines? Perhaps she could have a nice cool bath.

"Please let me in, Jameson," Jeff pleaded. "We need a doctor."

"Jameson, who's at the door? Is that the Parkingtons?" a female voice called.

"Mother … Mama, it's me!" Jeff called.

Noli tried to sit up at the sound of her mother's voice.

"Easy, Noli," Jeff soothed her. "We'll have you in a proper bed soon."

"Jeffery?" Warm air gushed from somewhere, not nearly as pleasant as the cold air. "What are you doing here?" Mama made a noise of alarm. "What's wrong with Noli?"

"I don't know." Jeff's voice broke. "We were coming to visit you for Thanksgiving. Noli fell ill on the way. I … I think Grandfather needs to send for the doctor."

"Noli, my poor girl. Come in. Jeff, it's been far too long." Their mother ushered them in and Noli felt the cold air leave completely, replaced by the hot air, so stifling it made her whimper. "Jeff, help me get her upstairs," she heard her mother say. "Jameson, get Father and send Ellen up. Oh, hello, who are you?"

"Mother, if I might present Victoria Adler, of Kentucky. She and I have recently become engaged. We were coming to visit you, in part so that I might introduce you to her." Jeff moved as he spoke, Noli with him. "Vix, this is my mother, Edwina Braddock."

"It's lovely to meet you, Mrs. Braddock. Jeff and Noli speak so highly of you," Vix said, as polite as could be.

"Why Jeff, you've gotten engaged?" Their mother's voice swelled with pride. "My word, I wasn't expecting that. Victoria, we'll talk. Jeff, let's put Noli in the nursery. We freshened it up for your little cousins, but they didn't come at the last moment."

Noli felt her mother's hand on her forehead.

"You don't think it's influenza, do you?" Mama's voice was tinged with worry.

"I don't think so—no one on the ship has fallen ill but Noli, and Jeff's barely left her side," Vix replied.

Noli felt herself being laid down on a bed. Ah, that was it. Now, if someone would open the window…

Mama repositioned her on the bed, helping her get comfortable. "Is she still in her corset?" Outrage colored Mama's voice. "How many days has she been in her corset? Truly, Jeff? Off with you now. Why don't you and your young lady help Grandfather summon a doctor? Ellen," she bellowed. "Noli, sweetheart, we're going to get you into something more comfortable. Ellen! I need your help."

"Mama." Noli's eyes flickered open, to make sure it was her mother and not a figment of her imagination. Or a croquet mallet.

"I'm right here." Her mother began to undress her. "Ellen!"

"Mama, I don't feel good." Heavy, Noli's eyes closed. It hurt to form words.

I don't feel good either, the sprite complained. *That bad man hurt us.*

He had indeed. There was no doubt this was Brogan's doing.

Her mother brushed her hair away from her face. "Hold on, Noli. Just hold on. We're going to get the doctor. Everything's going to be just fine."

All Noli wanted was a drink of water and a nap in a tree. When she opened her mouth, the words didn't emerge. But her mother would figure it out. Mama always knew exactly what she needed when she fell ill. This time would be no exception.

••••••••

James and Steven trudged through the cold toward Dr. Heinz's house. Rahel rode on Steven's back; it was faster than her walking through the ever-present muddy slush.

"Are we there yet?" Rahel asked. Again.

"Not yet," Steven replied, again, trying to keep the annoyance out of his voice.

James pointed to the horizon. "Look, I think it's up ahead. Rahel, let's race."

"Yessss!" Her squeal hurt Steven's ears as he set her down. Her dolls clutched in her arms, she raced James down the mucky road.

They beat Steven to the house. When James knocked on the door, Bridgid poked her head out. "Yes?"

"Oh, Bridgid, look who we found!" James' voice went singsong as Steven hurried to join them on the porch.

"Bridgid, Bridgid!" Rahel flew past James and wrapped her arms around the young housekeeper's legs.

"Rahel! Oh, Rahel. Dr. Heinz, come quickly!" Bridgid shouted as she hugged Rahel tightly right there in the doorway. "Come in." She ushered all of them inside. "Dr. Heinz," she called.

Tasty smells from the kitchen made Steven's belly rumble. Dr. Heinz appeared, looking much like the last time with his leather apron over his clothes and magnifying goggles on his head.

"Popi!" Rahel flung herself at her father.

He caught her and swung her into his arms. "Rahel, oh, my Rahel." Sobbing with joy, for several moments he just held his daughter, murmuring her name over and over. Bridgid bustled off to get everyone tea.

"Thank you so much," Dr. Heinz told them, still clutching his daughter. "I cannot express how grateful I am."

"It was our pleasure." Steven couldn't help but smile at the man's happiness, though "thank yous" always made him uncomfortable.

"You have the automaton?" James asked.

"James," Steven hissed, elbowing his rude little brother.

James shot him a wounded look as he rubbed his side. "You didn't have to do that."

"Please, be my guest for Thanksgiving, I insist." Dr. Heinz gave his daughter a kiss. "We'll have a feast indeed. Yes, your automaton is ready. Tomorrow, you can be off."

"We would be honored to share your Thanksgiving meal," Steven replied. A hot meal and a real bed sounded splendid. However, he couldn't truly relax until the automaton had been delivered and the quest declared completed. "Oh, I finished your book."

Dr. Heinz smiled. "And what did you think of Machiavelli?"

"It was interesting to learn more about his philosophy." Even if he didn't agree with most of it. Things such as "it is much safer to be feared than loved" seemed far more like his mother and uncle's philosophy than his own.

Rahel frowned at them, her lower lip jutting out in a pout. "You're leaving?"

Steven nodded. "Not until tomorrow. We have to get the present back to our mother—"

"In time for her birthday," James added, ignoring Steven's hard look at both the lie and the interruption.

Rahel clutched her dollies tightly. "When will you find Noli?"

At least Noli was safe with Jeff. But perhaps he should dream-search for her, as he'd done when she'd gone missing. At least he could talk to her that way, make sure she was all right. He felt like smacking himself for not thinking of it sooner. Yes, he'd dream-search for her tonight.

"Soon," he told Rahel, feeling lighter at just the thought. "I'll find Noli very soon."

....

"I can't believe we're going to a bawdy house with an automaton," Steven muttered as James led him back into Mathias' burlesque hall in New York City. "I'm sure there's a naughty joke in there some place."

James opened the door. At least this time his coat wasn't squirming with a fluffy cat.

Steven lugged the blanket-wrapped, child-sized form into the lobby, his brother tossing the doorman coins and elbowing past him. Neither of them felt like playing games. Also,

Steven hadn't been able to find Noli last night when he'd dream-searched for her, and that made worry ball up in the pit of his stomach. Either she'd stayed up all night or something was wrong.

The same dark-haired girl in the same scanty red outfit sauntered over to them. "I thought I told you to be properly dressed next time," she sniffed, swinging her hips for emphasis. Her eyes lingered on Steven's bruised jaw.

"Sorry." James gave her a disarming grin. "We're here to see Mathias."

What they needed to know was the location of the closest portal back to the Otherworld. The quest wouldn't be over until the item was delivered—which meant they could be harassed by "helpers" until then. Steven still hadn't forgotten the gunmen over Deseret—or Igan and his friends.

"What is that?" The hostess gestured at the blanket-covered automaton as she led them back through the curtain and down the passage, glancing provocatively back at James in the process.

James grinned at Steven. "My brother brought his own date."

Steven thumped him in the arm. "Lay off."

Rolling his eyes, James rubbed his arm and snorted. "You are such a fussy old bodger."

Noli. Every time James called him "V" or "fussy old bodger" it sent pangs through his heart sharper than any sword. He looked over at James, who was as laid back and flirtatious as ever, even after losing the love of his life. How did he do that? Steven knew that if anything happened to Noli, he might not be able to carry on. Certainly not like James.

The woman sat them at a table in the corner with a good view of the stage show, which seemed more subdued than last time. Today, those present seemed more interested in food and conversation than the performance, which currently featured a woman sitting in a giant birdcage, singing. Steven placed the wrapped automaton in her own chair.

"Mathias will see you shortly." Waggling her fingers at James, the girl left them alone.

"How do you do it?" Steven asked. "I know you miss Charlotte—I know you loved her—I just don't understand how you carry on, flirting and joking as if nothing ever happened."

James' face darkened like a storm cloud. "I miss her so much."

"Of course you do." Steven couldn't even fathom his brother's pain.

"I could either lie in bed and pine for her, or continue on with my life—and *someone*"—he shot Steven a look of mock-annoyance—"wouldn't let me stay abed. Also . . . " He sighed, running his fingers through his wayward curls. "Moping won't bring her back. All the yearning in the world won't bring her back. She made me promise to go on with my life, and this"—he held out his hands—"is the only way I know how."

Steven clapped him on the shoulder. "You're a stronger man than I."

"Am I?" James flashed him a grateful look. "You're the smart one; I'm just the funny, cute, charming one."

Steven laughed. "You *are* the better swordsman."

"True." James signaled the serving girl for a drink. The girl in the birdcage changed songs; this one was in some other mortal language.

Mathias strode over to them. "Stiofán, Séamus. Were you successful?"

Steven patted the bundle in the chair. "Yes, we were. Now, to get this back—which is why we're here. We're hoping you can direct us to the nearest safe portal back to the Otherworld. We didn't want to simply bumble all over New York only to use someone's private portal, which could take us to who-knows-where."

Mathias joined them at the table, not seeming as jolly as he had last time.

"I'm sorry we didn't bring you a gift," Steven added.

Mathias shook his head. "It's all right. Tiny will live."

The hound's name was *Tiny*? Even as pups, fae hounds weren't tiny.

The serving girl set drinks before them all. Mathias picked his up and held it, examining the contents in the light of the gas chandelier. "Your question is prudent. Most portals here are private. Also, I'm glad you stopped by."

Mathias' words made Steven's blood run cold. "Something's wrong."

"Someone's trying to get a message to you." Mathias took a long drink. "Do you know someone named Captain Vix?"

"Noli." It came out like a half-choked noise.

James thumped him on the back. "We know Vix. What's the message?"

"Wait—how did Vix know where to find us?" Steven's heart raced. *Noli.* Something had to be wrong with Noli.

"Um, Hattie probably told Vix where we were going. Oh, and I may have told Hattie she could leave me a message here." James' cheeks pinked.

Steven put his head in his hand. "You are impossible."

"Do you want to hear the message or not?" Mathias' voice held gentle annoyance.

"Of course, please." Steven wrapped his hands around his glass.

"It's a very simple message: *Noli's ill. Come to Boston.*" He appraised them. All the blood had drained out of Steven's face. "I have a feeling that's not good news."

"No, it's not," Steven said. This could explain why he hadn't been able to find Noli last night when he'd dream-searched—Noli was ill. Ill enough that Vix, who despised him, had sent word. But why? Something seemed to be missing here. Still, they had to travel to Boston. Immediately.

"I appreciate you delivering the message." Shaking, Steven stood up.

"Focus, V. We're so close." James put a hand on his arm. "I think it's odd that *I'm* the one who keeps telling you to stay on task. Anyhow, why don't we take this to the queen, then find Noli, just like we planned?"

Steven didn't believe his ears. "She's ill enough for Vix, who did *this*"—he pointed to his bruised jaw—"to send word. Something's wrong."

"I care about Noli too, but we're nearly finished."

"There's a public portal near Boston. I'll give you directions to it. Why don't you check on your friend, then continue on with your quest?" Mathias suggested, taking another drink.

The sensibility of Mathias' suggestion startled him. "Yes, that sounds like a very good plan." He looked at James. "Don't you think?"

James stood. "I think that should work."

"Good." Mathias checked his pocket watch. "If you hurry, you can still catch the train."

TWENTY

Bittersweet Returns

Checking to make sure the magical protections on the place still held, Kevighn entered the familiar clearing. They'd indeed held, but he didn't follow the regular path to his cabin. No, he went around back, to Creideamh's gardens. All Magnolia's hard work had gone to seed, as once again everything around him ran wild, a cacophony of green and growth.

A pink rose among the tangle caught his attention. His fingers caressed petals, soft as silk. Magnolia. She'd be so happy here, with the gardens, roses, and the faery tree.

He crossed into the woods where Creideamh's grove and tree house lay. Thank the Bright Lady that Ciarán had used his own magic to keep the grove from disappearing when he was banished—something only the dark king could do. Gazing up at the giant faery tree, Kevighn studied the tree house in its branches. It was formed from the tree itself. Creideamh's laughter practically echoed through the clearing.

So did Noli's.

A glowing ball of purple tugged on his hair.

"Hello to you too." He held out his finger for the tiny wood faery to perch on. "I've just come to get a few things, but I'll return."

Ever since Creideamh's death he'd come and gone, doing his work as huntsman. It would probably be the same now that he was working for Ciarán, and he much preferred the joviality of the Thirsty Pooka to the formality of the high palace.

The wood faery flew off in a flutter of translucent wings, and he climbed up into the tree house. More wood faeries watched him curiously, but they didn't deny him entrance. Closing his eyes, Kevighn tried to picture his sister.

All he saw was sweet Magnolia, who'd loved this place just as much.

When he opened his eyes, ghosts of his little blossom lurked everywhere. The basket and Creideamh's dress lay discarded on the floor from the last time he'd been here—the dress Magnolia had been wearing when he'd tried to seduce her at the high queen's command.

He picked them both up and returned to the cabin. The basket went in the kitchen, the dress in Creideamh's bedroom. Kevighn looked around the room, which still smelled of Magnolia—of dirt, roses, and those berries she liked.

In the front room, he went to his cache of weapons on the wall and wrapped his hands around a bow he'd made long ago for one specific purpose. He grabbed a quiver of arrows. Then he selected a special arrow from its place—one with Quinn the Fair's name literally carved into the shaft—and slid it in. He threw the quiver and bow over his shoulder and slipped a knife in his boot.

After all these years, revenge was so close he could taste it.

Kevighn gave the cabin one last glance. "Creideamh, by the Bright Lady, I'll avenge you. I promise."

•••••••••

Steven and James walked up the tree-lined path of the giant white mansion with its wide porch and columns. The grand neighborhood was quiet, lacking the bustle of flying cars, hoverboards, and such. However, the walkway was so long he wished *he* had his hoverboard.

"Now this is a house." James whistled.

Lights flickering in one of the windows caught Steven's eye. Which room was Noli's?

They climbed the steps and Steven knocked on the door, glad they'd cleaned up and changed. However, he still carried the blanket-wrapped automaton, which he set on the porch swing for the moment.

The door opened and a *very* old butler peered out. "May I help you?"

"Yes, we're here to see Magnolia Braddock," Steven replied.

"I'm sorry, but Miss Noli is unwell. Would you like to

leave a card?" The man looked as if he might fall over at any moment.

"Is Mrs. Braddock here? We're her neighbors from back in Los Angeles." Not only did Steven not have a calling card, but he didn't have time for such niceties.

The elderly butler shook his head. "I'm sorry, but Miss Edwina is out. Would you like to leave a card?"

"Is Jeff or Vix here? Please, we've come a long way." And they still had far to go.

The butler's wrinkled face scrunched in thought. "I do think Mr. Jeffrey and Miss Victoria are in residence. However, given Miss Noli's health, I'm not sure if they're accepting callers. Do you wish for me to check?"

"Miss Victoria?" James snorted.

Steven shot his brother a look. Victoria was a fine name. "Please. I'm Steven Darrow, and this is my brother James."

The elderly man shuffled off, leaving the door half-open and them standing on the porch, their breaths making frozen clouds in the late-afternoon chill.

"That is one old butler," James laughed as the two of them shivered in the cold.

"I think Jameson left the door open again," a female voice called. A brunette, older than Noli but younger than Mrs. Braddock, came to close the door. Her brown eyes widened and her mouth formed an "o" of surprise when she saw them. "Oh, there are callers on the porch. May I help you?"

"We're friends of Magnolia and Jeffrey's. Your butler is checking to see if Jeff is accepting visitors." Steven hoped she would let them in. At least it wasn't snowing right now.

The uniformed maid gave them a warm smile. "You'll have to forgive Jameson. He's a little . . . elderly. Why don't you wait in the parlor, where it's warm?"

She ushered them into a sumptuous parlor. The room looked as if it were used more often for feminine meetings than for male ones. However, a fire roared, making everything else moot.

"Would you like some tea?" she offered.

The heat curled around them like welcoming arms. "That would be splendid," Steven replied.

She bustled off.

Jeff hustled over to the fire to warm his hands. "This is *nice.*"

"Noli's mother is from a very good old family." Steven took a seat in the floral armchair closest to the fire. A large piano stood in the corner. On the wall hung several framed portraits, including one of Noli as a little girl, a large bow in her hair.

"Steven, what in tarnation are you doing here?" Jeff strode into the parlor, a puzzled look on his face.

"I asked him to come." Vix joined Jeff and took his arm. The fierce airship captain looked elegant in a long, flowing dress, much simpler than anything Noli wore but well-suited to her.

Jeff stared at Vix in disbelief, his eyes bulging. "You did? Why?"

Vix frowned at James. "What exactly are you looking at?"

"You're wearing a dress." James continued to stare unabashedly.

"Well, don't you go a-telling now." Vix sighed, her shoulders slumping a little. "I'm trying to be a good daughter-in-law-to-be. Today, I allowed Mrs. Braddock to dress me." She smoothed the skirt self-consciously.

Steven took off this hat. "I think you look lovely, Captain Vix. Wait. Daughter-in-law-to-be? Jeff, are congratulations in order?"

Jeff gazed fondly at Vix. "Yes, yes they are."

"Congratulations, then," he said. Jeff, married? Even an air pirate deserved some happiness.

James grinned cheekily. "That's great news."

"Thank you." Jeff's gaze returned to Vix. "Now, why did you ask them to come here? And when did you do it?" His gaze shifted to Steven, which made his skin crawl. "I'm not very happy with you right now."

"I'm sorry," Steven murmured, looking at his feet. "I really, truly am."

Vix looked around, then shut the door. "I sent word when we stopped to refuel in Chicago. Hattie told me where to find them." She gave Jeff a hard look. "And you know very well why."

"You're still thinking that?" Jeff ran his fingers through his hair, the corners of his lips turning down.

"It's been days and she's still not better. The doctor has no idea why, and she's killing plants." Vix crossed her arms. "We have to do something."

"She's what?" James left his spot by the fire and joined them.

Steven's mind reeled. "Wait, what's going on?"

There was a knock on the door. "I have your tea," the maid called.

"Please come in, Ellen," Jeff replied.

They sat, and Ellen served the tea and left, closing the door behind her.

"This is awkward, so I'm just going to say it," Vix said from her perch on the settee next to Jeff. "We know what you are. We've been doing business with your kind, and well, something went wrong and now Noli's ill—and I don't think it's influenza."

Steven sucked in a sharp breath as the news punched him in the stomach. They knew? How did they know? But there would be time for questions later.

"Please, pardon Vix's conspiracy theories. *I* don't think Noli's sick with the faery pox or something." Jeff huffed with annoyance.

"Faery pox?" Steven would have laughed if not for the severity of the situation.

Vix's jaw jutted out. "Your uncle did something to her. I know what I saw—his hands *glowed* when he choked her, and he threatened her, and kept saying something about her being out of her element."

James snapped his fingers. "Out of her element? Wait. Did you say she was killing plants?"

"What do you mean, *my uncle*?" Tea sloshed into Steven's saucer at the thought of Uncle Brogan threatening Noli.

Vix nodded, her brows knitting. "King Brogan is your uncle, right? He stormed onto *my* ship, got into a magic shoving match with Noli, and threatened her. He threatened you as well. Ever since then, Noli's been unwell and we don't know what's wrong. She still loves you and insists you love her ... so I sent for you, hoping you'd know what's wrong." Vix turned her still-full teacup around in her hands. "I didn't know what else to do."

"Why are you doing business with the Otherworld?" James made a face. "That's not very smart."

"James," Steven hissed, then turned back to Vix and Jeff. "Could you please start from the beginning?"

"Of course." Vix and Jeff told them about their business dealings with the fae. "I'm still not sure what this artifact is that Brogan wanted the pieces for, but both Noli and Kevighn Silver insisted that allowing him to have it could be disastrous—"

"Kevighn's involved in this too?" Steven's hand went to his forehead. The whole idea of the fae hiring mortals to steal things made him uneasy, especially when it involved his uncle. And Kevighn ... anything involving him was bound to be disingenuous.

Also, the idea of Kevighn on an airship with Noli made him uncomfortable.

Vix helped herself to one of the tiny cookies Ellen had brought with the tea. "He took a position on my ship, which he no longer has. I don't trust him. Noli, however, does. And he *did* find a way to pay us for the artifacts."

Jeff and Vix explained the cancelled business transaction. "Brogan was very angry we didn't sell the pieces to him," Jeff said. "He stormed onto the ship, and that's when he and Noli had the ... encounter that made her ill."

"Who'd you sell the pieces to?" James asked. "Kevighn?"

"Kevighn said he would take care of the pieces. They're apparently in the mortal realm for a reason," Jeff replied. "I believe the money came from someone named Kyran."

"Kyran?" Steven looked at James, not ever having heard the name.

James shrugged. "I have no idea who that is. I'm not sure I believe Kevighn, though."

"Me neither." Vix took another cookie. "But that's not our problem."

Her brusque attitude rankled Steven. They shouldn't be stealing for the fae to begin with—and some artifact banished from the Otherworld? His uncle wanting something like that didn't bode well. But the business dealings of air pirates weren't the reason for his presence.

"Could we see Noli? Please?" The idea of anything happening to her made Steven's stomach churn. Their kind didn't usually fall ill.

"She thinks you broke up with her because your mother, the queen, made you. Noli's very trusting—too trusting." Vix gave him a menacing stare, as if Noli's innocent nature was somehow his fault.

The idea of Noli's family knowing about the Otherworld was just ... surreal.

"Yes, yes, her assumption is correct." He focused on his cup, not them, part of him glad she'd held on to that belief and not abandoned him—especially with Kevighn lurking around. "I can't disobey an order from the high queen. I wasn't allowed to tell Noli the truth. I can't tell you how much it hurt to do that." Steven continued to stare into the depths of the amber liquid. "I *will* find some way for us to be together, I promise you that."

"Why?" Jeff asked.

That simple word caused Steven to look up and meet his eyes. "Because I've loved your sister for a very long time. There's no one else in any realm like her."

Vix took a sip of tea, giving him a nod of approval.

"She loves you too," Jeff replied. "I still don't understand everything. Noli told us what happened to her between going to the school and coming home again, but I don't actually comprehend the part about her not being mortal and a sprite living in her head." He made a face of confused disbelief. "I *do* know that something's not right about her."

"It's odd," James agreed, shoving a cookie in his mouth.

"I take full responsibility, and I'll find a way to remedy this." Steven bowed his head. He'd made so many mistakes—ones Noli had paid for. He looked at Vix, still not truly understanding what was happening. "I appreciate you sending for me. There's a good possibility that your doctors won't be able to help her, all things considered." Not that he was an expert on Otherworldly, or even mortal, illnesses.

"Well, if she's out of her element, they won't." James leaned back in his chair, as casual as could be.

"What?" they all said at once.

"You said Uncle Brogan kept telling her she was out of

her element, right?" James asked. "You're *air* pirates. Noli's an *earth* sprite. It's obvious."

They all stared at James.

He made an exasperated noise. "We need to spend time in our elements. Too much time away can make you sick."

That sounded vaguely familiar. "But we're earth court and we're fine," Steven said, trying to work all this out in his head.

"But we're not sprites. They're tied more closely to their elements than we are—and I think she's been spending more time in the air than we have."

Jeff's eyes lit up with recognition. "Noli kept telling me how she wanted to be among trees and dirt—and she loved her little potted plants. She keeps asking for plants to hold when she sleeps, the way a little girl does a doll—and they keep dying."

"Because she's absorbing their life force." Steven began to make sense of what was happening to Noli. "But it shouldn't be happening so fast."

"Your uncle did something to her, I know he did," Vix repeated, her eyes flashing in annoyance. "Why aren't you listening to me?"

"I'm listening. He's king of the earth court—he could have done something." James drummed his fingers on the arm of his chair.

"Yes, but the idea that he *would* is appalling." Steven made a noise of disdain. "Will you allow us to see her?"

Hope danced in Jeff's eyes, eyes so much like Noli's. "Can you help her?"

Steven stood. "I'm no healer, but certainly, I'll try."

Anything for Noli.

Jeff and Vix led them up a sweeping staircase and down several hallways. Finally, they pushed open a door. Steven brushed past them and rushed to her side.

"Noli."

Darling Noli lay in bed in a ruffled nightdress, quilt up to her chin, looking so small and pale. A withered plant lay in her arms. It was as if all the life, everything that made her his Noli, had been drained right out of her, leaving her as lifeless as the poor bedraggled plant.

She didn't stir when he took her hand. Her breath rasped and her face looked drawn, cheekbones protruding.

"I'm not even sure how she's lasted this long," Vix whispered from the background as she leaned against Jeff. "We can barely get her to eat or drink anything."

Steven brushed Noli's cool forehead with his fingertips. "Noli, it's me. Will you open your eyes for me, please?"

What he wanted to do was climb into the bed with her, hold her in his arms, and kiss her until she woke up—but he wasn't about to do that with Jeff watching.

All Noli did was sigh. Hope flicked within him. Perhaps it was a happy sigh because she knew he'd arrived.

James joined him at the bedside and looked at the plant, his brow furrowing. He put his hand on her cheek and it shimmered slightly.

"James," Steven hissed, alarmed by the blatant use of magic in public.

His brother sniffed, his hand continuing to glow green. "Do you want to help her or not?"

"You have magic as well?" Jeff whispered, coming up behind them.

"Yes," Steven replied. The room looked like a child's room, with books on a shelf and a box of toys. A few jolly pictures hung on the wall.

Biting his lower lip, James turned to Steven. "She's very sick, V."

"Really, James?" Steven didn't hide his sarcasm as he continued to hold Noli's lifeless hand.

Jeff joined them at the increasingly crowded bedside, his brow creased with worry. "Can you do something about it?"

"I... I don't know." James bowed his head. "I'm not good at this sort of magic."

Steven tried to remember everything he knew about someone becoming ill from being out of their element. "If she's out of her element, we need to get her back into it... in the Otherworld."

"We can't bring her on the quest." James' shoulders rounded. "But if we go back, give the high queen the automaton, and then return... what if it's too late? I already lost Lottie. I don't want to lose Noli."

"We're not losing Noli. I won't allow it." Steven wished there was some way to give her some of himself. "We can't bring her on the quest, but that doesn't mean we can't bring her back into the Otherworld. We'll take her to the big house and then finish the quest."

Hopefully, he and James could do something once

they got there. He wasn't sure they could summon a healer to aid her, since it would mean asking his uncle or Tiana for help. The best healers came from the water court.

Jeff sighed. "Must you take her? I suppose I'll have to concoct a story to tell Mother as to why we permitted Noli to leave with you. After all, we can hardly tell her the truth."

That was for certain. "It's the only way I know of," Steven replied. Even then…

"Noli said there are spies at your house in the Otherworld. She recognized one of your uncle's men." Vix plopped down in the rocking chair in the corner, the only chair in the room. A sewing basket sat next to it.

A sinking feeling surrounded Steven at Vix's mention of spies. While he'd known his mother had spies at the big house, he hadn't realized that Uncle Brogan did as well. He should have suspected this. No, he couldn't go to either of them for assistance.

"If I do allow you to take her, who will take care of her while you're finishing your quest? You can't simply leave her alone," Jeff prodded.

An idea formed in Steven's mind, one that would eliminate the need for a healer. Noli was an earth sprite and still had a special connection to trees, just like when she'd been mortal. He could communicate with trees…

"She won't be alone. I think I know someone who can heal her." This could work, and hope bubbled within him.

"What if it doesn't work?" Jeff's eyes narrowed, as if he blamed Steven for all this.

In a way, it *was* all his fault. Noli being one of them.

His uncle targeting her. Steven stroked Noli's hand, gazing at her too-still form. "It'll work."

It had to. Or he'd never forgive himself.

TWENTY-ONE

Deliverance

Worry increasing with his every footfall, Steven approached the large faery tree that hid in the center of the hedge maze at his family's estate, Noli bundled in his arms. Once, the giant, gnarled oak filled with wood faeries had been under his father's care. Now, like the big house itself, it belonged to him. The little wood faeries crept out of knotholes in the tree, watching him curiously. A pink one flew over and gestured to Noli, a worried look on her tiny face.

"She's very ill," Steven told them as they gathered, the pink one sitting *on* Noli. A few others perched on him. "I've come to ask the tree to heal her. James and I must finish our quest. Will you please watch over her while we're away? We shouldn't be gone for long." He hoped.

Heads bobbed as the wood faeries chattered all at once, offering to watch over and protect her. A few even retrieved tiny wooden swords. A yellow one saluted him and took up a guard stance, sword ready.

"I appreciate this." Steven crouched at the base of the gnarled oak, Noli still unmoving in his arms, the pink faery perched on her shoulder. Colorful night-blooming flowers covered the tree's base. Setting her in his lap, he put his hand on the trunk and reached out to the tree's spirit. *Will you take care of her for me? She's been out of her element and near death.*

He'd chosen this tree for several reasons. The oak liked Noli, and it had been on these lands as long as his family had possessed them. Hopefully he would feel compelled to help. The old tree also possessed a great deal of magic; healing Noli could kill a lesser tree.

I will try, young prince, the tree whispered back. *I have served the House of Oak for a very long time and will do my best.* The bark of the tree separated, making a Noli-sized knothole.

Steven kissed Noli, his heart torn at leaving her alone. "I love you so much, darling. I'll return soon."

He placed her inside the knothole, hoping she'd be comfortable, and watched as the bark closed around her, sealing her inside. You'd never know she lay inside, which meant she was safe from both his uncle and his mother. Hopefully, the tree would be able to heal her. He put his hand on the bark. *Thank you,* he told the tree, deliberately acknowledging the debt he owed it. *Noli means everything to me.*

We'll try our best to aid you, young prince, the tree replied.

The wood faeries all repeated that they'd protect her. A

few more had joined the miniature guard at the tree's base, marching around or sitting on the star blooms.

Steven bowed in thanks and sent up a silent prayer to the Bright Lady and anyone else listening. *Please heal her,* he beseeched, still crouched in the dirt. *Noli means everything to me. I need her to be well.*

And whole. One thing at a time.

A gentle breeze, soft as Noli's kisses, whispered through the trees as if answering his plea. His fingers brushed the bark, his heart wrenching at the thought that even this might not be enough.

He kissed his hand, then pressed it to the bark one last time. "I love you, Noli."

With a body-shuddering sigh, Steven stood up and made his way back through the hedge maze and across the gardens to his rambling family estate.

James was waiting for him in the library, which had become the hub of the big house during James and Charlotte's occupancy. The comfortable room had always been Steven's favorite, filled with books, well-loved furnishings, a window seat with a view of one of the gardens, and memories. The still-wrapped automaton occupied one of the comfortable chairs. Supper sat on the low table.

"Is she going to be all right?" James handed Steven a plate from his place on the settee.

"I hope so." Steven didn't feel like eating.

"I put Noli's things in her room," James added, heaping his own plate with food.

Noli's room had been Elise's room. His family had

lived here once, when not busy at the earth court palace. That was back when they'd *been* a family. When his parents had loved each other, and their children, and his mother had been content to be queen of the earth court.

Steven sat next to James and helped himself to some tea. Charlotte had wanted to live here, not at the high palace, while awaiting her sacrifice. Not that he blamed her. James and Charlotte had been content to occupy this wing, the nursery wing where they'd lived as children. A small staff had helped make this corner of the rambling estate feel like home again.

It felt strange to be here without Charlotte. Without Noli. Steven kept expecting to hear Charlotte giggling, or to spy Noli reading a book in the tree outside the window. Those times when he and Noli had stolen away to visit James and Charlotte in the Otherworld had become some of his happiest memories.

"She'll be fine." James shot him a hopeful smile.

"I hope so." Holding his cup of tea, Steven gazed out the window; not that he could see that particular tree from here. "I suppose we should take Hilde to the queen and be done with this?"

"I think so." James looked at him, fork paused halfway to his mouth. "Then what?"

"Then we help Noli get better. We work on a way to make her whole again and for us to be together." Absently, he grabbed a firm, fuzzy fruit from the bowl on the table. "Noli also seems to think her father may have fallen into the

Otherworld. If he did, he's long gone, but I've been promising to make some inquiries."

"I'm glad you said *we*." James shoveled supper into his mouth.

"We make a good team," Steven replied. Even if his brother infuriated him sometimes. He took a bite of succulent fruit, its flesh dissolving in his mouth like spun sugar.

James made a noisy yawn, stretching his arms for emphasis. "I have a feeling we should wait until morning to deliver this."

The long and tiresome day pressed on him. "True." Steven gazed at the automaton perched in the chair. "I hope this is good enough."

If it wasn't, he didn't know what they'd do. But with Noli ill, there wasn't time to even consider that thought.

....

Steven plodded into the library, rubbing the sleep from his eyes, fully dressed. Morning light streamed in through the window. Nightmares about Noli had kept him awake. If she never recovered, his uncle would pay.

His eyes fell on the chair where Hilde the automaton sat. It lay empty. His heart skipped a beat, then two. James had moved her. Yes, that was it. No reason to panic.

He searched the library with his eyes. No Hilde. Still, no need to panic.

Running out of the library, he threw open the door to James' childhood bedroom, which had been redecorated.

The toys were gone, but James' weapon collection remained. Touches of Charlotte lurked everywhere, from the flowered dressing screen in the corner to the cosmetics scattered across the dresser.

"James, wake up." Steven shoved his brother.

"Go away," James muttered, rolling over so his back was to him.

"Did you move the automaton?" Steven prayed to the Bright Lady that James answered *yes*. Hilde didn't look to be in here, either.

"She's in the library. Now let me sleep." James pulled the blankets over his head.

Horror swirled around Steven's limbs, rooting him to the floor. "Wait. You didn't move the automaton?"

"Why would I do that? Now go away." The blanket muffled James' voice.

Steven threw back the covers. "The automaton is missing."

James sat up straight. "What?"

"She's not in the library. Are you certain you didn't move her?" Steven's heart was thumping a tattoo of terror.

"Flying figs, no." James leapt out of bed and left without even throwing on a robe or slippers.

Steven followed him into the library.

James was staring at the empty chair, his mouth gaping. "I didn't move it, honest."

"We have to get it back." There was no time to go look for something else, not that Steven even knew where to start. Defeat pressed on him. They'd been so close.

"Where do we start? It's not as if we can ask the chair." James plopped down in the chair and put his head in his hands.

Who had a grudge against him? Who'd broken into the big house before? Who had no morals or scruples? Who loved Noli and probably knew all about his quest?

Steven rubbed his chin. "Do you have any idea where we can find Kevighn Silver?"

"Kevighn?" James looked up, his face contorted in confusion.

"Can you think of anyone else?" Steven certainly couldn't. "Get dressed. We need to get that automaton back."

• • • • • • • •

Noli floated in a strange dreamlike state. She wasn't exactly sure what was happening. Wherever she was, Miss Gregory and Queen Tiana weren't there—neither were any pink croquet mallets or purple cannonballs. All around her was… nothing. Yet at the same time it was everything. Where was she?

You're here, a voice replied, familiar, yet, at the same time unidentifiable.

Where was that? Was she in a dream?

You're just here. It's everywhere and nowhere. But it's safe, and soon you'll be well.

Oh, wait. She was ill—she remembered that much. There had been a voice… a voice she remembered… telling her he loved her, telling her she'd be well soon. For the life of her, she couldn't remember who that was. But that didn't matter. The fact that he loved her did. Just recalling it made her feel warm and tingly all over.

Not that she could actually feel her body.

Will you tell me a story? I'm lonely, the voice added.

A story? Well, what else did she have to do? It wasn't as if she could go anywhere or do anything in this vast nothingness.

"Of course." Noli tried to think of a story. V had been the one who loved faery stories, not her. But there was one her father used to tell her. "Once upon a time there was a little girl..."

• • • • • • • •

"Steven, this is idiocy. We don't know where Kevighn is and we don't know he has it," James insisted as they walked through the wasteland in their vain attempt to locate Kevighn Silver. "You're letting your hatred for him blind you. I think we need to look at this rationally, and logic says Kevighn didn't take it."

"He had to—who else could have it? And I don't hate him. Wait. When have you *ever* relied on logic?" Desperation rode Steven like a horse. If they didn't find the automaton...

James grabbed his brother and shook him. "V, snap out of it. I know you hate him, but we have no proof he took it. Also, he's exiled."

"Just from the courts, not from the Otherworld. And get off." Steven pushed James away. "I wish we knew a finding spell that worked on *things* rather than people." Not that he was any good at them anyway.

"Why don't we look one up in father's library?" James suggested.

Steven stopped walking and looked at him. "What?"

"Let's go back to the big house, look up a finding spell for things, and find Hilde that way instead of running around blindly." James shoved his hands deep in his pockets.

"Well, I suppose that's one way to do it." Actually, it was a very good idea.

James put his arm around Steven's shoulders. "We're going to find the automaton. Noli will be *fine*. Now, let's finish this."

Once again, his little brother as the voice of reason felt odd. Gulping, Steven nodded. "Yes, let's."

....

They crossed the unfortunately familiar bridge that led from the wildwood to the grounds of the high palace. Steven's belly sank all the way to his boots. The tall spires of Tiana's palace gleamed like polished brass. The giant clockwork drawbridge was down over the pink moat, indicating that the queen was currently in residence.

"How did the automaton end up here?" he whispered to James. Unless the finding spell was wrong. Odds were it wasn't.

"Um, the Bright Lady works in mysterious ways?" James offered.

Steven harumphed.

Into the palace they went, saluting at the gold-and-purple-clad guards and winding their way down the long and twisty halls. Steven wasn't surprised when they ended up in their mother's tea room.

A purple fire burned in the hearth. LuLu napped on a purple cushion. Their mother, clad in an ocean of gold and bronze ruffles, sat at her ornate table, having tea. Hilde occupied the chair across from her, a teacup in her metal hand. Steven knew from experience that Hilde's opulent guest chair was actually quite uncomfortable, and the queen did this on purpose.

"I love tea parties," the automaton told the queen.

"I thought Hilde only sang and told stories," James whispered to him.

The queen looked over at them and sniffed. "Oh, you're back."

His heart sank. Great. She *had* sent them on this fool's errand hoping they'd die. Had he truly expected anything less? She'd stopped being their mother the moment she cast them out of the Otherworld.

"Yes, we are." Steven squared his shoulders. "I see you've found Hilde. Does she please you?" His stomach knotted. This moment defined his quest.

The queen took a sip of tea, every passing second feeling like an hour. "She'll do. I did have to make some adjustments using magic. Also, her name isn't Hilde. It's Aisling." Queen Tiana's look dared them to say differently.

"It's your automaton—you may name her whatever you

wish, Your Majesty," Steven replied with a stiff bow. "So, my quest is over?" His stomach had yet to unknot.

The queen waved him off. "Yes, yes. I have to say, Aisling is rather amusing in a simple way. I do hope you won't wander far. I like having you and your brother around."

"Yes, of course, Your Majesty." Steven bowed again.

She liked having them around? Sure. She probably meant it would be easier to plot their demise if she knew their whereabouts.

"Your Majesty?" Steven added, his chest tightening. "Since I accomplished my task to your satisfaction, may I take up with Noli again?"

The queen laughed. "My dearest Stiofán, truly you're better off without her. As I told you, she'll hold you back from your goals. Now, be off before I find something for you to do." She shooed them away with her hand.

"Of course, Your Majesty." With a final bow, Steven and James left the tea room.

James scratched his head. "How did the automaton get to the high palace?"

"Mother, most likely. She probably still has spies in the big house. For all we know, she came and took it herself —or used magic to bring it to her." Despite finishing the quest, his heart felt heavy as they plodded down the vast hallways. One task down, so many more to go. If this was what being an adult was like, perhaps he shouldn't have been in such a hurry to grow up.

"Let's check on Noli." James clapped him on the back.

They made their way to the big house in silence, finally

traipsing through the familiar woods belonging to the House of Oak. Giant rowan trees, old as the land itself, helped guard the ancestral home, and shaded them as they walked. Now that those of the House were in residence again, the grounds were in better repair than they'd been when Steven had first returned to the Otherworld.

"The queen gave Noli to you, right?" James asked suddenly. "When she came to the house that day, when Noli and Charlotte were there?"

Steven tried to recall that particular event. "Yes, she did." It had given another layer of protection to Noli.

"Did she take all that away when she told you to break Noli's stone?" James asked.

Steven dissected his mother's fateful decree, when she'd given them their task, word by word in his head: *Before you begin your quest, you're to end this nonsense with Magnolia—and that includes breaking the stone in her sigil.*

No, not one thing about revoking Noli herself… not that he was sure the queen could even do that.

"*I swear that Noli is yours until you decide otherwise, entitled to all rights and privileges therein,*" Steven whispered, repeating the words Tiana had said to him that day at the house. "That's what she swore… "

"So, Noli's still yours in some way—she just doesn't have the protections of the House of Oak anymore?" James asked as they entered the center of the hedge maze.

Steven went over everything in his head one last time. "I… I think you're right. And while the queen can keep

Noli from the protections of our House, she can't keep her from being *with me* unless she breaks her oath."

James snapped his fingers, his green eyes dancing. "If she breaks her oath, you could challenge her to a dual." Even queens weren't excluded from the bindings of an oath.

"You're right. Not that I relish the thought of challenging her to a duel," Steven muttered. Which wouldn't end well, but perhaps the thought that he *could* challenge her would prevent any oath-breaking on his mother's part.

James shook his head. "I wouldn't want to think about that either."

Steven still felt sorrowful that Noli had had to endure the pain of the stone being broken. "What would I do without you?" he asked his brother.

"Do you really want me to answer that?" James shot him a silly grin.

The oak came into sight. Little wood faeries sat on the roots and branches of the gnarled tree. Some still clutched little wooden swords.

"Do you think she's well now, or do you think we'll have to leave her for a little longer?" James asked.

"As long as she recovers, I don't care." Steven greeted the little wood faeries by distributing crumbs of a cake he'd brought from the house. The greedy little beasts scrambled over the gnarled tree roots as they fought over the sweet. Crouching next to the towering oak, he put his hand on the trunk and reached out to the tree. Time to bring his darling home.

• • • • • • • •

Will you tell me another story? the voice asked.

Noli yawned. Well, she would if she had a body. The nothingness still enveloped her. She'd been napping between telling stories to this faceless, bodiless voice. She liked sleeping here in the mist, where the nightmares couldn't get her.

"Could you tell *me* a story?" she replied, still half-asleep. That might give her time to think of a tale she hadn't told yet.

I could, if you promise to remember it, the voice replied.

"I'll try."

Once, long ago, the Otherworld was different. Only a few people remember, and most don't remember it correctly. Once, we didn't need to rely on the blood of mortal girls with the Spark. The high queen wielded a staff, and through it there was enough power for the land to live without blood sacrifice. Some grew jealous of the staff's abilities, and great power can easily be abused. One day, in anger, the Bright Lady broke apart the staff, scattering the pieces across the mortal realm. But even she couldn't break the staff's heart, a gem of great power. That, too, was hidden in the mortal realm. Without the staff, the land had to rely on her people to bring her nourishment. Gradually everyone, even the rulers, forgot that once we didn't need a sacrifice…

The impact of the story made Noli's mind reel. "The artifact? Are you saying that there is an artifact of great power that, if reassembled, will negate the need for a sacrifice every seven years?"

Not needing a sacrifice would be wonderful. However,

Noli knew enough about the Otherworld to know that there must be much, much more to the staff than this.

Keep that piece of the staff you have safe. It's in your valise, the voice added. *You must keep it out of the wrong hands.*

"But how does it work? I don't understand. And *why* did the Bright Lady destroy it?" Something must have gone very wrong. Perhaps the wielders of the staff went insane or were easily corrupted due to its power. Her entire being—well, what she could feel of it in the mist—began to tingle.

No, no, no, you can't go yet, the voice told Noli.

"What?"

They're trying to take you. You're not well enough to go yet… and I'm not just saying that because I like your stories and you're kind. Also, I haven't finished my story.

"Wait—who's taking me? Taking me where?" She wasn't even sure where she was, other than safe and cozy, not hot, cold, or thirsty. The urgency in the voice's statement made her skin crawl.

The princes. They wish to take you.

"Wait, V? Is V here? But I want to go with him." The thought of seeing V again made her heart soar. He'd come back for her. Did that mean his quest was over? She remembered now. A little.

You do?

"I… I love him. I love him so much." With every fiber of her being. Memories of V flickered through Noli's mind like a zoetrope. "Please, let me see him."

You do love him, and it's so beautiful. The voice made a happy sigh. *If you truly wish to go, I'll make you well enough.*

"You can do that? I don't even know who you are." Noli's body tingled in a way that almost hurt, and lights flashed in front of her eyes. What was happening?

She didn't feel afraid, just prickly.

Don't forget me, and remember my story. You must keep the staff out of the wrong hands. You're a good person, Magnolia Montgomery Braddock.

"I am?" Sometimes she wondered about that, with everything she'd done of late.

The voice didn't answer; other voices echoed through the fog. Familiar male voices.

"Noli, darling, can you hear me?" V pleaded.

"Maybe we should put her back in. I don't think she's done yet," James said.

She felt as if she were being tugged like taffy. The nothingness slipped away and the prickly sensation ebbed. Hands gripped her and a breeze caressed her skin.

Noli's eyes fluttered open, and two very concerned princes came into focus. "Not done yet? What am I, a cake?"

"Oh, Noli!" V's unspectacled green eyes grew as wide as saucers as he pulled her to his chest. "You're alive. I'm so glad you're alive and well."

Noli wrapped her arms around him. "You came! I knew you would. Everyone said you wouldn't, but I had faith in you."

"That makes me so happy." V buried his face in her hair. "I feared I'd lose you."

"Where was I?" It felt so nice to be in his arms again.

"We put you in the tree because you were sick." James

leaned back on his hands in the soft moss surrounding a faery tree. Wood faeries encircled them; some even had swords.

"How did I get to the Otherworld?" Noli waved at the wood faeries, who waved back. A pink one perched on her outstretched hand, translucent wings flapping, dress resembling flower petals, pointed ears poking out of her brown hair. They were in the grove at the center of the maze at the big house. She was wearing her nightdress.

"We brought you here." James crouched beside them.

V stroked her hair. "Are you feeling better? We were so worried."

Noli nodded. She'd been in a tree? But she'd been someplace… memories of where she'd been hung like a haze, present but not quite tangible.

"Oh, good." V caressed her face.

"Why did you put me in a tree?" Something was nagging at the back of her mind, something she wasn't supposed to forget… but she just couldn't remember. More things escaped with every second she tried.

"Let's return to the house. I'm hungry," James groused, standing and shifting his weight from foot to foot. "I'm glad you're better, Noli."

V moved her off V's lap and they stood up. He took her hands and pulled her to him, gazing so deeply into her eyes, it was as if he was looking right into her soul.

"I'm sorry I hurt you. I love you so much. When I saw you so ill… " V shook his head, his eyes misty. "I never would have forgiven myself if something had happened to you." He leaned in, his lips soft and sweet.

Noli's toes tingled in delight as she savored his deep and gentle kiss... and kissed him right back. Breaking it off, she caressed his face, trying to remember him with her fingers. "Apology accepted." Then she punched him in the arm. Hard. "Never, ever do that to me again, Steven Darrow, or so help me..."

V rubbed his arm, his eyes meeting hers. "I'll try not to, I promise."

"Good."

"First one to the library wins!" James took off through the maze.

V took her hand. "I think we made him uncomfortable." He turned to the faeries and saluted them, his eyes gleaming. "Thank you, thank you so much."

Noli's heart jumped. He'd *thanked* the faeries for saving her. The faeries chattered in response. She still couldn't understand them.

"Shall we?" V held out his hand to her and looked in the direction James had run.

"He misses her." Noli leaned her head on V's shoulder as they wove through the hedge maze and walked toward the big house. She'd missed V, and the idea that he'd worried when she was ill made happiness bubble inside her.

"Yes, he misses Charlotte so much." V put an arm around her waist.

"I miss her too." A little piece of her had died that day. After all, it could have been her.

V squeezed her. "We all do."

"And now we're in the Otherworld, together. Does this

mean your quest is over? Were you successful?" The dirt under her bare feet felt sinfully delicious, and part of her expected her mother to yell at her to put her shoes—or clothes—on at any moment.

"Yes, we were successful. May I tell you all about it as we eat? Are you hungry?"

Noli's belly rumbled in reply and she laughed. "That sounds perfect. Will you please explain to me how I got here? The last thing I remember is … " She froze as she recalled the previous events. "Your uncle! Your uncle attacked me, and threatened me—and you too."

Steven pulled her close. "You're safe, Noli. I won't let anyone hurt you."

"Will you teach me to use magic to defend myself?" she asked. "Could we continue fencing lessons?" Anything to be able to protect herself and those she loved.

"Of course." V took her hand and they resumed walking.

"But when? How? Mama went to Boston, and you aren't supposed to be with me anymore." She sniffed at the thought. It wasn't as if she *needed* V, but after being without him, she knew that she *liked* being with him. It felt … right. It always had. They had to find a way to stay together.

"We could remain here for now." Steven wiped away her tear with his finger. "While we figure things out. And while you might not be allowed to wear my sigil, you're still mine. Remember how I told you about the queen 'giving' you to me?"

"I'm not a marble, but yes, I remember something about that. It's protection, right? But different from the sigil?" Noli would never understand this concept, any more than she'd get used to V's name being "Stiofán" or him not actually having to wear glasses.

"Yes. And even the queen can't take it away from us, which means we can still be together … if you still wish to be with me." V looked at her with bashful eyes. "I'll understand if you—"

Noli's lips captured his before he even had the chance to finish, and she told him with her kiss what words couldn't say.

When she broke it off, he grinned at her. "So, it's yes?"

"I suppose." She grinned back. "I meant what I said. We're in this together. I'm not a marble."

He laughed. "But you'd make such a pretty marble." Noli shoved him, and V laughed again. "Yes, we're in this together. I promise."

"I missed you so much, you fussy old bodger." She squeezed him tight.

He leaned in and kissed her again. "I missed you too, darling. I missed you too."

TWENTY-TWO

Where Do We Go From Here?

"Where do we go from here?" Still in her nightdress, Noli leaned against V on the settee on the library, their finished supper sitting on the low table. She loved eating in the library instead of at a proper table. So delightfully scandalous.

Steven and James had filled Noli in on all their adventures, and she'd told them about hers. She was glad to hear that Rahel was at home with her father. It galled her that Vix hadn't told her about James and V's arrival when she'd returned to the airship. Nevertheless, Vix *had* been the one to summon V when she'd needed him. The idea of Vix and Jeff knowing about the Otherworld still seemed so strange.

It felt odd to be at the big house without Charlotte, and she kept expecting to see her friend cuddling with James in the window seat.

“This development with an artifact troubles me,” Steven replied. He rubbed his chin. “I think we need to ask Quinn about it. I can’t believe I’ve never heard about it.”

The artifact. Noli needed to remember something about the artifact. “My valise! Do you know where it is?”

“It’s in your room. Vix gave it to me when we took you from Boston,” James told her, his mouth partially full of food. “She said that everything you had on the ship was inside. Why?”

“There are important things in it.” Perhaps checking on it would help her remember whatever it was she needed to know about it. The watch chain was also inside her valise, and while that wasn’t important, it gave her an excuse. “I’ll be right back.”

She dashed out of the library and found the valise sitting on her bed—well, Elise’s bed. But she always used this as her room. Opening the latches, she fumbled inside the bag until she discovered what she sought—the watch chain and the metal piece. She tucked the metal piece away, glad it was safe, then pulled on one of her simpler gowns and ran her fingers through her hair, untangling it. Watch chain in hand, she returned to the library where James and V were still discussing whether or not Quinn would know anything about the artifact.

“James, I made this for you.” She held the assembled but unwrapped watch chain out to him, twitching a little in apprehension. But the sprite didn’t interject. She actually hadn’t heard a peep from the sprite since V had pulled her from the tree—perhaps she remained asleep. Noli wouldn't mind if she never woke up.

"What is it?" James took it from her. "Certainly, it's quite nice. You made this?"

"It's a watch chain, made from Charlotte's hair. So that she'll always be with you."

James stood up and embraced her, his eyes glistening. "This is this nicest gift ever."

"I'm so glad you like it." Noli's heart leapt at the idea that it pleased him, since it had taken longer than she'd expected to make.

"I still think the idea of weaving a dead person's hair into jewelry is odd," V observed as he took another bite.

"Well, it's a good thing it's not for you, then." Noli plopped down beside him on the settee, wiggling her still-bare toes. "So, you want to visit Quinn?" She didn't mind going to Los Angeles, but the idea of seeing Mr. Darrow—after, well, everything—made her nervous.

"He'd be the best person to speak to. Also, I should let my father know we're still alive." V looked less excited about that idea.

"If we're venturing into the mortal realm, could we send Mama and Jeff an aethergraph telling them I'm well?" Noli took a sip of tea. "I don't want them to worry."

V squeezed her hand. "That's an excellent idea."

"She'll want me to return to Boston, though." As much as Noli missed her mother, that's not what she wanted for herself.

"You don't have to go to Boston. Do you wish to rejoin

Jeff and Vix at some point?" V looked at her through veiled lashes. "I'll support you in whatever your decision may be."

Wait… for the first time in her life, she could do whatever she desired. Not what her mother wanted. Not what Jeff wanted. Not even what V wanted. What *she* wanted. She rather liked the idea of staying here for a while and helping V.

In answer, she kissed V so deeply that James cleared his throat in protest in the background.

"So, you'd like to return to the Vixen's Revenge? I think you're well suited to being a ship's engineer." V's cheeks pinked in embarrassment.

She liked bashful V. "You're a fussy old bodger. Is staying in the Otherworld together for a time truly an option? It feels… decadent. Though I still wish to attend the university at some point."

It wasn't as if she could return to her home in Los Angeles—or walk right into a university and start tomorrow. Nor did she wish to rejoin the Vixen's Revenge. Unless she went to Boston, where else did her choices lie?

"It's just until we figure things out… Perhaps we *should* apply to the university together, for next term," V suggested. "I don't think it's too late." His fingers intertwined with hers, but she didn't completely relax.

"I like that idea," Noli said. As much as he tried, V still didn't fully understand mortal conventions—or why she clung to them. But if she didn't cling to them, that would be admitting she was no longer mortal and no longer wished to be so. Then the queen would win.

Also, going to the university and becoming a botanist was still a goal of hers.

"You two could just go to the university here." James rolled his eyes, still toying with the watch chain. "That's what the Academe *is*, right? A university?"

"There are universities here? I didn't know that." Noli looked at V for confirmation.

"*A* university," V confirmed. "The Academe is very different from universities in the mortal realm. We can look into it, if you'd like. I've wanted to use their libraries for research. I'd also like to travel to the cloisters and visit their libraries."

"Cloisters, too? What sort?" There was so much she didn't know about this realm.

"Men and women who dedicate themselves to the Bright Lady. They have excellent records and libraries. If any information exists that would help return you to yourself, if would be in one of those places." V touched his forehead to hers, sending little shivers up her spine.

James yawned, not bothering to hide it. "That sounds *so* boring."

V looked down his nose at his brother. "What? Dedicating your life to the Bright Lady or researching in the library?"

"Both." James threw his legs over the arm of his chair, food abandoned, as he continued to finger the watch chain.

Researching wasn't Noli's favorite thing either, but if it would help return her to her old self, she was willing to try.

"So," she said, "the plan is to return to the mortal realm, speak with Quinn, let your father know you're alive, send word to my mother and Jeff that I'm alive, then come back here and visit the university and the cloisters?" It wasn't as if she had anything else to do. "While we're there, we could research the legendary artifact as well." For some reason this seemed important, but she still couldn't remember why. What was it she needed to recall about the artifact?

"Definitely. I'd like to know who this Kyran is—and I still don't believe that Kevighn actually scattered the pieces in the mortal realm." V made a face of disgust.

"Will you stop?" Noli shoved him. "He said he would and I believe him."

V held his hands up in surrender. "Fine. I'll believe you until proven otherwise."

"We could go find him, if you'd like," Noli goaded, feeling the need to make V squirm a little. "I know where to leave word for him."

"You do?" V cocked his head. "Why?"

"Because he told me." She met his eyes, daring him to say anything.

V sighed and pulled her closer. "I don't want to fight. No, we don't need to find him."

"Kevighn told me that if anyone could return me to my old self, it would be Ciarán. Do you think that's true?" she asked. Kevighn said a lot of things, and sometimes it was hard to know what was truth, especially when she wanted it to be.

"Oh—I didn't think of that," James interjected from his chair. "But that doesn't mean he *would*, or that his price would be something we'd be willing to pay. Ciarán is as dangerous as the high queen. More."

V's lips pressed into a hard line.

Right. There would be a price, and since Ciarán was the dark king …

"I don't know. It could be less scary than asking the Bright Lady herself, or the magic," James replied.

"You're barking mad," V retorted. He squeezed Noli's shoulder. "We'll fix things for you. I promise."

She nodded in agreement. "Of course we will."

Somehow.

....

Noli lay in the bedroom she'd come to think of as hers. The butterflies and flowers James had painted for Elise long ago danced across the walls. Ruffles and bows trimmed many a surface, but it didn't bother her. Usually she ended up sleeping in V's arms on the occasions they were able to stay the night in the Otherworld. Elise's room had become a place where she stored things and got ready.

As elated as she was that V had found a way for them to be together, there was still the fact that, oath or no, Queen Tiana would never permit them to marry.

Neither would Mr. Darrow.

She also felt torn. Where did she belong? This realm with

V, since ultimately he'd become the rightful king of the earth court? Or the mortal realm with Jeff and her mother?

Confusion swirling in her mind, Noli sobbed into her pillow. Somehow she'd thought getting V back would remedy everything. Instead, it merely exposed a new set of problems.

She hadn't told V that she felt odd; it was either from her illness, or her experience in the tree, or both. And also that there was something she *had* to remember, but couldn't.

Also, despite the sprite having been so quiet, Noli knew she still lurked in there someplace.

"Don't cry, darling. Please?" V whispered from the doorway.

"I'm not crying," she choked. He had enough to worry about.

"Come sleep in my room? I miss you." His shadowy figure entered the room.

"I miss you, as well." She sat up and peered at him through the darkness, wiping the tears from her eyes. "The queen will be angry, won't she, that we're still together? Your father, too." Her chest tightened, although Mr. Darrow truly had no power over her. Not anymore. The queen, however…

"I don't care. I nearly lost you." V's voice broke as he approached the bed. "I don't think you understand what seeing you lying so still and small in that bed in Boston did to me. Now that I have you back, I'm not letting you go unless you tell me to. I'm sick of being told what to do—and the queen can't take you away from me without breaking her oath. If you wish to stay with me, I won't allow them to keep us apart." He held out his hand to her.

She took it, his conviction giving her inner strength. "Queen Tiana scares me."

"She scares me as well. But we can't let fear rule our lives. Right?"

"Right." Noli gazed into his green eyes. Even though he hadn't worn his spectacles since he'd rescued her, she still expected to see them sometimes. "And your father?"

V exhaled heavily. "I don't care. I want to be with you."

"Good." Using his hand, Noli pulled herself to a standing position.

She followed him to his room. V climbed into his bed and patted the space next to him. Noli crawled in, and he wrapped his arms around her.

Curling into him, her face buried in his shoulder, she asked, "Where do I belong, V?"

Was it here? Los Angeles? Boston? Jeff's ship?

"Where do you want to belong?" His warm breath caressed her ear.

"I... I don't know," she hiccupped. Love and loyalty warred inside her. Wanting to belong and belonging were two different stories.

"We'll figure it out, Noli." V stroked her hair. "We'll figure it out."

They lay there in the bed, bodies entwined. It felt so nice to be in his arms, his body against hers, feeling the rise and fall of his chest, hearing him breathing.

“I love you,” she whispered. That much she knew for certain.

His lips brushed the top of her head. “I love you, too, darling.”

She closed her eyes. “I know, V. I know.”

TWENTY-THREE

Los Angeles

Kevighn stood on the Los Angeles street, gazing at the row of large houses. He had never liked Los Angeles as much as other cities. These houses weren't monstrous estates like some he'd seen in his wanderings, but they were certainly grand and well kept.

Except for one. It looked just a little more tired than the others, though not overly so.

The Braddock Residence, for certain.

It also appeared vacant. Then again, Magnolia's mother was in Boston and Magnolia was with Jeff.

A sigh reverberated through Kevighn's entire being. At least she wasn't with that whelp of a prince, who hopefully was still on his wretched quest and would die a miserable death.

His gaze shifted to the house next door, the one whose address matched what Ciarán had given him. It wouldn't be terrible if that prat princeling was currently dwelling within. It would be nice to have a reason to kill him. The corners of Kevighn's lips tugged into a smile.

However, nothing would beat getting the chance to slay Quinn the Fair.

Ah, revenge would be so sweet. Granted, Quinn hadn't *actually* killed his sister. But if Creideamh had never fallen in love with him, she never would have died.

A highborn such as Quinn never would leave the court in order to be with Creideamh. No, instead he lured her out of the safe haven Kevighn had built for her in the dark court and attempted to bring her into his world.

And she'd died. Kevighn would never forgive him for that.

Today, of course, his mission wasn't one of revenge, but to get the queen's daughter, Ailís. Unfortunately, the best way to accomplish this task wouldn't involve Quinn at all. It entailed convincing Ailís to come with him of her own free will—just like he'd enticed all those girls over the years to return with him to the Otherworld in order to be the sacrifice.

He may need to make repeated visits. Like with all those girls, it might take time, finesse, and presents. His rucksack held sweets, ribbons, and a mechanical bird—three items proven to tempt girls of nearly any age.

However, given her age, no seduction would be involved. Also, Ailís wouldn't be going to the Otherworld to meet her death, but instead would be their savior of a different sort, one day. Hopefully. Kevighn still didn't have a firm grasp on Ciarán's plan. But that wasn't his problem.

Instead of going straight to the house, he ducked into Magnolia's backyard. A tree house—built not of the tree itself like Creideamh's, but of a mishmash of odds and ends—drew his attention, the tree shaped like a "J." He remembered Magnolia telling him about her tree house and her tree, and how much she loved them. Plus, this hideaway could prove a good perch for some covert observation. And since the house itself was abandoned, there was little likelihood anyone would notice him lurking about.

Kevighn climbed up the bent trunk and stepped into the tree house. The sheer Magnolia-ness of the place nearly knocked him over. From the hammer on the ground to the long-forgotten dried blooms, he could practically hear her voice calling to him.

Surprisingly, a clan of wood faeries hadn't taken residence. They came into this realm, and who wouldn't want to live in a tree cared for by Magnolia?

The window of the tree house gave him an unobstructed view of the Darrow residence. As he observed their backyard, something caught Kevighn's eye. The back door seemed ajar—and not just cracked open, but crooked. He studied the house for several moments, watching for signs of life.

The longer he eyed the eerily still house, the more he got the idea that something was amiss. It was in the curvature of the back-fence boards, the too-many boot prints in the grass.

Yes, this required further investigation.

Had someone else gotten to the girl first? Ciarán wouldn't be the only one to remember that Tiana had a daughter—or recognize that something would need to be done sooner rather than later. Yet who would have the gall to make such a treasonous move? The dark king could get away with things no one else in the Otherworld could.

Climbing down the tree, Kevighn took his dagger from his boot and hopped over the fence into the other yard. The boot prints were from several different men, but all the same type, like they were soldiers. He made his way inside the Darrows' house, creeping quietly, using the slightest touch of magic to see if anyone lurked within.

Nothing. No one living, at least.

Blood streaked the floor of the ransacked kitchen, and he followed the trail. The already-decaying carcass of the former earth court king lay in what looked like a study. Kevighn grimaced at the sight and stench. He held no lost love for the former king; in fact, part of him seethed at the idea of never getting to settle the score they had. Yet at the same time, here was an exile who'd died all alone. A sad death for someone who'd once been king. Had Queen Tiana killed him?

Perhaps this lonely demise was justice enough. Kevighn's hand glowed as he used his magic to examine the body. The old king hadn't died from magic, but of mundane knife wounds.

No... he'd died of both. Interesting. A ploy to foil the mortal police, perhaps?

Leaving the body where he'd found it, Kevighn trekked upstairs to search for more bodies and clues. As miserable as finding the body had been, that wasn't his task. Also, he wouldn't be too upset if he found Stiofán's carcass, as long as he got to kill Quinn himself.

No other bodies hid in any of the rooms. When he went into a girl's room, presumably Ailís', he frowned. Drawers were pulled out and things strewn about. While some of the downstairs rooms looked to have been ransacked, none of the other bedrooms had been. Surely a king-killer wouldn't be looking for something hidden in a little girl's room?

She'd fled. Probably with her protector, Quinn the Fair.

Kevighn picked up a forgotten doll and stuffed it in his rucksack, along with a photo. Hopefully he could use the toy to locate the girl. As he walked down the hall, he gazed through the door of the bedroom that belonged to Stiofán. At least, he'd presumed it was Stiofán's, considering it had his name written on the many boring tomes lining the desk.

Did the prat know about his father? Probably not, since he would have properly disposed of the body. Most likely he'd return as soon as his quest concluded.

A devilish grin spread across Kevighn's face. He should leave the prince a little surprise here.

••••••••

"Ready, Noli?" Steven took Noli's hand as they strolled down the street toward his house, James behind them. They'd sent aethergraphs to Noli's mother and Jeff letting them know that she was still alive. Now it was time to let his father know that he'd survived his ordeal as well.

"I could wait." Noli gazed at the Darrow house and bit her lower lip.

Steven didn't blame her for being apprehensive. His father never had liked her much, and he'd given them nothing but trouble from the moment they'd declared themselves a couple. His belly didn't unclench, either. This act of defiance scared him. Steven had always been the first to obey his father—or mother. As the eldest son, that was his job. To mind them. To be perfect. At least his father hadn't been the one who'd ordered him to break the stone in Noli's sigil. Still, he wouldn't be happy that they'd found a way to stay together. Queen Tiana would of course be displeased, but that was another matter entirely. One that inspired terror. Still, Noli was worth it.

Steven shook his head and squeezed Noli's hand. "I told you—now that I have you back, I'm not going to let my father keep us apart. Not anymore."

"I'm glad." She returned his squeeze, giving him a faint smile.

"You two are so mushy." James made a face of disgust.

"I'm sorry." Noli's cheeks pinked and she dropped Steven's hand as if burned.

"I… I didn't mean it like that," James apologized. "I…" He looked away.

Noli put a hand on his shoulder. "I understand."

His lips so tight they went white, James nodded, gulping.

Steven joined them. "Well, we try to understand."

James gave him a weak smile, running his finger over the watch chain, which he'd attached to his pocket watch. "I do appreciate it. More than you know."

"Are you *sure* I should go with you?" Noli looked around

as if at any moment the propriety police would jump out of the bushes and give her a citation.

Steven took her hand again and kissed it. "I *want* you to come with me."

"Well, if you insist." She nodded, her lips pressed together.

They walked down the side of the house toward the back door. It looked empty. His father was probably working, and Quinn and Elise were most likely elsewhere. Given the time of day, they should certainly return soon.

Noli studied the back fence and frowned. "Someone's climbed over the fence. There"—she pointed toward her yard—"and there." She indicated the back wall.

"Look at all these footprints." James gestured to the grass around them.

Steven went cold. "Footprints. Why would there be footprints in my backyard?"

"He said you'd pay," Noli whispered. "Your uncle said you'd pay. This is all my fault."

"Noli, this is not your fault." Steven cupped her face with his hands, trying to reassure her while an odd feeling sat like a lump in his own belly. "We aren't even certain that something's amiss." That feeling of foreboding wouldn't leave him.

"The door's ajar." James went pale.

The bottom fell out of Steven's belly. "This doesn't bode well."

Something flapped from the bottom corner of the door. He bent down and picked off a piece of green fabric, then held it up to the fading light.

"Earth court colors," James whispered, his eyes widening in horror.

"It's Brogan. It's all my fault." Noli shook, but she didn't wail or cry.

Steven put an arm around her. "Let's go inside. Perhaps my uncle simply paid my father a social call. After all, they're brothers." He didn't believe this himself. His uncle had never visited them in the mortal realm. Why now? He opened the door.

Blood splattered the kitchen—it looked as if a skirmish had occurred. His knees went weak, and Noli's hand flew to her mouth.

"It's just blood," Steven told her—and himself—as he glanced around the kitchen searching for bodies. Drawers had been pulled out and cupboards opened. "You don't have to go any further. Do you want to go to your house and wait for us?"

She shook her head and grabbed his hand. "We'll do this together."

That was his Noli.

James shuffled over to them, frowning, something in his hand. "Earth court guard knife. This doesn't look good."

Steven couldn't form words as he took the knife from James and examined it. When their father was king, Uncle Brogan had commanded the earth court guard. All earth court soldiers had the same uniforms and weapons, and Uncle Brogan had trained them how to use knives that were just like the one in his hand.

His finger traced the earth court insignia burned into the handle and handed it back to James. "Let's continue on."

Not that he wished to. Steven had no desire to see who the blood belonged to.

They followed the trail to his father's study, his heart thumping the entire time. Noli was clutching his hand so tightly that it went numb. When they entered the room, Noli put a handkerchief to her face and turned away.

"Flying figs," James swore.

"Father." Steven's knees shook. They hadn't had the best relationship, but he was still his father. The stench of rotting flesh made his eyes water. Blood spattered the furniture, walls, and floor. The lingering pulse of magic tingled under his skin.

The room looked ransacked: drawers open, books off the shelves. Were they hunting for something, or trying to make it look like a robbery gone awry for the sake of the mortal police?

Even though he should do something—anything—all Steven could do was pull Noli to him and stare at the grisly scene. *Dead.* His father was dead, murdered in cold blood. He wasn't sure if he should scream, cry, run and hide, head off pell-mell to hurt whoever did this…

Everything pointed to it being Uncle Brogan's work.

James came up beside him, his eyes filled with disbelief. "I don't understand. Why would earth court soldiers do this? Father's done nothing to anyone, especially Uncle Brogan."

No, their father had left the Otherworld quietly and moped in the mortal realm like a good exile, bothering no one.

Anger welled up inside Steven. "Father didn't deserve to die, especially like this." Judging from the state of the house and lingering magic, he'd at least put up a good fight. "Uncle Brogan probably didn't even have enough honor to kill him himself and sent guards in his stead, knowing father would be outnumbered." Disdain dripped from his voice. That was the coward's way.

"It's my fault. King Brogan promised to get revenge because I prevented Jeff from giving him the artifacts." Noli pressed her face into his shoulder. "I'm so sorry; your father didn't deserve to die."

Steven wrapped his arms around her more tightly. This was no scene for a lady, even one as uncommon as Noli. However, focusing on her helped him keep his own emotions at bay. Right now he needed to be rational and figure this out.

"It's not your fault," he soothed her. "I have a feeling Uncle Brogan has been looking for a reason to do this. As long as we're alive, James and I are threats to his crown."

Noli looked up at him. "Why would he kill your father if you two are the threats?"

"Because Brogan knows I'll come after him in order to avenge my father." Steven had known for some time that this day might come in some way, shape, or form, but he hadn't expected it to be quite this soon.

A sharp breath hissed between her teeth. "Are you saying that Uncle Brogan killed your father because he knew you'd come after him, and he thinks you'll lose?"

Steven nodded, not ready to say the words out loud.

Noli shook her head slowly. "I will never understand Otherworld politics."

"I think he meant this to look like a robbery." James was poking around the room. "Nothing seems to be missing. But why? Why did he have to kill him?" He hit the wall with his fist.

Steven wandered over to the bookshelf, wondering if the contents behind it were something the perpetrators sought. "I think that was the plan. To make it look like it could have been anyone, even a mortal, but leave just enough evidence for us to know who was here. The knife was probably an accident. I'm pretty sure he didn't mean to be that sloppy. He'd want us, bereft with grief, to attack him with half-cocked revenge and no discernible proof."

James snapped his fingers. "Uncle Brogan's an excellent swordsman. He'll be betting that he'll win the challenge. If he wins, that will mean he's innocent, no matter what evidence you have to show otherwise."

"What?" Noli made a face, her eyes rimmed in red. "Winning proves his innocence? There's no due process in the Otherworld?"

"We don't have judges and juries in the Otherworld. We have monarchs, magic, and the Bright Lady." Steven pulled the statuette on the bookshelf. It made a popping sound, releasing a hidden internal catch. His hand glowed green as he muttered the words to make the seal dissolve. The secret compartment hadn't been disturbed. Good.

He pushed the bookshelf aside, revealing a safe. Putting

his hand on it, Steven recited the spell that would open it. With a deep breath, he opened the safe door.

Inside sat a suit of armor, a sword, a book, and a wooden box.

Opening the box, he removed a gold ring with a stone as green as the one in his sigil, and slid it on his right hand.

"Are you really?" James eyed the precious things his father had snuck into exile with him. Remnants of his father's former rank.

"They're mine now," Steven said. "Certainly, we can't leave them here." His fingertips brushed the elaborate sword that he had so many memories of. "When I kill Uncle Brogan and reclaim the earth court, I think it would be poetic justice to use father's sword. *Before all else, be armed.*"

James' eyebrows rose. "Finally, a quote I like. Who says that?"

"Machiavelli."

Noli's face contorted. "You're going to kill Brogan?"

V put a hand onto her shoulder and gazed into her eyes. She still didn't understand their world. But she tried. His throat swelled. "I know it's exactly what he wants me to try to do, but I can't ignore this."

Dead. His father was dead. Steven felt simultaneously angry and numb.

"As long as you don't die," Noli whispered. "But I understand. If anyone hurt my family, I'd kill them."

"I don't plan on dying. I have too much to do." Too many things to fix. He put a hand on her arm. "We should look for

Elise and Quinn." He prayed to the Bright Lady they were alive and unharmed.

"Should we summon the police?" James asked.

"No. We'll take father's body home and bury it ourselves." Steven swallowed hard. He'd give his father that much—a small token of how much he'd meant to him, even if he hadn't told him how he felt before he'd died.

"Yes, he'd like that," James replied, his voice hushed. "I still can't believe Father is dead."

Noli squeezed his shoulder. "I'll go with you."

"I'd like that." Steven hadn't ever told her this, but Noli had always held him together, especially when he disappointed his father. Whatever happened to either of them, they went through it as a team.

He didn't want that to ever stop.

They made their way through the house. Steven kept holding his breath, praying they didn't find more bodies. Elise's room stood empty. Clothes, toys, and books were strewn across the room.

"Someone packed quickly," Noli said.

"I hope Quinn took her away." James' face contorted in anger. "I know that you, as eldest, have first right to challenge Brogan, but I'll be more than happy to kill him if you want me to. Just say the word. He needs to pay."

V nodded. "That means a lot to me. If Quinn left with Elise, there will be a message." He turned to Noli. "Quinn and I knew there could come a time where something might happen, so we worked out a system to magically leave each other a message."

"That seems... organized." Noli looked pale.

Steven opened his bedroom door, recoiling as the stench of the human condition hit them. Noli put her handkerchief back over her mouth and nose.

"That is disgusting." James made a face at the mess on the bed. "I'm going to get some things from my room." He left.

Steven's nose scrunched and the corner of his lips turned down as he went to his bookshelf. "Truly, that is vile. I can't see Uncle Brogan's men doing that."

Pulling out a particularly old and dusty book, he flipped through the pages.

Noli peered over his shoulder. "Quinn left you a note in a book?"

"In a way. Here." He held open a page with his finger so she could see. "He used his magic to leave me a symbol on a specified page. No one would know what it meant but me. This narrow rectangle means that he and one other person have fled, in this case Elise." His finger traced the rectangle. "The circle means they're safe and will contact us soon."

"Only you would have a code that was so complex yet so useless," Noli teased. "How will he know where to find us?"

"I vote for leaving word with Mathias," James called from his room.

Steven tucked the book under his arm. "That's a good idea. I have a feeling they won't leave the mortal realm, but we should check the big house and leave a note when we depart from there."

James appeared in the doorway. "What's the plan?"

"Take father's body, as well as anything we want to keep,

back to the big house." Steven looked around, trying to decide what to take as the realization hit: this chapter of his life was closed. This would never be home again. Life would never be the same. He sighed as he tangled his fingers in Noli's hair. "I don't think we're coming back here. Ever."

EPILOGUE

A Plan for Revenge

Noli watched as V and James placed white stones on top of the fresh mound of dirt, making a tumulus. They'd buried Mr. Darrow by the faery tree in the center of the maze, the same one where she'd once buried a tiny wood faery that had died in her hands, the same one that they'd put her inside—which she still didn't quite understand.

Her fingers brushed the bark of the old oak. There was something she needed to remember.

Something fun, I hope, the sprite piped up.

Noli suppressed a groan. She'd known the sprite's silence wouldn't last forever.

"You put one on." V held out a stone to her. His father's sword bumped against his back. He hadn't taken it off since he'd removed it from the safe with the other precious things his father had kept there. The ring glimmered on V's hand.

Taking the stone, Noli carefully placed it on the tumulus. She looked over at the star blooms surrounding the oak. Crouching, she stroked the closed petals of one. *Bloom*, she told it. *Please?* She didn't know if she had to be polite in her magic, but it wouldn't hurt. The pink blossom opened, its sweet fragrance filling her nose.

Picking the flower, she went over and placed it on the tumulus. V flashed her a grateful smile. James and V bowed their heads. She took V's hand. Mr. Darrow hadn't deserved to die.

After a few moments, they walked in silence to the library, which was filled with piles of books and other things they'd painstakingly brought back from the house in Los Angeles. It seemed that Quinn and Elise hadn't been at the big house, nor were there any messages in the places V checked. Word had been left for Quinn with someone named Mathias. Noli prayed they were safe.

The staff had left supper for them on the low table in the library. Noli didn't feel like eating. Instead, she poured everyone tea to give herself something to do.

"What now?" she asked, taking a sip of tea, although she already knew the answer.

"I'm going to go challenge my uncle." Quiet determination colored V's voice. His knuckles whitened as he gripped his teacup.

Noli took another sip and looked up at him. "Tomorrow you're going to wake up, grab your sword, storm over to the earth court palace, and challenge him?"

It seemed so . . . simplistic, given the complexity of Otherworldly conventions.

V and James exchanged glances.

"Pretty much." Steven pulled her to him. "You don't have to come."

"You can't keep me away. If you're going to finally achieve your childhood dream of taking back your court, I most certainly am coming with you." She pressed her forehead to his. She'd stand by V's side no matter what.

"I . . . I'm not going to challenge him for the earth court. I'm not an adult yet—and I'm not ready. I'm just challenging him for the death of my father." He went pale as he said this.

"So, the duel *isn't* to the death?" The idea didn't make her feel any better.

"No. The particular challenge I'm going to invoke isn't to the death." V pressed his face into her shoulder and her arms wrapped around him.

Then what was the point?

"I don't understand Otherworld politics," Noli muttered into her teacup.

James shot out of his chair, anger burning in his eyes. "We're not going kill him? He killed our father and *we're not going to kill him?*"

A look she'd never seen before crossed V's face. "Oh, we'll kill him," V told his brother. "By the Bright Lady, I promise you that. Just not tomorrow. I'm not an adult, and neither are you, which means we can't legally challenge him to the death. Of course, there's still a chance someone could die in any duel, regardless of what kind."

As long as it wasn't V. That's what she feared most.

"Are… are you still in?" V's voice wavered slightly.

"Of course I am." James put in his hand. "That's what brothers are for."

Noli put her hand on top of James'. "Count me in as well."

V added his hand to the pile. "Let's do this. Tomorrow, we'll go to the earth court and avenge my father's death."

Noli raised her teacup. "To revenge."

James and V picked up their teacups as well. "To revenge."

V drank, then added, *"Between friends there is no need for justice, but people who are just still need the quality of friendship; and indeed friendliness is considered to be justice in the fullest sense. It is not only a necessary thing but a splendid one."*

"*Nicomachean Ethics*?" She couldn't help but grin at V. "I've missed your random quoting of things."

James huffed as he poured everyone more tea. "You two are *so* boring."

"But we're here." She snuggled closer to V.

V put an arm around her waist. "That we are."

A plan formed in Noli's mind as they drank their tea. James and V were still considered children in the Otherworld, but thanks to what the queen had done to her, she was technically an adult sprite. She was sick and tired of being protected. No one was going to coddle her or tell her what do any longer. Even if she wasn't much of a fighter, she'd find some way to destroy the earth court king, no matter what.

Oh yes, King Brogan would pay dearly. No one threatened those she loved and got away with it. No one.

THE END

Author's Note

Charmed Vengeance takes place in an alternate version of 1901, a peek into what might have been. I've taken liberties with history, moving things back and forth to suit the story. For example, there was no "pleasure pier" in Los Angeles until 1916, the carousel didn't appear until 1922, and the Los Angeles Museum of History, Science, and Art didn't open until 1910. I have great fun creating alternate histories, which I consider one of the perks of writing Steampunk. There are so many things that might have been but never were. For example, how would the landscape of our county be different if Hawaii had remained a sovereign nation instead of becoming a state?

The State of Deseret is also something that never was. I've made Deseret an official territory, not a state, and much smaller than originally proposed, occupying the approximate size and location of Utah. The MoBatts are a play on the Mormon Battalion, which served during the Mexican-American war as the only religiously based unit in United States military history. I entertained the notion that the battalion stayed in service after the war, eventually becoming a privatized security force for Deseret and chasing all sorts of baddies—especially air pirates.

Human trafficking was an issue during the Victorian era. Girls were abducted, then brought to America to work in brothels because the supply of willing girls didn't meet the demand. In 1910, the American government banned the interstate transport of women for "immoral purposes." Unfortunately, human trafficking is still a worldwide issue today.

Making art and jewelry out of human hair, as Noli does in the story, was a Victorian pastime; ladies' magazines even published instructions. I'm not sure if any faeries commissioned mortals to steal antiquities, but people aren't always who or what they seem—which is valuable to remember, no matter what age you live in.

—Suzanne Lazear

Acknowledgments

Books aren't written in a vacuum and there are many, many people to thank, too many to thank here. First off, thanks to you, the reader, since without you there are no books. I'd like to thank the cadets, skippers, and the first mate of my Airship Squadron for their unwavering support.

Here's a big shout-out to all the people on Twitter and Facebook who answered questions, gave me ideas, sent me virtual cupcakes, and generally cheered me on—especially Lauren for inventing Missy Sassafras and her perfect scones; Grammin for all his help with airships; The Time Traveler for all his research help, links, and the inadvertent idea for the human trafficking subplot; Natalie for telling me about hair weaving; and the Fiction Vixen for the Twitter joke that launched an airship.

Leanna, Saundra, and Zoridia, thank you so much for answering my random questions. Hugs and cupcakes to all my cheerleaders and beta readers, especially Harmony, Jenn, Julia, Julie, Rachel, Renia, Robin, Sarah, Susan, LARA, the Apocalypsies, and the Class of 2k12.

Also, huge hugs and kisses to the hubby and Missy for supporting me in my dream. I couldn't do this without you.

Finally, thanks to all the people at Flux who made this book possible.

Photo by John Lazear

About the Author

Suzanne Lazear (Los Angeles, CA) loves both faeries and steampunk and will one day build a working cupcake cannon. She's a regular blogger at *Steamed*, a group steampunk blog. *Charmed Vengeance* is her second novel.

To learn more about the world of the Aether Chronicles, please visit www.aetherchronicles.com.